SINS OF THE MOTHER

Recent Titles by Deborah Nicholson from Severn House

The Kate Carpenter Series

HOUSE REPORT
EVENING THE SCORE

SINS OF
THE MOTHER

Deborah Nicholson

This first world edition published in Great Britain 2005 by
SEVERN HOUSE PUBLISHERS LTD of
9–15 High Street, Sutton, Surrey SM1 1DF.
This first world edition published in the USA 2005 by
SEVERN HOUSE PUBLISHERS INC of
595 Madison Avenue, New York, N.Y. 10022.

British Library Cataloguing in Publication Data

Nicholson, Deborah, 1961-
    Sins of the mother
    1.   Carpenter, Kate (Fictitious character) - Fiction
    2.   Women theatrical managers - Alberta - Calgary - Fiction
    3.   Murder - Investigation - Alberta - Calgary - Fiction
    4.   Detective and mystery stories
    I.   Title
    813.6 [F]

    ISBN 0-7278-6219-7

Typeset by Palimpsest Book Production Ltd.,
Polmont, Stirlingshire, Scotland.
Printed and bound in Great Britain by
MPG Books Ltd., Bodmin, Cornwall.

Prologue

It was one of those days, you know. It was November and you would expect cold, maybe a bit of cloud, some snow on the ground and dried brown leaves rustling across the pavement with every gust of wind. It was nothing like that. It was a long, late and luscious fall. The leaves were still on the trees, in various shades of orange and gold. The sun beat down, not warming the earth quite as much as a hot August afternoon, but making its presence felt. I leaned on Cam's car, wearing a T-shirt and jeans, feeling the warmth of the metal radiating through the denim. On the other side I felt the warmth of Cam, as he too leaned against the car, standing very close to me, watching the scene unfold.

'Kate, can you focus a little bit here?' Ken asked gently, prodding my story in the direction he wanted me to go.

I looked at Ken and then quickly down at the table, remembering suddenly where I was. One of my fingernails caught my eye; a ring of dried blood stubbornly clinging to the cuticle, even though I'd washed three or four times already. Just call me Lady Macbeth, I laughed to myself, and then I tried to stifle the giggle because I didn't want them to think I was crazy. But the sound that came out probably didn't do much to alleviate that impression.

A hand came down and covered mine, where I had been staring at the blood, bringing me back to the present. How did he always know what I was thinking, I wondered? I looked up slowly and smiled at Cam.

'You doing OK, Katie?' he asked, looking so serious and caring. But I could see the twinkle in his eye. Of course I wasn't OK. None of us were OK. And he knew that. But I had things to do here that would help make things better. And now I remembered that.

1

'Just peachy.' I smiled back at him.

'You want a break or you want to keep going?' Ken asked me.

'Let's keep going,' I said, taking a deep breath and twining my fingers through Cam's.

It was one of those days . . .

'Kate!' Ken warned.

'Just kidding,' I smiled, trying to show him I was in control. But I was feeling pretty shaky inside still.

It was one of those days where you thought everything was fine, your boyfriend was standing right next to you and you almost had this whole mess sorted out. But things were going too slowly. Cam walked over to the policeman, Officer Strachan, I think, and asked him how much longer he thought it would be. We just wanted to know if we should call our lawyer or not. And we were just talking to the policeman; well, I was probably flirting a little. I mean he was really cute and I thought we would be done and out of here in another minute or so. Then, suddenly he wasn't standing anymore, but crumpled on the ground. The sound seemed to register after he fell. It was surreal. It sounded like thunder. It split the air, flew past my cheek and, when I looked down at Officer Strachan, there was blood pouring out of the right side of his chest. I had my first aid certificate, and I guess the training paid off, because I was actually down on the ground, beside him, my hands pushing down on the wound as hard as I could, while all of this slowly registered in my brain.

I kept telling him he was going to be all right. Everything was going to be fine. But it wasn't. I could feel air rushing through my fingers, as they pressed into his chest. A sucking chest wound, they called it. Not a good injury. But I smiled at the young man, even as I felt tears running down my cheeks. Cam was yelling for the other officer while he dropped to the ground beside me, holding the man's head in his lap, trying to help him get into a position where he could breathe easier. But nothing was helping.

And then the other officer finally ran from the house, his walkie-talkie out, screaming into it.

'Officer down, officer needs assistance. I repeat, officer down.'

That voice would echo in my head for ever.

2

Saturday November 8

'Oh, my God, I can't believe it's you!'
My life had been gloriously normal forty-five minutes ago. Peaceful, alone with the man I loved. Cam had held my hand as we walked slowly back up to the apartment from the store on the main level. It had been a trip for munchies. You can't watch movies without munchies. I was in a salty mood and came back with salt and vinegar chips. Cam was craving chocolate tonight and he had a super-sized caramel bar, which was great because I knew he would share with me, so I got the best of both worlds. Every time I looked at him I realized how lucky I was; beautiful thick brown hair just starting to show some grey, laugh lines around his eyes, giving him that slightly weathered look, just tall enough to fit me under his shoulder when we cuddled on the couch, and he put up with me. And my family. I didn't think there was much more a girl could ask for. Especially the putting up with me part.

We had just recently packed my mother and her boyfriend off in a taxi to the airport and were finally, gloriously, alone for the first time in several months. Cam sat me on the couch with a glass of red wine and he had a beer. We had our munchies and he put a movie in the DVD player and sat down beside me. The perfect night in as far as we were both concerned. We were just cuddled up and comfortable when the phone rang. I started to get up to answer it, but I got a dirty look from Cam and I decided to let the answering machine pick it up. He obviously had other ideas because he disappeared into the kitchen and came back with a hammer in his hand. He calmly unplugged the phone, set it on the floor and then proceeded to demolish it with the hammer. When he was sure the phone wouldn't ring again, he set the hammer down and joined me on the couch, a smug look on his face.

'Feel better now?' I asked, trying to hide my shock at what he had done. Cam was usually pretty calm and in control. At least we did have another phone upstairs, which he seemed to have forgotten about at the moment.

'Much better,' he replied.

We could discuss it tomorrow; I decided I didn't want any sort of confrontation tonight. He sat back down on the couch and I tucked myself back into his embrace and turned my attention back to the movie. I was just snuggled comfortably, my eyes growing heavy with sleep, when there was a knock on the door.

I hesitated, fearing that getting up to answer the door might set the wrath of Cam upon me. For a moment there was an icy silence between us. Cam reached for the remote and pointed it at the TV, turning it off and calmly setting the remote back on the coffee table, thank goodness, because I didn't have a spare remote. Cam stood up slowly, meaning to answer the door, stopping to pick up the hammer on his way past.

'Cam!' I called after him and chased him to the door. I wrestled the hammer from his hand and he kissed me as he unlocked the door, a silly grin on his face. It looked like we weren't going to be alone after all.

'I wasn't really going to use it,' he told me. 'Just wave it around a little bit. It's probably just a salesman.'

'Yeah, right,' I said, reaching over him to open the door.

'Oh, my God, I can't believe it's you!' he exclaimed, his mouth dropping slightly in surprise.

I looked at Cam and at the lovely woman standing in our doorway. She was taller than me, almost as tall as Cam, short brown hair, cut in a fashionable bob, a figure with a few extra pounds but they all managed to land in the right places. And yet she looked frail or maybe just lost. She was somewhere around my age and I was beginning to feel a little threatened by her presence, given Cam's reaction to her arrival. I was about to speak up, when she dissolved into a pool of tears and fell into Cam's arms. Cam's open, waiting, even inviting arms.

'Cam, I can't believe I've found you. I've been to your last three addresses,' she sobbed. 'I didn't think I'd ever find you.'

'Carrie, come in.' He wrapped his arm around her shoul-

4

ders and shepherded her into the living room. 'Katie, will you grab her bag?'

'Uh, sure,' I said, already standing alone in the hallway, demoted from loving partner to bellhop with one fateful knock on my front door.

I picked up the suitcase that sat in the hallway and brought it in, closing and locking the door behind me. Then I hurried into the living room, overcome with curiosity about this mysterious, crying woman.

Cam had her sitting on the couch with a cup of tea in her hand and a box of Kleenex beside her. She looked up and noticed me for the first time. Cam also looked up and must have seen the confusion on my face.

'Katie, this is my cousin Carrie,' he explained.

She suddenly looked mortified and frantically wiped her tears. 'I'm sorry, this is a bad time.'

'No, Carrie, this is Kate. We live together; you're not interrupting a hot date or anything. Don't worry.' Cam tried to comfort her. 'Tell me what's going on.'

'I'm sorry, I shouldn't have come. I haven't seen you for ages and then suddenly I show up on your doorstep in this state.'

'It's OK.' I tried to reassure her too, taking a seat on the other side of the couch and handing her another Kleenex. 'Everyone turns up on our doorstep eventually. Why don't you try and tell us what's going on? I'm sure Cam can help, whatever it is.'

'I left Hank,' she said, breaking into a fresh stream of tears. 'Or more exactly, he locked me out of the house.'

'Hank?' I asked.

'Her husband,' Cam explained and then turned to Carrie. 'It doesn't matter how it happened. You know it's for the best. He's no good for you.'

'I know. But he's got all my stuff, I have no money; all I got was a couple of shirts and a pair of jeans.'

'Where are the kids?' Cam asked.

'They're at their dad's house. They can stay with him for a couple of days until I figure something out.'

'Do you have any money in your bank account?' I asked.

'A little.'

5

'Is it a joint account?' I asked.

'Yeah.' She nodded half-heartedly.

'Well, first things first, let's get to a bank and clean out your account. That'll take care of the money. As for clothes and things, I have more than enough to share,' I suggested, trying to be practical.

'And we'll find you a lawyer,' Cam said. 'It's about time somebody taught that bastard a lesson.'

I opened my mouth, about to ask why Cam seemed to hate this Hank so much, anxious to hear the story, and then decided maybe there would be a better time, like later tonight when we were in bed and Carrie wasn't sitting in between us.

'I don't think I have the strength to do this,' she said softly.

'You don't worry about that, we're going to be with you every step of the way,' Cam said, looking to me for reassurance.

I smiled back at him, promising him my help, but a little voice in the back of my mind was pointing out the fact that once again we were not alone.

Monday November 10

My name is Kate Carpenter. I am thirty-three years old, blonde still, with many thanks to the local drugstore and my hairdresser, blue eyed, with my first smattering of wrinkles framing those eyes when I smile. I work at the Calgary Arts Complex, for Calgary's largest theatre company, Foothills Stage Network, as the front of house manager. I live in a cute but tiny loft with my boyfriend Cam. He works at the Plex too, in the maintenance department. He is incredibly good looking and a fitness nut. I'm not. Cam had moved into my life a couple of years ago, but only moved into my apartment after there had been a murder in the theatre lobby, which I somehow got involved in. Cam was my knight in shining armour, moving in to protect me. Luckily he did a good job of it or I would have been just another grease spot on the stage by now.

I don't have a great track record with relationships and Cam is divorced, but we are struggling through so far. I had thought, when he first moved in, that it would only be temporary but I seem to have become used to having him around. And I always say that Cam's greatest attribute is that no matter how hard I push him away he keeps coming back.

Our effort had been frustrating. We had calmed Carrie down, washed her face and loaded her in Cam's car. A drive to the nearest bank machine had proven fruitless, as her inquiries with her bank card were just met with 'insufficient funds'. We dropped Carrie off to visit her kids for the rest of the day, as Cam and I both had to work.

Today we arrived at the bank, as soon as it opened, hoping they could help us out with this problem. I sat in the waiting area, flipping through an ancient magazine, watching Cam and Carrie stand in the interminable line for the tellers. I knew it was going to be a long day when first thing this morning we were lined up outside the bank, with about twenty other people already ahead of us. So here I sat, waiting. They finally made it to a wicket and Carrie handed her withdrawal slip over to the teller, who entered the information into the computer and then turned back to talk to Carrie. I saw the girl's shoulders slump and her back began to shake again. Cam put his arm around her shoulder protectively, but I could see he was angry by the way he was speaking with the teller. Finally, they gave up their argument and headed back in my direction. Carrie was frantically wiping her eyes, trying to regain some composure in this public setting.

'Well?' I asked Cam.

He shook his head and I followed them to the car. Cam helped Carrie in and held the door open for me before he walked around and got in himself. Cam had a prized 1971 white Hemi Barracuda, which was the only thing in the world that he liked more than me, or so he said. He definitely spent more money on it than he did on me. That's how I knew he was very angry, when he slammed his precious door.

7

'What happened?' I asked, afraid I might be taking my life in my hands by asking the question.

'The bastard cleaned her out,' Cam hissed through clenched teeth.

'Everything?' I asked.

'Everything.'

'My pay cheque was just deposited on Friday. I have nothing. I can't eat, I have no place to live, no clothes, nothing,' Carrie moaned from the back seat.

'Don't you worry about that.' Cam turned around, trying to put on a brighter face. 'You're staying with us.'

'I can't do that. I'd be intruding.'

'No, it's not a problem. You need help and we're going to be there for you.' He turned to me. 'Right, Katie?'

To my credit, I only hesitated a second before I agreed. I don't think either of them even noticed. Well, Cam probably did but he had the good grace not to mention it to me. I guess this was another one of those relationship things I would have to get used to, being there for each other's families. Lord knows mine was dysfunctional enough and he would probably have to return the favour sooner or later. And I wasn't counting my mother because he had gotten along with her just fine. So technically he still owed me.

We had a bunch of other errands to do, stopping at Carrie's kids' school to give them the new contact information, and then every government department that existed to change her address and dissociate her from Hank, and then groceries and home. The day was passed mostly in silence. Carrie looked exhausted when we finally got home but Cam insisted he call a lawyer friend of his and they set up an appointment for her to see him. Then, being the great caregiver he was, he made a big pot of soup and a fresh batch of biscuits and made sure we all ate until we were stuffed. While Carrie had a bath, we opened up the sofa bed for her and stayed downstairs just long enough to make sure she had everything she needed. Then I headed upstairs to the bedroom while Cam made sure she was tucked in safely before joining me.

I had already changed and was propped up in bed with a book when he came up with a couple of glasses of wine.

'Have I told you yet today that you're a really nice guy?' I asked him.

'Probably, but you can never say it too often.' He smiled as he set the wine on the nightstand.

'OK, you're the best, you're the best, and you're the best.'

He slipped out of his clothes, hanging them up neatly before climbing into bed beside me.

'Careful, it might go to my head,' he said, throwing my book on the floor and pulling me close to him.

'Boy, we haven't been to bed this early since we met,' I said.

'You mean after the first night?' he joked.

'That doesn't count, I was overcome by your pheromones,' I protested. 'And the way you looked in those blue jeans. Besides, I don't want you to think I'm easy.'

'I know you're easy.'

'I'm so lucky to have a guy like you. Every time I hear those stories or meet someone like Carrie, I thank God I've got a decent man.'

'How do you know I'm not going to drain your bank account one day?' he asked. 'Or are you actually beginning to trust me?'

'I know that the way I spend my money, my bank account is never going to be big enough to bother emptying.'

'That's OK, I only want you for your body anyway,' he teased. 'Do you want to watch some TV?'

'No, I just want to lie here for a while with you. OK?'

'That would be just fine with me,' he said, pulling me even closer.

And just when we were very close and really comfortable the phone rang. Cam reached over to grab it quickly before it woke Carrie. Luckily, we no longer had a phone in the living room since Cam had destroyed it, or that would have rung right in Carrie's ear.

'Hello?'

'Is Carrie there?'

'Who is this?' Cam asked.

I moved close to the phone, so I could listen in.

'It's her husband. Let me speak to her,' the voice on the other end demanded.

9

'Hank, this is Cam. How did you get this number?'

'Cam, how have you been?' he asked, his voice changing slightly as he tried to charm Cam.

'I asked you how you got this number,' Cam insisted.

'Look, Cam, I guess you know we had a little fight. Let me talk to her. I feel really bad about what happened and I want to try to make up with her,' he said, still trying to win Cam over with his gentle attitude.

'She's asleep, Hank. I'll let her know you called in the morning.'

'God damn it, I'm her husband and I demand to speak to her right now!' he screamed, giving up the act and reverting to what was apparently his normal behaviour.

'And I said she's sleeping,' Cam replied, his voice growing firm and quiet. 'She may not be strong enough to stand up to you, Hank, but I'm definitely ready to take you on.'

'You can't hide her from me,' he said menacingly. 'You can't protect her twenty-four hours a day. I'll find her and I'll get her back.'

'Well, you better not try it when I'm around,' Cam roared, losing the cool he had been working hard to maintain, and then he slammed down the phone. He reached over and turned out the light.

'Cam?' I asked.

'I'm OK.'

Not the response I was hoping for. So I tried again.

'He sounds like a real jerk,' I tried, hoping he would talk.

'He is.'

This wasn't the kind of conversation I was looking for and monosyllabic answers were never a good sign with Cam.

'Do you want me to get you a beer or something?' I offered.

'Katie, would you mind if I went out for a run?' he asked.

'Cam, it's like ten o'clock at night.'

'Do you mind?' he repeated.

'No. Do you want me to come with you?' I asked, being the good girlfriend, while praying he would turn my offer down.

'No, I just need to run.'

'OK,' I agreed readily.

He got out of bed without turning on the light or saying

another word. I watched his silhouette as he pulled on a sweat-suit and running shoes, and then watched as he quietly tiptoed down the stairs.

It was very late before I heard him come back up the stairs. I was still wide awake, waiting for him, but I didn't say a word as he undressed and climbed back into bed with me.

'Feel better?' I asked, snuggling up to him. He was warm and had a lovely musky smell from his workout.

'Much,' he said.

'Good.'

'Did you wait up for me?' he asked.

'Not really, I just couldn't sleep.'

'Do you want a glass of wine or something?' he asked, repeating my earlier offer while nuzzling my neck.

'You need a shave,' I said, squirming away as his beard burned my neck.

'I think I'll wait till morning.'

'I don't want anything.' I finally answered his original question, feeling myself grow sleepy now that I was in his arms. 'I think I'll sleep just fine now that you're back.'

'Will you do me a favour in the morning?' he asked.

'Sure.'

'Will you call Detective Lincoln and find out if there's anything we can do to help Carrie?'

'Of course I will,' I promised. 'Do you think there's anything we can do?'

'Well, between the lawyer and the police, I'm sure there's something. We'll have her stuff back in a couple of days, help her find a new place and maybe, if we're really lucky, we'll even get that bastard thrown in jail.'

'You're sexy when you're incensed.'

'Good night,' he whispered in my ear.

'Good night,' I whispered back.

'Katie?'

'Yes?'

'Do you always have to have the last word?' he asked.

'Yes,' I told him and, wisely, he gave up.

Tuesday November 11

'Katie, are you awake?' Cam asked, gently shaking my shoulder, knowing full well I wasn't.

I thought about pretending I was still asleep, and maybe getting another couple of hours in bed, but then I remembered we had company downstairs and I decided I'd better get up and try and put on a good show.

'I'm awake,' I said, turning over to face him, forcing my eyelids to part. 'You're dressed already.'

'I'm going out for a run,' he explained. 'I want you to come down and put the chain lock on after I leave.'

'Why?' I asked, concerned.

'Just to be safe. If Hank can find our phone number, he can probably find our address. OK?'

'I'm coming,' I groaned, throwing the blankets back and trying to find the floor with my feet.

Cam held out my robe for me and helped me into it.

'Have you got coffee on?' I asked, following him down the stairs.

'I already have a cup poured and waiting for you.' He smiled at me.

'Thank you.' I smiled back.

He opened the door and turned to kiss me before he left.

'Now, lock this door up tight. And when I come back, don't open it until you check the peephole,' he commanded.

'Don't worry, I know the drill.'

'I'll be back in about an hour,' he promised and then headed off down the hall.

I locked the door, put on the chain and headed for the kitchen for my coffee. Gratefully, I took a big gulp. The coffee tasted great; the brain was very grateful for the big infusion of caffeine but the stomach wasn't too sure about it this morning. I pushed aside the queasy feeling and took another sip, a little slower, giving myself a chance to settle down. Two more sips and a much calmer stomach later, I turned to see Carrie coming into the kitchen.

'Good morning,' I said, much more cheerfully than I was feeling.

'Morning.' She smiled back but looked a little uncomfortable when she realized it was just the two of us.

'Would you like some coffee?' I asked.

'I'd love some.'

'Have a seat, I'll get you a cup.' I turned and opened the cupboard. 'Do you take anything?'

'A little milk if you have some,' she answered timidly as she made her way to the table.

I poured a coffee and pulled the milk jug out of the fridge. I set them both on the table and sat down across from her. She finally sat down and fussed with her coffee for a couple of minutes. I didn't really know what to say either, so I turned back to the safety of food.

'Do you want something to eat?' I asked, wondering what I would do if she said yes. The kitchen was Cam's area of expertise. I just did take-out.

'No, I'm still stuffed from last night. Cam is such a great cook.'

'He spoils me pretty good.' I smiled, patting my growing stomach. It felt like the freshman fifteen pounds from my college years all over again.

'I remember, even when we were kids, he was always making these huge family dinners. We always thought he'd become a chef.'

'Lucky for me he didn't,' I said. 'So do you have to go to work today?'

'No, I called one of the other girls and got her to cover for me. I figured I might need a couple of days off to sort this out,' she said.

'What do you do?' I asked, realizing I knew absolutely nothing about this woman.

'I'm a licensed practical nurse. I work at a walk-in clinic in Sunnyside.'

'Nice area of town,' I said. 'Good restaurants. You must meet some interesting people.'

13

'That's one way of putting it. But no two days are the same.'

I couldn't stand one more minute of small talk. This woman had appeared at my door, thrown herself into my boyfriend's arms, cried all night on my sofa bed, and somebody owed me some answers. It was time to try to find out what was going on. And since she didn't seem to be in any hurry to offer up any information, I was going to have to ask.

'Have you been married long?'

'I'm not really married to him. We just live together. The married story is for the family's benefit. My mother never liked Hank and she would have died if she thought I was only living with him. So we told her we eloped. The story just kind of stuck, even though my mom is dead now.' She paused to take a sip of her coffee. 'Imagine, I went to all that effort to be with Hank and look where it's gotten me.'

'Has he always been like this?' I asked.

'He's abused me for years,' she admitted. 'Never physically, but psychologically.'

'So what made you finally leave?'

'He hit me. I always convinced myself that he just treated me the way he did because he loved me and he was trying to make me a better person. But when he hit me that crossed the line somehow. Doesn't really make sense, does it?' she asked, nervously adding more milk to her coffee so she didn't have to make eye contact with me.

'It does make sense.' I smiled reassuringly, reaching over and patting her hand. 'Everyone has a limit to what they can bear. You found out what yours was. And you made a good decision, Carrie. You need to get away from someone like that.'

'But I still love him.' She sighed. 'Despite everything.'

'You can't just expect years of feelings to vanish overnight. But you got out of there while you're still in one piece. And after a while, when you start dating again, when you see how a nice man treats a woman, you'll never want to go back to someone like Hank again.'

'I already did,' she admitted, blushing a little.

'You're dating someone?' I asked.

'We're not really dating. I met him and he's wonderful. He asked me out and I went. I don't know what made me do it, but I did. We dined, we danced, he held doors open for me and told me how beautiful I was. I haven't felt that good in years.' She had a slightly sorrowful smile on her face. 'I just knew that nothing could happen until I finished this thing with Hank. The problem is I just didn't know how to finish things with Hank.'

'Well, good for you, it's important that you have found someone who treats you right. And it's important that you feel like you deserve to be treated that way,' I cheered her on. I grabbed the coffee pot and filled my cup. 'Do you want some more coffee?'

'Please.'

'So are you seeing this guy? Does he know what happened?' I asked.

'Yes. I mean no. Well, not really. He has kids, I have kids and our paths cross. But he said he'd wait for me, no matter how long it took. And he loves my kids. He seems to think we'll all make a great family someday. I suppose he knows what's going on but I haven't talked to him since the police came.'

'How many kids do you have?'

'I've got two. David is eleven years old and Emily is seven.'

'And your ex-husband?'

'He's great. Funny, I look back now and wonder why I ever wanted out of that marriage. It seems so calm and peaceful compared to what I've got now. But I think it's just because we get along so much better since we divorced. So the kids are fine with him until I manage to get myself together. The only thing I didn't anticipate was Hank's reaction when I told him I was going to leave him.'

There was a knock on the door.

'Hold that thought, I'll be right back,' I said, getting up and running to the door.

I dutifully checked the peephole and saw Cam standing there. I opened the door and let him in, making sure it was locked tightly behind him.

'How's it going?' he asked, giving me a quick kiss on the cheek.

'Great. Carrie and I are just having some coffee and getting to know each other. She's just about to tell me what happened last night,' I whispered, pulling him into the kitchen before she had a chance to get nervous and clam up, leaving the story unfinished.

15

'Still jogging, I see,' Carrie said.

'I've got to keep my girlish figure.' He smiled at her. 'Especially since I'm trying to keep this crazy woman happy now.'

He pulled me to him and gave me a big hug. I wrapped my arms around his waist and hugged him back.

'It's not your body I'm after, just your cooking.'

'So you say now. But what'll happen when I let myself go? You'll find yourself some little usher and have a cheap affair with him while I'm slaving away over a hot stove,' he teased. 'Now, where's the coffee pot?'

'On the table,' I said, crossing over and grabbing it for him. 'There's just enough for one more cup.'

'I'll make more,' he said as he took the pot and poured some for himself. 'And I'll even make breakfast.'

I sat back down at the table and tucked my feet up under me.

'Do you want to tell us what happened?' I asked Carrie, wondering if she might feel uncomfortable now that Cam was here.

'It's the least I can do considering how much you guys are doing for me.'

'You don't have to tell us anything,' Cam said.

I shot him a dirty look. I wanted to know what was going on.

'No, it's OK,' she smiled weakly. 'I imagine I'm going to have to tell this story several times. I might as well get used to it.'

'Take your time,' I said. 'Remember, we're on your side.'

'Well, I told Hank I was going to leave him, going to find my own place, and he just went crazy. He screamed, he threatened, he stormed around the place. I finally called the kids' dad and asked if he could come and get them. They were getting scared. Once they were out of the house, Hank really let loose. He locked and bolted all the doors and told me I was never leaving him. Well, I was scared but I had also had it with him and his temper. I tried to reason with him for hours and then I finally went into the bedroom and decided to start packing some stuff and get out of there. He followed me and when he saw me open the suitcase and start packing, he hit me. It came out of nowhere. One minute I was sitting on the bed opening my suitcase, and the next minute I was on the floor. My lip was bleeding and I was seeing stars. He picked me up and threw me against the wall. I grabbed the cordless phone, locked myself in the bathroom and called 911.'

'Oh, my God,' I whispered.

'It's funny, it all seems surreal. Like it didn't really happen to me,' she said, staring down at the floor.

'It sounds like Hank to me,' Cam added.

'Well, the police came and banged on the door for ages until he finally let them in. They took him into the kitchen and heard his story and then listened to my story. The bottom line was they told me they couldn't guarantee that I would be safe and I should probably stay at a friend's house for the night. So I packed up a couple of things and got out of the house. A friend lent me a car and I spent most of the day looking for Cam, until finally one of his old roommates gave me this address.'

'That's all the police had to say?' I asked.

'That's what they advised me to do.'

'No protection, he hits you so you have to leave?' I found myself getting as angry as Cam had been yesterday.

'Katie,' Cam warned me before turning his attention back to Carrie. 'Does he go out during the daytime?'

'I don't know,' Carrie said. 'Why?'

'Because when he's out we can go over and get some of your stuff. At least that will help in the short term.'

'Doesn't he work?' I asked.

'He hasn't worked in the last five years,' Cam said.

'He works at home,' Carrie defended him.

'Or so he says,' Cam added.

'Well, does he normally go out during the day?' I asked.

'He usually goes out for coffee in the afternoon,' Carrie said. 'Meets his friends and they talk about their day trading stuff.'

'Good. Then we can go over and grab some stuff later. Have we got any boxes, Katie?'

'Not here, but I've got a ton of them at the theatre.'

'I can't today,' Carrie said apologetically. 'The kids are off school for Remembrance Day and their dad has to work so I

17

promised him I'd go over and watch them for the day. I'm sorry.'

'It's OK. Tomorrow we can stop at the theatre and pick up some boxes, then to the lawyer's, then Carrie's place. Now, would anyone like a good breakfast?' he asked, setting plates in front of Carrie and me.

'God, that smells so good,' I said.

'Eggs Florentine,' he said, setting a third plate at the table and going back for the coffee pot.

'This is delicious,' I said, not waiting for him to get back before I started eating.

'I'm glad you like it. Would you like some fruit salad with that?' he asked, before sitting down.

'Do we have some?' I asked.

'You'd be surprised what we have,' he said, pulling a bowl of fresh fruit salad out of the fridge. 'You should try checking out the refrigerator sometime.'

I spooned some fruit salad on to my plate and took another bite of eggs.

'Why would I do that? Then I might actually have to cook something,' I said with my mouth full. 'Do we have any of those biscuits left from last night?'

'Anything else while I'm up, Your Majesty?'

'A little more hollandaise sauce?' I asked, holding out my plate.

He filled my plate and brought it back to the table for me.

'What time do you have to be at Alan's house?' Cam asked.

'He's going to be here any minute. I'm going to drop him off at work and then take the kids to the park for a while. We'll pick him up later and he'll drop me off here.'

'Great. Well, Katie, I guess you and I actually have most of the day to ourselves. What do you want to do today?'

'Is going back to bed an option?' I tried.

'Uh, no. Do you want to try again or should I just make a decision?'

'Take me to Bragg Creek and buy me some ice cream?' I tried again.

'It's five degrees out and you want to have ice cream?'

'How about pie?' Carrie asked. 'Have you ever been to the pie place there?'

18

'There's a pie place in Bragg Creek?' I asked. 'How could I not know about this?'

'It's yummy. They make a great Saskatoon berry pie with fresh cream. And they heat it until it's bubbly.'

'Cam, did you know about the pie place?' I asked.

'Finished with your plate, Carrie?' he asked, studiously ignoring me and clearing the table.

'I think I'll just get dressed and meet Alan downstairs,' Carrie said, excusing herself and hurrying for the bathroom.

'What else are you hiding from me?' I asked Cam.

'I don't know, but if you want to have a shower with me you can check me out thoroughly and see if I'm hiding anything else.'

We managed to get out of the shower with some of the day left to spare, filled up the gas-guzzling Barracuda and hit the highway. Cam was feeling frisky, since we hadn't been out on the highway for quite a long time. Luckily, he kept it mostly under control and we managed to avoid all RCMP officers along the way. He pulled into the mall and parked his car a safe distance away. We strolled over to the mall, stopping to admire some great bikes that were parked in the parking lot.

'Pie first?' he asked.

'No, I can show a little self-control,' I said, buttoning my coat up tightly around my neck. 'We can window shop first.'

Bragg Creek may have only been a twenty-minute drive from Calgary but it was all up hill and the temperature seemed to have dropped several degrees between here and home. But the air was fresh and crisp and the mountains glistened in the distance, iced by a fresh coat of snow that must have fallen overnight, and I was happy to wander along the outdoor mall and get my fresh air while we window shopped. It was a good combination for a city girl and an outdoor boy.

We wandered for almost an hour until my fingertips were getting numb as the sun was sinking lower on the horizon. We went into the last store on the strip, a nice little art gallery, and we both headed for a great painting on the far wall.

'I love this,' I said, drawn to the colour of the fall leaves that seemed to almost hop off the canvas.

'It's amazing,' Cam agreed with me. 'The colours are fantastic.'

'You really love it?' I asked.

'And you too?' he asked.

'I can't believe it. I think this is the first piece of art we have ever agreed on.'

'See, we're not doomed,' he said with a laugh. 'We do have some things in common.'

'I wish we had room for this. But none of the rooms are really big enough for it.'

'If we ever get our own place, I'll buy it for you as a house-warming present,' he promised.

'If we ever get our own place, we'll buy it for each other.'

'Wow, you realize you didn't actually choke when you said that?' he laughed at me.

'I'm just hiding it better,' I chuckled with him. 'So, can I buy you some pie?'

He looked at his watch. 'How about if I buy you some dinner and we have pie for dessert.'

'Is it that late?' I asked. 'I should probably call Graham and let him know I might be a little late.'

'Katie, I will get you to work on time,' he promised. 'The car is full of gas and the Mounties hardly ever catch me. Come on, let's go grab a bite to eat. We've got an hour before we need to be on the road.'

And that's what we did. And the plan was working just fine until I heard sirens and turned around and saw the lights flashing behind us.

'I told you not to speed.'

'I'm not speeding,' Cam said.

'Well, can we outrun them?' I joked.

He was already slowing down and pulling on to the shoulder.

'We probably could but eventually I'd get caught and I don't want to go to prison and become somebody's wife, thank you very much.'

'That would be such a waste.' I sighed.

Cam stopped, put the car in neutral and had his licence and registration out before the RCMP officer got to his open window.

'Good afternoon, sir,' the constable said, leaning down into the window and checking out the dashboard of the car. I didn't know what he was looking for but I didn't think we looked like gun runners or drug lords.

20

'Officer,' Cam replied, noncommittally.

'This is a fine-looking machine you have here,' the Mountie continued. '1970?'

'1971,' Cam said, still holding his licence and registration out. The officer finally waved that away.

'You do the work yourself?' he asked, straightening up, running his eyes up and down the side of the car.

'I did. I've been working on her for about five years.'

'Beautiful job,' the officer told him.

I leaned across Cam and started to say something, anxious to get on with the ticket giving and get back into town. Cam pushed me back to my side and shot me a dirty look.

'We're going to be late,' I whispered.

'Do you have a Barracuda?' Cam asked, turning his attention back to the policeman.

'Naw, my wife would never let me. You're a lucky man.'

'I have my moments.'

'Well, I just wanted to let you know that one of your running lights is out. Looks like you must have taken some gravel damage.'

'That's one of the hazards of actually taking this thing out on the road,' Cam said. 'But who could leave it in a garage?'

'I agree. I just thought you should know so you can get that fixed right away.'

'Well, thanks, officer.'

'Well, I'll let you folks get on your way. Maybe I'll see you at one of the shows next summer.'

'Well, I haven't exactly cleared that with the little lady yet, but you never know,' Cam laughed, sliding his licence back into his wallet.

The policemen headed back for their cruiser and pulled out around us, waving like old time friends as they drove past us.

'Little lady?' I asked.

'Katie, I was just playing the game.'

'You haven't cleared that with the little lady?' I asked again.

'Katie, we didn't get a ticket. That's a good thing.'

'I will just never understand testosterone,' I said, settling back in my seat as Cam eased his baby back out on to the road, a proud smile on his face.

'Oh yeah, and estrogen is so much easier to understand.'

*   *   *

21

Cam was right, as always. He had me at work a few minutes early. I managed to get the coffee on, the inventory done and lobby sales ready before anyone else arrived. Mind you, we were in the last few days of the play and we were running out of merchandise for sale, so it wasn't taking as long as it might have three weeks ago. I had raided a poppy jar in Bragg Creek, leaving a big donation, and I had poppies set out for all the staff and volunteers. I always felt a bit of obligation to ensure we looked the part on Remembrance Day, as my great uncle had died on D-Day.

I called Carrie a couple of times, ensuring she was doing all right being home alone. After she assured me that the only problem that she was having was trouble sleeping because the phone kept ringing, as Cam and I were checking up on her every fifteen minutes or so, I decided to leave her be until I got home. She promised she would call me if anything happened.

The play was a musical and that usually meant a happy audience and a peaceful night. I was right this time. I hitched a ride home with one of the technicians and tiptoed upstairs past Carrie, who was already in bed and sleeping, and crawled into bed myself. I woke up briefly when Cam got home around four o'clock or five o'clock in the morning, but I cuddled up to him and was back asleep in no time.

Wednesday November 12

'What time do we have to be at the lawyer's?' I asked, with my mouth full.

The three of us sat around the table, stuffing pancakes and turkey sausages into our greedy little mouths, as Cam had once again provided a tasty repast for us.

'We've got to be there at eleven,' Cam told me, checking his watch. 'Which should be no problem since you actually got out of bed at a decent time today.'

'I work nights,' I explained to Carrie, trying to defend myself. 'I need to sleep late.'

When Cam said a decent time, he meant before noon. But I had woken up bright and early today, with a very queasy stomach. I really hoped I wasn't coming down with a case of the flu, especially with Carrie here and everything else going on. But it seemed to have settled now. At least it wasn't stopping me from eating breakfast.

'Sleeping late is one thing, sleeping the day away is something else,' he teased.

'You are rude, treating me this way in front of company.'

'Eat up, we've got three people who need to shower and we need to be on the road soon. I don't want to be late, Eli's doing me a big favour by seeing us today.'

I obeyed his command and managed to totally stuff myself yet again. I stood in the bathroom, fresh from the shower, gazing in the mirror and I realized I was going to have to start working out or quit eating Cam's cooking. Neither option seemed all that appealing to me. There had to be a third solution somewhere. But I could think about it later. I figured I had about five more pounds to go until I really had to worry about it.

'You dressed, Katie?' Cam asked, pounding on the door. He and Carrie were both showered and dressed and were now waiting for me, not very patiently. 'We're ready to go.'

'Just a couple more minutes,' I called through the door. 'I've just got to dry my hair.'

'Hustle it up,' he called back.

I plugged in the blow dryer and cursed the time it took to dry my hair. Maybe it was time to get it cut. I'll never forget the day that my mother did that. I left for school in the morning and she had long flowing beautiful hair; when she picked me up at the end of the day, it was gone. She'd decided that a woman of her age shouldn't have long hair. She was thirty-three. I was a year older than that. I shivered at the thought of it. No, I was not ready to cut my hair yet. I turned off the blow dryer, put on a little blush, some eyeliner, mascara and lipstick. I put a scrunchy elastic on my wrist, in case I decided to put my hair up later, slipped into a broomstick skirt with an elastic waistband and an oversized sweater. Elastic waists were a gift from the gods.

'Katie,' Cam called through the door again.

'I'm coming,' I yelled, quickly wiping down the shower and hanging up my towels. I opened the bathroom door and found Cam standing there, holding my backpack for me.

'I'm ready,' I said. 'What's the rush?'

'I don't want to be late for the lawyer's appointment,' he said. 'I told you Eli is doing me a big favour by seeing Carrie today. He's the best in town, Katie, and it normally takes a long time to get an appointment with him.'

'We've got a half an hour. We're doing fine.'

'Better early than late,' he told me. 'And I thought we were going to stop and pick up boxes first?'

'Well, we could have been out of here three minutes ago if you'd just shut up.' I smiled sweetly at him. 'We'll do it after the lawyer's appointment. The boxes aren't going anywhere.'

'I love you too,' he said.

'You trying to remind yourself of that or do you really mean it?'

'Both.' He turned and grabbed his keys. 'Come on, Carrie.'

'I'm coming,' she answered from the living room. 'I'm scared to death, but I'm coming.'

Cam hustled us all down to the car and we buckled in and headed west along the river.

'I've never heard about this lawyer friend of yours before,' I said to Cam. 'Who is he?'

'Elijah Smith. We met in university. We did first year general studies together. Then he headed off to law school and I headed off to trade school. There's a few of us that keep in touch and we usually get together once a year.'

'Is he really a good lawyer?' I asked.

'Well, he handled my divorce for me and I came out of that OK,' Cam said.

'You came out of that with nothing,' Carrie said from the back.

'I came out with my sanity and a tiny shred of dignity. I figured I was way ahead at that point,' he said.

'I'm hoping to get a little more than that,' Carrie commented.

'We're here,' Cam said, pulling into a parking lot.

Cam got out of his car and inserted his credit card into the ticket machine, bringing the ticket back to the car and leaving it on the dashboard. I resisted the urge to ask him how much it cost us to rent this parking space for the hour or so we were going to be here, but I knew the truth would only make me angry. There were some definite downsides to living and working downtown. I took a deep breath and cleared my mind, focusing instead on the beautiful high-rise office structure, right on the river, surrounded by trees and picnic tables.

'Are you sure we can afford him?' I asked.

'It's OK; he'll give us a good deal. I'm sure he owes me for something,' Cam assured us.

We walked through the marble lobby toward the glass-enclosed elevators. Carrie stopped and looked across the lobby at a man reading a newspaper. I thought I saw a hint of a blush cross her cheeks.

'Someone you know, Carrie?' I asked.

'No, I thought it was someone else,' she said, turning back toward the elevator.

Cam pushed the button for the twenty-third floor. I turned and put my face into his chest so I wouldn't have to look out as the elevator climbed the side of the building. I was scared of heights, something I was trying unsuccessfully to get over. Cam put his arm around me and rubbed my back, gently pulling me out of the elevator when the door finally opened.

'You're doing better,' he whispered in my ear.

'Why, because I didn't scream?'

'It's a start,' he laughed.

'Well, I think getting dropped off a forty-foot tower has probably helped a little,' I explained, referring back to the murder that had brought Cam into my apartment and almost ended our life together when the killer decided to come after me.

'It's this way,' Cam said.

We followed Cam down the corridor and into the office.

'Hello, Mr Caminski,' the pretty receptionist greeted him, which immediately made me wonder how well she knew him. 'Mr Smith asked me to show you into the conference room as soon as you arrived. If you'd follow me, please.'

We followed her down the hall and into a conference room that reeked of money. Solid mahogany table, heavy leather chairs, brass trim and the best view I'd seen in years; the river

25

and edge of the city on one side, the mountains on the other.

'We really can't afford him,' I whispered to Cam.

'I have coffee on the credenza for you, please help yourselves. I'll just let Mr Smith know you're here,' she said, closing the door behind her but not before she flashed a hundred-watt smile in Cam's direction.

'I think you should have stuck to university and followed your friend to law school,' I told Cam.

'No, Elijah told me that I take home more than he does.'

'But he's definitely got the better office,' I pointed out.

'And the higher stress levels. I like coming home and not worrying about work. And Elijah has to hire people to fix things, I do it myself.'

'Good point,' I said, pouring myself a coffee. 'Anyone want coffee?'

'I'll have one,' Cam said and I handed him a cup.

'Carrie?' I asked.

'No, I'm afraid I'll throw up if I put anything in my stomach right now.' She laughed nervously.

'Don't worry,' I said, pouring myself a cup and moving to the conference table. 'Everything's going to be fine.'

The door opened and we turned as one.

'Cam!' Elijah smiled, crossing the room in a couple of huge strides and grabbing Cam's outstretched hand. 'Good to see you, man. You're looking good. You must be in love.'

'On that note, let me introduce my girlfriend, Kate Carpenter,' Cam said, pulling me forward.

I held out my hand and found it engulfed in Elijah's hand. The guy had to be six four at least, built like a football player with a mass of black curls on his head that looked like they would benefit from a good cut.

'Wow,' I said, watching his hand engulf mine. 'I mean, pleased to meet you.'

'Did I tell you Eli played football for the Calgary Stampeders?' Cam asked.

'Only for a season,' he said. 'It's hard to balance a football career and a law career and I would have broken my mother's heart if I gave up law.'

'But you must have broken your father's heart when you gave up football,' Cam laughed.

26

'Yeah, well, he got over it. Mom was the one that would have held a grudge.'

Cam laughed. 'Looks like it's working out well for you, though.'

'I'm doing OK. And Kate, great to meet you. So you're the one that's going to tame our boy here?' he asked, his baritone voice commanding the attention of all within earshot. I could imagine him in court. 'You guys just let me know when you're ready for a pre-nup.'

'Oh God,' I choked.

'I guess that means you're not ready yet,' he joked, a deep booming sound that almost made the pictures on the wall rattle. 'And you must be Carrie?'

'That would be me.' She smiled timidly.

'Why don't we all have a seat and find out what's going on here?' Elijah said, pulling out a chair for himself at the head of the table. He dropped a yellow legal pad on the table in front of him, pulled the cap off his pen, and scribbled today's date at the top of the page. 'So, Carrie, tell me all about your life.'

'I don't know where to start,' Carrie said, looking down at the table and studying her fingernails.

'She's really nervous about this,' Cam explained. 'Maybe you can ask some questions, let us know what kind of information you need to get us warmed up here.'

'OK. First of all, are you married?' Elijah asked. 'In the legal sense, I mean.'

'No,' Carrie said.

'Common-law,' he said out loud while he wrote on his legal pad. 'For how long?'

'Over five years. It'll be six years in June.'

'OK. Well that's definitely common-law marriage. Do you have kids?'

'I do, I have a boy and a girl with my first husband.'

'And where are they now?' he asked.

'They're with their father.'

'So you've decided it's time to end it with this man?'

'He hit me. He's been psychologically abusive for a long time, but when I told him it was over, he hit me.'

'Just once?'

27

'A couple of times. I managed to lock myself in the bathroom and call the police,' Carrie explained.

'Were there charges pressed?' he asked.

'I didn't know I could do that. The police told me they couldn't guarantee my safety and suggested I leave the house and stay with a friend for the night. I just packed my bag and took off.'

'So you're not in the house at this point?' he asked, an eyebrow raised.

'No.'

'Well, that's not a good thing.' He scribbled furiously on the legal pad. 'Whose name is the house in?'

'It's in both our names,' Carrie said.

'Wait a minute,' I interrupted. 'What do you mean it's not good that she's not in the house right now?'

'Well, unfortunately possession really is nine tenths of the law. At least until we get in front of a judge. It's doubtful that she'll get back in the house before the court orders it.'

'But everything I own is in there. I don't even have a change of clothes. And neither do the kids.'

'Well, we're going to try to get a court date next week to get some of your stuff. Now, off the record, you would probably be wise to give him a call and see if he will let you come and get some stuff. If he will, take some friends over and get what you can. If not, you can get some friends together and go to the house when he's gone and get whatever you can.'

'We were going to go over there this afternoon,' Cam said.

'Good. But of course we never talked about any of this and if you were to ask me about it, I would advise against it. OK?' He stared straight at Cam, making sure his message was received loud and clear. 'Now, do you have bank books with you or the deed to the house, anything like that?'

'It's all in the house.'

'OK, you should try to get everything you can while you're there. Otherwise, you're going to have to go to the bank and get your records and head to a registry to get a copy of the deed.'

'We'll try to get all that stuff,' Cam said.

'I want to know why the police suggested she get out of there if those are the ramifications. Why didn't they press charges against him?' I asked.

28

'Well, it's not a perfect world,' he said. 'The bottom line is probably that they were worried about keeping her safe. And there are still some police officers that have a certain attitude about domestic disputes even though it's not the way the force really thinks about it. The domestic abuse unit should have been called. I'll make sure this all gets forwarded to the right department, though, and that they have a record of everything.'

'So now she has to go through all this because they didn't want to bother with a domestic dispute?' I asked.

'Well, that's what the courts are for,' he offered.

'I don't think we should settle for that,' I said.

'Katie,' Cam tried to stop me.

'I'm sorry, they advised her to get out but they didn't bother to advise her that she would lose everything she owns?'

'We're going to try to make sure that doesn't happen,' Elijah explained. 'And unfortunately, as much as I would love a precedent-setting case against the police department, this isn't going to be the one. What we have to figure out is where we're at now and proceed from that point.'

'So women are still getting screwed?' I asked.

'Katie, Eli is trying to help us,' Cam reminded me.

'It's OK, Cam, this is what I do all day long.' Elijah smiled at him and then turned back to me. 'Yes, women are still getting screwed sometimes. Now it may take a little longer this way than it would if she were still living in the house and he were out on the streets, but I am sure that I will get Carrie what she deserves. She will get half the house and all her belongings. It is unfortunate that it had to happen this way, but at least she is safe.'

'I don't know if she is or not,' Cam said. 'Hank called our house last night.'

'Cam, why didn't you tell me?' Carrie asked.

'It was late, you were already asleep,' Cam explained. 'And all he wanted to do was threaten you.'

'But how did he find me?' she asked. 'It took me most of the day to find you.'

'There are ways to find people and it's much easier than both of you think,' Elijah said. 'Especially if honesty is not a big issue for you. Now, did he make any threats?'

'Several,' Cam said.

'And did you make any back?'

'Maybe,' he admitted.

'Well, if he calls again, don't. We want him to be the bad guy here, not you. So be good. But the good news is that I can probably get a restraining order against him. I'll just get you to swear out an affidavit before you go and that should be enough if I can get the right judge. Also, Carrie, are there any injuries from your altercation with Hank? Any bruises or lacerations we can photograph as evidence?'

'I have some bruises on my hips and buttocks,' she admitted. 'And I have a bit of a black eye under my makeup.'

'OK, we'll get a record of those before you leave.'

'Do you have to?' she asked.

'I'm afraid so. We need it all for evidence. Otherwise it's just his word against yours.'

'But I just want my fair share of things. And my money back.'

'He cleaned out the bank accounts,' Cam explained.

'Well, you should open up new bank accounts today, with your signature only. And make sure you arrange to have everything deposited into the new accounts.'

'I don't want to bring up his hitting me in the separation,' Carrie said. 'I just want it to be over.'

'Well, here's the deal. We won't use anything against him unless we have to. But these guys can play dirty, Carrie, and we have to be ready for that. So we'll take those pictures and we'll save them just in case we need them, OK?'

'Alright,' she finally agreed.

'Good. So I'll get to work on the restraining order and I'll get the paperwork ready for the rest of it. But I need to see some of your paperwork before we can move on any of that.'

'And I need to know how much this is going to cost,' Carrie said. 'I don't make a lot of money and I don't even have any right now, since he cleaned out the bank accounts.'

'Don't worry, you've got Cam's special rates,' Elijah assured her.

'And I'll help, Carrie,' Cam said. 'I don't want you to worry about money right now.'

She smiled weakly at Cam but nodded her head in agreement.

'OK,' Elijah said, pulling himself up out of the chair. 'I'll send my investigator in to take some pictures and then you call me when you get copies of all your records. And don't worry, my investigator is a woman. I know it usually makes people feel more comfortable to know that.'

'Thanks, Elijah,' Cam said, standing and shaking his hand.

'And I'll let Laurie, my receptionist, know that you're not available anymore,' Elijah laughed. 'But it'll break her heart. Nice meeting you, Kate.'

'Laurie?' I asked after Elijah had left. 'The receptionist?'

'That would be her,' Cam admitted.

'Do I want to know about this?' I asked.

'A couple of dates right after my divorce,' he said.

'Good enough for now.' I smiled sardonically. 'I'll expect further details later.'

The door opened again and a woman who reminded me a little of my grandmother came in.

'Hi, I'm Norma.' She smiled at us. 'Elijah asked me to take some pictures. Which one of you is Carrie?'

'I am,' Carrie answered, holding up her hand and waving.

'OK, dear, come along with me,' she said, taking Carrie's hand and leading her out of the room. 'We'll just be a couple of minutes. You two can wait in the reception area.'

'Kate?' Carrie turned and looked at me with fear in her eyes.

'Do you want me to come with you?' I asked.

'Please,' she whispered.

I turned to Cam. 'I'll meet you back in the reception area as soon as we're done.'

I followed Carrie and Norma down the hall and into a small room that looked almost like a doctor's examination room. There was an exam bed, a curtained changing area, a light box for reading x-rays and lots of camera equipment on the counter.

'OK, dear, if you'll just go behind the curtain and change into this.' Norma smiled, holding out a paper gown.

'I'll be right here,' I said to Carrie, noticing her hesitation.

Carrie walked behind the curtain and closed it after her. Norma busied herself by checking that her camera was loaded and setting out some extra rolls of film.

31

'How are you doing, dear?' she finally asked.

'I'm ready,' Carrie said, opening the curtain and taking a step forward. She held the gown closed behind her with one of her hands.

'Good,' Norma told her. 'Now, if you'll just stand in front of this wall.'

'Here?' Carrie asked, moving slightly.

'That's right.' Norma smiled again. 'Now, where are the bruises?'

'There's one on my shoulder, some marks on my arms where he grabbed me, and some on my hips and rear end.'

'OK, we're just going to focus on those areas and get nice clear pictures of the marks, OK?' she asked. 'Now, let's start with your arm. Can you pull up the sleeve of the gown and let me see?'

Carrie obediently did as she was instructed and the woman moved closer with her camera. She studied the bruise for a couple of minutes and then adjusted her camera and began flashing pictures. Carrie jumped at the first couple of flashes, but then started to calm down.

'OK, I think that's good for that one. Now, let's have a look at that hip. Just slide the side of the gown up a little,' she instructed and she repeated her picture-taking process. She did the same for the marks on her buttocks and then had a quick look over Carrie to make sure there weren't any other marks we might have missed. She took a couple of Carrie's face, but didn't think that they would show up very well on film.

'I think that should do it,' Norma told her. 'So we should be done with you for the day. You go ahead and change; I'm just going to run this straight down to the darkroom. I'm sure Elijah will want to see these as soon as possible.'

She left us alone and I smiled at Carrie.

'You did great,' I told her.

'I'm just glad it's over,' she said. 'I can hardly wait to get out of here.'

'Well, you get yourself changed; I'm just going to go and check on Cam. I don't want to leave him alone with that receptionist for too long.'

'You go ahead, I'll be quick.' She smiled weakly, trying to reassure me that she was doing better than she actually was.

I walked back into the lobby area where Cam sat waiting and watched the receptionist smile at him. I tried to come up with a great line to stop her dead in her tracks but, unfortunately, Carrie was back with us before I came up with anything and we headed for the car. Cam and Carrie took the elevator; I opted for the stairs this time. You could only fight so many fears in one day. Besides, going down stairs sort of counted as exercise, didn't it? I made it to the lobby and saw Cam and Carrie waiting out on the street for me. I pushed through the revolving doors, right behind the man who had been reading the newspaper. He looked back towards Carrie and then hurried down the street in the opposite direction. I shook my head and realized that I had a very suspicious mind. Some things were just coincidence.

It was almost two o'clock when we finally stopped by the theatre and loaded the trunk with boxes. I hadn't realized we had been at the lawyer's for so long. We had also stopped and picked up a new phone for the living room before we came to the theatre. When we were fully loaded, Carrie phoned home from my office to make sure there was no one there and we headed out to try to rescue some of her possessions.

We made great time cross-town to Carrie's house, just missing rush-hour traffic. I figured everything was going too smoothly, and I was right. When we pulled into the driveway, Hank's car was there. Cam and I both looked to Carrie.

'What do you want to do?' we asked simultaneously.

'Let me go talk to him. Maybe he's calmed down a little,' she said.

'I don't want you to go in there alone,' Cam said. 'I'll come with you.'

'No, Cam, that will only make him angry. Let me go in. If he gets worked up, I'll come running for you.'

'Leave the front door open,' I instructed her.

'I'll leave the door open,' she promised.

'I'm giving you five minutes,' Cam said. 'Then I'm coming in, no matter what.'

'OK,' she said, opening the door. 'But let's try to keep it cool. If he's calmed down I'd like to keep him that way.'

'I'll be calm,' Cam promised.

33

Carrie walked up to the front door and rang the bell. We sat nervously in the car waiting for the door to open. She rang the bell again and we still waited. She finally pulled out her key and let herself in. She disappeared into the house and we waited again. Cam was getting jumpy and checking his watch every thirty seconds. He was just about to reach for the door handle and race in after her when Carrie came back outside and leaned down to the driver's side window.

'There's no one home,' she said. 'Let's all grab a box and get what we can before he gets back.'

Cam and I were out of the car in a flash, grabbed some boxes from the trunk and followed Carrie into the house. She led us down the darkened hallway to her bedroom. I threw my box on the bed and pulled open a dresser drawer and started tossing underwear into the box. Cam and Carrie were in the closet, loading up clothes and shoes. I realized my earlier fears were just the product of my overactive and cynical imagination. There was absolutely nothing to worry about. We were going to get her stuff and get out of here without anything happening after all.

'Freeze!'

I turned to the bedroom door and froze. There were two police officers, guns drawn and pointed directly at me.

'I'm not moving,' I promised them. 'Cam, Carrie, time to come out of the closet, very slowly.'

'Katie, what the hell are you talking about?' Cam asked, coming out of the closet and stopping dead in his tracks when he saw the policemen.

'Drop the stuff on the floor,' one of them ordered in a loud barking voice. 'Come on, face down on the floor now!'

Cam and I slowly got to our knees and then on to the floor. Carrie stood behind Cam, with a terrified look on her face, like a rabbit caught in headlights.

'But this is my house,' she said.

'Get down now!' the officer yelled at her.

'Carrie, do what they say,' I suggested, not wanting my life to end here on this bedroom floor because she wouldn't lie down. 'We can tell them our story later.'

Carrie finally obeyed and one of the officers crossed over to where Cam lay, frisked him quickly and handcuffed his hands behind his back. Then he did the same to Carrie and me. They pulled us to our feet and led us out to the car, locking us in the back seat. One of them went back into the house and came out with a man I assumed was Hank.

'Thank God you got here in time,' he said to the officer, looking shaken. 'I was just working on the computer downstairs when I heard them break in.'

'Liar,' I yelled at him, leaning my head out the open window. 'We used a key.'

'Shut up,' the cop in the front seat told me.

'Do you know these people?' the other cop asked Hank.

'Never seen them before,' Hank said, staring straight at Carrie. 'I want to press charges.'

'Don't worry, they'll be charged,' the officer assured him.

'We could straighten this all out right here and right now,' I said. 'This woman is his wife. This is just a domestic dispute gone wild. Ask him.'

'I told you to be quiet,' the cop in the front told me again.

'Katie, why don't you listen to him,' Cam suggested. 'We can straighten this out at the police station.'

'We can straighten this out here,' I continued, ignoring him. 'She wants to press charges against him. He beat her up and she had to leave the house the other night.'

'Come on, Steve,' the cop in the front seat called out to his partner. 'Let's get this loudmouth down to the station. I'm getting tired of the sound of her voice.'

'You better watch it,' I warned him. 'I'll be more than happy to give your badge number to my lawyer.'

'Ma'am, let me remind you that you are charged with breaking and entering. I don't believe I was in any way remiss in my duties in my apprehension of you. Now what I suggest is that you respect your right to remain silent.'

'Does your mother know how you treat people?' I asked.

'Katie, just be quiet,' Cam said, a little more forcibly.

I decided I'd listen to him this time, as the first cop got into the car and pulled out of the driveway. I didn't say another word until we were deposited in front of a desk sergeant at the police station.

'Name?' he asked me.

'I want you to call Detective Ken Lincoln,' I demanded.

'Name?' he asked again.

'I'm sorry, are you hard of hearing?' I asked. 'I want to speak with Detective Ken Lincoln right now.'

'Katie, just give him your name,' Cam said. 'I'll call Elijah as soon as I can and he'll take care of this.'

'Ken can vouch for us,' I said. 'I am not going to be arrested for taking Carrie to her own house and packing up her own things.'

'Sarge, may I recommend a deal here?' the cop who had arrested us asked.

'What?'

'Call this detective if she'll agree to cooperate. Trust me, I drove down here with her and she's not going to stop until you cave in.'

The desk sergeant turned back to me. 'If I call the detective for you, will you agree to help me fill out my forms here?'

'Yes,' I promised.

'Fine. What department is he in?'

'Homicide. That's Detective Ken Lincoln,' I reminded him.

'I got it,' he said, picking up his phone. 'Detective Lincoln, this is Sergeant McKay at processing. I have someone here who says she knows you.'

I waited anxiously, hoping Ken wouldn't throw me to the wolves.

'Her name?' the sergeant asked. 'She won't give it to me.'

'Kate Carpenter,' I said.

'Kate Carpenter,' he repeated. 'OK, I'll do that. Thank you, sir.'

'Well?' I asked him, after he hung up the phone.

'Take them to the interview room. He'll be down in a few minutes.'

We were led into a small room, still handcuffed, and waited for Ken to appear.

'Katie, pissing off these people is not going to help us,' Cam said as soon as the door had closed.

'I'm sure Ken will get us out of here.'

'So would a lawyer,' Cam said. 'Which I would have been able to call by now if you hadn't started mouthing off.'

'Cam, this whole arrest thing is a crock of shit. I do not intend to be fingerprinted and body searched, OK?'

36

'Who is this detective?' Carrie asked.

I had almost forgotten she was here, she had been so quiet.

'I've worked on a couple of cases with him,' I explained.

'No, you interfered on a couple of cases with him,' Cam clarified. 'You were not supposed to be involved in any of it. Ken will probably tell them to lock you up.'

'Cam, there was somebody stalking me, I had to get involved.'

'Against the wishes of the entire police department,' he said.

'But we caught the killer.' I smiled triumphantly.

'And almost lost you,' Cam said. 'And the second time you got involved with a police investigation, you got shot.'

'You got shot?' Carrie asked.

'It was only a flesh wound,' I said, trying to play down the dramatics for once in my life.

'Because you were interfering, again,' Cam said.

'I was trying to help out my friend. They were going to arrest him for murder.'

'You don't know that,' Cam said. 'If you'd stayed out of it, I'm sure the police investigators would have discovered exactly the same thing and you wouldn't have gotten shot.'

'Cam, you don't know that. But you do know that I have to help my friends. Just like you with Carrie. And I don't have to point out just where that has gotten us.'

'I'm sorry I asked,' Carrie said.

'It's OK,' Cam said, finally cracking a smile. 'We're always like this.'

The door opened and I turned to see Ken Lincoln standing there, staring back at us. Ken Lincoln was the antithesis of everything that television made you believe a police detective should look like. Ken was young, good looking, fit, and new to homicide, just recently being promoted from street patrol. He wore designer suits and his shoes were always polished. His haircuts probably cost more than mine did. And he never drank a coffee or smoked a cigarette. But the combination of his innocence, lack of experience and personality were magnetic. You couldn't help but like Ken . . . if you were innocent. He seemed much tougher on the guilty ones. Maybe I should be a little more afraid of him right now than I was.

'Well, Kate, I must say that I've always dreamed of seeing you in this position,' he grinned.

'Ken, for whatever I've done to ever piss you off, I apologize, because right now we really need your help.'

'I can see that.' He crossed the room to one of the chairs, sat down, stretched out his legs, crossed his arms over his chest and looked very pleased with himself. 'Want to tell me what happened?'

'Maybe we could get out of these first?' I asked, turning around and showing him the handcuffs. 'I'm not exactly dangerous.'

'Oh, I don't know. You've got them pretty scared at the processing desk.'

'Ken . . .?'

'OK.' He smiled again and then turned to the door. 'Officer, would you mind releasing these dangerous prisoners from their shackles?'

A police officer came in and took the handcuffs off all three of us. I pulled out a chair and sat across the table from Ken.

'Now, you want to tell me what happened?' Ken asked.

'This is Cam's cousin, Carrie,' I said, introducing her. 'She is in the process of leaving her husband. He beat her up and threw her out of the house. And thanks to the bad advice your fellow officers gave her—'

'Katie,' Cam warned me.

'She's out of the house and doesn't have any of her stuff. We were just trying to get some clothes and things for her.'

'Apparently the home owner said he didn't know any of you,' Ken pointed out.

'If you check the deed to the property, you'll see it's listed jointly in his name and in Carrie's,' Cam said.

'Did you press charges against him?' Ken asked.

'No, I just wanted a nice quiet and quick separation,' she said. 'I didn't want to involve the police.'

'Did you contact a lawyer?' Ken asked.

'We saw a friend of mine this morning,' Cam said. 'Elijah Smith. He specializes in family law.'

'I know him,' Ken said. 'He's very good.'

'That is why I took her to him.'

'And how did you gain access to the house today?' Ken asked.

'Carrie used her key,' I said. 'Did anyone look at the door to see if it was jimmied?'

'I'll have to check the report. Have you got the key?' Ken asked.

Carrie pulled it out of her purse and handed it to him.

'OK, you guys sit tight, I'll go check some of this out and see what I can do.'

'I don't suppose we can get some coffee while we wait?' I asked.

'Kate, I know you have always treated me with great hospitality at your theatre. However this is a police station and we don't usually provide our suspects with room service. But I promise I'll be as quick as I can.'

When Ken was gone, Cam turned back to me with fire in his eyes.

'Why do you insist on pushing so hard?' he asked.

'Why should I change my style now?' I asked. 'It seems to be working.'

'Katie, we've been sitting in a police station for over an hour, waiting to be processed. How are we any further ahead than we were a few minutes ago?'

'Trust me, Ken is going to help us,' I said, feeling very sure of myself.

But my self-assuredness started to vanish as time passed and Ken didn't come back. Almost two hours later, I was just beginning to really sweat when the door to our little prison finally opened again. Ken walked in, followed closely by Elijah Smith, who had to duck his head to get through the doorway.

'Well, I see things went well today,' Elijah greeted us.

'Have you got news?' I asked, looking anxiously from Elijah to Ken and back again.

'Yes, I think we've straightened things out here,' Elijah said.

'We're not going to press charges,' Ken added.

'Told you,' I smiled at Cam.

'But Hank has filed for a restraining order against you,' Elijah said.

'Against me?' Carrie asked.

'Actually, against all of you,' Elijah explained.

'He filed against us?' I asked, shocked.

'Apparently he's worried about his safety,' Elijah said. 'And a judge believed him. But don't worry, I'm going to go to court first thing in the morning and do some filing of my own. We're on top of this.'

'He should be worried about his sanity not his safety if you're after him,' Ken joked.

'Thanks loads,' I smiled, too relieved to be truly angry.

'If you're through with these felons, can I drive them back to their car?' Elijah asked Ken.

'Please, take them away,' he said with a laugh. 'I'd like to get back to my real job.'

'Thanks, Ken,' I said, seriously. 'I really appreciate all you did to help us.'

'It seems like that's part of my job description, to get you out of trouble,' he answered.

'You and me both,' Cam added.

'I didn't get us involved in this, Cam. Let's not forget that.'

'Let's get you guys out of here,' Elijah said, interrupting us before we could really get started.

'Good idea,' Cam admitted. 'You sure you don't mind driving us? I can call a cab.'

'Don't worry about it, I'll bill you,' Elijah chortled.

He dropped us off and made sure we were well off the property before leaving us to head back to his office. The three of us drove home in relative silence and didn't say anything until we were in the safety of the apartment, with the door triple-locked behind us.

'Do you mind if I have a bath?' Carrie asked.

'No,' I said. 'The towels are in the cupboard in the bath-room.'

'Do you mind if I have a really long bath?' she asked.

'Why don't you pour yourself a glass of wine to take in with you,' Cam said. 'And don't come out until you're good and relaxed.'

She stood on her tiptoes and kissed him on the cheek.

'Thanks so much for taking such good care of me,' she smiled, tears forming in her eyes and then, embarrassed, she hurried off into the bathroom.

'Well, I guess it's just us.' I smiled at Cam.

'What do you want to do?' he asked. 'I could make dinner.'

'I'm not really hungry. How about a movie?' I offered.

'OK, a movie it is. You pick it out, I'll grab a couple of beers.'

'Want to watch it upstairs? That way if Carrie wants, she can go to bed after her bath.'

'Sure,' he answered from the kitchen.

'What do you feel like?' I called back to him, standing in front of the bookshelf and realizing we had too many movies.

'I don't care,' he said, slamming the fridge and heading upstairs.

I grabbed a musical and followed him upstairs.

He was already propped up on the bed, pillows behind his head and his beer resting on his chest.

'What did you pick?' he asked.

'*Moulin Rouge*,' I said, popping it into the VCR. 'And I'm going to sing along.'

'Alright.' He smiled. 'But I'm not singing Ewan McGregor's part. We have company.'

'I don't care,' I said, slipping out of my skirt and pulling off my sweater over my head. I grabbed one of his sweat-shirts and pulled it on, grabbed a thick pair of wool socks and sat on the side of the bed to put them on.

'I must be in love,' he said.

'Why?'

'Because, even in wool socks and a baggy sweatshirt, you turn me on.'

'Get over it, babe, we have company, remember?'

'I am going to close in this room if it's the last thing I do,' he said, grabbing me and pulling me on to the bed beside him.

'Where's the remote, the movie is starting?' I asked.

'I got it,' he said, pointing it toward the TV and turning the volume up.

'Where's my beer?' I asked.

He grabbed it from the nightstand and handed it to me.

'*Voulez vous coucher avec moi*,' I sang, but then the phone rang and interrupted me.

'Ignore it,' Cam said.

'It might be the lawyer,' I said, jumping over him to grab the portable. 'Hello.'

'Hey, Kate, it's Graham,' he greeted me. 'Hey, is that *Moulin Rouge*?'

'Yes, it is.'

'Great songs, I especially like the love song montage,' he said. Graham was my assistant at the theatre and was also a budding actor. 'So did you forget we had a play tonight?'

'Graham, I've had a rough day,' I explained, trying to hurry him up. 'I'm sorry I didn't get to the theatre and I'm sorry I didn't call you but can we do the whole guilt trip and humble apology tomorrow?'

'I've been trying to get a hold of you all day, where have you been?' he persisted.

'In jail.'

'What?' His voice almost cracked with excitement. 'Do tell.'

'Tomorrow, I promise. Cam'll shoot me if I stay on the phone too long.' I noticed he was already giving me a dirty look.

'OK, but you better promise to tell all.'

'I promise. So were you just calling to chat?' I asked.

'No, I just wanted to let you know that there's a pre-show party tomorrow. Starts at five o'clock.'

'OK, I'll be there early,' I promised. 'Do we need staff?'

'I've got it all taken care of,' he assured me. 'And I'll be there extra early so you can share your experience doing time with me.'

'If I have to.'

'Does this mean the Kate Carpenter Detective Agency is back in business?' he asked.

'Not on your life. I've got to go, Graham.'

'See you tomorrow, Kate.' He signed off.

'Bye.' Cam took the phone from me. 'He's very excited we were arrested.'

'Well, I'm glad someone is getting some enjoyment out of this,' Cam said. 'But I'd prefer it if everyone at the Plex didn't find out about it.'

'I agree. I promise, I'll just tell Graham and swear him to secrecy.'

'Like that'll do any good.'

'I'll threaten to fire him,' I promised. 'He'll keep his mouth shut.'

'We going to watch the movie?' he asked.

'Are you going to sing with me?' I asked.

'I give up,' he said, pulling the comforter over his head. 'I should know I can't win with you.'

Thursday November 13

I woke up in the pitch dark and felt like shit. I hated this time of year, when the sun came up so late in the morning. In the summer, I could tell what time it was by the height of the sun as it peeked through the curtains. Cam was still in bed beside me, so I knew right away it was somewhere between 5:00 and 8:00 a.m., and on either end of that scale it was much earlier than the time I normally woke up. I knew it wasn't later, because he would be out jogging or cleaning something or otherwise being efficient. And I probably wouldn't feel this terrible either, because it didn't matter what time I went to bed, I was not a morning person. I rolled over so I could see the clock. It was only seven thirty. A little late for Cam, although he was working the late shift, but really early for me.

'Are you awake?' Cam asked sleepily, feeling my movement, a heavy arm landing on my shoulder.

'Barely,' I mumbled.

'What time is it?'

'Seven thirty,' I forced out, wondering why my stomach was giving me such grief this morning. I started taking some slow, deep breaths, trying to settle it.

'Are you OK?' he asked.

'I don't feel good,' I admitted.

'What's wrong?'

'I don't know. Maybe I'm getting the flu or something.'

'I'll make you some tea,' he said, throwing back the covers and getting up.

The thought of tea made my stomach suddenly lurch and

43

I dove out of bed, throwing myself over him, and raced for the bathroom.

'Katie?' he called after me.

I slammed the bathroom door behind me, not caring at all that our guest might still be sleeping, and barely reached the toilet in time. When I finally stood up Cam was standing behind me, holding out a glass of water for me. I took it gratefully and rinsed out my mouth. Then he handed me a facecloth and I washed my face.

'Back upstairs to bed,' he ordered. 'I'll bring you a cup of tea and I'll call Graham and tell him you won't be in tonight.'

'Don't call Graham yet, I've missed a lot of work recently,' I pleaded with him.

'Katie . . .' It was the semi-menacing, semi-patronizing tone that I wasn't quite sure how to deal with yet.

'Let's wait until this afternoon and see how I feel?' I tried.

'Only if you promise to get back to bed right now.'

'I will,' I said, hanging up the facecloth and heading for the stairs. I climbed back into bed and pulled the covers around me. Surprisingly, I didn't feel bad anywhere else. No fever or chills, no aches or pains, and my stomach seemed to be settling down. Just a few hours sleep and I was sure I'd be fine.

Cam came up the stairs, carrying a tray for me. He set it on the bedside table, poured a cup of tea and handed it to me. Then he sat on the side of the bed and felt my forehead.

'You remind me of my mother,' I said, sipping the tea slowly.

'Katie, somebody has to take care of you.' He smiled. 'Because you sure don't take care of yourself.'

'I'm young, I'm healthy, and I don't have to worry.'

'Well, you should. How're you feeling now?'

'Better,' I said, 'Just tired.'

'You go to sleep,' he said, brushing my hair away from my face. 'I'm going to go out for a run, if you think you'll be OK.'

'I'll be fine.'

'OK.'

'Do you want me to come and put the chain on the door?' I asked.

'No, I feel a little safer with the restraining orders in place. I don't think Hank will risk going to jail.'

'OK. Well, you run for as long as you want, Cam, I'm fine.'

'Thanks,' he said, leaning forward and kissing my forehead. 'I'll check on you when I get back.'

I couldn't help but smile at him as he pulled on his sweats and runners and headed down the stairs. I heard him whispering to Carrie in the living room for a minute and then I heard the front door close. I took one last sip of my tea, pulled the blankets tightly around me and fell asleep.

'Katie.'

I heard the voice and prayed it was a dream. I didn't want to wake up yet. But it persisted.

'Katie,' he called again, gently shaking my shoulder. 'Time to wake up, Katie.'

'Go away,' I mumbled.

'Katie, it's two o'clock. Do you want me to call Graham and tell him you're not coming in?' Cam asked.

He hit on my sore spot, work.

'No,' I said, slowing opening my eyes and trying to push myself into a sitting position.

'How are you feeling?' he asked.

'Fine,' I said, wondering if that was true or not.

'Are you sure?' he asked.

I blinked a couple of times, trying to pull myself fully awake.

'Yeah, I think so. Why'd you let me sleep so late?'

'I thought you needed it, since you were getting sick. And I knew that no matter how you felt, you'd want to go to work tonight.'

'Well, I really do feel OK,' I said, feeling surer of it by the minute. 'Don't you have to go to work?'

'I'm just getting ready to leave,' he said. 'That's why I wanted to make sure you were up.'

'I'm up.'

'There's coffee on downstairs.'

'Where's Carrie?' I asked.

'She's reading on the patio. She called into work and updated them and they told her to take as much time as she needed.'

'What are we going to do with her tonight while we're both at work?' I asked. 'I hate to leave her alone again.'

'I had a talk with her this morning. She feels OK about being alone. And I made her promise not to answer the phone or open the door, so that we wouldn't worry about her.'

'But are you going to worry about her all night?' I asked him.

'Of course I will. I worried about her all Tuesday night, I'm sure I'll do the same thing tonight, too. But she's a little too old for a babysitter, so I guess we just have to trust that she'll be smart enough to stay safe.'

'OK,' I agreed. 'Want to have a coffee with me when I get in to the office?'

'Sure, get security to page me when you get there,' he said. 'I have no idea where I'll be or what I'll be doing, but I'm sure I'll be ready for a break in a couple of hours.'

'OK, see you later then,' I said, giving him a quick kiss and lying back down on the bed.

'Katie, the alarm isn't set. If you fall asleep—'

'I'm up, I'm up,' I said, reluctantly unpeeling myself from the comforter and getting out of bed.

'Want to walk me to the door?' he asked.

'Don't you trust that I'll stay up?'

'Something like that.'

'OK,' I said, grabbing my robe and tying it around my waist. I followed him down the stairs and into the hallway.

There was a letter shoved under the door and I bent over to pick it up. It was from the landlord. I ripped it open and read the letter quickly. The last time I got a letter from the landlord I had bounced a rent cheque and was about to get evicted.

'What is it?' Cam asked.

'Oh God,' I said, my stomach churning again, but for a totally different reason this time.

'What is it?' Cam asked again.

'The building is going condo,' I told him.

'What does it say?'

'There's a meeting next month to fill in the details, but basically it looks like we've got six months to decide. Either buy in or get out.'

'Six months is a long time, Katie,' he chuckled. 'We don't have to decide today. Besides, buying a house isn't like getting married or having a baby. It's only a little commitment.'

'Oh yeah, you're telling me that with Carrie sitting out on the patio. Look at what happened to her.'

'Katie, let's not get all worked up about this yet, it's only the first notice,' he said. 'Besides, I'm not Hank. What happened to Carrie is not going to happen to you.'

'I can't deal with this,' I said, crumpling up the letter and tossing it back on to the floor.

Cam bent over and picked it up, smoothing the paper where I had crumpled it. 'If you don't want to buy, we won't buy. We need to think about it and decide what the best way to go is. OK?'

'You're right,' I said, looking sheepish. 'Sorry, just one of those little commitment freak-outs I'm prone to having.'

'There are lots of solutions to this problem,' he assured me. 'But if I stay here and list them all for you now I'm going to be late for work.'

'I know.'

'You won't worry about this all evening?' he asked.

'Oh, I probably will. When I'm not worrying about Carrie being here alone.'

'Me too,' he agreed with me. 'OK, I'm out of here.'

I grabbed him and pulled him back in the door. 'Not without a kiss you aren't.'

And he gave me a kiss that kept me going for the rest of the afternoon.

I hit the shower, had a quick cup of coffee with Carrie, and then headed for the theatre.

I wasn't all that surprised to see Graham there waiting for me. Graham was nineteen years old, a recent high-school graduate and convinced his future held fame, fortune and the bright lights of Hollywood. He took any acting job he could get, sang all day and all night, and pranced around on the stage of our theatre until someone kicked him off. He was cute, blond and worked hard to keep himself in good shape. He told me that since he had seen Keanu Reeves make it big in *Speed*, he'd decided muscles were the answer. If Keanu could have a hit movie just because he had good biceps, imagine what someone who could actually act could do. Graham hadn't learned tact or diplomacy yet.

Graham was sitting at my side of the desk, working on something that I would probably rather not do, so I sat at the other side and let him keep working. He had a coffee poured and waiting for me, an ashtray out, and sat there, waiting anxiously for me to speak.

'Hi,' I said. 'What are you doing here so early?'

'Cut the small talk, Kate, I want to hear about this big arrest. What was it for?'

'Technically I wasn't actually arrested.'

'Did you get handcuffed?' he asked.

'Yes.'

'Did you ride in a police car?'

'Yes.' I sighed.

'In the back seat of that police car?' he pushed on.

'Yes, Graham.'

'Well, that's close enough for me. Now tell me about it.'

I took a sip of coffee and searched my purse for a cigarette. Graham opened my desk drawer and tossed a pack across the desk to me. I pulled one out and lit it, taking a long drag and another sip of coffee before I finally ran out of excuses for not talking.

'Well, Saturday there was a knock on our door and Cam's cousin Carrie turned up, in tears just after leaving her husband.'

'And you shot him?' Graham asked.

'Hardly. Not that I haven't thought about it. No, he beat her up, she left him, she came to stay with us and Cam took her to see a lawyer friend of his. The problem being that she left with just the shirt on her back. We decided to go over there yesterday and see if we could talk the guy into letting her take some of her stuff. Well, when we got there, he wasn't home. So Carrie let us in and we started packing up some of her stuff. Until the police appeared, guns drawn, and accused us of breaking and entering.'

'He was home?' Graham asked.

'In the basement, with a cell phone, calling 911, as we were letting ourselves in the front door.'

'He had his own wife arrested?'

'Claimed he'd never seen her before in his life,' I explained.

48

'Nice guy.'

'Yeah, whatever. So they took us down to the station to process us. Luckily, Ken Lincoln was in and he helped straighten everything out. Eventually. They move really slowly at the Police Department.'

'That's not exactly the dramatic story I was waiting for,' he complained.

'It was more than dramatic enough for me, thank you very much.'

'So are you going to try going back to the house and get her stuff?' he asked. 'I'd love to come and help. Maybe with four of us there, we can get her stuff and get out before the police get there.'

'No way, I am not doing anything like that again,' I said, shaking my head to emphasize my point. 'I'm letting the police and the lawyers deal with this one from now on. Speaking of which, she's home alone. I think I'll give her a call and just make sure everything's OK.'

I picked up the phone and dialled home.

'Does he know where you live?' Graham asked.

'Probably. He got our phone number so I'm sure he's got our address.'

'Hello.' I heard my voice on the other end of the phone line. 'Neither Cam or I can take your call at the moment. Please leave your name and number at the tone.'

I waited for the beep.

'Carrie, it's Kate. Pick up if you're there.'

I waited a moment until I heard the answering machine click off and the phone being picked up.

'Hi, Kate,' she greeted.

'Hi, Carrie, how's it going?'

'OK,' she said, her voice betraying her.

'What's wrong?' I asked.

'He called a couple of times earlier. The first time he was really nice, but the second time he got very threatening. I hung up on him and I'm letting the answering machine pick up the calls from now on.'

'Has he called again?' I asked.

'Not yet,' she said. 'But promise you won't tell Cam. I don't want him to come rushing home to look after me.'

'But are you sure you're all right?' I asked. 'I can come home easier than Cam can—'

'I'm OK, Kate. I'm a little shaken up, but it's nothing I haven't dealt with for the last five years or so.'

'OK, but you have to promise to tell Cam when we get home tonight,' I instructed her.

'I will.'

'And don't touch that answering machine tape. If he calls again and threatens you, we're taking that tape straight to the lawyer tomorrow.'

'OK.'

'Carrie, is there somebody there with you?' I asked, thinking I had heard a voice in the background.

'No, I have the TV on. Sorry, I'll turn it down.'

'OK, so you're going to be all right until we get home? We'll be there around eleven.'

'I'll be fine. Really,' she said.

'And have you been able to find everything you need?' I asked. 'You know to just make yourself at home, right?'

'Kate, Cam called just before you did and I went through all this with him already. I promise I'll look for whatever I need, I promise I'll make myself some dinner, I promise I won't answer the door, and I promise I'll be fine and take care of myself until you get home. Just like I've done a million other times in my life.'

'Sorry, Carrie,' I apologized. 'We're both just worried about you.'

'I appreciate it, I really do,' she said. 'So is there anything else you need to check on?'

'No. I promise I'll leave you be for now. Look, I left my work number by the phone. You have to promise you'll call if you need anything.'

'I promise,' she said.

'OK, I'll let you go. Bye.'

'Well?'

I turned and saw Cam standing in the doorway.

'Well what?' I asked.

'That was Carrie you were talking to,' he explained, assuming I would now know what he was talking about.

'Yes, it was.'

50

'Well, what did she tell you that she didn't tell me when I called her?' he asked.

'Nothing.' I always tried to fake Cam out but it never worked.

'You're lying.'

'No I'm not, you're interrupting. I was going to say nothing that she's not going to tell you when you get home tonight.'

'Why didn't she tell me on the phone?' he asked.

'Cam, why don't we go grab a coffee?' I asked, not wanting to do this in front of Graham. I tried really hard to keep my personal life away from work. It never worked, but I still tried.

'Fine,' he said.

'Graham, I'll be back in twenty minutes or so.'

'Take your time, boss,' he said. 'Things are under control here.'

I took Cam's hand and led him down the fire escape toward the street. As we took the stairs down to the street I tried to break it to him gently.

'Look, Cam, I promised Carrie I wouldn't tell you, so I want you to promise not to get all excited about this.'

'As long as she's safe.' He applied his own conditions.

'She's safe. Hank's been calling and threatening her. But that's it, just phone calls.'

'I should go home.'

'See, that's why she didn't tell you. She doesn't want you rushing off to save her. I think she feels bad enough that she's invaded our lives, she doesn't want to mess up our jobs too.'

'Well, why did she tell you and not tell me?' he asked.

'She didn't really confess,' I explained. 'I sensed something was wrong and I kind of pushed her into telling me. Besides, she probably felt that I wouldn't overreact quite as badly as you would.'

Cam held the door open for me and we started down the street toward Grounds Zero, the coffee shop at the end of the block.

'This may end up working out really well,' I added.

'How do you figure that?' he asked.

'Well, if he leaves a threatening message on the answering machine, we can take it to the lawyer tomorrow, and that's got to do Carrie some good.'

51

'That's true. But what if he decides to come over and threaten her in person?'

'Cam, we live in a secure building. We've got a solid core door with three really substantial locks on it. Do you really think that he could get in before the police got there?' I asked.

'That's not what I'm worried about,' he said. 'I'm worried that Carrie won't call the police. Or even worse, that she may let him in.'

'Cam, do you think she's that stupid?'

'Not stupid, Katie. But she's lived with him for years and he's been like this for every one of those years. She's conditioned. And don't kid yourself. No matter what she says, this is not the first time he's hit her. The family has noticed lots of suspicious bruises on her over the years.'

'So why did she finally leave him?' I asked.

'Who knows? He must have crossed a line, did something that she refused to take. I don't understand this whole abused woman syndrome,' he said. 'I'm just glad she's out. For whatever reason.'

Or it could be another man, I thought. Someone who showed her how she should be treated and she liked it. I had to get her to tell Cam about this guy; I didn't like having these kinds of secrets from him.

Cam opened the door to Grounds Zero and I walked in. Gus, the owner, stood over by the counter, and I crossed over to my favourite seat. Cam sat beside me and lit a cigarette.

'Can I have one?' I asked.

'Do you think you should?' he asked. 'The way you were feeling this morning?'

'I'm feeling fine, Cam. And remember, there's a fine line between caring for me and patronizing me,' I warned him.

He pulled a cigarette out of his package and held it out for me. I took it from him and then he reached over and lit it for me. I loved the way he cupped his fingers protectively around the flame, just brushing my fingers with his. So Bogie and Bacall.

'Thank you.' I smiled.

'How are you feeling?' he asked.

'Fine, actually. I think whatever I had, I managed to sleep it off.'

'Hey, Kate and Cam,' Gus said, setting our coffee down in front of us.

'Hey, Gus, I don't recall ordering yet.'

'I decided to cut out the middle man. You two are far too predictable for me to wait around while you pretend to look at the menus, discuss whether you should try something new or not and then order exactly the same thing. I thought it would be much quicker this way.'

I looked down at my cappuccino with extra chocolate sprinkles. I didn't like being predictable, I was going to have to find something new to drink. Cam seemed happy enough with his, though, but this was just another battle he was winning in the commitment wars, as far as he was concerned.

'So how's your cousin doing?' Gus asked Cam.

'She's fine,' Cam answered.

'Wait a minute, how in the world did you know about her?' I asked. 'Nobody knows she's staying with us.'

'Kate, you should know by now that I don't give away my sources.' Gus smiled at me.

'So I should ask what you don't know?'

'Nothing important,' he said. 'I just like to keep up on what's happening with my friends.'

'So what do you know about Cam's cousin?' I asked, testing him.

'That she's left her husband and he's not such a nice guy. That Cam's hired her a good lawyer. And that yesterday, you spent a good part of the afternoon in jail.'

'I wasn't in jail,' I protested. 'I was at the police station.'

'Well, you're lucky that Detective Lincoln was there, from what I hear, or you would have been in jail.'

'We were in the right,' I said. 'That was Carrie's house and those were her things we were packing up.'

'But Kate, the police may not have particularly cared about that if Detective Lincoln hadn't made such a fuss about it. I hope you thanked him.'

'I refuse to believe that I would have been arrested,' I continued. 'We were in the right and justice would have been served.'

'Is this what she was like at the police station?' Gus asked Cam.

Cam just smiled at him and then took another sip of his coffee.

'You're lucky she got out at all,' Gus said with a laugh. 'So where are you going now with all this?'

'Well, I believe we're going to let the lawyer handle it all from this point,' Cam said. 'However, I haven't officially checked with Katie yet.'

'That's OK,' I said. 'I'm happy to let the professionals take over. I'd rather not spend another afternoon with the police.'

'I'm glad to hear that,' Gus said. 'These divorces have been known to get nasty.'

'I think it's pretty open and shut, Gus. All they have to do is split up their stuff and it's over.'

'Remember the wise words of Yogi Berra, "It ain't over until it's over".'

'Gus, I don't like it when you talk like this. Last time you told me to be careful, I ended up getting shot.'

'So it was good advice,' Cam said. 'Maybe this time you'll listen.'

'I'm listening,' I promised. 'I already said I'm leaving it up to the lawyers to handle. If you have a Bible here, I'll swear on it.'

'Better not do that,' Gus said. 'I'd be too afraid that lightening would strike us.'

'You guys are too funny,' I said, finishing my coffee. 'And as much as I'd like to stay and suffer your abuse, I really should get to work.'

Gus brought over the coffee pot. 'Want to try some of my new Kenya Blend for the road?'

'Sure,' I said, sliding the cup across the counter for him to fill up.

'I think you'll like this. It's really strong.'

'Thanks,' I said, picking up my cup. 'Cam, are you staying here?'

'No, I'll walk you as far as the stage door,' he said, standing up and tossing some money on the counter. 'I take it this is my treat?'

'Sorry, I left my bag in the office.'

'I'm used to it,' he said.

'I'll pay you back,' I promised. 'One way or another.'

54

Once we were outside I took his hand and gave it a squeeze.

'She'll be OK, Cam,' I promised him. 'I think she must have a good reason for finally leaving and she'll stay away from him. She just needs you to believe that. I think if she starts feeling like you're worrying about her all the time, she's going to think she's causing you too much trouble. You know what I mean?'

'I think I know what you mean. So I can worry but I can't tell her that I'm worrying?'

'Yeah, I think that's pretty much it.' I smiled. 'She has a lot to figure out and I guess we have to stand back a little and let her figure it out.'

'I'm scared for her, Kate. We've all been scared for her since she first took up with that loser.'

'I know, Cam.' I sighed. 'But this is a good first step she's taking. And she came to you for help. That means a lot.'

'Thanks, Katie.'

He left me at the stage door with a kiss and I walked the rest of the way to the theatre, enjoying the sunshine. I opened the front door and heard Graham singing. He was in the upstairs lobby, belting out something from *Gypsy*, and I snuck up quietly behind him, finally reaching out and tapping him on the shoulder. Poor Graham jumped ten feet straight up and turned fifteen different shades of red.

'Shit!' he screamed, turning around to see who was behind him. 'Kate, don't you ever do that to me again!'

'Sorry, I used to do that to my brother, I just couldn't resist seeing if it still worked.'

'I swear you scared ten years' growth off me.'

'Good, then it still works,' I laughed.

'So are you going to tell me what you and Cam talked about that you couldn't say in front of me?'

'Graham, you know it's not good for us parents to fight in front of the kids,' I joked.

'Kate, don't patronize me.'

'It's nothing, Graham,' I promised him.

'This ex-husband is hassling her, isn't he?' he asked.

'Yes, he is.'

'So what are we going to do about it?' he asked.

'Absolutely nothing,' I told him firmly. 'The lawyer is taking care of everything. If Hank wants to make some stupid phone calls, let him. He can't hurt us with phone calls.'

'As long as he doesn't decide to come over and do it in person,' Graham suggested.

'It's not going to happen. Besides, you've seen the locks that Cam has put on my door. No one could get in there.'

'Kate, I want to snoop around,' Graham said. 'We're getting good at this.'

'Graham, there is nothing to snoop around about. That's what the lawyer is taking care of. You and I are back to running a theatre.'

'But that's so boring,' he whined.

'A couple of months ago you thought it was pretty good,' I said.

'That was before we got all this real-life excitement going on around us.'

'And it's working out real well, too; you have fun investigating and I get shot.'

'Or you get dropped off the fly towers. Don't forget that one!'

'Don't remind me,' I said. 'But that's my point. We're staying out of this. If Hank is stupid enough to keep calling us, he's just digging his own grave. We're saving the answering machine tapes and I bet I'll see him arrested before the week is out,' I said smugly.

'The way your life has been going, I'd like to take that bet.' He smiled at me.

'Nope, I'm not tempting fate by even betting. I'm just going to enjoy the end of this run; a few more days, a little *Rock and Roll* and happy audiences. It's going to be great.'

Luckily the phone rang and saved me from further argument. Graham reached for the phone, but I beat him to it.

'Kate Carpenter,' I answered.

'Hey, Kate, it's Nick here,' the security supervisor from the stage door greeted me. 'I have a caterer here looking for your theatre. You want me to send him around to the front?'

'No, I'll come down there,' I said, hanging up the phone and then turned my attention back to Graham. 'The caterer is here.'

'You want me to go?' he asked.

56

'It depends, what are you working on now?' I asked.

'Just doing the sales summary for the month,' he explained.

'Well, you just keep working on that and I'll gladly go pick up the food.' I smiled, standing up.

'You're lucky you have me to do all the dirty work,' Graham said.

'I know.' I smiled at him and then headed for the stage door. Back to running a theatre, just like normal, I thought.

The night had gone about as smoothly as one could ever go. I actually left Graham in charge for most of the show and sat in the theatre, watching the play for the first time through without interruption. *Rock and Roll* had been running for a couple of weeks and I hadn't had a chance to watch it yet, with the double duty we had with the piano festival being moved to our theatre during the past couple of weeks. And I always tried to let the staff see the show first. After all, there had to be some perks other than the terrible pay and lousy hours. The show got out on time and we cleared up the last of the pre-show reception mess from the private room quickly, signed the staff out and were done.

I was actually about a half hour earlier than I thought I would be, so I wasn't surprised when Cam wasn't waiting out by the stage door for me. I left a message with the security guard for Cam and wandered down the street to Grounds Zero. Gus was the first person to own this little gem of a business that kept open late at night. No one seemed to realize that theatre people were night people, and the previous owners had all closed up at eight o'clock at night, which is probably why they were previous owners and Gus was thriving. Nothing like a little caffeine at eleven o'clock at night when a show got out. None of us had to be at work early the next day, after all.

I made my way to the counter and waited for Gus to finish with one of the other customer's orders.

'Hey, Kate, you're done early tonight.' He smiled when he saw me.

'For a change!' I agreed. My nights tended to end later rather than earlier.

'So what's it going to be, regular coffee or cappuccino?'

'I'll have a latte,' I decided, being adventurous. 'Double espresso. It's been a long day.'

'Do you just never sleep?' he asked, starting to work at the big espresso machine he had brought from Italy himself.

'Caffeine doesn't affect me at all. I think I've built up a resistance to it over the years.'

'You're going to get a big shock when you hit forty, kiddo,' he said, pouring the extra shot of espresso into the large mug.

'If I make it that long.'

'Well, you have to quit spending the afternoons in jail,' he laughed. 'That'll age you too quickly.'

'I would just like to know how you find out this stuff,' I said. 'And some day, I am going to find out who your sources are.'

'Ah, Kate, you know it would just ruin the mystique if I told you my secrets,' he teased me, handing me my coffee. 'Tell me what you think of that. It's a new blend I just got in.'

I took a deep breath of the heady aroma of the rich espresso blend, appreciating my coffee as if it were a fine wine.

'Mmm,' I almost moaned as I took a sip. 'Hazelnut?'

'You're almost as good as I am.' He laughed again, wiping down the espresso machine carefully.

'Yeah, well, I can guess your other secret too,' I admitted. 'I'll bet my big mouth assistant Graham stopped by and you bribed him with one of those fresh squeezed wheatgrass things you make. Did he sell me out for a fresh squeezed orange juice, Gus?'

'OK, you got me on that one.'

'I've have to quit telling him stuff. He can't keep a secret for more than thirty seconds.'

'Kate, he's nineteen years old. This is exciting to him. He hasn't lived anything but high school yet and, since he's hooked up with you, it's just one adventure after another. Besides, this was yesterday, you didn't tell him anything, he overheard you on the phone with her.'

'Damn him, I'm taking away his phone privileges.'

'Told you, he craves excitement.'

'Well, that's going to stop now. I liked my boring life. I don't need all this excitement.'

'So what's this jail thing about then?' he asked.

'It's about time I learned to listen to Cam,' I said. 'But

don't tell him I said that. Do you know how much those hand-cuffs hurt?'

'No, actually I don't. Now 'fess up.'

'OK, OK. I'll tell you everything for one of those macadamia nut biscotti,' I tried.

'Is it a good story?' he asked.

'You'll just have to take your chances.'

He laughed and handed me a biscotti and a napkin.

'If you want a plate, you have to pay for it,' he joked.

'Thank you,' I said, dipping the biscotti into the coffee. 'So, Cam's cousin turned up at our doorstep a couple of days ago. She left her husband and apparently he was kind of abusive. I don't know too much about his family yet, so I don't know the whole story here. But we went over to her house to get some of her stuff and he had us arrested for breaking and entering. Bastard!'

'That's exactly what you told me this afternoon,' he protested.

'I know.' I smiled at him.

'Kate, you never tell me the whole truth when Cam is sitting beside you. What are you leaving out?'

'Well, maybe she's seeing someone else,' I admitted. 'But Cam really does not know that and I don't want him to find out.'

'Have you got a good lawyer?'

'We've got a really good lawyer for her. He sort of suggested we try this. But I think I'll just take Carrie shopping for some clothes tomorrow. It's easier than trying to get back into that house again.'

'Now that sounds like a sensible idea,' Gus agreed. 'Looks like your ride is here.'

I turned around and saw Cam's car pull into the loading zone.

'Well, I'm not finished my coffee yet. I left a message for him at the security desk. He should be in here shortly.'

'I'll just whip something up for him too, then,' Gus said, moving back to the espresso machine. 'Do you think he'll like that?'

'I think he will, just make his a single and don't you dare tell him mine's a double,' I warned him.

I took another bite of coffee-soaked biscotti and let it melt in my mouth.

'Hey, Cam,' Gus called out over the noise of the steamer.

'Hey, Gus.'

I turned my head and watched him walk over to us. He still looked good in those jeans.

'You're early tonight,' he greeted me, wrapping his arms around my waist and nuzzling my neck.

I could feel the heat from his body warming me and hoped he wouldn't let go for a while. I wrapped my hands around his and held him, encouraging him to stay.

'I know.' I smiled, totally at peace for just this one moment in time. 'Everything actually went smoothly for a change.'

He leaned his head on my shoulder and turned to Gus. 'And you're awfully quiet in here tonight.'

'Nobody wants to hang around on a Thursday night,' he said, sliding Cam's coffee across the counter to him.

I finally let Cam go, and he slipped on to the bar stool beside me. I moved over toward him, leaning on him instead of the counter. I don't know what it was but he just looked and felt good tonight.

'What's this?' Cam asked.

'A new blend,' I answered for Gus, who was back to pampering his machine again. 'Try it, it's really nice.'

'You're right,' he said after sampling his. 'And I'm betting yours is a double and you're not going to sleep tonight.'

'Oh, Cam, the caffeine has nothing to do with my not being able to sleep. It's because you're lying there, right beside me, distracting me.'

'What has come over you tonight?'

'I don't know but I wish we didn't have company back home,' I whispered into his ear.

'I told you, I am buying the lumber this week and closing in that loft if it's the last thing I do.'

'But you probably can't get that done tonight?' I asked.

'Probably not. I promise as soon as we get Carrie settled and in her own place, I'll get the guys over and we'll put up some walls.'

'My office is empty right now. There's no one around, the theatre's dark—'

'OK,' he said, jumping down off the stool. 'We're getting you home. You must be sick.' He put a hand on my forehead, to check for fever.

'Stop it, Cam, I'm just feeling good tonight. The show went well, I'm not sleeping in a jail cell and things almost feel normal right now.'

'Well, I'd like to get home, anyway. Gus, can we have a couple of take-out cups for these?' Cam called.

Gus poured what was left of the coffees into paper cups and I tossed some money on the counter for him, enough to cover the biscotti too.

Cam put his arm around my shoulder and pulled me toward the door.

'See you tomorrow, Gus,' he called, pushing mc through ahead of him.

'So, we going up to my office?' I asked.

'We're going home,' he corrected me. 'We have company expecting us.'

'Fine.' I finally realized I was not going to get my way on this one. 'She's probably asleep anyway.'

He just opened the car door and stood there, waiting for me to get in, which I finally did.

Friday November 14

I woke up late the next morning. And I knew it was late because the sun was actually shining through the space where the curtains didn't meet in the middle. The apartment was very quiet. I was going to turn over and go back to sleep, but decided I'd better get up and see if anything was going on. I threw back the covers and crawled out of bed. Cam seemed to be missing, but he usually went for his run early, so that wasn't anything unusual. I pulled on a pair of sweat pants and kept Cam's sweatshirt on, figuring since Carrie had been around for a few days now, I didn't have to try and impress her and sweat pants were fine for morning wear. It was my own apartment, after all. I did run my fingers through my hair and try and straighten it out, though. I climbed slowly down the stairs, feeling my stomach start to get queasy again.

'I have to stop drinking coffee so late at night,' I said, knowing I was lying to myself.

The apartment was empty but there was a note from Cam underneath my coffee cup, a place where he knew I'd find it. He just told me that he had taken Carrie to work and then was going in early himself. He'd see me at the theatre later. I poured myself a cup of coffee but then felt another wave of nausea overtake me. Maybe a cup of mint tea would be a better option this morning. I put the kettle on to boil and went to the bathroom to brush my teeth, stopping to turn on the stereo. I wasn't alone very often anymore, and I missed having some good, loud music to get me going in the morning. I couldn't decide between my two favourites but finally chose a classics CD I had just bought, nothing like a little classical overture to get you moving in the morning.

After I brushed my teeth and drank a half a pot of tea, I showered and dressed and realized I still had a couple of hours before I had to be anywhere. I looked around for something to do, and realized I also wasn't very good at being alone anymore. Nothing caught my attention. It looked nice out, so I thought it would be a nice day to walk to the theatre and do a little paperwork. I really shouldn't let Graham do it all. A good manager knows how to delegate, but a good manager also reviews the books every once in a while.

I turned everything off, grabbed my backpack and keys and poured some tea into a go-mug before I hit the streets. I walked over to the French doors to make sure they were locked and then I noticed Carrie's purse sitting beside the sofa. I checked my watch and realized I had lots of time to get to work and decided to take a little detour and take her purse to her. I tucked it in my backpack, made sure the place was locked up tight, and then headed for the street.

It was bright and sunny out, a lovely day for November. There was a light breeze blowing from the west and I could smell the crisp, sweet mountain air. I walked a few blocks and crossed the Louise Bridge over into Kensington, one of those areas that had managed to save itself from the low tax bracket it had fallen into with a revitalization program that had made it one of the priciest areas in town. At first, house prices had risen but businesses had turned over at an amazing rate. There were a couple of times we had gone down to try out a restaurant only to find it was already closed and turned into a video store. But the area seemed to have settled into its new identity. I loved the little boutiques and great furniture stores. I had enough furniture picked out for my first five houses. Too bad none of it would fit in my tiny little loft. I turned on to Kensington Road and headed for the medical centre down the street. I passed the local Starbucks, the smell of the coffee threatening to pull me off my latest mission, but I managed to refocus and carry on. I opened the door to the Walk-In Clinic and was overwhelmed by the number of people in the waiting room. I smiled at one of the gentleman sitting at the far end, thinking I recognized him from somewhere. He was probably one of the regular subscribers at the theatre. I always ran into people that I recognized from the theatre but didn't know by name. I made my way to the desk and was greeted by a very young receptionist.

'Hi there, what can we help you with today?'

'I'm actually looking for Carrie Palmer.'

'Are you a patient?'

'No, I'm a cousin.'

'Oh,' she giggled. 'Have a seat and I'll page her for you.'

I stood in the corner, hoping to not actually be there long enough to need a seat. Shortly, the door to the back rooms opened and Carrie's head popped out.

'Kate?' she asked. 'Come on back with me.'

I followed her through the hall and into an exam room. She closed the door behind us and turned to face me.

'Oh my God, what's wrong?' Carrie said, her face filled with worry.

'Nothing, Carrie, you just forgot your purse at the apartment and I thought I'd bring it over.'

'Oh, thank God. When they told me you were here I was afraid something horrible had happened.'

'Oh, Carrie,' I said, going over and giving her a big hug. 'I'm sorry, I never thought I'd worry you. Trust me, though, if anything bad ever happens I'll send Cam to tell you.'

Carrie grabbed a Kleenex and dabbed at her eyes.

'I'm sorry,' she apologized again.

'Don't worry. Are you having a hard day on your first day back?'

'Well, I'm more stressed out than I thought I was. But I have to admit, it's nice to be busy. Even if it is mostly giving flu shots and doing urine dips.'

'Good. Well, you going to be OK or do you need me to spring you for the day?'

'No, I think I can get through a few more hours. Do you want a little tour around here?'

'You guys look pretty busy.'

'It's always busy,' she said.

'And I really should get to work . . .'

'Don't like doctors, right?' she asked.

'Not much.'

'OK, well I'll get back to work and let you get on your way.'

'You sure you're going to be OK?' I asked, not sure if she was just trying to be brave or really doing OK.

'I'm sure.'

I pulled her purse out of my backpack and handed it over to her.

'All right. We will see you sometime later tonight at the apartment.'

I headed out of the office, the smell of disinfectant spurring my fight or flight reflex, and landed back out in the sunshine only an hour behind my original schedule. I made good time and felt better as I approached the Plex. It really was a white elephant of a building, not fitting into the surroundings very well, but it was my home for the last several years and I had grown to love the place. This is where all my friends worked, where I got to see all the performances I could ever want for free and where I had found Cam. And I was looking forward to being alone in my office for a couple of hours. There I knew I could find something to do and probably get some work done. I thought I'd start working on the schedule for next month. My hopes sank when I saw the light on in my office. I wasn't alone after all. I hurried through the stage door, down the back hall and up the stairs to my office. The

64

door was propped open and I saw Graham sitting at my desk, thumbing through a book.

'Graham?' I said, poking my head through the door.

'Oh, hi, Kate.'

'I know you like your job, but you do realize you're two hours early, don't you?' I asked him.

'I have an audition in thirty minutes. I thought I'd just use the office for some prep time,' he explained. 'I can't always get time alone at home.'

'Time to get an apartment of your own?' I asked.

'Only if I get the matching raise to pay for it. Besides, you'd break my mother's heart. She doesn't want her only son to leave her. Why are you two hours early?'

'I was going to start working on the schedule for next month,' I told him, sitting down in the chair across from him.

'Well, I'll go rehearse in the lobby,' he said. 'Since it's getting hard to get alone time here, too. Do you want me to put on some coffee for you before I go?'

'No, I'm not feeling very well today, I'm sticking to herbal tea,' I explained, holding up my go-mug. 'Will you be back in time to work the matinee?'

'Should be. Will you be OK if I'm a little late?'

'Graham, you know I wouldn't do anything that might get in the way of your big break,' I laughed. 'Plus I actually ran this theatre for a couple of years on my own before I hired you. Now leave me alone and go prepare yourself. What are you trying out for?'

'*The Pied Piper of Hamlin.*'

'Oh, well, everybody has to start somewhere.'

'Acting is acting,' he said, starting off down the hall. 'I'll start wherever I have to start and I'll take whatever I can get.'

'Break a leg,' I called after him. Then I spent the next hour remembering why I let Graham do all the paper work. He seemed to like it, I didn't.

After an hour, I needed a break. I decided to put on some coffee because my stomach was feeling a little more settled finally and my brain was craving caffeine. I filled the pot, turned it on and then searched my desk for a cigarette. I was in a never-ending battle to quit smoking. I decided I was going to try to only smoke at the office, yet I still carried a package in my backpack, just in case. Cam was one of those people who could smoke or not smoke and never became addicted. I was sure he wanted nothing more than to see me quit, as did everyone else I knew. And I should, I thought, as I brought the cigarette to my mouth and lit it, any time now. I was almost ready to quit.

I poured a cup of coffee, sat back at my desk and took a sip. One sip and suddenly my stomach was churning again. I ran for the ladies' room, where I spent the next ten minutes. When I came out, holding a wet paper towel to my forehead, Graham was sitting at my desk.

'You back already?' I asked, trying to hide my discomfort.

'Yeah, I got the part,' he said, breaking into a huge grin.

'Way to go, Graham.' I sat down heavily in the first chair I came to.

'What's up with you?' he asked, concern in his voice.

'Oh, nothing,' I lied.

'Kate, I heard you in the bathroom. Are you OK?'

'I think I'm just fighting a flu bug,' I confessed. 'I just haven't been feeling great the last couple of days.'

'You were fine earlier.'

'Well it comes and goes. And I'm probably drinking too much coffee.'

'And smoking too much. Have you been to the doctor?' he asked.

'What is this?' I asked, feeling he was crossing that line between our personal and business relationships. 'Your Cam impersonation?'

'I'm serious. You never get sick, Kate.'

'What is the doctor going to say? You've got the flu. Go home, rest and drink plenty of fluids.'

'But then at least you know what you're dealing with.'

'I'm dealing with the stomach flu, Graham, we've all been there, and we've all lived through it. I will too.'

'You're a little touchy,' he said. 'Maybe you should go home and rest.'

'I don't need rest, I just need people to stop bugging me about everything.' I took a deep breath and decided to change the subject. 'So, tell me about the part.'

66

'It's the Pied Piper. What's there to tell?' he asked, settling back in his chair and looking hurt. 'I wear tights and play a flute.'

'Well, what colour tights do you get to wear?'

'Very funny,' he answered. 'Whatever happened to "You have to start somewhere"? It was you who used to tell *me* that all the time.'

'That's when I was being supportive. Now that you've got the role, I can go back into full teasing mode.'

'Well, then, I'm out of here. I'm going to go and get changed for the show.'

'Alright.' I changed places with him at the desk. 'I'm almost done here. Can you get everything started in the lobby while I finish the schedule?'

'Sure. Just come down and join us whenever you're ready.'

Graham headed off to the change rooms and I closed the door to finish the schedules.

Our matinee had been jammed to the rafters with high-school students, who had loved the play and stayed for hours afterward, asking questions and taking tours of the theatre. Most of the girls had been quite interested in having Graham conduct their tours personally and he had taken great pleasure in accommodating them. When we finally got the place cleared out, I sent Graham out for a break, declined his invitation to join him and headed back up to my office. I was planning on calling my friend Sam for a nice little chat when Cam came in.

'Don't you ever knock?' I asked him.

'I have keys to the entire building. I don't have to knock.'

'But what if I was in here with my Italian lover Roberto?'

'Well I already walked in on you with your French lover Stephan, so I guess I'm getting used to it,' he joked.

'Hey, that was last month – you know we're over,' I joked, but still able to feel the sting of Cam walking into my office and finding me in the arms of my old flame from my university days.

He came closer, leaned on my desk, his face just inches from mine. 'Besides, Katie, if I can find someone to take you off my hands, I might just be grateful.'

'Nice thing to say to the woman you're supposed to be in love with,' I chided him.

67

He kissed me and then sat down in the chair across from me.

'Not that I wouldn't love to stay and banter with you all evening.' He changed the subject. 'But have you heard from Carrie yet today?'

'No, but we just got the matinee cleared out. Do you want me to check my voice mail?'

'Please.'

'Wouldn't she call you?' I asked him, punching in my code.

'Probably, but I want to make sure she hasn't tried one of us before I start freaking out.'

'She probably just got tied up at work,' I said, still skipping through my voice mails. A million volunteers calling to change their shifts. I just flipped over those for later. 'Nope, nothing from Carrie.'

'Man, she knows we're worried about her,' Cam said.

'How about if you just try calling the apartment first to see if she's there?' I suggested, handing him the phone and dialling.

He let it ring through to the machine before he hung up.

'Not there,' he informed me.

'So, now we try work,' I said. 'Did she give you the number?'

'Yeah, she gave me her card,' he said, tossing it across the desk to me.

I dialled the number and handed him the phone again.

'Hello, is Carrie Palmer there?' he asked the receptionist.

'Great!' He tucked the phone under his chin and turned to me. 'She's there.'

'See, not everything is a crisis. Some things in our lives can be normal.'

'Hi, Carrie, it's Cam.' He turned back to his phone conversation. 'I'm just about done here and Kate's working tonight, so how about if I pick you up and we grab some dinner . . . Great, I'll see you then.'

'Well?' I asked.

'She's working some extra hours to make up for what she missed this week. Nothing to worry about after all. She said she was just going to phone me.'

'So where are you two going to go for dinner?' I asked.

'I don't know. We always used to do pizza and beer when

we were kids. Maybe a game of darts or something. What time are you done?'

'Probably by 11:00. There aren't any receptions or anything tonight.'

'Well, then, we can come and pick you up when you're done and all head home together.'

'Sounds good to me,' I agreed. 'I'll meet you at the stage door?'

'I'll be there. I'm going to go and get changed.'

'Well, have fun,' I said, standing up to kiss him goodbye.

'That should keep me going for a while,' he said with a smile, as he slipped down the fire escape and the short cut to his office.

I sat down, smiling at the taste of his lips on mine, and I turned back to pick up the phone and call Sam. It rang just as I touched the receiver and I jumped. I picked it up, half expecting it to be Sam, who had an uncanny knack for calling me just as I was about to call her.

'Kate Carpenter.'

'Where is she?'

'Who?' I asked, realization slowly sinking in. 'Is this Hank?'

'Where is Carrie?'

'I don't know right now, Hank. I'm sure when she feels ready she'll call you.'

'Don't you get all patronizing with me,' he threatened me.

'No, Hank, I'm not. I'm just not sure that Carrie's ready to talk to you yet. If you just give her a little more time—'

'You know, I kind of liked you until you got this attitude. Now tell me where my fucking wife is!'

'Hank, I'll tell Carrie you called but I think—'

'I'll tell you what, Kate, sweetie, you're not as safe and sound as you think and next time I call, I think you better answer my questions better. Carrie has probably told you it's not good to make me lose my temper!'

And then he hung up the phone.

I found my hands shaking as I hung up the receiver. I opened my desk drawer and searched around for a cigarette to calm my nerves. I pulled out the package and dropped it on the desk. There was an elastic band holding a piece of paper wrapped around the package that hadn't been there before the matinee. Gingerly, I picked up the package and slipped the note out from under the elastic, and opened it carefully.

I want my wife back or you're going to be sorry was all it said.

'Oh, shit,' I said out loud.

I pulled a cigarette out of the package, lit it and picked up the phone. I should have this number on speed dial by now.

'Detective Ken Lincoln,' I said, when the switchboard answered.

'Ken Lincoln,' his voice said, answering on the second ring.

'Ken, it's Kate Carpenter. I need some advice on what do to about something.'

Ken sat across the desk from me after having turned down the coffee I offered him and sipped on his bottled water instead. I should know better but I kept hoping I could bring these health nuts over to my side.

'You know, Kate, it's a good thing the theatre is on my way home. It just saves me all that extra driving when I have to come over here all the time.'

'Very funny,' I scolded him. 'You know I'd much rather the four of us went out to dinner or something, instead of us always getting together over some sort of gory crime scene.'

'So, what's the problem?' he asked.

'You remember Cam's cousin and her abusive husband?'

'Yep. Something about breaking you out of the big house, I think?'

'Yeah, yeah. Anyway, the abusive husband just called me and threatened me and then I opened up my desk and found a note from him.'

'I have got to talk to Lazlo about the security around this place,' he said, referring to the building's head of security.

'Did you just hear the words that came out of your mouth?'

'Yeah, I guess you're right. I at least have to talk to Nick about this. Too many people can just come in and out of this office as they please.'

'Well, it doesn't make me very happy either, but I'm not allowed to change the locks myself.'

'So is that the note?' he asked, glancing across my desk.

'That's it.' I moved the paper over to him with the tip of my pen. 'And I already touched it.'

'I doubt they'll fingerprint this. The problem is that this is a public building. It's not really like it's breaking and entering.'

'But he threatened me,' I explained.

Ken picked up the note and read it. 'He didn't actually sign it or anything.'

'Yeah, I noticed that.'

'What you need to do is give this to your lawyer. There's just not much I can do with this. Maybe your lawyer can attach it to the restraining order, keep him away from the theatre. Then if he tries this again or something else happens, we can pick him up. But it's pretty hard with just a few scribbles on a piece of paper.'

'This is just so frustrating,' I said, lighting another cigarette. 'Carrie is the one that got assaulted and yet she's the one who seems to have no rights.'

'Yeah, well, the law is changing with domestic abuse cases, but it's changing very slowly.'

'Well, thanks, Ken. I'm sorry to waste your time on this.'

'It's not really a waste of time for me,' he said. 'Because I was actually going to give you a call and see if there was any chance we could get a couple of tickets to this show. My wife really wants to see it.'

'Sure, that's easy. What night were you thinking?'

'She was hoping for Sunday, if that's OK?'

I turned and made a note on my calendar. 'The tickets will be waiting for you at the box office under your name. Make sure you pick them up by 7:30.'

'Are you sure about this?' he asked. 'I don't want to cause you any trouble.'

'It's not illegal, Ken. I always have some house seats available. So enjoy.'

He stood up and pulled on his coat. 'Well, thanks, Kate, I owe you one.'

'Well, you can pay me back by not telling Cam anything about this little note.'

'You're right I won't tell him a thing. Because you're going to tell him,' he urged.

'No way, you know how overprotective he gets when he

71

thinks I'm in danger. I'll be walking around here with armed guards.'

'Against my better judgment I won't say anything. But I really think you should tell him.'

'Well, I'll call the lawyer, but I think that falls under the category of what Cam doesn't need to know won't hurt him. And I appreciate your discretion in the matter.'

'Well, what can I do? I'm taking free theatre tickets from you. Wouldn't it be bad form to betray you after you have bribed me?'

'Yes, it would,' I agreed, taking his empty bottle from him. 'So I'll see you Sunday.'

'Great. Rebecca is going to be so happy. You guys want to go out for drinks afterward?'

'I'd love to but can we hold off on confirming? I don't know where we'll be with Carrie and all this stuff by then, you know how it goes.'

'Yes, I've been through this with you before,' Ken said.

Ken headed for the exit and passed Graham in the hall, who then ran excitedly into the office.

'Detective Lincoln was here? What's going on, Kate?'

'Nothing, Graham,' I said firmly, grabbing the note quickly off my desk and shoving it into my backpack.

'Kate, come on, tell me.'

'Graham, he was here to get some theatre tickets and that's it. And if you tell one single person that he was here, and I mean anyone, your ass will be fired so fast that you will not know what hit you. Do we understand each other?' I threatened him.

'Yes, ma'am. You're hiding something from Cam. We understand each other perfectly.'

I just looked at him and growled under my breath. Everyone thought they knew me so well.

I sent Graham off to do some work and I finally picked up the phone to call Sam, only to get her answering machine.

'Hi, it's Kate. It's a little crazy in my life again and I was just calling for a sanity break. OK, OK, I was just calling to whine and get a little sympathy. See, I can't even lie to your answering machine. Anyway, I'm at work now and I'll be home late so I'll probably talk to you tomorrow.'

72

I hung up the phone and decided to do some actual work myself. But my secret had remained safe from the Plex grapevine, so when Cam picked me up at eleven o'clock, we didn't fight or argue about anything, because I had actually managed to keep a secret from him for at least one night.

'How was your day?' he asked, giving me a quick kiss as he opened the door for me. Carrie was sitting in the back seat, holding a take-out pizza box on her lap.

'It was a fine day,' I said. 'And it's going to be a fine night if that's a Supremo from Karouzo's Pizza.'

'Yes, it is,' Carrie said. 'Or at least what we managed to save for you.'

Cam looked over at me and smiled, waiting for me to add something, but I just smiled back. I could never lie to Cam and get away with it. Unless he let me.

Saturday November 15

I woke up and immediately knew something was wrong. My spider sense was tingling. It was morning; I knew that because there was light peeping through a crack in the curtains and I heard the morning sounds of the bottle pickers' shopping carts careening through the alleyway. But there was a warm man laying beside me, snoring softly, his arms wrapped around me, holding my head gently against his chest, where I could hear the slow, steady beating of his heart. I wriggled a little and looked up. Yep, it was Cam all right. I couldn't see the alarm clock, but it had to be well past his normal "hit the streets for a run" time of seven o'clock or some other disgustingly early hour that I refused to acquaint myself with.

'Cam,' I whispered, hesitant to break this idyllic moment. Nothing but that gentle snoring.

'Cam,' I tried, not really any louder. I just had to try enough so that I could tell him I tried to wake him up. I really planned on turning over and going back to sleep and wanted to do that with a clear conscience.

'Hmm?' he grumbled from deep within his throat.

Damn, I thought, now we were up.

'Did you forget to set the alarm?' I asked, still whispering, hoping he wasn't totally awake.

'Hmm?' he asked again.

My hope sprang up, renewed. Monosyllabic grunts were a good sign. I laid my head back down on his chest and tried to slow my breathing, feigning sleep.

'No,' he finally managed an entire word. He released his grip on me and rolled over, stretching his arms until they hit the wall and dumping me unceremoniously back on my side of the bed.

'No?' I asked, pulling the comforter up around me and settling in again.

'Nope, I thought it would be a good day to sleep in. Carrie has gone to work early, I don't have to be at work until three o'clock and I'm assuming you don't have to be in early.' He nudged me with his elbow under the covers.

'Ouch, Cam, if that is your idea of foreplay, you are going to be waiting a long time for any sexual satisfaction,' I said, rubbing my ribs.

'How about this, then?' he asked, pulling me back on top of him, his mouth on mine before I could give him any sort of a smart answer and his hands tracing the outline of my spine, slowly going lower and lower until I felt a shiver run through me.

'You might have a slightly better chance now,' I said, finding my voice suddenly hoarse.

Cam laughed, but he didn't stop what he was doing.

The second time I woke up that morning, a couple of hours later, things were right back to normal. The sun was streaming through the curtains that Cam had opened, hoping to encourage me to get out of bed, the aroma of brewing coffee wafted up from the kitchen and the bed next to me was empty. A typical morning at Kate's house. I rolled over, pulling the comforter over my head, and closed my eyes again, hoping for another hour or two before Cam decided I had to get up because I was wasting the day.

74

The covers were slowly and gently pulled away from my head, sunlight drifting under my fluttering eyelids, Cam's fingers running through my hair. Now this was the way to wake up in the morning. I slowly opened my eyes all the way, rolled over to check the time on the alarm clock, in order that I could protest the hour at which I was being awoken, and was surprised to find it was already almost two.

'Yes, it really is two o'clock,' he affirmed.

'Wow, is it my birthday?' I joked.

'No, but you can consider this your early present and then I won't have to get you anything later.'

'And you're not going to nag me about wasting the day?'

'Nope.'

'Or tease me for the amount I sleep?'

'Well, I can't promise that it won't come up some time later.'

'And you're not going to get me a birthday present?'

'I think that sounds like a really good deal.'

'Well, that's a nice dream for you, too bad it's not going to happen.' I stared up into those beautiful eyes, wondering if he had time for a repeat performance of this morning.

'I have to get going.' He smiled down at me, reading my mind yet again. 'I promise I'll be home on time if you will.'

'Yes, I'll be home on time and so will Carrie,' I whined, reaching up to try and pull him down to the bed. But he'd been awake for longer and was much quicker than I was, dodged my half-hearted move and was up off the bed before I could try again.

'I really have to go,' he said. 'Is it safe to kiss you goodbye?'

'Enter at your own risk,' I teased.

He was brave and leaned over to kiss me and then stood up quickly again.

'There's coffee on the night table,' he called as he trotted down the stairs.

'See you later,' I called after him, hearing the door slam and the bolts turn.

I wanted to curl back up under the covers, but I knew that would be a really bad idea. I had a bad habit of falling asleep again and, though Graham could run the theatre without me, I'd rather he didn't have to do it too often. I snuck my feet out from under the comforter and pulled myself into a sitting position. I reached for the coffee and took a sip. It smelled funny this morning; maybe Cam was trying a new brand or something. And then it made its way down to my stomach, which started twisting and turning. I made it to the bathroom in record time and, luckily, just in time. I had to make a doctor's appointment, I thought; I can't afford to get the flu and, virus or not, there had to be something modern medicine could do.

Cam had laid some breakfast out for me. But one look at it sent me back into the bathroom. After my stomach was empty of anything I'd eaten for the last week, and I had brushed my teeth and showered, I figured I was settled enough to try and clean the kitchen. I turned off the coffee pot, dumped the coffee, washed the pot, and emptied the grounds from the filter. I put some plastic wrap over my breakfast plate and popped it back in the fridge. Then I went and stood out on the patio and gulped in the fresh air, as just the lingering smell from the pot of coffee was still turning my stomach. When I was strong enough to face the kitchen again, I bundled up the garbage and took it out to the garbage chute. I sprayed air freshener around the room, which usually made me nauseous, but seemed to help today.

After I was finally satisfied with the smells in the apartment I managed to get dressed and walk the several blocks to the Plex. Downtown Calgary was fairly clean and safe and the fresh air was doing me nothing but good. I took the stairs up to the theatre and heard Graham puttering around in the office. And then I smelled the coffee. All that fresh air apparently hadn't done me as much good as I thought it had.

When I came out of the bathroom Graham was standing outside the door, offering a cup to me.

'No, I couldn't drink anything right now,' I explained.

'Kate, it's mint tea. It'll settle your stomach,' he told me.

'Where'd you get this?' I asked.

'I ran down to Gus's while you were otherwise occupied.'

'That was incredibly nice of you,' I said, taking the cup and setting it down on my desk.

'You have to drink it to make it work,' he explained.

76

'I don't feel like anything, really.'

'It'll help, Kate, I promise. Ginger and mint are the best things for an upset stomach. I promise.'

I took a sip and the warmth of the mint soothed my throat and I felt myself relaxing. Something I had no intention of telling Graham.

'There, are you happy?' I asked him.

'Yes, I am,' he said.

'Good, now maybe you can quit nagging me for a minute or two.'

'Actually, I just have to run down to the pharmacy for a minute, if you don't mind.'

'Nope, I don't. Can you get me some Smarties?'

'Do you think that's such a good idea with an upset stomach?'

'When I was a kid, my mom always gave me Smarties and chocolate pudding when I was sick,' I told him. 'I'm sure it will still make me feel better. Nothing against your tea, of course.'

'Fine, I'll get you a small box, but I won't be responsible for what it does to you.'

Graham grabbed his coat and backpack and I was gloriously at peace for almost an hour, until the ushers started to arrive for the evening's show. Leonard was the first to arrive. He was twenty-two, tall and gangly and working his way toward a PhD in philosophy. He managed to regale me with his latest research on Nietzsche and the new slant he had planned for his thesis. I don't know how many times I had sat in this office and listened to a first-year philosophy student wax about Nietzsche, knowing that next year a new professor would turn them on to the Greeks or Romans and I'd be suffering through Socrates and Plato.

I was just about to give my opinion on typefaces and bibliographies when we were saved by the arrival of Martha. She was in her sixties and had started working for me the day her husband had retired, much to my benefit. She was nowhere near as indulgent as I and she would never sit and listen to Leonard. She may ask after his grades or exam results, in that polite, grandmotherly way, but would never listen to him for as long as I would. Martha, instead, was much better at rapidly turning the subject to something that other people in the room might also be interested in. Today, however, since no one else was here yet, the subject turned to the latest photographs of her grandchildren. I also sat through these with the patience of a saint, until a few others arrived and she passed them around for everyone to see. They had lightened my mood and my body seemed to be feeling better.

I managed to get everyone signed in, went over my briefing, chatted to all the volunteers and got them all into position. We moved the audience in to the theatre and the play started on time, something I always considered a success, meaning I didn't have to explain to some irate actor why I had kept him waiting for two minutes while trying to handle a double-sold ticket. I headed back to my office to finally eat my Smarties, followed by Graham.

'Who's watching the lobby?' I asked him.

'Leonard,' he informed me.

'What are you planning on doing tonight then?'

Graham followed me into my office, holding a brown paper bag, and sat across the desk from me.

'I bought you something else at the drugstore,' he said.

'What?' I asked, actually excited. Maybe it was more chocolate.

'Before I give it to you I want you to promise something.'

'What?'

'I want you to promise not to get mad at me.'

'Graham, I don't think I want it.'

'Kate, I mean it. You know I care about you a lot. I'm honestly thinking only of your health. Please don't get mad at me.'

I held out my hand for the paper bag, not willing to make any promises until I knew what he was talking about. He finally, reluctantly, handed me the bag. I set it on the desk and opened it.

'Graham!'

'Kate, don't get mad,' he reminded me.

'Graham, I want to know what the hell you were thinking when you actually bought this?' I demanded.

Graham got up and shut the door to the office.

'You're getting a little loud,' he cautioned me.

'I know I'm getting loud. I'm in total shock. I think you have a lot of nerve buying this for me!' I pulled the box out of the bag and sat it on the desk for him to see. 'A pregnancy test?' I asked, still not believing it.

'Kate, I have four sisters. They are all older than me and they all have kids. I know about these things.'

'I am most certainly not pregnant.'

'You've been throwing up for how long now? And the smell of coffee is making you sick? Do you think that's normal for you?' he asked.

'I have the flu,' I protested.

'So then take the test. No harm, no foul.'

I took several deep breaths, trying to calm myself down. I wasn't really mad at Graham, I was mad at myself. I don't know why I hadn't thought about it, that I could be pregnant. It made sense; I was on the pill but sometimes birth control failed. But I was mad that Graham had noticed the signs and had to tell me before I noticed them. And I didn't want him to know these things about my personal life, either.

'OK, I'm calming down,' I told him.

'You can yell at me all you want,' he said. 'Just promise me you'll take the test.'

'Graham, you're crossing those lines again.'

'Kate, if you are pregnant you need to know. You're smoking and you're drinking tons of caffeine. Don't you think you should find out early so you don't hurt the baby? Just in case?'

He had me there.

'OK, I'll promise I'll take the test, but I won't promise to tell you the results or talk with you any further about this at all. Do you understand that?'

'That's fine with me,' he promised. 'Just know you can talk to me if you want to.'

'Fine,' I said, still not totally happy with this situation.

There was a knock at the door. Graham got up to answer it and I grabbed for the pregnancy test and stuffed it quickly into my backpack before he got the door opened.

'Hey, Leonard, do you have problems down there?' Graham asked.

'Just a little thing called intermission,' Leonard said. 'I thought you two might like to know; maybe join us in looking after the eight hundred or so patrons we have visiting us tonight?'

I realized my office speakers were off and we had missed the end of Act One. We both ran downstairs. Graham headed for the main bar to see if they needed any help, and I for my spot by the door of the technical booths, available for anyone that needed me. Luckily, no one had needed me, either before or after intermission.

Once everyone was settled again, I snuck back up to my office and dialled my friend Sam's number.

'Hello?'

'It's Kate.'

'Kate, what's wrong?'

'What do you mean?' I asked. 'I told you I'd call you sometime today.'

'But it's late, it's almost ten o'clock.'

'Oh, God, I'm sorry. Were you in bed?' I asked.

'No, it's just that I always worry when the phone rings this late. And you sound funny.'

'I sound funny? How?'

'You sound worried.'

'Oh, it's nothing. Life has just gotten a little bit crazy,' I said. 'But I'll call you back tomorrow. You're right, it's late.'

'Kate, I'm rolling out four dozen tart shells and then I'm going to bed. That's how long you have. Now tell me what's up.'

'Cam's cousin is staying with us.'

'Is he?'

'She.'

'Oh?'

'She left an abusive relationship and showed up, covered with bruises, on our doorstep.'

'That's why you sound funny,' Sam said.

'Why?'

'You've got company again, you're not getting your regular bunny-rabbit sex life that you're always bragging about.'

'Funny,' I told her, my voice betraying the fact that I didn't really find it funny.

'You're a little touchy today,' Sam pointed out, as only a best friend could.

80

'I'm sorry. How many have you done so far?'

'The first dozen. Keep going.'

'Well, it's just been really stressful. I don't think she's getting fair treatment. She's out of her house and can't get any of her stuff. We tried to go get some things the other day and her husband actually had us arrested.'

'What?'

'Yes. Thank God for Ken Lincoln or I'd be making license plates right now instead of managing a theatre.'

'A little melodramatic there.'

'Well, you sit in an interrogation room in handcuffs and see if it doesn't make you melodramatic.'

'Is that all?' she asked.

'I guess.'

'Then tell me why you're so touchy and hardly responding to my wittily sarcastic repartee?'

'I haven't been feeling well recently. I think I'm getting the flu.'

'So go to the doctor.'

'Remember who you're talking to?'

'So stay home, stay in bed. Cam loves taking care of you; let him.'

'Sam, I just hate to miss any more work. I've missed a bit recently and drawn a lot of attention to myself. I'd kind of just like to fade back into the woodwork,' I explained. 'How many tarts have you done now?'

'Just finished the fourth dozen.'

'You're fast.'

'Kate, I'm not going to hang up on you if you need me.'

'No, I'm just out of sorts but it's nothing serious,' I said. 'You've probably got an early job tomorrow, you need to get to go to bed.'

'Another few minutes won't kill me,' Sam promised.

'No, really, I'll talk to you tomorrow. I'll be fine.'

'OK, well, you know where to find me, Kate. Just take it easy, OK?'

'I promise. Sleep well and give Bonnie a kiss for me.'

I hung up the phone and headed back down to the theatre lobby, joining Graham on the couch and watching the end of the play on the monitor.

81

We emptied the place and closed it down. I feigned staying to wait for Cam so I didn't have to walk out with Graham. I was afraid he might want to discuss this whole pregnancy thing again. When I saw Cam's car pull up outside the stage door, I quickly turned off the lights and locked up my office. I made sure the pregnancy test was packed tightly down in the bottom of my pack and headed out.

We rode home in silence. I knew I should try to talk and act normally, but my mind was just so distracted I couldn't quite focus. Cam and Carrie wanted to go out and have a beer and play darts, but I told Cam I wasn't feeling well and made them drop me off at home, insisting I wasn't going to need them for the next couple of hours and sending them back out into the night.

When Cam got home, I was wide awake, my mind still churning over all the possibilities, arguing that there was no way I could be pregnant and then wondering what it would be like to hold the baby. I was making myself psychotic with the thoughts racing through my mind.

'How are you feeling?' Cam asked, when he climbed into bed.

'All right,' I said, not really lying. 'I just have a bit of a headache.'

'Do you want some aspirin?' he asked.

Were aspirin OK when you were pregnant? I knew you had to watch what medications you took, but how did you find out about this stuff? What would probably help was some coffee, as I hadn't had any yet today, but I had promised myself I wouldn't touch another drop of caffeine until I knew for sure if I was or wasn't pregnant.

'Katie?' he asked, reminding me I still hadn't answered his question.

'Uh, no, I'm fine. I'm sure I'll be even better after a good night's sleep,' I promised.

'We should get you to a doctor.'

'I promise I'll go tomorrow, when I see how I feel,' I told him. What I meant was if the test was positive.

I felt his hand move to my forehead again, and I brushed it away.

'What are you doing?' I asked.

'Feeling for a temperature,' he said. 'You just agreed to go to the doctor tomorrow.'

'Depending how I felt,' I said irritably. 'Sorry, I'm just on edge with this headache. I guess it's not a good time for sarcasm.'

'Sorry, sweetie,' he said, rolling over and giving me my space. 'Do you want anything or just to sleep?'

'No, I'm sorry,' I apologized. 'But I would like just to sleep.'

He kissed the top of my head and then I heard him softly snoring in a matter of minutes. Sure, he could sleep; he had nothing to worry about. Yet.

Sunday November 16

I woke up early, when the alarm rang signalling Cam to get out of bed for his run. Well, I guess saying that I woke up would imply that I'd slept, and I hadn't really. I tossed and turned and worried and dozed until the image of a box of diapers or a case of baby formula would pop into my mind and then I'd start all over again.

'Morning,' Cam smiled at me when he noticed I was awake. 'You tossed and turned a lot last night. Bad dreams?'

'No, just a lot of stuff on my mind, I guess.' I stretched and tried to look normal. Did you actually look different if you were pregnant? 'Are you going for a run?'

'No, Carrie has to work at eight. so I told her I'd drive her in. I have to be at work at nine today, so I'll just head to the Plex. I can go for a run at lunchtime.'

'Wow, you're a rebel today,' I teased.

'It's all for the sake of Carrie. I don't think she's been sleeping too well, either. This way she can get another half hour or so of sack time.'

'And so can you, Mr Stay-Out-All-Night.'

'I was winning at darts. That doesn't happen very often you

know,' he said, finally pushing himself out of bed and grabbing some clothes from the closet.

'So I've heard.'

'What time are you heading in today?' he asked me.

'Well, I don't have a matinee today, so I'm just going to toss and turn for another couple of hours.' I gave him a weak smile and he came over and sat on the side of the bed.

'You sure you're feeling OK, Katie?' he asked. 'You just haven't been yourself the last few days.'

'I'm fine,' I lied to him, knowing he would know it was a lie but not caring right now.

He looked at me and just smiled, then tucked the comforter tightly around me and kissed me lightly on the forehead. 'Call me if you need anything.'

I lay in bed, listening to him shower, followed by Carrie. Then they had breakfast, gathered up their stuff for the day and were out of the apartment. I waited another half an hour, just to make sure that Cam really was gone, before I finally climbed out of bed and headed downstairs with the pregnancy test.

By this time I had to pee so badly I could barely read the directions on the box. I pulled out the stick, did what I was supposed to do, and left it on the bathroom counter while I went and had a cup of coffee. I knew I shouldn't have caffeine, I had promised myself I wouldn't, but it was that or a stiff scotch and a cigarette right now and I figured caffeine was the lesser of all those evils.

Strangely, this morning the coffee didn't seem to bother me. As a matter of fact, it tasted really, really good. As did the second cup I had while I avoided going back into the bathroom. Finally, I worked up the courage to go back and look. I walked slowly, suddenly understanding what an inmate on death row must feel like, walking that last mile, condemned to his fate, as I was to mine. I looked at the stick and I knew what it meant. But I picked it up and compared it to the picture on the box, just to make sure. I carried the stick and the box into the living room and sat down on the couch. I reached over for the phone and pushed speed dial number one. The phone rang twice before it was picked up.

'Hello?'

'Sam,' I sobbed.

'Kate, what's the matter?' she asked, her voice rising in alarm.

'Sammy, I need you.'

'I'm on my way,' she said, hanging up the phone without even asking what I needed. She just knew I needed her.

I don't know what kind of traffic laws she broke to get here, and I didn't ask. But the intercom buzzer rang and I let her in, I opened up my front door and stood there, waiting for the elevator to arrive. I heard the door open and she hurried down the hall toward me.

'What?' she asked, seeing me standing there. 'Tell me right now, I've been going crazy with worry the whole time I was driving here.'

I held up the stick and let her look. I could tell she recognized what it was right away. The look in her eyes softened and she smiled.

'Oh, Kate,' she said, holding out her arms.

I melted into her hug, breaking into wracking sobs, while Sam held me and rubbed my back. She slowly worked me into the apartment, closed and locked the door and got us to the couch. She grabbed a box of Kleenex and put a bunch of tissues in my hand. I pulled away from her and wiped at my eyes, which were now red and swollen, and finished up by blowing my nose very ungracefully.

'Thanks for coming,' I sobbed, grabbing more Kleenex to staunch the fresh tears.

'I knew something was wrong with you last night.'

'What do you mean?'

'You sounded really funny on the telephone.'

'But I didn't know yet.'

'But you suspected, didn't you? You had the test already. Why didn't you say something to me?'

'I didn't suspect, Sam, not for one minute. Graham did.'

'What?'

'Yeah, he put everything together and went to the drugstore and bought the pregnancy test for me.'

'Boy, he's a brave young soul.'

'And then he had to argue with me to try and convince me to use it. I just couldn't believe he might be right at first.'

'Wow. He argued with you.'

85

'And won,' I sniffed.

'I guess there's a first time for everything,' Sam said, laughing at me.

'He only won because he was right. He said if there was even an outside chance that it might be true, then I had to know so I didn't do anything to hurt the baby.' And then I dissolved into that sobbing again, the out of control kind that I always hated. 'Thank you for coming over.'

'Oh, sweetie, you know I'm always here for you. But, man, I thought someone had died or something.'

'I'm sorry, I didn't mean to worry you,' I said. 'But don't you think this is worse?'

'Uh, no, actually. I mean it's a shock but there are lots of choices you can make here.'

'No, there aren't,' I said, pausing to take in a deep ragged breath between the tears.

'Sweetie, you're not thinking clearly. Once you get over the shock of this, you and Cam can sit down and talk about your options.'

'I can't have an abortion,' I sobbed. 'Remember what happened to him and his wife?'

'Oh, yeah.'

'She snuck out and had an abortion without telling him. That would kill him. I mean this is what he's been waiting for, praying that I would finally be ready to start a family, but I don't know if I'm ready for it.'

'Well, the thing about being pregnant is that you don't really get to decide if you're ready for it or not. Fact is you are pregnant and now you have to figure out what you're going to do about it. The part about whether you're ready or not no longer applies.'

'Oh, Sam,' I sobbed, dropping my head into her lap and breaking out into a fresh round of tears.

She let me lie there and cry for a good thirty minutes or so before she decided enough was enough. And, truth be known, I was probably starting to get a little dehydrated.

So, after being made to have a brisk, cold shower, dry my hair and put on some decent clothes, I headed out with Sam to the local coffee shop to grab some breakfast to go. Then she decided a little shopping was just what I needed.

Sam seemed to be enjoying her new role as my keeper, happily ordering me herbal tea . . .

'No more caffeine for you, young lady.'

. . . and a muffin filled with bran, fruit and oat bran, all the things that were going to send my digestive system into shock, I was sure. It actually tasted pretty good, but I had no intention of telling her that.

We wandered downtown, picking at our muffins and sipping our drinks, being oh so very cosmopolitan, and peeking in shop windows.

'That would look amazing on you,' Sam told me, pointing to a cute little summer dress hanging in a store window, with an end-of-season sale tag on it.

'You're right, it would, if I weren't about to gain a million pounds and totally reshape my body forever.'

'Oh, stop feeling sorry for yourself. You're not the first woman to get pregnant and you won't be the last, either. Besides, look at Cindy Crawford or Kate Moss. They got pregnant and they both got their bodies back.'

'Yeah, but did you see their bodies before? They had a head start. I'm doomed.'

'Oh, Kate, it's not that bad, you know? You get this great little baby at the end of it, and they even let you take it home and keep it.'

'I just don't think I can talk about this yet,' I said. 'I think I have to get used to the whole idea of it first, and then maybe we can have these great heart-to-heart, woman-to-woman things. But right now, I need to spend money.'

'Well get that dress,' she insisted. 'If nothing else, it will give you something to shoot for afterwards. It can be your goal dress.'

'My goal dress?'

'Don't tell me you haven't done that before? Hung up a dress that didn't fit but that you swore you were going to diet and exercise back into?'

'Well, maybe,' I admitted. 'But at least that was personal choice, not enforced.'

'Enough.' Sam laughed. 'Come on, we're going in and trying that thing on.'

'Sam—'

'Look, it's on sale,' she said, saying the magic words. And I followed her into the store.

I bought the dress and decided I was going to wear it at work tonight. It was a little summery, but we were still having this amazing warm, late fall and I thought I wouldn't look too ridiculous. Maybe with a nice cardigan . . . Two trained shoppers like us and yet it still took us another four hours to find a cardigan in exactly the right shade of red to match the dress. But we were women on a mission and there was no stopping us.

Sam dropped me off at the theatre and, as tempted as I was to head to Grounds Zero and grab an illicit coffee, I realized there was much more at stake here than my craving for a little caffeine, so I resisted and took my new purchases up to my office.

For a change, Graham wasn't sitting in the office, smugly working his way through something I'd come in early to complete. Sometimes it was like he could read my mind. Today his absence gave me a few minutes of solitude as I made the coffee for the volunteers, emptied and cleaned my ashtray, something else I was going to have to deal with, and then changed into my new outfit. I was feeling pretty good when I heard the door open at the end of the hall and heard Graham's happy voice singing down the empty corridor. He turned into the usher's changing room and dropped off his coat and backpack before making his way into the office. He sat down across from me and opened his bottled water, tossing the bottle cap into the garbage.

'Two points,' he cheered for himself.

'You know, that gets a little tiring after hearing it for the ten thousandth time,' I told him.

'You look nice tonight, boss,' he said, appraising the new outfit. 'What's the occasion?'

'A good sale at my favourite store,' I lied.

'Oh, my God.'

'What?' I asked, looking up from my file, alarmed.

'Oh, my God!' He broke out into a huge bug-catching grin.

'What is the matter with you?' I asked him.

'It was positive.'

'Graham, I have no idea what you're talking about,' I said.

'You took the test and it was positive and you're pregnant!'

For a minute I just stared at him, sitting across my desk from me, smiling smugly. And that's when I knew I really could kill a man if I had to. Before I realized what I was doing, I was out from behind the desk, had Graham by the shirt collar and threw him up against the wall. I could literally feel my nostrils flaring as I stared at him, his shocked face just inches from my burning eyes.

'You will never, ever say that out loud again.'

'Kate, calm down,' Graham said, the voice of a man practised in the art of brotherhood and unclehood.

'That is an absolute secret and I swear I will castrate you if I hear of anyone finding out about this.'

'Kate.' Graham tried again, *The Horse Whisperer* coming to mind. 'Kate, let go of my shirt, please.'

Suddenly, as I realized what I was doing, I did let go, took two steps backward and broke down in tears. I looked at Graham's worried face and ran for the washroom, throwing myself into one of the stalls and sobbing. I only sat there for a minute or two, when I felt strong hands reach down and pull me out of the stall, and then I looked up and there was Cam. He took me in his arms and let me cry, rubbing my back gently.

'Did Graham call you?' I asked, when I was finally getting my breath back.

'No, I just came up to see if you wanted to have a coffee before the show,' he explained. 'I didn't even have to ask Graham where you were, I could hear you halfway down the stairwell.'

'Sorry,' I said, taking the wad of toilet paper he offered me and wiping my face.

'Katie, this is just not like you. What is wrong with you?' he asked, concern on his face.

'Nothing,' I lied again.

He put his hands on my shoulders, holding me still, making me look him in the eyes.

'Katie, really, what is wrong with you?' he asked, not breaking away until I gave him an answer he could believe.

'I really don't know,' I admitted, not quite the outright lie. Tears filled my eyes again and he let me go.

'I'm going to take tomorrow off and get you to a doctor,' he said, running a paper towel under the cold water tap for me.

'I'll go,' I promised, meaning it. 'You don't have to take a day off.'

'No, you won't go,' he argued. Under normal circumstances he would have been right. But not this time.

'OK, but you don't have to take the day off. I'll get Sam to take me and then we can have brunch or something. OK?' I hoped this would satisfy him. I could go and get the home pregnancy test confirmed and not have to tell Cam just yet, either way.

'You promise me?' he asked.

'Yes, I do.'

Cam took the damp paper towel and wiped my face, dabbing at the mascara that was migrating down my cheeks.

'Do you want me to take you home?' he asked.

'I can finish the show,' I assured him. 'I'll just concentrate and quit being such a wimp for a couple of hours. Really, I'll be OK.'

He felt my forehead and seemed to be reassured that there was no fever.

'OK, but I'll be back here at eleven o'clock tonight to pick you up, no arguments. And if you're not done, Graham can finish up for you. I think you should try and get a good night's sleep.'

'I think you're right.'

'Oh, Katie, it really scares me when you agree with me. You sure you don't want to go to the doctor right now?' He tried out a smile.

I actually laughed in return.

'No, I'll be fine. But I'll be waiting at the stage door for you at eleven sharp, I promise.'

I finally convinced Cam that I wasn't going to die in the next hour or so and then managed to persuade him it was safe for him to go back to work. Then I tried to find Graham but, as a smart man with a lot of sisters, he had known what to do. He made himself scarce. I finally tracked him down to the second balcony and tried to apologize. I didn't feel a lot better,

90

but I was horrified by my behaviour earlier and had to say something. Graham gave me a big talk about hormones and how he understood and not to worry because he could keep a secret, so I knew we would be OK.

And I was OK, until at about half past seven when I saw Ken Lincoln and his wife Rebecca walking up the stairs. I had totally forgotten they had tickets to the show tonight. So, being the brave and adult woman that I was, I sent Graham over to talk to them and I spent the evening bartending in the Rodeo Lounge.

Cam was at the stage door at 11:00 sharp and I was waiting for him. We drove home in silence, me feigning utter exhaustion. When we got home Carrie was already asleep on the sofa bed, so we made our way upstairs quietly, changed and climbed into bed.

Cam pulled me close to him and wrapped his arms tightly around me and I felt safe and warm, as I always did in his arms. But I also felt something else. I felt this strange sense of distance. Even though I could feel his heart pounding against my back and his warm breath on my neck, there was something between us. There was the secret. And this wasn't just one of those little white lies I told him that he pretended not to know about to make me feel better. This was a huge, gaping omission. And I didn't know quite what to do about it. Luckily, this one time, he didn't seem to notice as he held me tight and fell asleep long before I did.

Monday November 17

About every four weeks I get a glorious Monday all alone. Cam works a day shift and I get the day off, if I'm lucky; if I'm not then I work a rental in the evening. Rentals are usually a piece of cake for us. It is a night when the play isn't scheduled to run and a company will hold its annual general meeting or an educational seminar or something like that. We get them in, we close the doors and then we smile at them on their way out. But whatever way it happens I get the day all to myself to do what I want, when I want. A small remembrance of my single days, oh so many months ago, when every day was like that. This was one of those Mondays. And, to top it off, Carrie had gotten up bright and early to go and spend the day with her kids, as they were off school for a professional day for their teachers.

I had woken up early and given Cam a happy, smiley send-off, promising again that I would go to the doctor. Then I went back to bed for an hour or so. After waking up feeling fairly refreshed, I put on my robe, grabbed a cup of decaf tea and sat in the sunshine on my balcony. I had the Sunday newspaper with me, which I hadn't read yet, but I just didn't have the energy to check up on the world this morning, so it sat on the table while I sipped my tea. I suddenly realized I had one hand protectively over my belly, in that stereotypical pregnant woman pose. This was so ridiculous; the baby, if you could even call it that, was probably the side of a pea pod or something, and I wouldn't be able to feel a thing for months. And yet, there I sat, a stupid grin on my face and a hand protectively over my belly. Already I was one of those women that I used to love to ridicule.

I didn't have a stupid grin on my face as I sat in the examination room at my doctor's office. I had given them a urine sample and was awaiting the arrival of the doctor with the pregnancy test results. Anxiously awaiting his arrival. Every time I heard footsteps outside the door, my heart started racing and my stomach lurched. I had called Sam and promised her I was going to the doctor, but I'd wanted to come alone. I'd already done the incredibly emotional thing yesterday, which was when I'd really needed her. For this, I wanted to be on my own. I wanted to discuss my options and start to get some sort of realistic plan put together about what I was going to do about this very unexpected situation.

I had been so busy thinking about what I was going to tell Cam that I actually missed the sound of the doctor walking down the hall and turning the doorknob. Suddenly, he was just there.

'Good morning, Kate.' He smiled at me.

92

Normally, that smile, those dark good looks and those piercing eyes would get my immediate attention. Today, it just didn't seem to do it for me.

'Hey, Brock.' I smiled weakly at him. 'Don't you ever take a day off?'

'I work just like your theatre; we're here seven days a week to serve you better. And how about you? Just got up on a Monday morning and thought you might want to take a pregnancy test?'

'Well, not really. I took a home test yesterday and it was positive. I figured I should let you have the final say.'

'Where's your man?' he asked.

'At work.'

'I'm guessing he doesn't know about this yet?' Brock asked, raising an accusatory eyebrow at me.

'Nope. Cam really wants to have kids, so I really didn't want to say anything to him until I knew for sure.'

'And . . .?'

'And this wasn't exactly planned,' I confessed. 'I thought the birth control pill was 99.99 per cent effective?'

'It is, but somebody has to be the 0.01 per cent, don't they?' He smiled. 'But, since this is one of those accidental happenings, I'll put on my serious face and manner for you, OK?'

'Is it positive?' I asked.

'It is positive.'

'Can you tell how far along?' I asked.

'Do you remember when your last period was?'

'It ended about four weeks ago, I think. I'd have to check the calendar to be sure.'

'Well, my best guess right now is that you're three or four weeks' pregnant.'

I felt tears burning the corners of my eyes but I refused to let them escape. I took a deep breath and steeled myself for the rest.

'OK. So what we need to do is send you for some blood work and schedule an ultrasound. Your last physical was about six months ago, and I'm confident that everything else is in working order. I'd like to do an examination but I'm willing to defer that to another day after you've had a chance to let all this sink in. How's that sound so far?' he asked.

'It's fine,' I agreed.

'Now, do you want to talk about the other options we have?' he asked.

'I need to know what's available,' I said. 'I have no idea what I'm going to do and I have to talk to Cam, but I guess I need to know.'

'OK, well, I've got some brochures here. Your options are pretty much having the baby and keeping it, having the baby and giving it away or not having the baby. Both of these brochures are from the Regional Health Centre and they talk about the latter options. This book is provided by the hospital's Maternity Centre and it tells you everything there is to know about having a baby. And there are probably a few things in there that you'll wish you didn't know.'

I took all the material from him and wondered where I was going to hide them from Cam.

'Kate, seriously, I want you to talk to Cam and then I want to see you back here by the end of the week.'

'OK.'

'No, I really mean it,' he said, putting his hand on my shoulder. 'This baby business is pretty serious stuff, you know?'

'Last guy that touched me almost lost an arm.' I smiled at him. 'I haven't had a cigarette or a coffee in two days.'

'Feeling a little edgy?' he joked, but pulled his arm back quickly.

'Yes.' I laughed. 'That would be putting it mildly.'

'Well, good for you. If you have a problem, we can talk about things to help you with it. But, meanwhile, I am serious about talking to Cam about this and I'd really like to see both of you by the end of the week, if that's possible.'

'I'll do my best,' I promised and jumped off the table. 'Thanks for everything.'

Brock opened the door and walked me out into the waiting room.

'Kate, I know this is a big surprise and it's scary, so you call me if you need anything, OK?'

I did something very unprofessional; I hugged him. Then I pulled away, blushed and ran from the office. Who was this woman that I was turning into?

94

If I had turned right when I left the doctor's office, I would have been at work in under five minutes, because it was less than a block away. But, instead, I turned left. I wandered two or three blocks and then found myself heading north, toward the river. I didn't know why I was going there. There are beautiful river pathways in Calgary, meandering along the wavy path of the Bow River, with ultra-expensive luxury condominiums on one side and the natural river habitat on the other. I wandered through downtown, avoiding all the shops and things that would normally take my attention, and found myself at the edge of the river.

I wandered down as far as Kensington and then turned back toward the centre of town. Near Prince's Island there was an elderly man selling bags of bread crusts, to feed the ducks and geese. I hadn't done this since we had brought Sam's little girl down here, when she was only about two and a half years old. But I felt compelled. I crossed over to the island, sat myself down on the rocks at the edge of the lagoon and tossed some bread crusts into the water. Soon there were lots of ducks swimming around, waiting for me to toss in more. It seemed late in the year for this many fowl to still be in Calgary, but I think our milder winters and the excellent food supply are keeping more and more of them in the city year-round.

When my bag was empty and my brain clearer, I scrunched up the bag, pulled myself up and found a garbage can to dispose of it. I checked my watch and found I still had plenty of time before I had to be at work. It was getting a little chilly, as the sun was sinking lower and lower on the horizon, but I would rather the chill than running into anyone I knew just yet. I still wasn't quite ready to face people. So I wandered around the island, talking to the ducks. An hour later I was getting cold, the sun was setting, and I knew it was time to go back.

I walked along 9th Avenue slowly, looking up toward my office. The lights were on and I could see Graham moving around, getting things ready. Soon, Leonard appeared in the office with him. Good, I thought, there was safety in numbers. I'd rather talk about Nietzsche tonight than my pregnancy with Graham.

I climbed the stairs and plastered a nonchalant smile on my face, joining them.

'So, Leonard.' I smiled. 'Did you manage to find that obscure reference you were talking about last night?'

Graham shot me a dirty look, not believing that I had actually brought up philosophy, let alone an incredibly boring thesis on Nietzsche. Leonard, too, looked unbelievingly at me, but wasn't about to question this gift horse.

'Well, actually, I went on that website I was telling you about, and it linked me to this chat room started by a University of Toronto doctoral candidate who, frankly, I think needs to get out more. But, regardless of all that, he has a copy of a book that he found in a little-used book store in Amsterdam and he's going to be able to fax me some of the appropriate quotations. It's not quite what I was hoping for but it's a tremendous clue. And then he actually knew someone who wrote on my topic, I think at the Sorbonne, so if I can get someone to translate when I go to London next summer, I should be able to get a good lead . . .'

A half-hour later Martha appeared and managed to stealthily turn the conversation from Leonard's mysterious book to her trip to London and her favourite stops on her bus tour there two years ago. I joined in with my comments from my summer spent studying there, and soon we had everyone offering suggestions as the ushers and volunteers slowly filed in.

I assigned positions and had to put Graham in the VIP lounge for the night, because we had a semi-famous actor with us this evening. He was in town filming his latest made-for-TV movie, with his latest very young, very blonde girl-friend. We offered him the private lounge and snuck him into the theatre just as the lights went down, so as not to cause a stir for him or disturb the actors in our little play. He wanted to go backstage afterwards and meet the cast, so I also assigned that one to Graham. I signed the others out, shut out the lights and was waiting for Cam at the stage door by eleven.

We went home. I was terrified he was going to bring up the doctor's appointment. But I guess he was hoping I would bring it up and I was just hoping to get to bed and pretend to be asleep before he gave up hoping and started asking.

'What did you end up doing today?' he asked.

'I slept in a bit, read the weekend paper and then took a

wonderfully long walk down by the river. It was really beautiful out today, wasn't it?'

'We are having a lovely fall. Do you think we're going to pay for it when winter finally arrives?' he asked.

Small talk. The love of my life and I were reduced to small talk.

'I hope not,' I sighed. 'I fed the ducks today. I haven't done that since Bonnie was a tiny little thing. It reminds me of summers with my grandma.'

'You used to feed the ducks?'

'The swans, in Crescent Park in Moose Jaw. Grandma always had a bag of stale bread crusts waiting for us when we arrived.'

I climbed into bed and plumped up my pillow. Cam climbed into bed beside me, wrapping himself around me and pulling the comforter up and over us. I loved these crisp fall nights, snuggled under a down comforter with the window open a crack and the air brisk in the room. I especially loved it since Cam was the brave one who got up first in the morning and closed the window and cranked up the furnace. Those hardwood floors could be mighty chilly.

'I hear you had a movie star in tonight,' he whispered, a shiver running down his back from the chilly night air.

'No secrets at the Plex, are there?'

'Not many. Was he well behaved or did you have to peel his grapes for him?' he asked.

'He was fine. No tantrums, no special requests, just a very young girlfriend.'

'Oh?'

'Yeah. He had a blonde on his arm who's probably spent more on plastic surgery than I've made in the last ten years and was young enough to be his daughter. Maybe even his granddaughter, depending on how much plastic surgery *he's* had. But he didn't cause a stir with the rest of the audience or anything.'

'Nothing else happen today?' he asked. I know this was his idea of a gentle opening and he was really hoping I would talk, but I just wasn't ready yet. And I didn't have any more lies for him. The truth was weighing me down too much to spend any more energy on lies.

'It was nice out today, wasn't it?' I mumbled, sounding as tired as I felt. 'I went for a long walk down by the river. Didn't I tell you about that already?'

'Why did you have a show tonight? Aren't you usually dark on Mondays?'

'It's because the play was held over. With the rental schedule this was the way it worked out. Tomorrow night there is a banking seminar booked,' I mumbled, not even pretending any more, as I felt myself dropping off to sleep.

'Night.' He kissed my cheek, but I felt his arm growing heavy around me. The chill left us as his body warmed the bed and he too drifted off to sleep.

'Night,' I mumbled back.

And then it popped into my mind. How was I going to tell him? I wondered. But I pushed the thought out of my mind and drifted off. I really needed a good night's sleep for a change. I could deal with everything else tomorrow.

Tuesday November 18

Cam was still working days and, though I heard him up and getting ready, I gave him a quick 'Good morning', rolled over and pretended to go back to sleep. I was off today. I was going to let Graham run the bank seminar tonight. It was an easy gig and I was only a phone call away if anything happened. I was very happy not to have to face Graham or Gus or anyone else at the Plex, because they all seemed to be able to stare right through me and figure out exactly what I was hiding. I heard Cam leaving with Carrie and I decided I really might just go back to sleep after all. I rolled over, pulled the comforter up around me and settled in, just as the smell of the morning's coffee wafted up and over the loft and started to wreak havoc on my over-sensitive stomach.

I finished in the bathroom and came back out into the living room. With three people living in such a small space, things got really messy quickly. It was different from when I lived alone and things landed exactly where I dropped them. And it took at least a good week or two before the mess started to make me crazy. I started picking things up and then decided that, with the bonus of both Cam and Carrie being at work, I might as well surprise Cam and actually clean the house, so he didn't have to do it on his day off for once.

I had the laundry going by nine o'clock and talked to a couple of neighbours I had never met, even after all these years in the building. The laundry room seemed to draw a whole different crowd in the morning. We had a lively discussion on the whole issue of the building going condo while I waited for the rinse cycle; then I dropped in the fabric softener and said my goodbyes. Before I knew it, I was vacuuming carpets, washing floors and even cleaning toilets, albeit with thick rubber gloves on, you couldn't expect me to recover completely in one day. By noon the place was fairly sparkling and I was pretty proud of myself. I hoped Cam would notice when he got home later.

The phone rang and I set down the dust cloth and picked up the receiver.

'Hello?'

'Hey, Kate, it's Sam. What's up?'

'I'm just cleaning house. What are you doing?'

'You're what?'

'Cleaning house,' I repeated. 'You know, vacuuming, dusting, laundry, that sort of stuff.'

'I didn't know you knew some of those words.'

'I just said I was cleaning, not murdering someone. What's wrong with that?'

'Well, nothing is wrong with it,' she explained. 'But I just don't think I've ever heard those words come out of your mouth before in that order. More like "Cam's cleaning and I'm watching him while drinking coffee." That's what I would expect to hear.'

'Don't get smart,' I said. 'Did you just call to give me a hard time or did you actually want something?'

'Well, my little daughter says it's a bright, beautiful, sunny day outside and she thinks her Auntie Kate should buy her an ice cream at the zoo this afternoon. You game?'

'Well, yeah, actually I am. I'm feeling a little nostalgic these days. I was out feeding the ducks all alone yesterday, so it'll be nice to have some company today.'

'That's not nostalgic, that's nesting,' Sam teased me.

'I'm ignoring that remark as I'm neither discussing fowl nor nesting today.'

'Did you go to the doctor yesterday?'

'Yes.'

'Why didn't you call me like you were supposed to?'

'Because I spent several hours wandering around down by the river and when I got to my office, I wasn't alone for more than ten seconds.'

'Well, what did the doctor say?'

'He said I was pregnant.'

'Kate.'

'Sam, not yet. Give me another day or so. Let me spend the day at the zoo with your daughter and eat ice cream.'

'We have to talk about this eventually, you know.'

'I am aware of that,' I promised. 'Anyway, I'd like to be home by four so I can have dinner with Cam and Carrie. They were talking about maybe going to look at some apartments tonight. Anyway, I just don't feel like I've been around much and I'd like to get caught up with them.'

'All this nesting, that's a good sign, Kate.'

'I told you, don't even start with that.'

'OK, OK. Well, you know that Bonnie never lasts much more than a couple of hours at the zoo so, if I meet you there at one o'clock, I'm sure we'll be ready to go home by three.'

'OK. The place is looking pretty good here, so I think I can stop dusting for a couple of hours.'

'Well, that's good. You know, you don't want to jump into these things too quickly. Maybe you should save something for another day.'

'You're very funny. I'm just trying to be a good partner for Cam. I mean, there's no reason he should be responsible for all the chores and the cooking and the laundry around here.'

'Whatever you say, Kate,' she said, pretending she was giving in to me. But her voice had that 'I know better than you' attitude. 'So, north entrance at one o'clock?'

'It's a deal,' I agreed. 'See you then.'

I hung up the phone and gathered my pile of cleaning stuff and took it back to the utility closet. The phone started ringing, so I dropped everything and ran back.

'Hey, Sam, what did you forget to tell me this time?' I asked.

'Kate? It's actually Carrie,' the timid voice told me.

'Oh, Carrie, I'm sorry,' I apologized. 'I was just trying to be a smart aleck. Everything OK with you?'

'Everything's fine,' she told me. 'I was just wondering if you guys could meet me at my old house tonight instead of me coming to the apartment first?'

'Are you sure that's a wise idea?' I asked.

'Yeah, it'll be OK. The kids need to pick up a bunch of stuff for school. So I called and Hank said it was OK. I guess he doesn't want to get my ex-husband involved. Hank doesn't like to take on men, you know?'

'Yeah, I do,' I told her. 'Cam isn't home right now, but I know he was talking about taking you apartment hunting tonight, so I don't think he has any other plans. I'm sure we can get you over there tonight.'

'No, I just want you to meet me there. I was actually planning on picking up the kids after work and borrowing a friend's car. Then I can load it up with their stuff and take it back to Alan's place. I was just hoping you could meet me there in case Hank causes any problems, and then pick me up from Alan's house?'

'Carrie, honestly, anything we can do to help. Just tell me what time.'

'Well, I think I'll probably be there around five,' she said. 'Is that too early for you guys?'

'I think it's just fine. I'll double-check with Cam but, if you don't hear from me, we'll meet you at the house at five.'

'Thanks, Kate, you're really great for taking on me and all my problems. I hope you know how much I appreciate it.'

'It's no problem at all.' I laughed. 'Cam had to live with my mother for a week! Now, Carrie, just promise me that if you get there first, you won't go into the house until we get there.'

'That I can absolutely promise. I'd really rather not get arrested again.' She giggled.

'OK, well, we'll see you later then.'

*   *   *

101

It was November, so I had put on my jeans, wool socks, hiking boots, T-shirt, shirt and heavy sweater for the zoo trip. Now I sat at a picnic table, eating a melting ice-cream cone, and had stripped off the heavy sweater, which was draped over the stroller. Bonnie sat on my knee, happily dripping ice cream all over both of us. None of us cared. We had already seen the lions and tigers and bears (oh my) – a must since she'd seen *The Wizard of Oz*. After that, Bonnie was happy to see the monkeys that were in the outdoor enclosures, as long as they didn't fly and take her to the Wicked Witch of the West. That's why she didn't like going inside the monkey house. Her dad had scared her once in there with what he thought was a funny Wizard of Oz monkey story and she seemed to still be traumatized by that incident. After we'd checked those items off our list, we had our ice cream. If our timing was right, we could go and pet the elephants. After that, Destination Africa, as she was starting to like the hippos, too, now that their river was glassed in, so you could watch them while they were under the water.

In the summer we'd put Bonnie in the stroller after seeing the elephants. She would fall asleep and we would see the things that she hadn't yet expressed an interest in. For Sam, it was always the Australian exhibit. She and Ryan had spent six months in Australia on a job exchange just after they got married. For me, it was the Siberian tigers. I could watch them and their kittens for hours, playing with their giant-sized cat toys. It always seemed slightly surreal, because they looked like super-sized house cats.

But since it was November, and the sun set earlier these days and we both had obligations later, we packed things up and headed home right after the elephants, promising Bonnie that the hippos would wait for her next visit. Why she was scared of the cute little monkeys but liked petting the huge, rough-haired elephants I could never understand. But they made her giggle and I loved that little baby face when it broke out into one of those full little belly laughs that only a five-year-old can produce, so we petted the elephants every chance we got.

Sam dropped me off at home, even though I insisted that I could take the C-train, and I hurried upstairs to get changed.

I had called Cam before I left for the zoo and confirmed everything with him. He was home at four fifteen, changed into
jeans and a sweatshirt and we were parked outside Hank's
house by four thirty, awaiting Carrie's arrival.

We'd been sitting in the car for about ten minutes when I
decided it was too hot and stuffy. I pulled on my jean jacket
and climbed out, leaning against the hood of the car and letting
the sunshine beat down on me, as it slowly made its way
toward the mountains in the west. Cam turned off the radio
and came out to stand beside me. He pretended he just wanted
to be with me, but I knew he was making sure that one of
the rivets on my jeans didn't scratch up his precious car.

Once I had actually jumped up and sat on the hood, and Cam
had almost had a heart attack. After I scurried off, realizing my
sin, he had spent an hour polishing the hood, looking for the
most minute of scratches that might turn into rust at the first
sign of moisture. There had been no scratches, but I had certainly
learned to treat his car with more respect. I might not understand it, but he loved that car, so who was I to question that?

I heard a car coming around the corner and craned my head
to see if it was Carrie. It wasn't, it was just a police cruiser.
I looked down at my watch and wondered how much longer
she was going to be, when I noticed that the police cruiser
wasn't driving by yet, rather pulling over in front of us. The
car pulled up in front of us, parked and two officers got out,
approaching us slowly, one a little farther back than the other,
with his hand on his holster.

'Oh, shit, what is this about?' I asked.

'Kate,' Cam warned me, poking me in the ribs none too
gently with his elbow.

'Good afternoon,' the officer said politely. 'Anything we
can help you folks with this afternoon?'

'Nope,' I said.

'Officer, if you'll try really hard to ignore my smart-mouthed
girlfriend, I'm sure I can answer your questions.'

'We've had a complaint that there are two people hanging
around; I believe it was suggested you were casing the neighbourhood,' the officer said, talking directly to Cam this time
and ignoring me, which was probably for the best.

'Hank,' I suggested.

103

'And I'm sure it's from this house,' Cam said, pointing over his shoulder to Carrie and Hank's house.

The officer just nodded noncommittally.

'Look, officer, my cousin lives here. She and her husband have just separated and there's just a little bit of animosity. She has made arrangements with him to pick up some stuff for her kids and we just came along to meet her here, in case he decides to cause any trouble. That's all we're doing. We weren't even going to go in.'

'Do you have some ID?' the officer asked.

'In the car,' I said, trying to be polite. 'In my wallet.'

'You want to get that for me?'

I opened the car door and grabbed my backpack. I pulled my driver's license out from the wallet and turned it over to the police officer. I grabbed Cam's wallet and gave it to him; he did the same.

'OK, I'm just going to call this in and make sure everything is OK,' the officer explained. 'You two just wait here, I'll only be a minute.'

'Detective Ken Lincoln can vouch for us,' I told him. 'He's in homicide but he knows what's going on here.'

'OK, just let me check this out.'

The other officer stayed back and smiled politely at us, while his partner climbed into the police cruiser and got on the radio. In a couple of minutes he was back out and looking much more relaxed. He handed us back our ID.

'All right, so I talked with Detective Lincoln and he gave me the scoop, so here's what we're going to do. You two are going to stay here with my partner, Officer Strachan. When your cousin gets here, I'll go in with her, just to make sure there aren't any problems. Then we can sit here and watch you all drive off and that way we'll just avoid any of the problems you folks had when you were here last time.'

'That would be fine with us.' Cam smiled, putting his wallet in his back pocket and nudging me again.

'Absolutely,' I agreed. 'I would really rather not be hauled down to jail again.'

'All right.' He smiled and waved his partner over. 'Pete, let me tell you what Detective Lincoln had to say about these folks here.'

Carrie drove up just as the officer finished his instructions and pulled her car into the garage. Officer Danko walked around the large hedge that blocked the view into the front yard, and up the driveway to try and get to Carrie before she went into the house so he could explain everything to her.

'Pete.' The first officer poked his head back around the hedge. 'The kids are in the back seat of the car and the wife has already gone into the house.'

And his point was made by the sound of arguing coming from the house through the open windows.

'OK, I'll keep an eye on everyone out here,' Officer Strachan reassured his partner. 'You go on and settle them down in there. Do you want me to call for back up?'

'Yeah, why don't you bring a supervisor down here. Then Detective Lincoln will trust we did everything on the up and up.'

Officer Danko headed back into the house and Officer Strachan stepped a couple of paces away from us and talked quietly into his radio.

We heard the doorbell ring once and the arguing stopped. The doorbell rang again and then Hank opened the door. We heard the officer talking calmly and quietly and Hank yelling back at him. Finally the men came to some sort of agreement because we heard the officer enter the house and the front door close. Then all was silent. Officer Strachan's radio crackled to life again and he turned and listened.

'Is everything OK?' Cam asked.

'He seems to have them calmed down,' Officer Strachan explained to us. 'The woman is in the kitchen packing some things and the husband is in the living room talking to Officer Danko. It seems to be that they're fine with each other as long as they're in different rooms.'

And then it was quiet again. Except for the sound of Hank's voice, which seemed to rise every time he heard something he didn't like from the policeman.

Silence was hard. Time slowed down and crawled past. I fidgeted, looking in my backpack for some gum but really wishing I could find a cigarette. I settled on the gum and started chewing quite vigorously. Officer Strachan was kind of cute, and I flashed him one of my flirty smiles, hoping for a little conversation, but he seemed pretty serious about his duty out here. I looked at my watch for the hundredth time, wondering how much longer this was going to take.

'I'm just going to go and make sure the kids are still OK in the car,' Officer Strachan told us.

'Do you want me to come with you?' Cam offered.

'No, I'd really rather you two stayed right here, please.'

'Not a problem,' Cam assured him.

I was going to ask Officer Strachan how much longer he thought this was going to take, or if we should call our lawyer, when I heard it.

I didn't know what the noise was at first. It was loud, so loud it hurt my eardrums. And then I heard it again, another crack through the silent neighbourhood, this time followed by the sound of shattering glass. We all turned toward the house, but Officer Strachan's reaction was quicker than ours.

'Get down,' he screamed at us, not waiting for a response.

He shoved me aside, pushing me down, and shouted again, telling Cam to get down as well. Then I felt a puff of air pass my cheek and, instead of me being down, Officer Strachan was down. He was lying on the ground, the right side of his uniform rapidly turning red as blood gushed out of his chest and spilled over on to the asphalt.

I dropped to my knees, my hands trying to plug the hole in his chest and I looked up at Cam.

'Cam . . .?' I didn't know what else to say.

Cam dropped down beside me, taking the policeman's head in his hands and trying to hold it steady.

'Hang on there,' he said to both of us. 'We'll get some help here. Just try not to move.'

My hands pushed down hard into the officer's chest, but blood still seeped out between my fingers and I could see his face growing pale. I could also feel air between my fingers, as he tried to catch his breath, and I felt a sinking feeling in my chest as I realized how serious this was.

But I smiled down reassuringly at him. 'I've got you here.'

He opened his mouth and tried to gasp something.

'Don't try to talk,' I told him. 'It's going to be OK. You've lost some blood but as soon as the ambulance gets here, they'll get you off to the hospital and you'll be good as new.'

106

We heard the front door of the house open and the sound of feet scrambling over the pavement.

'Over here,' Cam bellowed, rewarded by the sight of the other policeman, Officer Danko, racing around the hedge and taking in the scene instantly.

'Officer down,' he screamed into his walkie-talkie. 'This is unit 52, officer down, officer needs assistance. I repeat, officer down.'

I heard that voice in my head, over and over again. I'm not sure if he actually kept yelling it or if it was just my mind, trying to cope with the scene around me. Suddenly there were sirens and lights flashing everywhere around us. I saw paramedics running over with a stretcher just as I felt Officer Strachan let go of a last ragged breath. I looked down at him and allowed myself to be pushed out of the way as they scooped him and ran, the ambulance screaming off into the twilight.

Someone gave me some paper towels to wipe my hands with and Cam and I were asked to wait in the back of one of the police cars. The police took the kids out of the back seat of Carrie's car, and put them into another police cruiser. I saw one officer with a gun in an evidence bag and Carrie being led in handcuffs to a third police cruiser.

I don't know how long we sat in the back of the car. We didn't appear to be locked in or anything, but no one was rushing to see how we were doing. There was too much else going on. I sat, leaning against Cam, staring out the back window. It seemed like a thousand police cars had appeared. There were lights flashing up and down the street. Twilight was descending and the lights were casting an eerie glow. Ken Lincoln had arrived and made his way through the scene. Many other men in suits accompanied him, detective badges flashing everywhere. People were measuring things and picking up items and putting them in bags and asking questions up and down the street. Finally, Ken made his way over to the car that we were sitting in and opened the back door. I got out, followed by Cam and looked up at Ken, waiting for some answers.

'So, guys, we're just finishing up here and we're going to have to get you down to the station for a statement,' Ken said.

'What's going to happen?' I asked. 'Was Carrie trying to shoot Hank?'

'I don't really know,' he admitted. 'We're just piecing some of it together. But it appears your cousin got a hold of a gun and brought it with her when she came to pick up the kids' things today. Unfortunately, that makes it look a little like she was thinking about hurting him or at least threatening him. And premeditation is not good news for her,' Ken explained.

'Oh God.' It seemed that was all I could get out of my mouth just now.

'Can we see her?' Cam asked, glancing toward the police car where she sat.

'No. I'm sorry, Cam, but I have to play this one by the book. There was a cop shot and we don't know yet if he's going to make it or not. They'll be taking her down to processing in a couple of minutes. The best thing you can do for her is to call her lawyer. I just don't know what else to suggest right now.'

'That's OK,' Cam said, shaking his hand. 'I appreciate you letting us know what's going on.'

'What about her kids?' I asked.

'We've contacted their father. He's on his way to pick them up.'

'Maybe we could sit with them in our car until he gets here?' I suggested. 'Then they don't have to sit in the police car and watch any more of this.'

'That's fine with me,' Ken agreed. 'Just don't go anywhere with them where we can't find you. Come on, I'll make sure the officer turns them over to you.'

We walked past Carrie, who stared straight at us, without any recognition crossing her face, and Ken opened the door to the police cruiser where the kids were sitting.

'Hey, David, Emily,' Cam said, kneeling down so he could see them. 'How are you guys doing?'

'I want to go home, Uncle Cam,' Emily said, while David just stared at him.

'I know,' Cam sighed. 'Your dad is on his way. How about if you come and wait with us until he gets here?'

'That's way better than this yucky car,' Emily said, scurrying out, her brother right behind her. 'There's gum on the back of the seat.'

'Oh, who the hell cares about that?' David screamed at his sister. 'Don't you realize someone's been shot?'

'Hey, dude,' I said, holding out my hand for him to take. 'We're all a little stressed out right now. Why don't we go for a little walk and maybe talk about it a bit.'

After staring at my hand for at least a full minute, David finally reached out and took it. I smiled reassuringly and helped him out of the police cruiser and guided him away from the mess, leaving Cam to bring Emily along. David slowed as we passed the police car where his mother sat. His hand slowly came up and he rested it on the glass of the car window, against where his mother's cheek rested. Slowly, Carrie's face turned to him and tears began to spill down her cheeks.

'Don't worry, Momma.' He was crying now, too. 'It'll be OK.'

'Come on, David,' I said, applying a little more pressure to his shoulder and guiding him to Cam's car. 'The police are going to look after your mom right now. We'll see her soon.'

He let me steer him out into the street.

'Did you see what happened, sweetie?' I asked him.

'No!' he said quickly. 'Emily and I stayed in the car, just like mom told us to.'

'That was lucky, huh?' I asked him. 'Were you sleeping?'

'No, Emily was. I was playing with my Gameboy. I used the headphones so I wouldn't wake Emily up.'

'That was very nice of you,' Cam said.

'I should have protected Momma,' the boy protested. 'I should have been in the house with her and I could have protected her.'

'Oh, David, I don't think so. I don't think anybody could have stopped what happened today. It was just a very bad accident.'

'It should have been Hank that got shot,' he told me calmly.

'I know Hank has been mean to your mom . . .' I began.

'It should have been Hank,' David insisted. 'That was the way it was supposed to be.'

'What do you mean?' I asked.

'Hank was the bad man. He was the one that should have been shot.'

I was about to argue when, thankfully, the kids' father pulled up beside Cam's car and jumped out.

'David, Emily?' he shouted, running to his kids and scooping them up in his arms. 'Are you guys OK?'

'We're fine, Daddy,' Emily said. 'I slept in the car for the whole thing. Those loud sirens woke me up.'

'David?' he asked, looking at his son.

'I want to go home, Dad,' was all David had to say.

The man looked up and reached out his hand to Cam, who took it and shook it.

'Good to see you again, Alan,' Cam said.

'Are they OK?' he asked, looking down at the kids.

'Yeah, they missed everything. They were just waiting in the car,' Cam reassured him. 'You can take them home.'

'I was so worried when a police detective called . . .'

I put my hand on his shoulder, trying to reassure him.

'I'm sorry,' he apologized. 'I'm Alan Palmer.'

I shook his hand.

'Kate Carpenter. I'm with him.' I nodded toward Cam and smiled.

'Why don't you just take them straight home?' Cam suggested, letting go of Emily's hand and giving it over to her father. 'We've got to go down to the police station. We can call you from there and let you know what's happening.'

'OK,' he agreed. 'Is there anything else I can do?'

'I don't think there's anything any of us can do,' Cam said with a sigh.

We watched Alan secure the kids in his car and then drive away. I turned to get into our car and I noticed a very familiar face standing behind the police barricade across the street. I started to cross the street toward him.

'Where are you going, Katie?' Cam asked.

'I just wanted to say hi to someone,' I explained.

'Now?'

I crossed the street and the man with the familiar face turned away and started to walk down the block.

'Hey,' I called after him. 'Hey, you, slow down.'

He turned and looked at me. 'Sorry, were you talking to me?'

'Do I know you?' I asked.

'I don't think so.'

'But I'm sure I've seen you around recently.'

'Sorry.'

'I'm Kate Carpenter,' I said.

'Nice to meet you.'

'And you are?'

'Uninterested. Now if you'll excuse me I've got to get home.'

'Why are you leaving before all the excitement is over?'

'I'm going home to see my children and give them a hug. My kids go to the same school as those kids and it just gave me a bit of a chill.'

'So what are you doing in this neck of the woods then?' I asked.

'Miss, was it Carpenter?'

'Yes.'

'Are you with the police department?'

'No.'

'Goodnight then.' He smiled politely and turned and walked away.

I looked around the interrogation room; four boring walls, all institutional grey and chipped and cracked from years of wear and tear. I was searching my memory, trying to find something I had forgotten, something that might make all this look better, make Carrie seem not quite so guilty.

'. . . And that's all I remember,' I told Ken, feeling a catch in my throat as the words tried to come out.

Ken reached over and shut off the tape recorder.

'OK, well, that should do it for now. That's pretty much the same story we're getting from everyone. No one actually saw what was going on.'

'What about the officer that was in the house with her?' I asked.

'He was in the living room. Carrie was in the kitchen, packing up some things. He couldn't see into the kitchen so he doesn't know exactly what happened either, just heard the shots. When he got into the kitchen, Carrie was standing there, with a gun on the floor in front of her and you guys were screaming for help.'

'That's bad, right?' I asked.

'It's sure not good,' Ken offered.

'Should we wait for Carrie?' Cam asked.

'No, I'm sorry but she's going to be a while, probably over night at least. Her lawyer is with her now and he'll take care of everything. I'm sure he'll call you if he manages to get her out.'

'Oh,' was all Cam could muster. My turn to be brave.

'So, are we done here then?' I asked.

'Yeah, I guess,' Ken said, looking at all his papers. 'You're not planning on leaving the country or anything, are you?'

'No, but we should have done that yesterday.' I made a half-hearted attempt at a joke.

'Good. Just let me know if anything else comes to mind,' Ken said, pushing his chair back and standing up.

I stood up too and pulled Cam up with me.

'Come on,' I said. 'I need you to take me home.'

Wednesday November 19

The rest of the night had been a somber one in the old loft. We tried watching TV for a while but kept getting news flashes with pictures of Carrie's face appearing on all the channels. And as if that wasn't bad enough, suddenly, there we were, in living colour, sitting in the back of a police car, and neither of us was up for watching any more of that. We turned off the TV and went to bed, pretending to read for a while, until we finally pretended to sleep.

Cam tossed and turned all night long. He finally gave up trying to sleep and got up at seven o'clock, showered and headed for the police station, to see if he could find out what was going on with Carrie. I got up with him, figuring there was no point in lying in bed and tossing and turning all by myself for another few hours. I made some coffee and pretended to drink it and happily ate the breakfast he made, finding that I was starving and my stomach was a little more settled this morning.

I had a big problem, though, and that was that I had to figure out what to do about mornings and my coffee addiction. I knew the minute I asked for decaf or turned down a cup of coffee, Cam would know something was up. Maybe if I switched the coffee with some decaf he wouldn't be able to tell. I didn't think I could go the entire nine months without a sip of coffee. I'm sure it was all psychological, just like thinking I was eating for two when number two was the size of a walnut right now, but there had to be an upside to this whole thing and this morning it was going to be the fact I could eat without guilt. And cigarettes. I wanted one so badly right now that I could scream. I was going to have to figure out how to tell Cam soon that I was pregnant because, if I had to go much longer without a cigarette, his life was going to be in danger the first time he lit up around me and he should be forewarned. I was struggling to work this all out while I was putting the last of the dishes in the dishwasher when the phone rang.

'Hello?' I said, grabbing it by the second ring, another big advantage to living in a small place.

'Well, how'd he take it?'

'Sam?' I asked. 'What are you talking about?'

'Cam. You told him, right?'

'You've got to be kidding.'

'Kate, we talked about this.'

'Look, Sam, I know, and you're right, but something came up and . . .'

'Something else is going to be coming up really soon, too, you know. Are you going to wait until you start showing before you tell him? Or until Graham lets something slip? How do you think he's going to feel about that?'

'Sam,' I sobbed. 'Just stop it.'

'Kate, I know your hormones are a little out of whack right now, but you cannot just start crying every time something isn't going the way you want it to.'

'Sam, have you been out of town for the last day or something?' I asked sarcastically, not intending to sound quite as mean as I did.

'Uh, no,' she said, her voice sounding hurt. 'What's up with you?'

113

'Maybe you should bring your newspaper in from the front stoop,' I suggested, still sarcastic but trying to rein it in a little. 'Carrie ran into a little bit of trouble last night.'

I heard Sam open the front door, then the phone dropped as she bent over to pick up the paper.

'Hello?' I yelled through the receiver.

She was taking a very long time to pick it up.

'Kate, sorry,' she apologized. 'Hang on one more second.'

I heard the door slam and then I imagined her scurrying back to the kitchen and opening up the newspaper on the table.

'Ryan!' she screamed upstairs to her husband. 'Sorry, Kate. I can't believe this. What happened? Is that Cam's car in the background of the picture? Oh, my God, were you there? Are you OK?'

She was suddenly off the offensive and sounded like she was in shock.

'Calm down,' I said. 'I'm OK, Cam's OK.'

'What do you want?' I heard Ryan yelling down the stairs.

'Come down here, you have to see this,' Sam yelled back up the stairs, nearly blowing out my eardrums. 'Sorry, Kate. Now tell me, what's going on?'

'Well, I don't really know. It looks like Carrie took a gun with her yesterday when we went over to pick up some stuff from her place. I guess she thought that if Hank tried anything, she could hold him off long enough to get out safely. Well, she ended up firing it; it missed Hank and hit the police officer that was standing next to me.'

'Oh, my God.'

I was expecting more but that was all she could get out.

'Yeah, I think I said that, too.'

'Sorry, Kate. I'm speechless. What do you want me to do? Should I come over? I can be there in fifteen minutes.'

'No, no,' I insisted. 'You don't have to come over. Cam should be home soon. He went down to the station to see if there was anything he could do. But I'm pretty sure there is *nothing* he can do and that Eli will just send him home to get him out of the way.'

'But are you OK?' she asked. 'And I don't just mean that you didn't get shot, I mean, are you OK?'

'Yeah, well, not really. I think I'm totally in shock. It was

114

horrifying. But today it just seems like something I watched on TV, not something I actually witnessed, you know?'

'Kate, sweetie, we're coming over. I need to bake you some muffins or something, and I think it might be good for Cam to have Ryan there when he gets back. You know how sometimes guys can only talk to other guys. And Ryan being a firefighter and all, sometimes people open up to him because they know he's seen stuff like this.'

'I'm not saying no,' I said.

'All right, we'll be there in twenty minutes or so.'

'I thought you said fifteen?' I tried a half-hearted joke.

'Well, since it's not urgent I should probably change out of my pajamas. Is there anything you need that we can pick up on our way?'

'Decaf coffee?' I asked, feeling a little catch in my throat.

True to their word, Sam and Ryan were in my living room within a half an hour. Sam had brought a big canister of decaffeinated coffee. She even poured the coffee into my regular canister, so I wouldn't have to explain to anyone why I was drinking decaf. One crisis at a time was her theory. Although, even though she was my best friend and sworn to secrecy, I was pretty sure Ryan knew my big news as well. Within an hour of their arrival Sam had two different kinds of muffins cooling on the kitchen table, with a jar of homemade jam she had brought with her and a big pot of decaffeinated coffee that was probably the best thing I had tasted in days. She was working on a casserole for dinner that looked big enough to feed a small army. But when Sam was stressed, she cooked. When I was stressed, I either smoked or had a fight with Cam. I was feeling a little out of sorts that I couldn't do either right now.

Cam finally got home in the early afternoon. He wasn't feeling much better than when he left. He hadn't had the chance to see Carrie, but he had spent lots of time with Eli, Carrie's lawyer, who outlined for him in no uncertain terms how bad things looked and how it just got a whole lot more expensive. Apparently, we had a bit of a chance because there was no actual eye witness to the shooting. Officer Danko was in the living room and by the time he got into the kitchen where Carrie was, the gun was on the floor and Carrie was in shock and not talking. Eli wasn't sure how he was going to build a defense out of that, but he was going to try. And, if not, there was insanity. We might be able to have a psychiatrist see her and state that she had obviously had a dissociative break from reality, the years of abuse, etc. The only problem was the fact that she had brought the gun with her, which definitely showed premeditation.

'So it's not looking good,' I said, my arm around Cam's shoulder.

'Nope.'

'Eli's a good lawyer, though,' Ryan piped in. 'He won that big case last year, you know, the young prostitute that shot her pimp? And everyone said that was open and shut.'

'You're right,' I said. 'We have to try and think a little more positively about this. There's a long history of abuse, and Eli is the best. He'll be able to get her off.'

'It was a policeman that got shot, though,' Cam reminded us. 'A young policeman with a young family. If Carrie had actually shot Hank, we wouldn't have half these problems.'

'Anyone want another beer?' Ryan asked, already half way to the fridge. Cam nodded his assent and Ryan opened two cans and brought them over. 'How about we have this on the balcony and the women folk can call us when luncheon is ready?'

Cam got up without much enthusiasm and followed him out to the deck. Ryan closed the door so they could have their man talk in private. I didn't care, as long as Cam could get some of this off his chest and start feeling a little better.

Sam headed back into the kitchen to dice something else and I sat down at the table and dug into the now-cooled muffins with a fresh cup of coffee.

'Thanks for the coffee,' I said with my mouth full. 'And the muffins. These are great.'

'You're welcome. So when are you going to tell him?'

'Shhh!' I scolded her. 'I don't want him overhearing you.'

'I am being quiet.' She washed her hands and sat down beside me, having a muffin of her own. 'Kate, I am so sorry this whole tragedy has happened and that Carrie felt she was forced to do this. But, regardless of any of that, you still have to deal with this. You have to talk to Cam.'

116

'I know. Just not today. He's distraught, I'm in shock, and I can't add anything else to that today. I have to give him a day or two to recover.'

'A day or two is fine,' she assured me. 'But that's all. I'm going to be checking up on you, Kate.'

'I know you are.'

'I just want to make sure you're dealing with it. I'm worried about you, sweetie.'

'And I'm worried about him,' I said, pointing to Cam sitting out on the balcony with Ryan. 'This is all incredibly bad timing for him. How is he going to deal with all of this at once? I mean, look at him.'

And it was true. Cam was hunched in his chair, his shoulders rolled forward, his brows furrowed, the wrinkles around his eyes seeming to be etched deeper than they were yesterday.

'He'll get through this with your help,' she said. 'That's what family is for and you're his family now.'

'And what about me?' I asked, tears suddenly filling my eyes. 'How will I get through it?'

Sam pulled me close to her and wrapped me in one of her big hugs. 'We'll get you through this, don't you worry.'

I had called Graham earlier to let him know what was going on. I really didn't know if I was going to go to work or not tonight, and I told him he was in charge unless notified otherwise. But by the time we had eaten our late lunch/early dinner and Sam and Ryan had headed home to pick up Bonnie from the neighbours, I was starting to feel edgy. I'd been stuck inside all day and had energy to burn. I didn't know how I was going to manage to sit at home all night and be a good, supportive girlfriend for Cam. I really was terrible at all this.

That's when Cam offered to drive me to work. I protested that I certainly couldn't leave him tonight; he protested that he'd be just fine and, in the end, I went to work.. He let me out at the stage door and I made my way through the lobby up into my office. I was a little bit late and Graham was at my desk, just starting to sign in everyone. The robust conversation stopped immediately as I crossed the threshold.

'Good evening,' I greeted them. 'Sorry I'm late but I've had a bit of a hectic day today.' There was a nervous giggle that ran throughout the room. 'Now, I'm sure you've all seen

117

the newspapers today and would love me to tell you what happened, but I'm not going to. I hope you can all respect that I just can't talk about this yet and that, when I can, I will try and answer all your questions.'

'No problem,' Martha said. 'Leonard can fill all the empty silences with some more talk about those incredibly boring dead philosophers of his. Apparently he's found another dusty book somewhere with some incredible insight into sado-masochism or some such thing.'

Everyone burst out laughing at that one and we returned to a semblance of normal. I got all the positions assigned, got everyone in their places and then we opened the doors. I was standing by the technical booth as the audience started to meander in. I noticed a couple lined up by the bar, whispering to each other and glancing toward me. Then a couple that I handed a program to did a double-take and quickly crossed the lobby, whispering to their friends and pointing back toward me.

I quickly turned away, pulling open the door to the technical booth and stepping inside. I took a couple of deep breaths, trying to quell the tears that were threatening to escape my rapidly blinking eyelids.

'Kate?'

I saw Trevor's head poke out of the stage manager's booth.

'Hi, Trevor,' I greeted our stage carpenter, putting on my brave front.

'What are you doing in here? Is something wrong?'

'No, no. I just needed a minute to myself.'

Trevor came down the short hallway from the booth to where I stood.

'Why'd you come to work tonight, Kate?' he asked.

'You know?'

'Lordy, woman, everyone in the city knows. Now, are you OK?'

'Please don't be nice to me.'

'What?'

'Don't hug me or be nice. I've been crying for ever and if you do that I'll start all over again and I just want to try and get through tonight.'

'OK, I'll be mean.'

'Well, not too mean.' I laughed.

'Look, why don't you come and have a beer with us after the show?' he asked. 'And for now, don't let the bastards get you down.'

'Thanks.'

'Look, Kate, if you can't do it tonight, just call me. I'll hide you out in my office until everyone's gone,' he suggested. 'I know it's not a pretty office but it's private.'

'That's threat enough to get me through the evening!' I laughed and then I opened the door for him and headed back out.

As the size of the crowd grew as show time approached, the attention I was getting lessened. But I was manic at work, all of that frustrated energy bursting to come forth. I cleaned out bar fridges, filing cabinets and storage rooms, and I actually felt a little better by the time the night was over. I had no idea how the second half of the play had gone, as I'd been in the storage room the whole time, but everyone was smiling, including Graham, so I thought things must be OK.

After I got the lobby cleared and my staff signed out and on their way home, I made my way backstage to the green room. The actors were gone, but the techies were all lounging on the couches, most with a beer in hand. I poked my head around the corner.

'Anyone welcome at this party?' I asked.

Trevor, Scott and Dwayne were all as different as night and day. Trevor was the technical director and head stage carpenter and in charge. He had worked in the theatre for years, all over the US and Canada. He always liked to act very serious and professional, hence the glasses, which I was never sure he really needed. Despite the serious demeanor he always had a twinkle in his eye, for me at least. And after work, he always seemed to have a beer in his hand, which is why his T-shirts were losing their battle to meet his pants in the middle. Scott was the goofball, but an incredibly handsome one. He was the assistant stage carpenter, trying desperately to figure out how to get a girl to go out on a second date with him. And Dwayne was the lighting technician for the theatre. Dwayne was as skinny as a beanpole, with café au lait skin and a hint of an accent that made him seem very exotic. He was the

119

quietest member of this trio, whether by choice or because he could never get a word in edgewise with the other two, I didn't know. And though he never said much, you knew he didn't miss a thing.

'Kate, we haven't seen you back here for a while,' Scott said. 'Pull up a beer and join us.'

I brushed off a free end of the couch and took a seat.

'I'll skip the beer but I'll take the company,' I said.

'Tough night?' Trevor asked.

'Tough week,' I admitted.

'Is that Graham acting like a butthead again?' Trevor asked.

'Kate, if you would just let us hang him from the catwalk for a couple of hours, I am sure he would be much more compliant with any orders you might give him from now on.'

'Actually, all your staff probably would be.' Dwayne chuckled.

'You are not hanging any member of my staff from anything, do you understand?'

'You sure know how to kill a good idea,' Scott pouted.

'So is it personal problems of a romantic nature?' Trevor asked, playing dumb in front of the guys.

'No, it's the fact that her cousin is in jail for shooting a cop yesterday,' Scott said. 'Good thing you're a carpenter because you're a terrible actor.'

'Yeah, but thanks for trying,' I said. 'And rest assured that if it were romantic problems, I'm pretty sure I wouldn't be discussing it with any of you three.'

'It's the shooting,' Dwayne agreed. 'It's Cam's car in the picture in the newspaper, isn't it?'

'Yes.'

'You were there, weren't you?' Dwayne asked.

'Yes.'

'What?!' both Scott and Trevor said almost simultaneously.

'The woman that got arrested is Cam's cousin, not mine,' I explained. 'She's been staying with us for a little while. We were over there trying to get some stuff from her husband's place when it happened.'

'Wow, I can't believe you didn't tell us this sooner,' Scott said. 'I thought it was just that your cousin got arrested. I had no idea you were there.'

'It just happened yesterday,' I explained.

'I know, but if it had been me I would have come racing in to tell everyone.'

'Well, I've been in shock, I think. I was just relieved Graham didn't manage to get me alone tonight. He would have made me go crazy asking for details and stuff. I think I've talked about it all I can for one day.'

'Is that a hint?' Trevor asked.

'Sort of,' I said. 'I don't want to be rude; I'm just so tired. It feels like when somebody has died. You know how emotionally exhausted you get from talking about it over and over and over again?'

'We get it,' Trevor said. 'Is Cam coming to get you tonight?'

'He wanted me to call him when I was done, but I think I'm just going to call a cab.'

'No, you are not,' Trevor said. 'My assistant butthead will get you home safe and sound tonight.'

'I will?' Scott asked. 'I mean, I will.'

I laughed. 'I really can just call a cab. You guys are having your beers, I don't want to bring your party to a total halt.'

Scott turned his beer bottle upside down to prove it was empty.

'Done and I've only had one so I'm safe to drive.' He smiled at me. 'And I've been with these guys for eight hours already, I think I can last one evening without them.'

'Scott, really, I'll be fine. Have another beer with your friends.'

Scott stood up and held out his hand. I finally decided it would be easier to take it and not argue with him. He helped me up and draped my coat around my shoulders. Then he wrapped his arm around me and pointed us for the door.

'Say goodnight to the boys,' Scott told me, stopping and turning us around to face them.

'Goodnight, boys.' I smiled.

'Goodnight, Kate,' Trevor said, opening another beer for himself.

'Take it easy,' Dwayne added.

Scott got me home safe and sound, dropping me right at the front door. I let myself in, turned to wave to Scott that I was inside and all was well, and then took the elevator. I opened the apartment door quietly, not wanting to disturb Cam if he was asleep already. I found him asleep on the couch or passed out, I thought, as I counted the number of empty beer bottles on the coffee table. He was snoring heavily and, even if I could wake him up, I wasn't sure I could maneuver him up the stairs. So I got a blanket, tucked myself in beside him on the couch and covered us tightly against the spirits of the night.

Thursday November 20

Despite the fact that Cam was the one drinking all night, I was the one that woke up sick. I carefully extricated myself from the blankets and his grasp. This time I took no chances and turned on the faucet in the tub so he wouldn't hear me, although I was pretty sure by the way he was still snoring that he wouldn't hear anything at all. I crawled carefully back under the blanket and tried to sleep, but that snoring in my ear and the beer breath was getting to me, so I gave up. I got up again quietly and put some coffee on to brew. The poor guy was really going to be hurting since it was the decaf Sam had snuck in for me, but there was nothing I could do about that right now.

I tiptoed upstairs and took off what was left of the clothes I came home in and put on some sweat pants and a sweatshirt. I'm sure it was all in my head, but I definitely felt bloated and out of sorts. I just didn't feel like I had a tanktop type of body anymore, sigh.

I heard a crash. Cam must have rolled over and fallen off the couch, taking the coffee table with him.

'Cam,' I called out, racing down the stairs. 'Are you OK?'

I stopped to stifle a giggle when I saw him lying on the floor, covered in beer bottles. I didn't dare laugh out loud until I found out if he was hurt, how bad he was feeling and what kind of mood he was in. I hurried into the living room and picked up the coffee table, piling everything back where it belonged while Cam pulled himself upright.

'You OK, sweetie,' I asked?

'Fine,' he answered gruffly, storming off to the bathroom and letting me finish with the mess.

I managed to get everything put back where it belonged, folded up the blanket and straightened out the cushions on the sofa. I was waiting at the kitchen table with a cup of coffee and the newspaper for him when he came out of the bath-room. He wore his bathrobe, having scraped off yesterday's clothes, and had managed to wash his face and brush his teeth as well. Pleasant for me but it also seemed to have bright-ened him up a bit.

Cam sat across from me and sipped his coffee. I slid the bottle of aspirin across the table toward him and he gave me a rather sour look but opened the bottle and took a couple with his next sip of coffee.

'Thanks,' he said.

'You're welcome.'

'So do you mind telling me how I wound up on the sofa last night?'

'You don't remember?'

'I remember rolling over at one point and you were in bed beside me. I can't figure out how I went from that to the sofa.'

'You were on the sofa when I found you,' I laughed. 'I came home and you were passed out. I tidied up a bit of your mess and tried to get you moving, but you were down for the count. So I grabbed a blanket and joined you down here.'

'That couldn't have been very comfortable.'

'It was comforting. I didn't want to sleep alone, you know? Probably for the same reasons that you drank all that beer.'

'I know,' he sighed, grabbing the coffee pot and filling up both of our cups.

'Any word?' I asked. 'Anything happen while I was at work last night?'

'Nope. Eli said he'd call if anything happened and, until he called, to assume nothing new was going on.'

'Can we go see her, Cam?'

'I don't know. I'll ask Eli today and see if we can arrange something.'

'Do you want something to eat?'

'You planning on making breakfast?' he asked, eyebrows

raised. 'Because I couldn't help but notice that the place looked pretty clean and tidy when I got home.'

'Did it?' I asked innocently.

'And was it my imagination or did I notice there was a bunch of clean laundry upstairs?'

'Maybe.'

'And it was even put away in the dresser?'

'Well, isn't that where it goes?'

'But I did notice that my shirts weren't ironed.'

'Hey, don't go expecting miracles, buddy.'

'And now you're offering to make breakfast?' he asked.

'Cam, do you actually have a point here?'

'You just seem to be turning into a little housewife and I wanted to say I really appreciate the old team spirit thing. But when it comes to cooking, don't you think it's best if we leave it up to me?'

'There are muffins and jam from Sam's baking spree yesterday. I figured I could manage putting those on a plate and digging a knife out of the drawer without poisoning you. If you're really nice, I might even warm up the muffins in the microwave.'

'You know how to work the microwave?' He laughed, some good humour slowly working its way back into his demeanor.

'I've made popcorn for you before,' I reminded him. 'That was in the microwave. Now, before I get all cranky and rescind my offer, do you want a muffin or not?'

'That would be lovely, dear,' he teased. 'Have you got a cigarette?'

I could almost hear the orchestral crescendo that was about to happen right there and then if my life came with a sound-track. Caught. Trapped in my deceit.

'No, sorry, I must have left them at work.'

He got up and went off to rummage through his pile of clothes in the bathroom.

'Found them,' he said, joining me at the table. 'Would you like one?'

I felt myself almost drooling at the thought. Yes, I thought, oh God, yes, please give me a cigarette. I'd smoke two at once right now if I could. Maybe three.

'Cam, promise you won't make a big deal about this?'

'What?' he asked.

Tell him, tell him right now, I thought. Just blurt it out.

'Well, I'm trying to cut down and hopefully quit. But I didn't want to say anything because I don't want anyone making a big deal out of it,' I said, trying to convince myself it wasn't really a lie.

I saw his face light up. Cam wasn't a real smoker like me. He could take it or leave it, and I hated him for it. But I knew he would be really happy to see me quit. I'm sure the next step in his evil plan was to get me out jogging with him every morning. Well, wouldn't he be surprised when he finally found out the rest of the story. And then I felt my eyes well up with tears from those out-of-control hormones.

'I'm going to go have a shower and get ready for work,' I told him, kissing him quickly on the cheek as I raced to the safety of the bathroom, the only room in this whole apartment that actually had a door on it. He was right, we had to do some renovations. Or move.

Oh God, I was going to have to give up my beloved loft, as well as my cigarettes and coffee. I sobbed quietly in the shower while I shaved my legs, and felt quite a bit better after that bit of soul cleansing. I wrapped myself in a towel and joined him back at the table, greedily having a second cup of coffee.

'So how you doing today, Mr Caminski? Did your little binge last night help you blow out some of those emotions?'

'Well, Ms Carpenter, I think I'm starting to get over some of the shock of all of this. I'm just so worried about Carrie, though. I don't know how she's going to survive this.'

'I know.' I sighed, laying my head on his shoulder. 'So, how about if I go to work and get some stuff done and then I'll be free later if we can see her. Unless you want me to stay home with you?'

'I'm fine,' he insisted

'No, seriously, Cam. If you want company, I'm here for you. Graham can manage the theatre for a day or two. The play has been running for a while, there's nothing new or exciting for him to deal with.'

'Honestly, Katie, I really am OK. You can go to work.'

'You're really telling me the truth?' I asked, one last time.

'Except for this splitting headache, yeah, I'm doing OK. I promise. I can call you if I need you, you know. You're only a few minutes away if you have to come home to rescue me.'

I smiled at him. 'OK. I'm going to go get dressed and pretend I believe you're telling me the truth.'

'And I'll do a little tidying up down here. It smells like beer.'

'Uh, yeah, I believe I noticed that, too. And after I spent all day cleaning and working my poor little fingers to the bone.'

'Uh, Katie, I'm not sure that cleaning the apartment once qualifies you for martyrdom yet.'

'Fine.'

'And then after I've restored the place to its former brilliance, I think I'll lie in the bathtub for an hour or maybe even use some of that nice-smelling stuff you always put in there.'

'I highly recommend the lavender if you're feeling stressed,' I told him.

'That sounds pretty girlie,' he said. 'Don't you have anything like Cuban cigar scent?'

'Try the sandalwood, that's as manly as I can manage without a trip to the store,' I called from upstairs. I was skimming through my closet, trying to find a pair of dress pants that was pressed, hemmed and not missing any buttons. I just didn't feel that jeans were appropriate for a visit to the local jail.

'OK, I'll give it a shot,' he called up to me, dishes clinking as he started tidying up.

I found some pants, a blouse and a matching cardigan. Pretty boring and conservative, but I was sure it would make me look like an upstanding citizen. After all, I'm pretty sure they will be judging Carrie by the company she kept. It was probably time to start cleaning up my act a bit anyway. This impending parenthood made everything else seem so important. How I dressed and presented myself could effect how the baby's school teachers felt about her and treated her, or maybe even effect what schools she got into. And every time I start to think this way, I get overwhelmed by the rush of feelings that came along with it. How was I ever going to get this under control enough to tell Cam?

126

I did manage to get myself under control enough to finish getting dressed and back downstairs without getting all teary-eyed again.

'Do you want a ride?' Cam asked from the balcony. He was out sweeping off the deck in anticipation of another beautiful fall day.

'No, I could use the walk,' I said. 'Besides, you don't exactly look dressed to drive me to work.'

'Didn't your mom ever drive you to school in her pajamas?'

'Cam, you've met my mother. Can you actually picture her ever doing anything even remotely like that?'

'Good point. I can slip on a pair of jeans in about two seconds and drive you in.'

'I'm fine. I'll grab a newspaper and a coffee and pretend it's a normal day.'

I found my backpack and jacket in the living room where I had dumped them the night before and got myself ready to go. Cam grabbed me in his arms before I could turn for the door.

'I love you, Katie, and I'm very proud that you're trying to quit smoking. And I promise that's the last I'll say about it.'

'I love you, too.' I gave him a big kiss and then pulled away and headed out of the door, as I felt my tear ducts begin to betray me again.

I discovered it was a lovely, crisp fall day outside, as I pushed through the doors of my building. I stood outside for a moment to let my eyes adjust to the sunlight. There was no predicting how long this weather would last, but I was sure enjoying it while it was here. Eventually winter would hit and it would seem interminable, as it did every year. It was when I pulled my sunglasses out of my backpack that I noticed him, across the street, on the bench with a newspaper. The man from the day of the shooting. The man who said his kids went to the same school as Carrie's kids. What was he doing sitting across the street from my building, watching my front door? I wondered if I should run across the street and talk to him, but then he noticed me looking at him and got up and hurried away. I must remember to tell Cam about seeing him again.

I tried to keep up a brisk pace, feeling my muscles screaming; I didn't do as much walking now that there was Cam and the car in my life. I walked past Grounds Zero and smelled the lovely aroma of the roasting beans, resisting the siren song they sang to me. Gus was going to be really suspicious that I hadn't been in for a while but I was ready with the whole story of Carrie to throw him off the track. No one was going to question that this week's events would be affecting my normal routine.

I got to the front of the theatre and was surprised to see Detective Lincoln sitting on the steps.

'Ken?' I asked. 'Did something happen to Carrie?'

'No, I—'

'Oh, my God, Cam?'

'Kate, he's fine.'

'Did I miss an appointment with you, then? I thought you were going to call if you needed us for anything.'

'Kate, it's none of that. Relax. This is one of those purely personal visits. I was downtown interviewing someone on another case, and I just thought I'd drop by and see how you were doing.'

I sat down on the step beside him, dropping my backpack on the ground and wishing I had a cigarette. It was when I wasn't busy that I missed them the most.

'I'm OK.'

'I've been thinking about you a lot. Well, truth be told, I've been worrying about you.'

'Me? God, why?'

'Well, this has been a pretty traumatic week for you,' he started.

If you only knew, I thought, but let him finish.

'You know, there are lots of counselors I can refer you to, ones that work with this type of post-traumatic stress. You may not even feel it yet, you might think you're doing just fine,' he explained. 'But when you're least expecting it, that's when it hits you.'

'I think I'm mostly worried about Carrie,' I told him.

'I figured you might be so I checked up on her, too.'

'And?'

'Well, I'm not going to tell you she's fine,' he said. 'Would

128

you be? But she's doing OK. She's not saying much, but we've got a counselor talking to her. She's as comfortable as she possibly could be in the Remand Centre.'

'Thanks, Ken, I appreciate that. Are we going to be able to see her?'

'I think her lawyer is working on that. I'm sure he'll let you know as soon as he has things arranged. This stuff never works quite as fast as it does on TV, you know.'

I laughed. 'I'm sure you're right about that.'

'So, where's Cam?' Ken asked.

'At home, recovering. He got a little intoxicated last night and has a bit of a headache today.'

'And he's doing OK, too?'

'I think he's doing better than he was. I wouldn't say he is his normal self right now.'

'OK, well, I was pretty sure you would both say you were just fine, but I brought this card along anyway. This is one of the counsclors we refer victims to and she's really great. As a matter of fact, my wife and I have seen her a couple of times. I want you to promise to keep the card and call her if things start going sour, OK?'

'OK,' I agreed, surprising him with my ready acceptance.

'I did call her and tell her what happened, so she'll know who you are if you call.'

'I appreciate that, Ken,' I said, taking the card and slipping it into my wallet.

'Just remember, you're not alone in this,' he said, standing up and offering a hand for me. I accepted and pulled myself up.

'That seems to be the theme of my week,' I said, praying I wouldn't get all weepy in front of him, too. 'And we appreciate it.'

'Good.'

'Ken, I've been noticing something strange in the last week or so.'

'What's that?'

'I think someone is following me.'

'Following you?'

'Well, yeah, I kept seeing this guy and I thought maybe I just recognized him from the theatre or something, but then he turned up on the day of the shooting. And this morning he was across the street from my apartment, watching the entrance.'

'You know, Kate, sometimes things are just coincidental.'

'I know. But I just have a feeling this isn't.'

'You and your feelings.' He laughed. 'OK, what can you tell me about this guy?'

'Well, his kids go to the same school as Carrie's kids.'

'Uh-huh.'

'Well, that's all I know.'

'That's not much to go on.'

'I know. I'm probably being overly suspicious, right?'

'People have a tendency to get that way at times like this.'

'And you can't check him out because there's no way to identify him, right?'

'I'm glad you said it for a change.'

'OK. Well, I guess I just had to tell someone.'

'Kate, I'll call you if anything new comes up,' he promised.

'Thanks,' I called after him as he made his way down the street.

I walked into the Plex and let myself into the theatre. I stopped on the other side of the door and listened carefully. Nothing. Absolute silence. For one of the rare moments in my life, I was absolutely alone in the theatre. I climbed the stairs and dumped my stuff in my office. I wandered into the theatre, intending to do a bit of a walk-through inspection, even though it was really early, but, instead, I sat down in orchestra centre. I let the darkness and silence envelope me and finally relaxed, feeling some of the stress draining out of me. I leaned my head back and watched the slowly swaying lights above me, moving in tempo to some unknown and unfelt breeze.

'Kate?'

I jumped out of the chair, shocked out of my reverie by the harsh tones of someone looking for me.

'Kate, you in here?' It was Graham. And then the lights came on, blinding me for a minute.

'Kate, what are you doing in here?' Graham asked.

'Relaxing,' I said, blinking my eyes and trying to adapt to

the sudden change in my environment. 'What are you doing here so early?'

'Early?' he asked. 'Kate, it's four o'clock. This is always when I get here.'

'Four in the afternoon?' I asked, shocked.

'Yes. What time did you think it was?'

'I got here about noon, I think,' I told him, getting up and trying to straighten the creases that had developed in my pants. 'I can't have slept here for four hours.'

'Welcome to the wonderful world of pregnancy.'

'Shh!' I scolded him. 'You promised you wouldn't use that word.'

'You can chastise me later. Right now I just came to tell you that Cam's on the phone.'

'And it took you this long?' I asked, running past him and to the office. 'Damn, I don't want him to get suspicious.'

I sat behind my desk and took the phone off hold.

'Cam?' I asked. 'Everything OK?'

'Everything's fine,' he assured me. 'I just wanted to let you know that I talked to Eli and we can't get in to see Carrie until tomorrow morning, if that works out for you.'

'I'll make it work,' I promised him.

'How's your afternoon going?' he asked.

'Fine,' I lied. 'I'm getting lots accomplished.'

'Do you want me to come and get you tonight?'

'No, I'll just catch a ride home with Scott. Unless you need to get out for a while?'

'No, I think another night at home might be good for me. I promise if I feel the urge to drink that much beer again that I'll do it in bed so you don't have to try and get me up those stairs.'

I laughed at him. 'That would be very considerate of you. So, I should be home around eleven thirty or so. Call me before then if you need me to pick anything up, OK?'

'OK. Love you.'

'I love you too, Cam.' I smiled at him, even though I knew he couldn't see over the phone. But I couldn't help myself.

The evening went like clockwork, boring and predictable, which was my favourite kind of evening. Usually, near the end of the run of a play, this is how it got. It was nice because it gave us all some time to hang out together, which never

131

seemed to happen at the beginning of a run, with all the receptions and stress and running around we had to do. I did have a greatly diverse group of ushers working for me, but they seemed to genuinely like each and like their jobs and we usually had a good time together.

About an hour before call time, I decided I'd better check with Scott and see if he could drive me home tonight. I wouldn't want to take the chance that he might actually have a date or some life of his own and be stuck here. So I wandered down to the green room and had a coffee with the techies and a couple of actors who were in early. The guy who was playing Elvis's ghost brought in a couple of dozen donuts and I undid my belt another notch and dove in with the best of them. I was really happy he wasn't imitating the early skinny Elvis.

Once my ride was secured and the donuts gone, I headed back up to my office and we got the audience in and out, managing to keep them all happy for the time in between. I met Scott at the green room and we snuck down some secret back stairs that took us right to his parking spot in the underground parkade. He held the door open for me, which I thought was a little strange for him, and then went around to the other side of the car and let himself in. He put the keys in the ignition but didn't turn the car on. Slowly, he turned to me.

'Pregnant?'

'What?' I asked, my heart racing at that word.

'You're pregnant?'

'I don't know what you're talking about.'

'I was in the sound booth when Graham came into the house and woke you up and said you were pregnant.'

I didn't know what to say to that, so I waited.

'And Graham knows about it? How the hell does Graham know about it and I don't?'

'Cam doesn't even know yet,' I whispered. And then I started crying. Damn.

Scott quickly pulled several Kleenex out of the box that was sitting on the back seat and shoved them at me.

'Don't cry,' he said, looking really uncomfortable. 'I didn't mean to upset you.'

'No, it's not that,' I sobbed. 'I just cry at everything right now. It seems to be a hazard of the condition.'

132

'Oh. I wouldn't know.'

'This is terrible.'

'What, that you're pregnant?' he asked. 'Well, I'll admit it's a bit of a shock. I personally thought that you two would wait for a couple of years but—'

'No, not that,' I paused to blow my nose. 'It's just that Cam doesn't even know yet but both you and Graham do.'

'What?'

'I haven't figured out how to tell him,' I sobbed.

'And yet that junior butthead knows?' Scott asked. 'Are you crazy?'

I sobbed harder at that one. 'I think I may be.'

'Oh, geez, Kate, I wish I'd known that earlier,' Scott apologized.

'Why?' I asked.

'Because I already told Trevor and Dwayne.'

'Oh, God!'

'I'll call them,' he promised, trying to prevent me from going off the deep end again. 'As soon as I get home I'll call them both and tell them not to say anything.'

'You know how word travels around this building.'

'I promise, we'll keep it quiet until you are ready to tell.'

'You'll never be able to do that.'

'We will,' he promised. 'We'll kill anyone who even says anything about it. That'll stop them from talking.'

This time I laughed.

'And we'll start with the junior butthead.'

'You are such a goof.' I smiled as I pulled down the sun visor and checked my reflection in the little mirror. I dabbed at my smeared makeup, trying to make it look like I'd just had a hard day at the office rather than I'd been crying my eyes out.

'You OK?' he asked.

'I'd better be, I don't think you'd know what to do about it if I wasn't.'

'You're right,' he said. 'Crying women make me really uncomfortable.'

'It shows. When I'm a little more steady on my feet I can teach you some of those compassionate moves that the chicks really like.'

'Wow, maybe I can get me a second date with somebody then.'

'Scott, I'm good, but I don't know if even I am that good.'

'Ready to go home?'

'Very ready,' I admitted. I gave up on the mirror and just put on some fresh lipstick.

'You look fine.'

'Like five miles of bad road,' I argued.

'Naw, it's fine.'

'Cam will be able to tell,' I insisted.

'It's late, it's dark.'

'Is it that bad?'

'If you're lucky he'll be asleep.'

'Thanks a lot, Scott. Way to make me feel better.'

'No, really you look OK. I think that whole thing about pregnant women glowing may be true.'

'You want me to start crying again?' I threatened.

'OK, I'm driving, I'm driving.'

Friday November 21

I woke up in bed, with Cam beside me and no mountain of empty beer bottles in sight. The alarm was ringing and Cam's arm snaked out from under the covers to push the snooze button. Nine minutes later, when it rang for the second time, he had it turned off and was up and in his running clothes, kissing me on the cheek almost before my eyes were open. As the aroma of a fresh pot of coffee reached the loft, my stomach started twitching again. I threw back the covers and got out of bed, deciding I had to quit fighting this morning sickness thing and just get used to it. Morning sickness would probably last the first trimester and I had another two months to go. But the doctor had assured me it was a good sign that it was a strong and healthy pregnancy. I believed him but it didn't make me feel any better as I kneeled in front of the toilet.

I brushed my teeth and then went into the kitchen and poured myself some coffee. I took a sip and waited. It seemed to be settling OK. I risked another sip, a bit bigger and bolder, and that did it. Once back in the bathroom, after throwing up, I decided to have a shower. I came out with the towel wrapped around me to find Cam sitting at the table with the newspaper and a cup of coffee.

'Did you have a good run?' I asked, trying to sound cheerful.

'Katie, are you all right?' Cam asked.

'I'm fine,' I said, worried about the turn the conversation was taking. Time to take control and change the subject. 'Why don't you call Eli and see if we can confirm while I run upstairs and get dressed.'

'There's lots of time.' He reached out for my hand and I let him take it. 'Have a seat and have a coffee with me.'

He pulled me around the table and I sat down in a chair beside him. He got up and poured a coffee for me and pulled a muffin out of the microwave and put a huge pat of butter on it, setting it all down right in front of me. He gave my knee a little pat and then turned back to his sports section, acting very nonchalant.

'You're shaking,' he noticed, without turning and looking at me.

'I'm just a little chilly, I guess.' I smiled, moving the muffin around on the plate.

'Eat up, sweetie, and then we can get going.'

'I'm not really hungry,' I said decisively, pushing the muffin across the table from me.

'I really think you should eat something. I mean, who knows how long we're going to be?' He smiled as he pulled the plate back in front of me.

I took the littlest piece of muffin I could manage and shoved it in my mouth, trying to swallow it whole before the taste or aroma sent my stomach rolling again.

'Your coffee is getting cold,' he said, flipping the page of the newspaper and moving the coffee cup closer to me.

That was it, the final straw. I ran to the bathroom, closing and locking the door behind me. When I came out, face washed and teeth brushed yet again, Cam stood in the hallway, waiting for me with a look on his face that almost broke my heart.

135

'What's the matter?' I asked him.

'That's what I should be asking you. Katie, you've been throwing up for two weeks. You went to the doctor and you tell me he says everything is normal, yet you still keep throwing up. There's no such thing as a two-week virus.'

I felt myself break out in a cold sweat and begin to sway. I turned back into the bathroom and ran the facecloth under cool water and held it to the back of my neck until I felt the desire to faint pass. Here we go.

'Cam, why don't you sit down,' I said, trying to lead him back to the table. 'I'll pour you a coffee.'

'I'm not going anywhere. I'm going to stand right here until you finally tell me the truth. Are you sick?' he asked. 'I don't care how bad it is, tell me the truth.'

'I'm not sick,' I said, running the water over the cloth again, then turning off the tap and sitting on the counter. Cam came in and stood right in front of me, his hands either side of me on the counter. His face was way too close for me to lie to him.

'I said I wanted the truth. Katie. No matter how bad it is, I'll be there for you,' he assured me. 'Whatever it is, we can get through it together. You've got to know that.'

I took a deep breath and then let the words spill out before I could change my mind.

'Cam, I'm so sorry. I'm so sorry I haven't told you and I'm so sorry it even happened. And I'm so very, very sorry I've been lying to you; well, not really lying but avoiding telling you about it because I was just never sure how you would react and then the time never seemed right and then this whole thing with Carrie came up and—'

'Katie,' he yelled, stopping my rambling.

'I'm pregnant.' I told him. It was now out there for all to see.

'What?'

'I'm sorry. Oh, God, I'm really so sorry. I mean I didn't plan this and it was an accident and I don't know how it happened because I've been so careful and the doctor says I'm just one of those .01 per cent of cases where the pill didn't work,' I told him, knowing I was rambling again but not being able to stop myself.

'You're pregnant?' he said, his voice cracking.

'Cam, I know you really wanted a baby but we didn't plan this. I don't know how you must feel about it. All I can do is keep telling you how very sorry I am to have let this happen.'

'How do you feel about it?' he asked, taking the cloth from me and holding it against the back of his neck.

'I don't know,' I said, being honest with him for the first time in weeks. 'I'm totally confused. One minute I think it's the greatest thing that has ever happened to me, the next minute, I'm in an utter panic.'

He came close to me and wrapped his arms around me, hugging me more tightly than I had ever been hugged before.

'I think that's what it's supposed to feel like,' he said. 'I don't think anyone is ever ready to become a parent.'

'We need to talk about this,' I said, when he finally pulled away.

'I know we do. And I'm not going to pressure you into keeping it,' he told me. 'God, no wonder you've been freaked out. Have you been thinking about my ex-wife and the abortion?'

'Yes,' I admitted.

'Honey, that was her. This is us. They are two totally different things. You and I are going to be together no matter what. And we're going to make our decisions together. We're already a family and that's the difference between you and her.'

My eyes welled up with tears.

'A baby would be a nice bonus,' he continued. 'But it is a big surprise and we need to make a decision we can both live with.'

'Cam, I want you to know, right now, that I've already decided there's no way I can give up this baby. That I know for sure. I mean, it's the only thing I know for sure. I think I've already bonded or something, it's so strange. But there are so many other things we have to try and figure out; like when I'm going to have my nervous breakdown.'

'I love you, Katie,' he said, pulling me tightly to him again.

'I love you too,' I told him, hugging him back this time. 'But this isn't how I was supposed to tell you. I had this all

137

planned out for some time next week when Carrie was moved into her new apartment and this whole shooting settled. A little candlelight dinner, a nice bottle of wine, you know? Now we're going to have to tell everyone that you found out about our first baby in the bathroom. I mean, what kind of a story is that going to be?'

'Our *first* baby?' he asked.

'Look, I'm pregnant; you can't hold me to anything I say for the next eight months. My brain is under the influence of some very powerful hormones right now.'

'Well, everything important in our lives seems to happen in very strange places and in very strange ways,' he admitted. 'Why should this be any different?'

'I suppose,' I agreed. 'So, are we going to the police station to see Carrie?'

'We have to,' he said. 'I told her we'd be there to see her today.'

'We better finish getting ready,' I said, checking his watch. 'We're wasting the day away here.'

'You're right but I don't want to leave. I want to stay here and hold you,' he said. 'Hey, can you feel anything yet?'

His hand went to my tummy.

'Nothing except for the dozen donuts I ate last night.'

He leaned over and kissed me, laughing at me. 'I hope you can be half as happy about this as I am.'

'I promise I will be as soon as I stop throwing up,' I laughed.

'OK, give me two minutes in this bathroom and I'll be ready,' he said.

'Why don't you take three and I'll clean up the kitchen?' I offered.

'OK, three minutes. And then I'll bring the car around and pick you up out front,' he said. 'If that's OK with you?'

'Cam, if I have to spend the next nine months telling you I'm OK, I'm going to go crazy.'

'All right, then, you clean up the kitchen and I'll meet you out front,' he told me, pretending to be all forceful and in charge.

'That's better.' I smiled and gave him a quick kiss. 'Anything else?'

138

'Lots,' he said. 'We just don't have time right now.'

'By the way,' I called from the kitchen.

'Uh huh?'

'We can't tell anyone yet, you know. Not until we're past the three-month mark.'

'Really?' He sounded disappointed. 'How much longer is that?'

'Probably another eight weeks or so.'

'Really? I can't talk to anyone about it for that long?'

'Well, a couple of people accidentally know. There's Sam, which probably means Ryan knows, too. And Graham sort of found out. And then I think Scott told Trevor and Dwayne—'

'Everyone at the Plex knows?' he asked, now sounding really disappointed. 'I mean, I can understand you telling Sam, but Graham? Or the technicians?'

'Yeah, well, it's a really long story.'

'Were you ever going to tell me about it?' he asked. 'Or just everyone else and then hope someone let it slip?'

'I was only going to tell you if I had to.'

'So are you going to tell me how everyone knows?'

'Only if I have to.'

'I think it's only fair, don't you?' he asked. 'Me being the father and all?"

'I'll tell you all about it tonight,' I promised him but then I saw an argument starting in his eyes. 'I promise I will tonight. Just not here and now. Please, Cam?'

'Fine. Well, I'm glad that Ryan knows. I think I'll get a lot more out of talking to Ryan than to Graham,' Cam said. 'So, really, when were you planning on telling me?'

'Oh, I only had a few hundred other people to tell first,' I teased. 'You were definitely moving up the list.'

I tidied up and finished dressing and met Cam out front of the building. He reached over and took my hand and held it almost the entire way to the police station. He kept smiling at me every time we were stopped at a red light; a silly, stupid incredibly happy smile that was making my stomach dance all over again but for a totally different reason. What have I done? I wondered. He found a parking spot about a block away and parked the car. He started to ask me if I could walk or if he should drop me off in front of the building and then park. Cam was always incredibly polite and thoughtful, but this was getting to be a little much, even for him. I shot him a dirty look and he just parked the car. He did race around to my side to help me out, though. I let him have that one without an argument and took his hand as we walked down the sunny street toward the station. We were in for quite a shock when we saw Carrie and Eli sitting on a bench in front of the building, smiling in our direction.

'Carrie?' I shouted down the street, shaking Cam's hand free and running toward her. I wrapped her in a big hug and, even though I felt her in my arms, I still couldn't believe she was out here on the street.

'So, I guess you've been busy since I talked to you yesterday,' Cam said to Eli.

'A little. I didn't really do anything, I just took advantage of an opportunity that presented itself.' He sounded self-effacing but he looked proud.

'So are we off the hook here?' I asked anyone who would answer.

'Well, we've had some lucky breaks,' Eli explained. 'Firstly, there was no one in the room but Carrie when the gun was fired, so no witnesses. Secondly, there was no gunpowder residue anywhere on Carrie. All the tests are negative. And there is no way she could have fired that gun and not have had some residue somewhere. For bonus points, Officer Strachan's status was changed last night from critical to serious but stable. So he's not out of the woods but things are definitely looking up on that front. And then I filed the right papers with the right clerk, who got it in front of the right judge, who decided that we couldn't really hold Carrie with the evidence or lack thereof that we currently had.'

I couldn't help myself; I let go of Carrie and hugged Eli almost as hard as I had hugged her.

'You are the greatest,' I told him, feeling tears in my eyes again. I blinked them away quickly before pulling away from him.

'It has really helped that Carrie hasn't confessed or said anything to the police yet.' Eli smiled reassuringly at her.

'This is wrong,' Carrie said softly. 'I shouldn't be out here.'

'It's OK,' Cam said, reaching out and putting a hand on her shoulder. 'They'll find out what happened and this will all be over soon.'

'I know,' she whispered. 'I know they'll find out.'

'Look,' Eli said. 'Why don't you take her home? I'm sure a hot bath and a square meal will have her feeling a little better. And probably some sleep. It's hard for most people to sleep in this place.'

'We'll do that,' I told him.

'And I've got a business card from the counselor she's been seeing. Dr Thomas, I think,' he said, fumbling in his pocket trying to find the card. 'She wanted you to give her a call if Carrie needs any help with anything.'

'Will do,' Cam promised, taking the card and putting it in his wallet. I'm sure he was worried it would end up in my black hole of Calcutta backpack, never to be seen again if I were to take it. 'Anything else we need to do?'

'I'll be in touch. I'm sure they're not finished with us yet, but for now I suggest you just go home and keep your heads low. OK?'

Cam shook Eli's hand. 'Thanks for everything.'

'No problem. You'll get my bill in the mail,' Eli joked, picking up his briefcase and heading off down the street.

Cam and I each took one of Carrie's arms and led her back to the car. I put her in the front seat, settled myself in the back and we headed back to the apartment.

Eli was right; Carrie had a huge meal, a hot bath and then settled herself on a chaise lounge on the balcony in the late afternoon sun, wrapped in a warm wooly blanket.

'Go talk to her,' Cam whispered to me while he washed the dishes.

'You know the dishwasher is working now. We don't have to do these by hand,' I protested.

'I am aware of that, but this will keep me busy and give you an excuse to be out there. Now go talk to her.'

'You go talk to her. You know her better than I do.'

'You're a girl,' he informed me.

'So?'

'You're supposed to be good at girl talk. Women let their guard down and tell each other things, right?'

'How the hell should I know? Sam's the first female friend I think I've ever had.'

'Well, then, it's time you learned,' he told me. 'Besides, you're going to have to small talk with all the other mothers at nursery school. Maybe it's time you learned how to do it.'

I tossed the dishtowel on to the counter. This was the same argument I'd been having with myself.

'Fine,' I warned him. 'But if you intend to use the pregnancy to win every argument for the next nine months, you are going to be sleeping on the couch a lot!'

Of course, being mad only works when you don't break out in giggles afterward. But he had that look on his face again, that silly, bug-catching grin he had been wearing since I had told him this morning, and I just couldn't help myself.

I tiptoed out on to the balcony. I couldn't tell if Carrie was awake or asleep and I didn't want to disturb her if she had fallen asleep. I sat down quietly on a chair beside her and watched the sky for a few minutes.

'It's OK,' she finally said. 'I'm awake.'

'Did I wake you?' I asked.

'No, I've just been daydreaming. Enjoying the sight of the wide open sky while I can.'

'What do you mean while you can?' I asked.

'You can't see the sky very well from the windows at the jail.'

'Carrie, you're not going back,' I assured her. 'They'll investigate and find out what happened and you'll be exonerated.'

'Nope, it's not going to happen that way,' she insisted. 'I'm going back to jail.'

'But you didn't do it, did you?' I asked.

'No, I didn't.'

'Did you see who did it?' I asked. 'If you did, you have to tell the police, Carrie, or at least Eli. This is your life we're talking about here.'

'Did you know there's a bluebird nesting over on the eaves above that balcony?' she asked, pointing at the building across the street.

'Carrie, you can tell me what happened,' I tried. 'Maybe I can help you decide what to do.'

'I can't tell anyone what happened.' Then she seemed to

shake off her fugue. She pulled her chair into a more upright position and turned to face me. 'Forgive me. I'm just really tired. I don't even remember what happened. It's just all a blur in my mind from the minute Hank started threatening me.'

'Tell me about it. Maybe something will come back to you.'

'I went into the house and Hank started yelling at me. I went into the kitchen, trying to get away from him, but he wouldn't leave me alone. And then the doorbell rang and it was that police officer. Hank went and let him in and he was yelling at him, too. I just wanted all the yelling to stop,' she said, her voice almost a whisper now. 'I was standing at the kitchen counter, packing up some of the kids' lunch stuff and wondering if my life was ever going to be any different. If I was ever going to get away from Hank and start over.'

'So you decided that if he wasn't around, you could get on with your life?'

'No, I was only going to do something if he threatened me. I swear it.'

'So what happened.'

'I don't know. I was packing and crying and then I heard this noise and the next thing I remember is I was sitting in a police car.'

I relaxed a little, seeing her acting a little more normal, as she began to talk. I stretched out on the lounge I was sitting on and sipped the coffee I had brought out with me. I should remember to let Cam know I was slipping him decaf. He might start going into withdrawal soon and I'm pretty sure I would be the one to suffer the consequences.

'You really don't remember anything else?' I asked her.

Carrie turned back toward the sky, watching a bird fly past.

'Not a thing,' she said. 'I just wanted the yelling to stop. It was so loud. It's very peaceful here. And I just wanted it to be like that. Peaceful.'

Part of me really wanted to believe her. But I didn't. And I didn't know why. But I was just about to start digging deeper when Cam opened the balcony door.

'Graham's on the phone, Katie. He wants to know if you're coming in to work tonight or not?'

I looked at my watch, surprised to see how late it was. I

looked over to Carrie and thought about staying home but the mood seemed to be gone. She was turned back to the sky, her chair back in the fully reclined position, not paying any attention to either Cam or I. I turned back to Cam.

'Tell him I'll be there in half an hour.'

I reluctantly gathered my mug and looked over at Carrie, hoping she might ask me not to go but to stay with her instead. But she was lost to me and the rest of the world right now.

'I'm going to find out what your secret is,' I promised her silently. 'You're not going to jail for something that you didn't do.'

And then I ran upstairs to get ready for work.

That night at the theatre turned out to be punishment for all my missed days and inattention of the past week. Everything that could possibly go wrong did. Bartenders mis-poured drinks, T-shirts went missing, we ran out of programs, tickets were double sold, patrons were complaining about the heat or the cold or both, and I was generally run off my feet trying to please everyone.

By the time intermission was over, I felt like hiding in the locker room until the theatre was empty, but I resisted. Instead, I stretched out on the couch in the private lounge with my shoes kicked off, when Graham walked by me and made some sort of a comment about being pregnant. He didn't see the three other ushers standing behind him, nor the way their eyebrows raised and jaws dropped in shock at that announcement. I did. I heaved a huge sigh, sat up, put my shoes back on and dragged them all up to my office.

'All right, everyone. Forget the fact that Graham has a mouth he doesn't know how to control and let my big secret out. I need to ask you all a big favour.'

'You *are* pregnant?' Martha asked.

'Really?' Charlotte asked.

'Really,' I admitted. 'But it's early and we aren't supposed to tell anyone yet.' I shot another dirty look over at Graham

'I'm sorry,' he apologized again.

'I know, I know,' I sighed. 'So how about it, guys, can we keep this between us? Not even husbands or wives or sisters or friends? No whispers between each other where someone else might overhear? Please?'

144

Martha and Charlotte glanced at each other; Graham and Leonard just studied the floor.

'I understand totally,' Charlotte said. 'My mother-in-law found out with my first baby before I had a chance to tell anyone and she sure took the wind out of my sails. I'll keep your secret.'

'Me, too,' Martha said. 'Absolutely.'

'And I'll be happy never to have to discuss the female reproductive system in this room again,' Leonard said.

'I second that,' Graham said. 'As a matter of fact, I'm just never going to talk to anyone again.'

'Thank you all,' I said, not really believing the secret would be kept.

They all left my office except Graham.

'So I know you're having a bad night,' he started. 'Do you want more bad news or should I wait until tomorrow?'

'How bad?'

'Mild to moderate.'

'OK, pile it on me.'

'Susan called and left a voice mail. She is quitting.'

'Oh, that's not so bad. We can handle being one usher short right now.'

'And so is Mahmoud.'

'Both in one night? What's going on?'

'Well, I'm not sure if you'll see the irony in this, but they've been dating for a while and it turns out Susan's pregnant.'

'Graham.'

'I swear to God it's true. Anyway, they are going to elope to Vegas. They leave tomorrow. And then they're moving to Vancouver Island and moving in with her parents until the baby is born and he gets his degree.'

'You're enjoying the humour in this, aren't you?' I asked.

'Well, I would have been enjoying it a little more if I hadn't slipped and given away the pregnancy thing again,' he apologized. 'Have I told you how sorry I am? I was just trying to be a smart ass and—'

'Graham, go count ticket stubs or something. I can't handle you apologizing any more.'

'OK,' he said. 'I'll stop. As long as you know it really was a stupid accident.'

'Graham!' I warned.

'I'm gone,' he said, racing off down the hallway.

I finally got the theatre cleared, made my way home and found everyone already in bed, sound asleep. Thankful for that, I crawled into bed for a peaceful night's sleep, knowing Carrie was home safe and sound and that I wasn't hiding anything from Cam for a change.

Saturday November 22

If I had slept so well and all was at peace last night, why was I sitting at the breakfast table feeling like I hadn't slept in a week? And I didn't dare say anything because I was already sick of everyone blaming every problem I had on my pregnancy. I was not in the mood for either a lecture about taking care of myself or that stupid smile of Cam's again. As a matter of fact, I was feeling a little mentally queasy about the whole thing and really wanted to avoid the topic for at least a day or two. I wondered if there was a support group for people like me, something like 'Unplanned Pregnancy and How to Get Used to It.' But for now I was trapped behind my kitchen table with Carrie on one side and Cam on the other. I smiled at them, hoping they wouldn't figure out it was a fake one.

And Cam, he was a whole other story. I came down for breakfast this morning to find a big glass of milk, a multi-vitamin, a coffee, a slice of whole-wheat toast, half a cantaloupe with cottage cheese inside and a cherry on top. And I had lost track of how many times he had winked at me behind Carrie's back. Thank God it was pay day at the theatre. I had to go in early for payroll and no one could argue with me, as payroll was the one thing Graham couldn't do.

So I wolfed down my ever-so-healthy breakfast and was surprised that my stomach seemed to stay settled after all that food. Then I found some clean jeans that still fit and a sweat-shirt and headed for the C-train before anyone could stop me. Once on the train, I started to enjoy the fact that I was alone and no one was circling over me, being overly solicitous. I got off a block early and wandered slowly to the theatre, enjoying the fresh air and sunshine. I passed Grounds Zero and waved inside to Gus, as I continued down the street toward my theatre.

'Kate!'

I turned to find Gus hurrying down the street after me, a take-out cup in his hand.

'Hey, Gus.' I smiled at him, the thought of having to throw out that beautiful mochaccino breaking my heart.

'Kate, I haven't seen you around for a couple of days,' Gus said. 'So I wanted to make this for you. I think you'll find it surprisingly satisfying.'

'Thanks, Gus,' I said, taking it and starting to turn away. 'I'll catch you later.'

'Kate, try it, just for me.'

'I will as soon as I get to my office,' I promised him.

'Kate, it's decaf. I brought in the decaf espresso just for you. Sorry it took so long for me to get it in but it's not exactly like you kept me in the loop on this one!'

'What do you mean?' I asked.

'About the baby,' he whispered.

'Gus, you know?' I asked.

'I don't know nothing,' he said with a smile, his eyes twin-kling at me. 'I just think you drink too much caffeine so I've got a decaf espresso for you and from now on everything you order will be made with that. That's all I know.'

'Thanks, Gus,' I said, raising my cup to him and then taking a giant-sized sip, gulping it down greedily.

'You're welcome.'

'Oh, my God, I have missed this so very, very much,' I said, tears filling my eyes again.

'Now don't go getting all weepy on me. Just go to your office and enjoy your mochaccino.' And he turned and hurried back into his shop.

I took my mochaccino and my weepy little self up to my office and got started on my paperwork.

Payroll actually balanced on the first try, for the first time ever since I'd been doing it, which is why Graham found me sitting at my window, staring up at the sky when he came in.

'What are you doing, boss?'

'Staring,' I admitted. 'Carrie was staring at the sky for hours today and I was trying to figure out what she was seeing up there.'

'Carrie's at your place? What, did you guys stage a jail break or something?'

'Oh, did I forget to tell you that part?' I laughed. 'Eli had her sprung yesterday morning. Something about lack of evidence so they had to drop the charges. There was apparently no gunpowder residue anywhere on her so I guess that means she couldn't have fired the gun.'

'Right on. So have they charged anyone else?' he asked.

'I don't think so. And she says she doesn't remember anything at all. But you know I think Carrie knows exactly what happened. What I don't know is why she won't tell us.'

'Well, don't they call it post-traumatic stress syndrome or something like that? Maybe she really can't remember. I thought it was common.'

'I guess. And I would probably believe her more if she had been looking me directly in the eye when she said it, rather than staring up into the sky. Plus, she kept going on and on about how she was going back to jail and would never see the sky again.'

'It sounds like you'd better get her to a psychiatrist.'

'She's been seeing someone,' I told him. 'I don't know, it's probably just me, but this just doesn't feel right. And after being dropped off a forty-foot fly tower and shot at, I seem to be getting a good instinct for this kind of thing.'

'So are we checking this thing out?' he asked.

'Well, not so much checking things out,' I said, knowing that would be the final straw for Cam. 'More like just seeing if we can make things add up a little better than they do now.'

'Oh, I see the difference. One way Cam has you locked up because he's afraid something horrible is going to happen to you again and the other way you feel safe and vindicated?' he laughed at me.

'Vindicated?'

'Mandi has been teaching me big words. Don't try and change the subject on me.'

'Yeah, well, don't get so smart. You may have been right about a lot of things recently, but you're still replaceable!'

'So what are we going to do?' he asked.

'I'm going to draw a picture,' I said. 'Can you sneak into the set designer's office and grab some of the graph paper?'

'You're going to draw a picture? Is this one of those pregnancy-related hormonal things? Suddenly you're going to get artistic?'

'No,' I said, tossing a wadded-up napkin at him. 'I want to draw a picture of the house. Where it happened. I need to be able to visualize where everyone was and what happened at the moment of the shooting.'

'OK, now you're talking,' he said, his eyes lighting up with excitement. 'But I have a computer program at home that does set designs for theatres. If you want me to, I can go and get it and we can do it on the computer.'

'That would be cool,' I agreed. 'Do you want to go now? I think I can manage things here if you hurry back. I believe I have run a show once or twice without you.'

'Yeah, but it's been so long, I wasn't sure if you actually remembered how.'

'Goodbye, Graham. Hurry back.'

Graham got back in time for intermission, worked the main bar and then went upstairs and loaded the software on to the computer in my office. We spent the rest of the second act trying to load in the dimensions of Carrie's house, as near as I could guess from my one visit there and my incredibly bad spatial awareness.

'You want to start this tonight?' Graham asked, after we got everyone cleared out of the place.

'Yes I do,' I told him. 'But I can't. I have responsible adult things I have to do tonight.' Much as I really wanted to stay and start trying to plot out various scenarios, I was sure Cam would expect me home on time. Especially now; I was sure he would want to talk about things. Even though I didn't want to talk about the pregnancy, Cam had just found out and he was just starting to get used to this whole idea. I hated having to be understanding, it was so unlike me.

149

'No worries,' Graham told me. 'Tomorrow. I'll meet you here early and we can play around with it.'

'Graham, I'm disappointed. I was expecting an argument from you.'

'Well, Kate, I have young and irresponsible things to do tonight, so starting tomorrow would be just fine with me.'

'Young and irresponsible?' I asked.

'You keep saying you don't want too much information but then you keep asking me all these questions.'

'Oh,' I said. 'Oh, I get it. Well, say hi to Mandi for me.'

And with that, I hitched a ride with Scott and was home right on time, raising no suspicions and requiring no lectures. It was well after eleven when I opened the door, and the place was dark and quiet. I tiptoed past the living room, noticing Carrie settled on to the sofa bed and the lights out. She must still be totally exhausted from her ordeal, I thought. A dim light dribbled over the edge of the loft and I knew Cam was awake and waiting upstairs for me. I let out a quiet little sigh, my one moment of self-pity, and then climbed the stairs quietly. Cam sat in the armchair, the light on behind him and a book in his lap. He looked up and saw me and a big smile cracked his face.

'Hi, sweetie,' he whispered.

'What are you doing up? Are you waiting for me?'

'No, I just honestly wasn't all that tired. I haven't had this much sleep since I started dating you and I think it's starting to get to me.'

'I know. If we're going to continue to have a bunch of company, we're going to need a bigger apartment.'

'If we're going to continue to have kids we're going to have to get a bigger apartment.'

'My loft,' I moaned.

'It's a single person's apartment,' he explained.

'I know, I've been thinking about that, too,' I admitted. 'Maybe it's not so bad that it's going condo now. But I don't know if I can handle all this change at once.'

I took off my sweater and tried to hang it up in the closet but he grabbed me and pulled me on to his lap, tossing the book aside.

'Honey, kids or no kids, we definitely need a place with more doors. I never realized you got so much company.'

'Neither did I. But you're right,' I said.

He rubbed my tummy and that smile crossed his face again. 'Soon us two will be three, remember?'

'Oh, yeah. You know, I actually had a moment today where I wasn't actually thinking about it or freaking out about what we've done.'

'Yeah, it is scary.'

'You can't be scared,' I said.

'Of course I'm scared,' he said.

'You're the one that's wanted this for ages. You're the one that's been planning and begging and hoping and praying for a baby.'

'Yeah, but, Katie, that was the dream. Now it's real. In less than a year we will have a little tiny human being that we will be totally responsible for. Someone that we will have to raise to survive this big, cruel world.'

'Oh, my God, I'm growing a person.'

'Yes, you are.'

'It's like the movie *Alien*, you know, if you really stop and think about it.'

'Quit thinking so much.'

'See, that's the other thing I've been thinking about. Is it really responsible of us to bring a child into this world? It's not in such great shape, you know.'

'I don't think it's our responsibility to decide whether children should still be born or not.' He smiled at me, running his fingers gently through my hair. 'I think it's our responsibility to teach our children how to live in the world. The world has always been troubled but children are still born into it every day.'

'Wow, you're deep,' I teased him. 'At least this baby will do really well in the daddy department. And you can make up for all the mistakes I'm going to make.'

'Katie, this baby is going to have an amazing mommy. There is no one in the world like you and if you can teach our baby to be half the person you are, we will be blessed.'

And there went those damn hormones again, as the tears welled up and then overflowed. Cam just laughed at me and held me tightly until it subsided. The holding part mostly made up for the laughing at me part. I managed to pull myself

151

together and finished getting into my pajamas and then tucked into bed. Cam turned out the light as I cuddled up, tucked under his arm, but I could tell he wasn't ready to go to sleep yet.

'It's OK,' I said.

'What?'

'You can talk.'

'No, you need your sleep.'

'Cam,' I said, frustration in my voice. 'I know you just want to look after me, but I just hate feeling all dependent. Please try to stifle that whole patronizing thing that keeps coming out, OK?'

'I'll try.'

'Yeah, that sounded sincere. Now tell me what's on your mind?'

'I just wanted to know how come Graham, and everyone at the theatre, knew.'

'Oh, God, are you really hurt by that?'

'Well, a little.'

'Oh, Cam, it was mostly accidental. I swear,' I explained.

'I feel like I've missed out on a whole part of the pregnancy,' he told me.

'I know. It's just that I was sick all the time and Graham related it to the smell of coffee and that reminded him of when his sister was pregnant. And then the obnoxious little brat went out and bought me a pregnancy test. It was positive and then I went to the doctor to confirm it. Since then I've been trying to figure out how to bring you into this magical little circle of ours.'

'And everyone else?' he asked.

'Well, you know how bad Graham is at keeping his mouth shut. It just happened.'

'Were you scared to tell me?'

'No, not of you. I was just scared, period. It was such a surprise. I mean, even if we'd been planning it, it would have been on my mind. But this just came out of the blue and just totally shocked me. I didn't know what to do. But I was never scared of you. I guess I was scared of the baby.'

'OK, well you're forgiven everything then. But you're telling me I can't tell anyone?' he asked.

152

'Well, the risk of miscarriage in the first three months is higher, so I really didn't want anyone to know until then.'

'Maybe we're closing the barn door after the horse has already left on this one. What do you think?'

'Well, maybe. I just don't want to talk about it with everyone yet. I want it to be between us for a little while, until we get used to it, I guess.'

'So what do we do?' he asked. 'Pretend I don't know yet? And then you get to talk about it with everyone and I don't.'

'Well, I guess that's not going to work.'

'I'll let you make the decision, Katie, but maybe it's too late and maybe we should just accept that half the world knows about the baby and the other half is going to find out, no matter what we do.'

'I guess you're right.'

'Sleep on it,' he said. 'Let me know what you've decided in the morning.'

'You're a nice man not to be angry about all of this.'

'How could I be angry about a baby?' he asked.

'I mean about everyone knowing and all that stuff.'

'Well, I am a little upset. I'm just hiding it really well.'

'Do you still love me?' I asked.

'I'll sleep on that and let you know in the morning,' Cam said with a laugh.

Sunday November 23

I woke up Sunday morning, anxious to get to the theatre and try out Graham's computer program. But I was also quite sure I didn't want Cam to find out about it just yet. I knew he wasn't going to be happy about my investigating anything right now. So I didn't dive out of bed and arouse his suspicions but lay there and cuddled for a few minutes while we discussed our day. I did have a matinee at the theatre today and I knew Cam had to go in to work a little bit early, so we finally got out of bed at around nine o'clock. I told Cam I'd catch a ride in with him.

We had a quick breakfast alone. Carrie took her wool blanket, coffee and muffin out to the chaise lounge on the deck again, after assuring us repeatedly that she really was fine. Neither of us believed her, but we had decided to give her a few more days before we staged any sort of a major psychiatric intervention. We tidied up, got dressed, checked to make sure Carrie was OK one last time, and then Cam dropped me off at my office before parking the car.

This was the last day of the run of this play and, as of Tuesday, the new show would be on stage rehearsing prior to opening. The Christmas show was always a big one. Every year we ran *A Christmas Carol* and it was becoming a family tradition. I had a week to get everything cleared out from *Rock and Roll* and get the merchandise in for Christmas. Graham and I were going to be working hard and I still had Carrie to deal with and this pregnancy. I was getting a headache just thinking about it all.

It was still two hours before call time and Graham wasn't at the theatre yet. Though I was happy he seemed to have found himself a steady girl, I missed the days when his life circled around my wants and needs and he would be here waiting to get started. It was so sad when ushers grew up. I decided to get the sign-in sheets and other stuff ready for the show, patience not being one of my virtues. Graham finally came running down the hallway about a half an hour later, just when I pretty much had everything done.

'Sorry,' he apologized, racing in and dropping everything in the corner. 'I got tied up.'

'Not literally, I hope,' I joked, and then saw the blush start on his cheeks. 'Graham, don't even take me there. What you and Mandi do in your free time is your own business but I have a definite rule about too much information, remember?'

'Trust me, I have no intention of divulging anything,' he said, turning to his backpack and pulling out a bottle of juice while he tried to regain his composure.

'All right. We need to put the people into this little design,' I instructed him, rapidly changing the subject. I vacated my desk so he could sit down and run the computer program.

154

'OK.' He sat down and adjusted everything to his satisfaction. 'Let's start with you and Cam. Where were you guys standing when this all happened?'

'Cam's car was parked here,' I said, pointing at the screen, 'And we were standing here, with our backs toward the house, facing across the street.'

Almost magically, two figures appeared where I had pointed on the screen, and then a picture of Cam's car gradually filled in behind them.

'How'd you do that?' I asked.

'I found it on the web and decided to go for a little realism. Do you like it?' he asked.

'Yes, you're very clever, Graham. Now, Officer Strachan was over here, facing us.'

I continued to point to various places on the computer screen and Graham continued to program everyone in until we had all the participants plotted in their designated locations at the moment of the shooting. We played with it for almost an hour; trying out this and that to see if we could make everything fit the way Carrie had described it to me. And we couldn't. As near as I could figure, if Carrie had pulled out the gun from where she stood, she would have killed the refrigerator. We kept playing it back, moving everyone around a few inches at a time, until the rest of the staff started to wander in.

'Morning,' Martha called, coming down the hall.

'Your staff is here,' Charlotte added. 'Better hide whatever it is you're working on that you don't want us to see.'

'Yep, remember our rule. If this is something you're trying to hide from Cam, don't tell us. We're terrible liars.'

'We're not doing anything, you two,' I said. 'Graham has a new set-design program he was showing me.'

'A lot of whispering going on,' Charlotte said.

'That's not a good sign of innocence,' Martha giggled.

'Well, everything's turned off and we're actually going to do theatre work now. So, anyone that doesn't want to get stuck doing coat check had better start showing me a little respect!'

'I'm just going to get changed,' Graham said, turning off the computer and heading for the change room.

Charlotte poured coffee for herself and joined Martha on the window ledge seat.

'So, it's getting harder and harder to talk to you,' she said. 'With all these things we can't talk about.'

'I told Cam,' I admitted. 'But I also told Cam we would keep it quiet so he would have a chance to tell a few people. Plus it still is a little early to be talking about it, don't you think?'

'I don't know,' Martha said. 'Things are so different these days.'

'I know, I couldn't even get a pregnancy test until I was almost three months along,' agreed Charlotte.

'And now people can find out in days,' Martha continued.

'Five days, I think,' I added.

'And they seem to tell everyone right away.'

'And no one worries like they used to.'

'I worry,' I said. 'About everything.'

'Good,' Martha said. 'At least that seems a little more like my day.'

'Yeah, you should worry a bit. It is a huge responsibility,' Charlotte said.

'Well, I'm glad my sleepless nights make you two happy.'

'It'll get better, Kate,' Martha promised. 'Especially now that you're sharing it with Cam.'

The door opened at the end of the hall and a group of volunteers trundled in.

'And speaking of not sharing the news with the world just yet—'

'Lovely weather we're having, aren't we?' Martha asked, changing the subject with an evil wink of her eye.

Our well-oiled machine got the staff assigned and in place. Since we were in a hold-over week, everyone here, volunteers included, had worked this show at least once already. So very little explanation was required and they were out of the office and in position in record time.

'I think you're right, Kate, I think there's something that Carrie isn't telling you,' Graham said, when we were alone in the office and he had opened the computer program again.

'I know she's hiding something,' I insisted. 'She was looking directly into my eyes when she said she didn't do it. I believed that part of it. It was when she said she didn't know who did it that I started to think she was lying. I don't know why she's

156

doing this. We've only been trying to help her since she first turned up on the doorstep.'

'Kate, some people are very good liars, you know,' he said. 'Basically that's what all us actors are.'

'I don't think so,' I said. 'I just don't think she's just lying. I think there's another explanation; we're just not seeing it. Yet.'

'Hey there.'

I almost jumped out of my chair and so did Graham. We had been so intent in our studies that we hadn't heard Cam walking down the hallway. And now I was pretty sure I was going to catch a great deal of hell from him for trying to get involved in solving this mystery.

'What are you two up to?' he asked, entering the office.

I got up quickly and wrapped him in a big hug while Graham saved and closed our little computer model.

'Hi, sweetie, how is your day going?' I asked, planting a big kiss on him.

'Get a room, you two,' Graham said.

'My day is good,' Cam said. 'So what are you two staring so intently at on the computer?'

'I was just looking at a set design that Graham is working on for a friend's play,' I lied. You know, I really hated lying to Cam, but it just always seemed necessary in these cases because he never agreed with what I was doing. I always convinced myself it was OK, because I wasn't lying about great big life decisions, but about little things that didn't really matter except for the way they might affect his day-to-day peace of mind. And he always found out, which also made it OK, right?

'Oh, cool. Is that Auto-Cad?' he asked Graham, pulling up the chair I had been sitting in and leaning over so he could see the computer.

'It's a theatre-specific program based on that,' Graham explained.

'Have you got any coffee on, Katie?' Cam asked, not turning away from the computer. 'Show me what it does.'

'No, Graham needs to get back to stuffing programs now,' I told Cam.

'Please, Mom, just five more minutes,' Cam whined, 'I love these programs.'

157

'Yeah, please, Mom.' Graham seconded the motion.

'Fine,' I said.

I shot them both my worst dirty look and then turned to pour coffee, knowing that Cam's ire might be aimed at me in another few seconds.

'Well, the play is set in an old haunted castle, like a Dracula-style gothic setting,' Graham began. 'And the challenging part is that the author of the play has scenes set in the tower, the main entrance and the dungeon, which is way too heavy in scenery changes for a small theatre stage. I mean, it's not like you can build a real working castle on a stage as big as ours and have it look effective and work for the actors with the kind of budgets we have. And this play was written for an even smaller venue than this. But I think I surmounted the problem by doing this . . .'

I stopped listening to Graham and turned around. There on the computer screen was a castle, with gargoyles staring down at the stage from a tower, and diagrams for lighting and prop placement. There was even a drawbridge.

'. . . I thought we could use Gobos to change the light for the dungeon so it would be coming from above through the grates, and the tower light would be diffuse and look like it was shining through an open window.'

'That's really cool,' Cam told him, taking the coffee from my outstretched hand. 'Maybe you can teach me how to use this. Someday, I might want to try a renovation on wherever we're living at the time, and this would sure help to lay things out.'

'You're moving?' Graham asked.

'The place is going condo,' Cam explained. 'We're out next spring.'

'Kate, are you keeping things from me now?' Graham said with a laugh.

'See, Cam,' I said, swatting the side of his head playfully. 'This is how things leak out around here and how everyone knows everything about my life, whether I want them to or not.'

'Sorry,' he apologized. 'I guess we're even now.'

'I will absolutely teach you how to use it,' Graham said, smiling up at me as he brought the subject back to where we had started. 'I better get back to stuffing those programs now, huh?'

'Yeah, I guess you better.' I smiled back. I couldn't believe he had loaded another set design in there and saved the day. I don't know if it was something he had been working on or something he had planned to use to cover our butts if we had been caught but, either way, he deserved a raise.

Graham shut down the computer and grabbed a box of programs to carry down to the main lobby.

'So what brings you here this fine afternoon?' I asked Cam, feeling quite confident that I hadn't been caught as I took a seat behind my desk.

'I brought you a present,' he said.

'What?' I asked, excitement creeping into my voice.

He reached into his tool belt and pulled out a take-out container of milk and set it on the desk in front of me, smiling brilliantly.

'Very funny.' I slumped into the chair, disappointed.

'No, seriously, three glasses a day from now on. You had one at breakfast and here's your midday serving.'

I reached over and grabbed the milk, opening it and taking a sip. I wasn't even going to bother to fight him on this one, because it was one of those immutable facts and I could never win.

'Is this the only reason you came?' I asked.

'Well, no, let's call it a happy coincidence,' he told me. 'Carrie's ex-husband is going to bring the kids over for a visit tonight. I thought we might do a barbecue if you can get off early.'

'I've missed a whole lot of time recently,' I said. 'I'd rather not take much more if I have to. What time were you thinking?'

'Well, they were going to come over around seven o'clock this evening, I think.'

'OK, I'll get the evening show in and then leave it to Graham. I can take a cab home and be there by eight fifteen or so, if that's OK?'

'That would be lovely, dear.'

'You know this is my closing night.'

'I know, but it's a hold-over, so it's not like there's a big party planned or anything.'

'Yeah, and I guess my partying days are over for a little while. OK, I'll be there as soon as I can after I get the show in.'

'Good. I just thought it would be nice to have you there. And I thought you might like to get to know all of them, under better circumstances than last time. They are all potential future in-laws you know?'

'I know that but I also know you and I'm guessing that the real reason you want me there is you think it might be an uncomfortable situation for everyone and you want me there as the master of small talk, to fill those uncomfortable silences.'

'Well, that thought may have crossed my mind, I admit. You still coming home early or you going to punish me and stay and work all night now?' he asked me.

'Yes, I'm still coming! But only if you let me get back to work now for a while.'

He leaned across the desk and kissed me. 'Your wish is my command.'

'God, why can't you say that when I'm asking for something expensive?'

I watched him walk down the hall, partly for the view but mostly so I knew when it would be safe to turn the computer back on and see if I could find whatever vital piece of evidence it was that we were missing. Graham turned up in the office again about fifteen minutes later and we kept trying different scenarios, but we could not make the scene fit the crime. Carrie might have been there with a gun at her feet, but the police had released her. And we couldn't make the trajectory match either, from where she was positioned. I left the program with Graham for the night to see if he could come up with any interesting ideas, and then I headed for home and our houseful of company.

For a change, the house was ablaze with light and life when I arrived home. The kids were on the balcony, tossing birdseed out for the pigeons. Cam and Alan were managing the barbeque and Carrie was in the kitchen, tossing the salad. They had the table filled with condiments, buns and plates and, I assumed, with the number of us, we would be eating in the living room.

'Hi, Carrie,' I greeted her, dropping my coat and pack behind the kitchen table.

'I'm so glad you made it home,' she said, smiling at me. 'Cam said you were going to try to join us.'

'Do you need help with anything?' I asked, hoping she wouldn't ask me to do anything that revealed my less than lackluster kitchen talents.

'No, I've got this part all under control, but thanks.'

'OK, I'm just going to get changed,' I said and ran upstairs. I undid my tight skirt and found a nice stretchy pair of sweat pants. I wondered if it was too early for pregnancy weight gain and if this was coming from all the food Cam was forcing down my throat. Not that I had a problem eating his cooking before, but now he was so concerned about me getting a balanced diet and vitamin and mineral content that I knew I was going to have to take charge soon. I had hoped all the morning sickness would balance that out. I looked at my reflection in the mirror, with just the sweat pants and bra on. I was going to have to take control really soon. I pulled on a sweatshirt to cover what I thought was my very obvious middle and turned around to see Cam standing at the top of the stairs.

'Carrie said you were home,' he said.

'How long have you been standing there?'

'A minute or two.' He blinked. Was that a tear in the corner of his eye? So why was he now the weepy one and I feeling very sarcastic.

'Don't say it,' I warned him.

'But Katie—' he whispered.

'I was not standing here marveling at the brilliance of my body, growing a baby or anything weird and miraculous like that, Cam. I was standing here thinking just how fat I was getting and that I really had no excuse for it at this point.'

'And I was just coming to tell you that dinner was ready,' he told me.

'Liar.'

'You'll never know for sure, will you?'

'You still going to love me when I'm fat and bloated?' I asked.

'Yes.'

'And my ankles and toes are swollen?'

161

'Yes.'

'And I can't tie up my own shoes?'

'Yes.'

'And I have varicose veins and hemorrhoids?'

'Well . . .'

'Yeah, I know your type,' I said with a laugh.

He strode across the room and pulled me over to the window. He wrapped his arms around me, his hands resting protectively over that bloated belly. I resisted the urge to push them away to some other part of my body that I still liked. We looked down on to the balcony, as Carrie and Alan and the kids tried to sweep up the birdseed that had spilled everywhere. The kids giggled and messed up the pile every time Carrie started to get it swept up, while Alan tried to shoo away the marauding crows that had invaded the pigeon's picnic.

'Tell me that isn't worth a little bit of weight gain,' he whispered in my ear, pointing down at the balcony.

'They're pretty cute.' I sighed, feeling myself being pulled into this whole dream of his, whether I wanted to be or not.

'You know, Katie, I have been thinking a lot about the future recently.'

'Yeah, me too,' I admitted.

'Well, I think there is probably something else we should talk about before things get too much farther along.'

'What?' I asked naively.

'Well, about whether or not we want to get married before the baby arrives.'

'Cam,' I said, pulling away from him. 'Don't.'

I almost felt like I was hyperventilating.

'Don't what?'

'Please, this isn't a rejection or anything like that. But please let me get used to the idea of having a baby before we broach the subject of marriage. Please. I just can't take two big things like this in one week.'

'Katie?' he said, that look on his face.

'Cam?' I asked, my eyes pleading with him not to go back there.

'Come on down and have dinner,' he said, holding out his hand for me. I took it and followed him down the stairs.

162

We got hamburgers fixed for the kids and sat them at the coffee table. Then the adults got themselves food as well and sat in the living room. I found myself between the two kids on the floor, enjoying our burgers and salads. I had even been talked into trying some hideous blue Kool-Aid drink that wasn't half as bad as it looked, and green ketchup.

After dinner the men retired to the balcony for a cigar and Carrie volunteered for clean-up duty while the kids kept me in the living room and tried to refresh me in the finer points of Go Fish. I managed to find a complete deck of cards and get them shuffled and dealt out. I had figured I might have to let the kids win, but they were beating the pants off me. I was pretty sure they were cheating but I couldn't prove it.

'So what did you guys do today?' I asked.

'We went to the gun range after school. What did you do today?' David asked me.

'I went to work. Did you say the gun range?' I asked.

'Yes I did. Where do you work?'

'I want a two,' Emily whined.

'Go fish.' I told her. 'I work at a theatre. Why did you go to the gun range?'

'Daddy's teaching me how to shoot guns properly,' he informed me. 'Daddy is an expert gun shooter. And he and Joey's dad go hunting together. Do they play *Harry Potter* at your theatre?'

'No, we have live plays. You know, like Storybook Theatre. You've seen them at your school, haven't you?'

'I want a three. Do you have a three?' Emily asked.

'It's not your turn,' David said. 'I want a Jack.'

'Storybook Theatre did *The Princess and the Pea* this year,' Emily informed me. 'Do you know the Princess? She was very beautiful.'

'No, I don't,' I said. 'And I don't have a Jack either. Aren't you a little young to be shooting guns?'

'No, they have a kids' club. Do you have a Queen?'

'Hey! It's not your turn. Do you have a five?'

'How did you know?'

'So do you like shooting guns?'

'I want a five too,' Emily said.

'From which one of us?' I asked.

163

'You.'

'Go fish.'

'Do you like shooting guns, David?' My spider sense was tingling again

'It's OK. I want to be able to go hunting with Daddy when I get bigger. And . . .'

'And what?'

'I want a ten,' he asked Emily and she reluctantly pulled out a card and handed it to him.

'And what, David?'

'And I want to be able to protect Mommy better.'

I was shocked into silence for a minute by what David had said. When I finally regained some sense and was about to ask him what he meant, Cam and Alan appeared back in the living room, stifling my questions. We finished up our game, cleaned up the cards and I helped Carrie put away the rest of the dishes she had washed up.

'I like your kids,' I said to her.

'They cheat at cards,' she said. 'But other than that they're OK.'

'Yeah, I figured that out about the cards a little too late,' I said.

'Well, I'm going to drive home with Alan, if you don't mind, and stay for a while. I'm missing the kids, so we're going to do some homework together, and then I'm going to read them their bedtime story and tuck them in.'

'Do you want me to send Cam to come and get you later?' I asked.

'No, I'll either borrow Alan's car or maybe I'll just sleep on his sofa if it's late.'

'You two seem to have a pretty good relationship,' I commented.

'Yeah, too bad we worked it all out after we got divorced.'

'It might have been easier to do it the other way around,' I agreed. 'What about this other man you've met? You haven't said much about him.'

'No, and I'm not going to. I don't want him involved in any of this. We decided we were going to wait until Hank and I had separated, so that's what I'm sticking to.'

'But surely he must be worried about you?' I asked.

'He is. He calls me at work and checks up on me.'

'Carrie, don't you want someone around, someone that you can lean on?'

'I don't want him involved in any of this,' she insisted. 'Kate, I know how this is all going to end. It's going to end badly, and I don't want him involved. I shouldn't have even gone out with him in the first place. He's already way more involved than he should be.'

'How come you are so convinced that this is all going to end badly?' I asked. 'I know Detective Lincoln is going to do everything in his power to figure this all out.'

'I know.' Carrie sighed but was interrupted when Alan came into the kitchen with her coat.

'OK, we're ready,' Alan said. 'All aboard that's coming aboard.'

'All aboard,' Emily echoed from the front hallway. 'Toot, toot.'

Carrie finished with the dishtowel and hung it up.

'I'll be right there.' She smiled and then turned to me. 'It has to end badly, Kate, there is no other way. And trust me, I've thought about it a lot.'

'Just tell me what I can do?' I begged her.

'Have a good night,' she said with a sad smile. 'I'll see you guys in the morning.' And then she grabbed her coat and purse and followed her family out the front door.

I finished putting things away in the kitchen while Cam cleaned up the devastation on our balcony. I sat on the couch and flipped channels on the TV until he joined me.

'Anything on?' he asked.

'Is there ever?'

'Well, that doesn't seem to stop us from watching it.'

I handed him the remote. 'You do it tonight. I don't feel like making a decision.'

Cam got comfortable with a beer in hand and flipped through the channels, finally stopping on a documentary about great white sharks.

'Cam, I really think something is up with Carrie.'

'You mean other than the fact that she's just been involved in a shooting and is under investigation and has left her abusive husband and spent several days in jail?' he asked.

'Yeah.'

'What? God, what else is there?'

'She just keeps saying this thing is going to end badly and that she's going back to jail.'

'Katie, I think she's just in shock and not thinking straight.'

'Cam, I really think Carrie knows something and she's not telling us.'

'Women's intuition again?'

'Maybe.'

'Or is it that part of you that wants to get all involved but remembers that she promised me she wouldn't do that any more?'

'I just get a bad feeling.'

'So, how *is* that bullet wound on your arm from when you got your last bad feeling?'

'I get it, Cam. But I am so worried about her.'

'Why don't you call Ken Lincoln and tell him some of the things she has said to you?' Cam asked. 'Maybe it will help him figure things out; which, by the way, is actually his job.'

'But I don't know what she's covering up. What if she really did do it and my talking to Ken ends up getting her convicted?'

'Well, what do you want to do?' he asked.

'I want her to tell me what happened. And then I can decide what to do.'

'And is she going to do that?'

'Probably not.' I sighed. 'But I just can't help—'

'You can't help wanting to be involved in this,' Cam finished my sentence for me. 'But there is one thing I want you to remember, Katie, and that is that you are now responsible for two people, not just one. So I'd rather you didn't get involved. Remember, the first time you got dropped off a forty-foot tower, the second time you got shot. Do you think that's fair to the baby? To put her at that kind of risk?'

'Uh, no, I understand that part, Cam. That would be why I'm sitting here on the couch, wondering what's going on, instead of following Carrie half way across the city to see where she's really going to go tonight.'

'She's going to Alan's,' he informed me.

'No, she's not.'

166

'Yes, she's going to spend some time with the kids.'

'That's where she's starting out. I don't think that's where she's going to end up.'

'And what makes you think that?' he asked.

'If you were in serious trouble, like this, and you were alone, staying at a stranger's house and you couldn't go home, what would you want the most?' I asked.

'To be with you,' he said. 'I'd want you to come to me if I couldn't get to you.'

'Well, I think Carrie's going to find comfort tonight. Regardless of what she said.'

'She's going to see a boyfriend?'

'I think she is. And I'm just wondering if he knows what is really going on.'

'Wow,' Cam said. 'You have the craziest imagination I have ever seen.'

'It's true,' I protested. 'I'll bet you a hundred dollars that she is telling Alan she's going to take a taxi back here. She told me she's just going to stay on Alan's couch tonight. What did she tell you?'

'Katie, you're insane. Just watch the sharks attack the nice surfers and give your imagination a rest.'

'I dare you to call Alan's place in the morning if she's not back here.'

'I will do no such thing. And neither will you. Carrie has a right to go wherever she wants and not explain it to us. I don't want her to think we're checking up on her.'

'But she's not telling the truth,' I said. 'She knows what happened in that house when that gun went off and she's not telling.'

'And that's why the police are investigating it. And please note, I said the police.'

'You are the most frustrating man I have ever met in my life!'

'Me? You are the most frustrating woman I have ever met and there are days I wonder why I stay here.'

I looked angry at those last words, not sure whether I was about to burst into tears. Instead, I grabbed him and kissed him.

'Oh, yeah, that's why,' he said with a laugh.

'And don't you ever forget it,' I said, kissing him again to ensure that he wouldn't.

167

Monday November 24

Sunday night we had fallen into bed around midnight and fallen asleep much later than that. Nothing like a good fight to keep you up all night. I was exhausted by the time the lights finally went out. But I hadn't slept well. I'd had strange dreams and tossed and turned all night. I had this horrible feeling that I knew something, something I wasn't supposed to know. I didn't know what to say to Cam, if anything. The fact that David belonged to a gun club bothered me. The fact that the mysterious neighbour kept turning up bothered me. Why couldn't I get these things out of my head? Cam had gotten up already to go running and I wandered down to the kitchen and found a breakfast plate in the fridge that he had made up for me, right beside the big glass of milk that he had poured. I laughed but obediently took them to the table. I picked at my food, feeling a little queasy, and had just opened the newspaper when Carrie came out of the bathroom, her robe on and her wet hair up in a towel. She poured herself a coffee and sat down beside me.

'Morning,' I greeted.

'Good morning.'

'Did you have a good time with your kids last night?' I admit it. I was fishing for information.

'I did.' She smiled. 'I actually fell asleep while Emily read me a bedtime story and Alan left me there overnight.'

'Well, you look almost happy to be alive today.' I smiled at her.

'You know, seeing that the kids are OK did a lot for my mood. I am feeling much more optimistic today. I might even try going to the gym before I go to work today. I think it might make me feel a little better, to get back into my normal routine.'

'Well, just don't overdo it. You know there are going to be people out there that recognize you and that can be a little creepy.'

'I know, I've been dealing with stares and glares all week long. But my gym is pretty private and at work I can hide out in the back room if things gets too bad,' she assured me. 'What about you?'

'Well, *Rock and Roll* closed last night and *A Christmas Carol* starts rehearsals on stage tomorrow, so we've got to clean up all the merchandise and stuff from the first one and bring all the stuff in for Christmas for the next one. I've got deliveries and pick-ups starting around noon and, by the time we finish our inventory and bank deposits and all that other stuff, the day should be pretty well shot.'

'You looked like you were having fun with the kids last night, Kate.' Carrie smiled.

'I was. Your kids are great. But I felt guilty for keeping them from spending time with you.'

'No, the last thing I wanted to do was force them to spend time with me. Just being in the same room is good enough. I just wanted them to have some fun and see that they were doing all right. Their lives have been a little out of control for the past couple of years.'

'I know. The things we do for love, huh?'

'So are you and Cam going to be having some kids of your own?' she asked. 'I mean, I'm not trying to be pushy or anything, but I know Cam is ready for a family and you just looked so good with the kids, I couldn't help but ask.'

'We're in discussions right now, and that's all I have to say on that subject.'

'Point taken.'

'You know, Cam is a good man and I know he wants kids really badly. But he is willing to give me time to adapt to all this stuff, like marriage and commitment and responsibility, so that's kind of where we stand right now.'

'It's OK, Kate, you don't have to explain.'

'It's just that you're the first person I've met in his family. I want you to know that I really love him and appreciate him and not think that he's giving up everything for me.'

'You'll make a good mother, Kate, when you're ready,' she

assured me. 'My kids were thoroughly enchanted by you last night. How did you find so much to talk to them about?'

'Oh, I don't know. I just started to ask them what they did during the day and stuff. I had to because I was trying to distract them from the card game. They were beating the pants off me.'

'They cheat, you know.'

'So you said.' I took a deep breath. 'David said he's in a gun club.'

Carrie looked up at me. Was that a hint of sudden panic in her eyes? But her voice remained calm.

'Yes, his father is quite the marksman. David joined the gun club recently.'

'I just find it interesting that after what happened you were all right with that.' I concentrated on spreading cheese on my bagel and not making a lot of eye contact.

'Well, I don't really have a lot of say in their lives right now. Alan and I agreed that I would give him complete custody temporarily until this was all over and, in return, he wouldn't have to take me to court to sue me for custody as an unfit mother.'

'I see,' I said, sorry I'd said anything when I heard the sadness in her voice.

'Kate, I do understand your concern, but don't you think it's better that, if he's going to be around guns, he knows how to use them properly?'

'I really can't say. I'm not much of a gun proponent myself. Especially now.'

'I understand. I just don't want to risk him finding a gun and hurting someone,' she almost whispered, and then pulled herself back. 'Besides, they are my kids and I think Alan and I can figure out what's best for them.'

'Of course,' I assured her. 'I was just curious.'

'You'll know, when your time comes to have kids, you'll know what it's like. Weighing all these decisions and trying to figure out what's the right thing to do. And sometimes the right thing and the best thing aren't the same, you know.'

'I can see that.'

'Oh, well, you probably won't see them again for ages, so no worries.'

'What?' I asked, not following her train of thought.

'Oh, nothing. I was just going to say that the single biggest fallacy about having kids is that you're ever going to be ready for them. Basically, you never will be, so you just have them and adapt along the way.'

'Boy, you can say that again!' I said, realizing how true that was.

'Huh?'

'All my friends with kids say that.' I tried to recover.

'Oh, right.'

It seemed both Carrie and I had things to hide.

'Oh, look at the time,' I said, happy to be saved by the clock. 'I'd better get in the shower and get going. Sorry to eat and run.'

'It's OK. I'm leaving in another hour or so. I'll read the paper and have some more coffee. I'm quite good at entertaining myself.'

'Well, just give me or Cam a call if you need anything today.'

'Sure thing.'

I put my dishes in the dishwasher and started for the bathroom.

'Kate,' she called after me.

'Yeah?'

'Do you know what you'll find is the most interesting thing about having kids?' she asked me.

'What's that?'

'It's how fiercely protective you will be of them. You would literally kill to protect them, you know what I mean?'

I felt a shiver run down my back as I returned Carrie's piercing stare.

'Yeah, I guess I do.'

Carrie turned back to the newspaper, dismissing me.

Cam came home in time to drive me to the theatre, a treat since I was running a little bit behind. I had a few ushers in to help out and got everyone assigned, counting inventory, packing up old stock, moving things into the lower lobby for pick-up. Graham had drawn up a plan on his fancy set-design program for our Christmas displays in the lobbies and we had

171

done some fine-tuning on the plan and then pinned it up so everyone would know where the new stuff was going. We moved a few tables around and replaced the table linens. Then I decided I could spare a few minutes, so I went back up to my office and stared at the computer screen for a good half an hour before Graham came up and interrupted me.

'Does staring at it endlessly help?' he asked.

'No. But I think I might have got a little hint last night. I think I may have figured out what happened in that house. I think I may know who fired the gun.'

'What?' he asked. 'Who?'

'I'm not ready to share yet. I have to see it run on the program to see if it really works.'

'What are you talking about, a re-enactment of the shooting?'

'Graham, can you ask everyone to stay after we get all the stock delivered?' I asked.

'Sure,' he said. 'You calling a staff meeting?'

'Nope, I'm going to throw a pizza party. Tell them I'll order pizza but I need their help with this. Main lobby, ten minutes after we get it cleared of all these merchandisers and the doors locked.'

'Are you going to tell me what you're thinking?' he asked.

'Nope, you have to wait and see like everyone else. It's just a theory I have.'

'OK, main lobby it is. I must say I'm a little hurt that you won't tell me what's going on.'

'I'm still working it through in my mind,' I tried as an apology. 'If I was sure what I was thinking, I promise I'd tell you.'

Looking slightly mollified, Graham headed off to find everyone and pass the word around. I dialed my favourite pizza joint and placed an order, hoping my credit card could handle it. When the lobby was clear, I ran inside the theatre auditorium and yelled for the technicians, trying to see if the place was empty or not. Monday would normally be their day off, but I suspected they might be in, making plans for putting up the new set tomorrow. Trevor liked to make sure everything ran smoothly.

'Scott, Trevor, anyone here?' No response. Maybe I was going to get lucky.

172

'Scott, Trevor, anyone? Hello?' I called more loudly.

Still nothing. I jumped up on to the stage and snuck into the stage carpenter's office, rummaging around in Trevor's desk drawer.

'Just what do y'all think you're doing?'

I turned around and faced Trevor guiltily. Scott stood just behind him.

'I always said she had a sneaky side and we shouldn't trust her,' Scott teased.

'Did you get lost trying to find your office?' Trevor asked. 'Tell us the truth. We have lots of things we can torture you with back here.'

'I confess. I'm sorry. Didn't you hear me calling you?' I asked, innocently.

'Yeah, we did. We just wanted to see what you'd get up to if you thought you were alone.'

'And she turned to a life of crime,' Scott sobbed. 'Where did we go wrong?'

'I don't know.' Trevor sighed. 'You think you raised them right and then look what happens.'

'OK, OK. I'm just looking for a tape measure.'

'Why on earth do you need a tape measure?' Trevor said, crossing to his desk, pulling one out from under a pile of blue-prints and then holding it just slightly out of my reach.

'Because I need to measure something.'

'Well, I knew there would be a simple explanation for all this.' He smiled at me. 'What did you want to measure?'

'I can't tell you.'

'Sure you can,' Scott said. 'Because, you know, we have standing orders from Cam that if you're getting yourself messed up in something that you shouldn't be messing with . . .'

'Cam is not my father!'

'Kate, tell us,' Trevor commanded.

'I want to re-enact the shooting. I've got the ushers to stay for pizza and Graham's laid out the design of the house and I just need to measure it out in the lobby. And since now you know everything, can I have some gaffer's tape, too?'

'What?' Scott asked. 'Have you lost your mind?'

'That would definitely be one of those things we should tell Cam about,' Trevor said.

173

'You're right about that one,' Scott agreed.

'Go get the walkie-talkie,' Trevor ordered.

'Trevor, I just want to try it. I think I know what happened that day but I just have to test out my theory. If I'm right, not only can you call Cam but you can call the police as well.'

Trevor and Scott exchanged glances and then Trevor turned back to me.

'I guess you'll need a stopwatch, too,' he suggested.

'That would be very helpful.' I smiled at him.

I arrived back in the lobby with the two technicians, a measuring tape, a stopwatch and an armful of gaffer's tape in every colour imaginable. The pizza had arrived and luckily I didn't have to take up a collection to pay for it. Everyone grabbed a slice or two and then I took the ushers into the Rodeo Lounge to explain what we were going to try to do. And to swear them to secrecy. Scott and Trevor stayed in the main lobby with Graham and his drawings, moving furniture, laying tape and designing the general outline of Carrie's house and front yard as best we could.

When they were all done, I assigned a character to each usher and then we put them in place. We ran through what the police had initially thought had happened, with Carrie as the shooter. Of course that was possible but with the fridge in the way and no gunpowder residue, it wasn't the answer. And none of us could come up with any viable reason for the lack of residue on Carrie. She didn't have the time to change clothes and shower. Then we ran through the other scenario, my new hypothesis. The one where David took the gun from the glove compartment of the car, where Carrie had left it, and snuck in the door between the garage and the kitchen. He would probably have walked into the kitchen right around the time Hank was screaming at Carrie, watching like the terrified little child that he was, behind the door. Then, as Hank went into the living room, to let the policeman in and argue with him for a while, David would have taken aim and fired at Hank through the doorway from the living room to the kitchen. Carrie probably had her back to him, so she wouldn't have seen him until it was too late. I thought he had probably pointed the gun at Hank, but the gun had been too heavy for him or it had recoiled when he fired and the bullet had

174

missed its target, and gone through the living-room window. Maybe he panicked or maybe he lost control of the gun, but he could certainly have managed to get off another couple of shots before Carrie had been able to turn and see that it was him. And one of those stray bullets had gone on the same trajectory as the first, through the living-room window, past where I stood and into Officer Strachan's chest. From one innocent little boy pulling the trigger to protect his mom.

The timing was perfect. Carrie would have turned and seen David there with the gun. She probably screamed at him to stop and he dropped the gun and ran back outside. David could have made it back to the car before anyone even reacted to the gunshot. He probably would have dropped the gun right at her feet, and that's what Officer Danko would have found by the time he made it into the kitchen. Carrie was in the perfect physical location to be found guilty and protect her son. Office Danko would have grabbed the gun just as Cam started screaming for help and raced outside to see what had happened. There would have been no time for him to do a proper evaluation of the crime scene.

'Wow, an eleven-year-old boy protecting his mom,' Martha sighed. 'That is a very sad state of affairs.'

'I know,' I agreed. 'There was this creepy neighbour guy hanging around and I thought it might have been him. But when I saw the look in Carrie's eyes this morning when I was asking her about David, I knew it was him she was protecting.'

'Mother's will do everything in their power to protect their children,' Martha said.

'Then why did she never try to protect him while she lived with that violent man?' I asked.

'I don't know if we'll ever know that,' Martha said. 'But she's paying for her sins now.'

'Why did you think it was the neighbour?' Graham asked me.

'I just had a feeling he might have been her new boyfriend. But maybe I was wrong.'

'So he hasn't been following you then?'

'No, he's been looking for Carrie, making sure she's all right,' I said. 'Let's try this one more time just to make sure.'

We ran the scene twice, timed it all out and realized it worked perfectly. When I was sure, we called Cam. After we ran through it twice for him, answering his questions over and over until he was finally satisfied, we called Detective Lincoln. He saw it once and sent a detective to Alan's house to talk to David. When the police got to Alan's house, they radioed Ken to let him know David wasn't there and that they discovered Carrie had picked him up earlier in the morning. Ken then drove to our apartment with lights and sirens flashing and Cam following closely behind, something I'm sure he would have enjoyed a lot under different circumstances. We raced upstairs but none of us was surprised to find all of Carrie's stuff gone. At least she had been polite enough to fold the sheets that had been on the sofa bed, leaving them in a tidy pile on the arm of the couch.

'I can't believe she's gone,' I said, tossing my backpack angrily across the kitchen.

'Kate, criminals run,' Ken said simply.

'She's not a criminal.'

'I know, but she is trying to protect her son and it's the same difference.'

'What do we do now?' I asked.

'We do nothing. Carrie is technically the custodial parent. Any agreement she and Alan made this week was purely informal and between them. And if the custodial parent has the child there is nothing I can do about that. It's not kidnapping,' Ken told me. 'I, however, will be watching the airport, train station and bus depot. I'll put an APB out on Carrie and then we'll just wait and hope we can find her. With any luck, she'll come to her senses and turn herself in.'

'I don't think she will,' Cam finally said.

'Why not?' Ken asked.

'She's stubborn,' he said. 'She stuck with Hank for years while we were trying to get her out. And now she thinks she's protecting David and she won't care what anyone else has to say. She thinks she's doing the right thing.'

'Well, if she calls—' Ken started.

'Don't worry,' Cam assured him. 'We'll do everything we can to get her back.'

'And let me know,' Ken said.

'And we'll make sure you know everything,' I promised.

'Wow, Kate, are you reforming your ways?' he asked.

'Hey, I'm just worried about the kid.'

'OK, well, you know how to get a hold of me,' Ken said. 'I'm going back to my office. There's nothing else I'm going to find here.'

Cam walked him to the door and I heard them say their goodbyes and the door get locked. I kicked the couch, knocking off the sheets and blankets she had meticulously folded and laid out for us.

'Feel better?' he asked, bending over to pick up the sheets and refold them. He handed me two corners while he took the other two.

'No. I feel fucking stupid.'

'Why? Because you didn't figure this out sooner?'

'No, because she was practically telling me this morning she would do anything to protect her kids and I didn't even suspect she might disappear. If I'd called Ken this morning, he might have been able to stop her.'

'You don't know that,' Cam said, taking the newly folded sheet from me and handing me the edge of the next one. 'We don't know what time she left or when she suspected you might be on to her. We didn't know anything for sure. She might have been planning this since last night or for several days. And if you'd called Ken this morning, what would you have said: that you had a bad feeling? And what would he have said to that?'

'He would have told me to leave the police work up to him,' I admitted.

'Yes, he would have. And nothing else would have happened and we would still be in the exact same position we are right now.'

'I suppose,' I said, handing him the folded sheet.

'No supposing about it. You know I'm right.'

'So, do you want me to take you back to the theatre to finish up?' he asked me.

'I probably should,' I said, but sat on the couch instead.

'Or would you rather just call Graham and see how things are going?' he asked, handing me the phone.

'That's a really good idea. And then when I find out that everything is fine, I think I'll just go to bed.'

'Tired?' he asked.

'Exhausted. Aren't you?'

'Getting there.'

'So, who's family do you think is more trouble so far,' I asked. 'Mine or yours?'

'I'd say it's a neck and neck race right now,' he said with a laugh.

'Good. Now I won't feel so bad next time my mom comes to stay.'

'Is she coming?'

'The way my luck goes with my mom, she'll probably just drop in tomorrow.'

'Katie, I love you a lot but, if that happens, I may have to move into my office for a couple of days. There is only so much a man can take.'

'I may move in with you.'

I almost jumped out of my skin when the phone rang in my hand. I recovered quickly and answered, hoping it would be Carrie.

'Hello?'

'I want to talk to Carrie.'

'Hank?' I asked.

'Put my wife on the phone.'

'She's not here.'

'Don't give me that crap. Put her on the phone or I'm coming over there to find her.'

'Hank, I swear she is not here right now and I have no idea where she is. I'm going to hang up. If I hear from her I'll let her know that you called.'

'Don't you fucking hang up on me.'

Cam ripped the phone from my hand.

'Hank.' His voice was quiet and calm, in that scary angry way of his. 'If you call this number again, I'll report you to the police. If you talk to my girlfriend that way again, I'll kill you.'

'You can't protect her twenty-four hours a day,' he said. And then I heard the line go dead.

Cam slammed the phone back down on the cradle. I could feel the anger seething out of his pores. I was about to say something to try and calm him when the phone rang again. Cam grabbed it before I could and pushed me away.

'I told you to quit calling this fucking number,' he swore into the phone.

'Cam?'

'Oh, my God, Alan?'

'Cam, is everything alright?'

'No, Hank's been hassling us. God, Alan, I am sorry. Is everything all right there with you? Have you found David?'

'Yes, that's why I was calling. He just came home. His mom put him in a taxi and paid the fare and he just got dropped off.'

'Is he OK?'

'He's great. He just thinks he had a regular day with his mom. He doesn't have a clue anything else happened or how worried we've been.'

'And Carrie?'

'He doesn't have any idea where she is. He's not even sure where they were today. I spoke with Detective Lincoln and they are going to talk with him in the morning, but I don't know that it will help.'

'OK, well, I'm really glad to hear that. Give us a call tomorrow if there's anything you need.'

'Will do. Goodnight.'

Cam hung up the telephone much more gently than the last time.

'What?' I asked.

'Carrie just sent David back to his dad in a taxi.'

'Well, thank God for small mercies.' I sighed. 'And Carrie?'

'Nothing.'

I smiled and squeezed his hand, but there really wasn't anything to say. We finished cleaning up, turned off the lights and climbed upstairs to the bedroom.

'She's got keys to the place,' Cam said, while we were changing.

'She's not going to hurt us, Cam. She's disappeared.'

'I don't think she has.'

'What, now you're getting woman's intuition feelings?'

'I just don't think it's her style.'

'David's safe, she's said her goodbyes to him and now she's gone. We will probably never see her again,' I said.

'I think she's going to turn herself in,' Cam said.

'Why would she do that?' I asked.

'To finish protecting David.'

'You mean, she'll confess so that no one will really suspect he had anything to do with it?'

'Yes, I think she will.'

'Cam, we've already proven that Carrie didn't do it and that David did.'

'What if she can come up with a reasonable explanation that proves that *she* could have done it, not him?'

'I don't know if that would work,' I said. 'Detective Lincoln is pretty certain that we've come up with the right solution.'

'But she's protecting her son,' he said. 'Think about it, Katie, if this was our child. Wouldn't you do it? Wouldn't you try anything to save your son?'

'You know what I think?' I said, sitting on the edge of the bed and pulling on the really attractive thick wool socks I had taken to wearing to bed.

'What do you think?' he asked.

'I think it's going to cost us a fortune if we have to change our locks every single month.'

Tuesday November 25

It was morning, I had been up once already, morning sickness overtaking me when it had still been dark. But I had managed to get back into bed and sneak another couple of hours sleep without disturbing Cam. I could tell it was late because the sun was shining though the window. The bonus was that I was still in bed with no one trying to wake me. I yawned and stretched like a lazy cat and found my arm blocked by a warm body lying in bed beside me. I decided not to question why he was still in bed with me, but instead I moved closer to him and wrapped my arms around his waist, snuggling into his warm back.

'Morning,' he mumbled, sleep still making his voice slightly gravelly.

'Go back to sleep,' I whispered.

'It's OK, I've just been dozing on and off for a little while.'

'How come you're still home?' I asked. 'Aren't you

supposed to be running or working or whatever else it is you morning people do?'

'Aren't you supposed to be throwing up or whatever it is you pregnant people do?'

'I did that already,' I explained. 'I just managed not to wake you up.'

'Oh, sorry I missed that. Well I'm burned out and stressed and worried sick about my cousin and I decided I needed a day off. I couldn't think of a better way to spend it than going to the doctor with you this afternoon.'

'What do you mean?'

'You have a doctor's appointment today.'

'No, I don't.'

'Well, yes, you do actually, you just don't know about it because I made it for you.'

'Are you trying to go behind my back again?'

'Katie, I swear I'm not. Well, not intentionally anyway. The doctor's office called and said you were supposed to come in soon, with me apparently, and you hadn't. So I made an appointment for you. And, since I was invited, I'll be joining you.'

'OK.'

'Don't argue with me,' he said.

'I'm not.'

'I mean it. Having a baby is serious stuff and we're not going to mess around about doctor's appointments and that kind of stuff.'

'Fine,' I agreed.

'Katie?'

'Cam?'

He rolled over on his back and looked me in the eyes.

'What's wrong with you?' he asked.

'Nothing's wrong with me. What are you talking about?'

'You're not arguing with me,' he informed me.

'Should I be?'

'Well, you usually do.'

'But I promised that I wouldn't. About this at least,' I added quickly.

'But that's not like you.'

'I know. And I have to admit it feels kind of weird to agree with you like that. But it's like you said; this baby business

181

is serious stuff. I honestly forgot about the doctor's appointment last week with everything else that was going on. But I'm not going to mess with anything about the pregnancy.'

'So you're not mad at me?' he asked.

'Nope. As a matter of fact, I should probably thank you. But that might be a bit too much of a change for me all at once,' I said with a laugh.

'Want me to make some coffee?' he asked.

'No, my stomach actually feels settled right now, so I'd rather not push it,' I said.

'So you get pregnant and I have to stop drinking coffee?' he asked.

'Well, small price to pay since you don't have to push a ten-pound baby out of a ten centimeter opening.'

'Point taken,' he said. 'I won't bring that up again.'

'Besides, it's warm and cozy here. Don't leave me just yet.'

'You've got a good point there, too.'

I cuddled in, tucked against his shoulder and both our eyes started to grow heavy again. And then my bladder sent one of those urgent messages to my brain.

'Oh no,' I moaned, extricating myself from his embrace.

'What?'

'I have to go to the bathroom. I hate this part, too.'

I climbed over him and headed for the stairs.

'Well, I'll come down and make some breakfast then,' he offered.

'Nope, I forbid it. I'll be back in a minute.'

'OK,' he said, already snuggling back under the covers.

I ran down the stairs and to the bathroom, thinking how nice it would be to have an en-suite bathroom right now. I finished up, washed my hands and was looking forward to crawling back under those covers when there was a knock on the door.

Carrie! I thought, racing to the door before thinking of anything else. She's finally come to her senses and come back. I double-checked that I had something semi-presentable on; my sweatshirt was long enough to be a dress, safe to greet company. I pulled open the door, ready to arrange my face into a gentle and compassionate look, and then realized my mistake. I tried to slam the door but found myself pushed up against the wall, wondering what had happened and how exactly I had gotten there. Stars were swimming in front of my eyes. There were two hands on my shoulders, holding me there, and angry eyes just inches from my face.

'Where the hell is she?' Hank growled at me.

'Let me go,' I hissed, trying to catch my breath and recover from the shock.

'I just don't understand why you are making this so hard,' he said, his breath warm on my cheek he was so close to me.

'I don't want to make this hard,' I whispered, all I could get out as one of his hands had moved to my neck.

'I just want to know where the hell my wife is. You know, we've been doing this for years. We have a little fight, she gets her panties in a knot and disappears for a while, and then she realizes it was all her fault and comes back and we carry on. It's a real good life we have had up to now. I don't like this new version where she disappears and I don't know where she is! And since you are the meddling bitch that convinced her to take off, I'm pretty sure you'll be able to tell me where I can find her.'

'I have no idea where Carrie is,' I told him.

'You know, I'm being nice here. I'm trying so hard to be nice and you just aren't doing anything to help me,' he said, shaking his head sadly, like I was an errant child.

'Hank, I honestly don't know where Carrie is. We're looking for her right now, too. I swear that's the truth.'

'Where the hell is my wife?' he roared, slamming my head against the wall, his elbow pushing harshly against my neck.

'Get the fuck out of my house!' I screamed back at him, struggling for breath. I knew that was my last chance. Really scared now, I tried to push him away. I didn't want to die down here with Cam sleeping peacefully upstairs.

And then he was gone and I was hanging on to the door-knob, trying to stay upright and catch my breath. Hank was lying flat on the ground at my feet. I was feeling quite proud of myself and my unknown strength and agility until I blinked away the stars swimming in front of my eyes and saw Cam on top of him, holding him down, rage in his face.

'Are you OK?' he asked me, turning from Hank for a moment.

'I'm fine,' I coughed. Physically fine, at least, I thought.

In that one moment Hank tried to slip out from under Cam,

who reacted by slamming him roughly back down into our carpet.

'You sure?' he asked, not looking away this time.

'I'm sure.'

'OK, go call 911, please.' I hated it when his voice got that quiet rage. I was never sure what he might do. 'This bastard is going to jail.'

I obeyed without argument, grabbed the phone and started dialing. Agreeing twice in one day before noon; this must be a record for me.

The police arrived quickly. They took our statements and escorted Hank off to the police station. I was never more relieved to see the cuffs go on someone and also relieved that Cam had avoided doing anything that would put him in jail for the day, too. Cam closed the front door, secured the locks and turned to me.

'You really OK?' he asked.

'I think so.'

'The baby?' he asked, his hand going over my tummy.

'Yes, if anything got hurt it was my head or my neck. He didn't hit me or kick me or anything.'

'You're sure?' he asked again.

'Yes, Cam, I'm sure,' I said turning toward the kitchen. 'Lets go make some coffee or something.'

But he grabbed my arm and pulled me roughly back into the hallway.

'What is the matter?' I asked. 'You're hurting me.'

'Funny, just what I was going to ask you. What the hell is the matter with you? Fuck, Katie, opening the door for him?'

'Well, I didn't know it was Hank,' I said. I immediately wished I could reach out into the air and pull those words right back inside of me.

'What?'

'Cam, I thought it was Carrie. I forgot to check the peephole.'

'And the three locks and the chain bolt?' he asked.

'I'm sorry.'

He just stared at me, and then dropped my arm and stormed past me into the kitchen. I turned and followed him. He was already sitting at the table, angrily flipping pages of the newspaper.

'Shall I make coffee now?' I asked timidly.

184

'Yeah, shall we have a celebratory breakfast since you're still alive and managed not to get the shit kicked out of you by that incredibly abusive man who has no problem beating up women?'

'Sure,' I joked, hoping to break his mood.

The newspaper got thrown across the kitchen, followed by an ashtray that made a small dent in the wall by the fridge.

'You think this is funny?' he roared at me.

'No, I don't,' I roared back, hormones surging and readying for a fight. 'I am a little freaked out too, right now. I'm not sure if you noticed, but it was actually me that was in danger back there.'

'Yeah, Katie, I actually noticed that. I picked up on the fact you were in danger right away. That's why I threw myself at him and pinned him to the floor while you called the police. And if you recall, I asked you if you were OK.'

'Don't yell at me.'

'What else am I supposed to do?' he asked. 'I put in extra locks, I put on chains and deadbolts. I tell you a hundred times to check the peephole and never let anyone in unless you're sure you know who they are, and what do you do the minute my back is turned? You race to the door and throw it open without checking anything.'

'I told you I thought it was Carrie,' I reminded him.

'And if it were, stopping to look in the peephole would have resulted in what?'

'I was afraid she'd get scared and leave.'

'Do you think that's about the stupidest thing you've ever said?' he asked me.

'Probably.' I gave up. 'Cam, I am sorry. I just didn't think.'

'Well, try to think, just once. And think about this. Think about how I feel when I'm at work and worrying that you'll do the same stupid thing. Think about what would have happened just now if I wasn't home. Think about anything for a change but just try thinking.'

I just stared at him. Anger still flared in my stomach, but my brain was beginning to realize that I had been really stupid and my heart was breaking that he was talking to me this way. My heart won out, as I suddenly broke into wracking sobs.

'I'm sorry,' I cried. 'I'm so sorry.'

'Katie?' he asked.

You couldn't blame the poor guy for being thrown, this wasn't exactly a normal reaction for me.

'I did do a stupid thing and I'm sorry. But please don't hate me.' I continued to sob. 'I hate it when you're mad at me.'

'Is this a trick?' he asked.

'It's the hormones,' I said. 'I can't help myself.'

He pulled me down on to his lap and wrapped his arms around me.

'I'm sorry I yelled,' he said. 'But I am just so scared of losing you.'

'And I'm scared of losing you. I don't want you to leave me because you think I'm stupid.'

'Katie, I don't think you're stupid,' he said. 'I think you do some stupid things sometimes, but I don't think you're stupid.'

'Really?' I asked.

'Really,' he promised.

'I swear I'll never ever do anything like that again,' I promised, wiping my eyes with the sleeve of my sweatshirt.

'Well, you probably will, but I'll just try and be more understanding.'

'I swear I won't,' I insisted. 'I learned my lesson. I won't even let you into the apartment without the secret password.'

'Will you at least tell me what the password is?' he asked.

'Maybe.'

'Feeling better now?'

'Yes. Cam, I'm really sorry. I don't mean to use tears as a weapon or something. I just seem to be out of control right now. These things happen and I don't know where they come from.'

'It's OK. I'm going to cut you a bunch of slack for the next little while.'

'And I am sorry about the fact that I opened the door like that. I really don't know what I was thinking.'

'I'm glad to hear you say that. Sometimes, you lead with your heart and your head can't keep up.'

'I know.'

'You want some breakfast?' he asked.

'I am kind of hungry,' I admitted.

'For anything special?'

'Oh, any sort of Cam food will do.' I smiled at him, hoping that would be enough to encourage his endeavors.

I got up and let him stand up and then took his place at the table. I tucked my feet under me and turned to the entertainment section of the newspaper, where I always started. Cam got the coffee going and brought me a cup and I sipped and read contentedly, dabbing occasionally at my eyes, until he finally sat down beside me with a breakfast plate in each hand. I happily moved the newspaper out of the way so he could put my plate in front of me and then I bit into my wonderful Gruyère and asparagus omelet. You know, if this was what marriage was like, I couldn't really understand what I had been so freaked out about. This wasn't so bad.

I understood the downside a little better later in the day when we were at the doctor's office and I was half naked on the exam table with my feet up in the stirrups.

'Everything's looking pretty good,' Brock told me, pulling down the sheet to cover me and snapping off his rubber gloves. Why did they snap those things anyway?

'And we get to do this every month from now on?' I asked, not exactly sounding thrilled.

'Yep, we have to watch that little tyke and make sure he's growing properly. And make sure mommy's doing OK, too.'

'Oh, my God, it could be a boy?' I asked, sitting up and covering up in one quick motion.

'Yes, Kate, a boy or a girl, those are your choices.'

'Well, a girl I could manage, but a boy? I don't know anything about taking care of boys.'

'I have books all about babies. I promise we'll help you figure it out.'

I took a deep breath and realized I must be sounding pretty silly.

'OK, I'm OK.'

'You sound like you're hyperventilating,' he said. 'Should I be getting my stethoscope or maybe a brown paper bag?'

'Brock, I'm fine,' I said, concentrating on breathing slowly. 'It's just been a stressful day today.'

'Why don't you get dressed and then bring Cam into my office.'

'Happily.'

I hopped down off the table and dressed quickly, then I

brought Cam from the waiting room into Brock's office. The doctor was prepared. He had duplicates of all the materials he had already given me set up and waiting. We sat in the chairs on one side of the desk while Brock sat behind his desk. Cam reached over and took my hand.

'I already have all that stuff,' I said, pointing to the pile of handouts.

'I know, but did you show any of them to Cam or did you hide them somewhere?'

'Uh, I refuse to answer on the grounds I may be incriminated,' I admitted reluctantly.

'So these are for him. I also want you to buy *What To Expect While You're Expecting* at the bookstore. It's a good book; it will take you through your pregnancy day by day and then we can talk about some of the things that are going to happen and some of the things that are probably going to freak you out, as well as some of the things you're going to need to make decisions about,' he said with a laugh.

'Like names?' I asked.

'Uh, no, you'll be making that decision all on your own,' he teased me. 'I was thinking of other things that I might need to be involved in, like where you want to deliver and what kind of delivery you want and how you feel about episiotomies and many, many other things.'

'Episiotomy?' I choked, suddenly understanding why men held their crotches every time the word vasectomy was mentioned.

'Katie, this is all way off in the future,' Cam said. 'We've got months and months to deal with this stuff, so don't go getting all worried about it now.'

'He's right,' Brock agreed. 'But you should probably look into birthing methods. I just know some of the birthing classes fill up quickly and I highly recommend first-time parents take one, especially you two.'

'Me in particular or expectant mothers in general?' I asked.

'You in particular,' Brock said pointedly.

'We'll take care of it,' Cam promised.

'This is your requisition for the lab work. We'll be doing this every month, too. And here's a specimen cup. Bring me in some morning urine next time you come.'

I took the little plastic cup and stared at it uncertainly.

188

'Just put it in this and hand it to the receptionist when you come in,' he explained, handing me a brown paper bag. 'She'll know what to do with it.'

'It'll be done,' Cam promised on my behalf.

'Now, do you two have any questions?' he asked us.

'Is it too late to change my mind?' I asked.

'I think we just need to get used to this whole idea,' Cam said. 'Having a baby is a little overwhelming right now.'

'I imagine it is. You just start reading through the stuff and you know I'm here whenever you need me.'

Cam stood up and shook hands with him. 'Thanks for everything, Brock.'

I followed suit. 'Yeah, thanks.'

'Just call me if you need me,' he repeated. 'And don't get all stressed about this.'

'I know, hundreds and hundreds of women have done this . . .'

'Well, I know hundreds of women have had this talk,' he said. 'But I was going to give you the talk about how stress doesn't do either of you any good.'

I thought about hugging him again, but stifled that feeling and tried to maintain some composure. Once again, I felt my eyes tearing up but managed to get out of the office without turning into a gushing fountain. When I was outside, I convinced Cam to take me for a decaf mocha. Gus was only a block away after all.

After our coffee, Cam let me poke my head into the theatre. There was a definite flurry of activity, but it was mostly on stage as stagehands and flying crew were everywhere, building our own little piece of Victorian England. A few actors were wandering around the lobby, doing warm-up exercises or reading lines. But there was nothing that really required my presence and I was happy to let Cam pull me out of the theatre and toward the park.

A decaf mocha, a walk in the park and an early dinner at home, just the two of us, without a single thought for anyone else, just for one night. That was how I wanted to spend my evening. And I was sure Cam would be more than happy to comply.

We made it home as the sun was setting, and Cam took his bag of groceries into the kitchen and happily started making cooking sounds. I let him be and put a CD on the stereo and sat down on the sofa with a novel. There wasn't more than two minutes of peace before the phone rang.

'I have to answer it,' I said to Cam, who was looking in my direction from the kitchen.

'I know.'

'Hello?' I said, picking up the phone and praying nothing was seriously wrong.

'Good evening, ma'am, I am calling to see if you have a few minutes of time so that I could tell you about a wonderful new product that's available in your area now.'

I started laughing.

'Ma'am?' the voice on the phone said. 'Would you like me to continue?'

'No.' I laughed and hung up the phone.

'What?' Cam asked, not sure if he should be worried or not.

'You know how you get so crazy sometimes that you forget that real life is still happening all around you?'

'Yeah.'

'It was just a telephone salesman.'

He laughed too.

Wednesday November 26

Before I went to bed, I had searched the Internet and found the name of the patron saint of pregnant women. It had been a long time since Sunday school and I was a little rusty on the saints. But I had said a prayer to Saint Anne before going to sleep, asking for a good night's sleep, a strong bladder and a settled stomach. She had seen fit to grant my requests and I had woken up rested and relaxed and ready to roll today.

It wasn't until I was in the bathroom, dealing with my first wave of morning sickness, that I thought about Carrie for the first time. I wished I knew where she was. I racked my brain while I brushed my teeth; trying to remember every conversation I'd ever had with her, everyone she'd ever mentioned. I knew the police were following up with the people she worked with, her previous neighbours, other parents from school and from the kids' extracurricular activities, but I just kept hoping that something might pop into mind. And yet it didn't.

Cam and I had decided to go into work at the same time, so I got a ride. We took a little detour and decided to stop at Alan's house and see if there was anything we could do for him and the kids. I had a big excuse worked up about how we just happened to be in the neighbourhood, even though it was a twenty-minute drive in the wrong direction, but it turned out we didn't need it. Cam parked in the driveway and rang the front doorbell. I got out of the car and peeked into the garage window. No cars in sight.

'I don't think they're home,' I said.

'Well, we didn't exactly call in advance.'

'I hope everything's OK.'

'Trust me,' Cam said. 'With my family you always hear when it's bad news. They're probably just off to school or a field trip or something really mundane.'

I wandered over to the side gate and peeked over the fence into the backyard. Nothing. I turned back toward the car when the door opened in the house next door.

'Hi there,' the handsome face said to us, but without a smile to match the pleasant tone. 'Anything I can help you folks with?'

It was him, I thought, my mystery stalker. But I kept silent.

'We were just looking for Emily and David,' Cam said, coming around the car, hand extended in greeting. 'I'm Cam, Alan's cousin.'

The neighbour took Cam's hand and shook it, but didn't offer a name in return.

'And you are?' I asked.

'Stan.' He smiled. 'I've lived next door to these people for several years and they have been good neighbours. I don't want anyone poking their nose where it don't belong and causing them any problems.'

'We're not going to cause any problems,' I assured him. 'We're as worried about the kids as you must be, Stan. Or at least as worried as you seemed on the day of the shooting.'

'Well, that's good to know you're not going to cause any

problems. And yes, I was quite upset the day of the shooting,' he said, finally offering a small smile. 'Nice to meet you finally.'

'Did you know Carrie when she lived here?' I asked.

'I moved in after they had split up,' Stan told us, and then turned back into his own yard. I noticed a face peering out of the front window through a crack in the curtains. But then the face pulled away quickly and a hand pulled the curtains back together.

'Well, maybe we can all get together for a drink next time we're in the neighbourhood,' I shouted after him as he walked back to his house. 'Why don't you have your wife call me?'

'I'm widowed,' he said.

'I'm sorry, I thought I noticed a woman in your living-room window.'

'It's the maid's day in,' he said.

'Well, you know where we live.'

'What do you mean?'

'I saw you watching my apartment a few days ago?'

'I think you're mistaken. I work downtown, perhaps you saw me around.'

'Perhaps.'

'Well, we should get together. I'll just watch for your car and poke my head over the fence the next time I see it. Mighty fine car, by the way.'

And then he disappeared back into his house.

'What was that about?' Cam asked.

'Cam, don't you think it's strange that all his curtains are closed so tightly on a beautiful sunny day like today?' I asked. 'And he's a widower and yet I saw a woman in the house?'

'Oh, my God! Call the police. A single man has a woman in his house. I guess I should probably turn myself in for being with you too?'

'I'm serious.'

'Get in the car,' he told me. 'I'm going to be late for work.'

I complied but not happily.

'Do you know who I think was in that house with him?' I said to Cam, once we were on Crowchild Trail and headed back downtown.

'The Pope?'

'Cam!'

192

'Princess Grace? I know, she didn't really die in the car accident and has been hiding out in Calgary for the past few years?'

'I think Carrie was in there.'

'You are crazy,' he said, as we crossed the river, almost hitting a Canada goose that was brave enough to try and cross the busy highway.

'I am not crazy. I think that's the man she's been seeing.'

'He said he moved in after they split,' Cam reminded me.

'But what he didn't say was that he didn't know her. He totally avoided the question. God, don't you notice anything?'

'I notice that the hormones seem to be getting to you again.'

'And I think the fumes from that ancient car of yours are addling your brain.'

'Katie, I'm sure the police have canvassed the neighbourhood. And if Carrie were hiding out in that house, they would have figured it out.'

'How?' I asked.

'What do you mean how?'

'How would they have figured it out? Would he have suddenly felt so guilty that he would have confessed to them? Did she forget she was in hiding and answer the door?'

'OK, if you're so convinced that's true, call Detective Lincoln and tell him what you think.'

'I might just do that.'

'Fine, then.'

'Fine,' I agreed, getting the last word in again.

We drove through the downtown corridor in silence. I was trying to figure out what it was about that neighbour that had set off my radar. I'm sure Cam was just hoping I was over it and had started thinking about knitting booties or something; anything other than the neighbour. He parked the car in its spot across the street from the stage door, ensuring no other cars were too close for comfort. Every single little door chip or ding was lovingly fixed almost immediately, so I don't know why he was so overprotective about it all. I thought he looked forward to them, so he had an excuse to spend an hour or so alone with his car. I guess I would just never understand this thing between him and the fish.

'See, I don't understand boys,' I said out loud, unfortunately.

'What?' Cam asked, locking the doors and holding out his hand for me.

'Nothing,' I said. 'Just the hormones talking again.'

'Is it something I said?' he asked.

'No, it's more like something you did.' I patted my stomach and winked at him.

'I think you were there at the time, too,' he said.

'Is that Ken Lincoln?' I asked, as we waited for the traffic to clear so we could jaywalk across the street to the stage door.

Cam looked where I was pointing, to a man sitting on the steps leading up to the stage door.

'I think it is,' he agreed.

'Cam, don't say anything to him,' I warned him.

'I thought—'

'I just need to think about it for another minute or two. Please don't say anything. Like you said, it's probably just my pregnant brain kicking into overdrive.'

We ran across the street to where Ken sat waiting, praying it wasn't bad news.

'Ken?' Cam said. 'What's up?'

'Are you looking for us?' I asked, more to the point.

'Yeah, I am,' he said, and then read the worried looks on both our faces. 'But it's nothing serious.'

I sat down on the step beside him and Cam leaned against the railing.

'It must be pretty serious,' I said. 'You've got a Diet Coke in your hands. Have you been drinking while on duty?'

Ken was a bit of a health nut and I had never seen him drink anything during the daytime that wasn't organic.

'OK, you caught me. It's my weakness when a case is stressing me out.'

'Diet Coke? Do you know what's in that?' I asked. 'I mean if you're going to stray, shouldn't you start small? Maybe a little frozen orange juice without the pulp or something like that? Won't the amount of sugars and chemicals in this can send your body into shock or something?'

'You're very funny. Now let's get back to the case at hand. Have either of you heard from Carrie?' he asked.

'Not a word,' Cam said, looking to me to confirm his statement and I nodded in agreement.

'Is there anyone else you can think of that she might have gone to?' he asked. 'People usually don't just disappear; they usually turn up somewhere or with someone that they know. And I just can't help thinking that she'd want to be close by to make sure her kids were OK.'

'I don't know.' I was frustrated, too, but I just wasn't sure what I should tell Ken. But since my conscience was feeling guilty, I felt I had to add something. 'I know she said she had met a man, but that is pretty much all she said. I don't know anything else about him. And she did say she didn't want him involved in any of this, so maybe he's not even a factor. Maybe she's just staying in a hotel somewhere.'

'Well, we've talked to everyone at home, at work and even at the supermarket she shopped at and you're the only one who even knew she might be seeing someone else. How do you get all this information out of people anyway?' he asked.

'It's just a natural gift I have.'

'She's a snoop,' Cam said. 'She'll ask anything and stare you down until she gets an answer.'

'Well, due to the extreme circumstances here, I'm going to ignore both of your smart-ass comments. But I don't think she would be too far away from her kids, either.'

'No, you're right,' Cam agreed with me.

God, I wanted a cigarette. I could think so much more clearly with a cigarette. Or maybe it was thinking about having a cigarette that was clouding my mind so badly.

'Ken, have you—' I stopped. I knew I should say something but I couldn't do it.

'What?' they both said, turning to me in unison.

'What I mean is, I have an idea that might just bring her out,' I said, my mind darting around at warp speed to come up with a plan that didn't take too much explanation and that these two would buy into.

'What?' Ken asked, finishing his Coke and then tossing the can in the recycling bin.

What would bring Carrie out and keep Ken from asking me too many questions? And then it appeared, like a flash from my muse.

'Take David in for questioning,' I said proudly.

'What?' Ken asked.

'Take David in for questioning,' I repeated.

'What are you talking about?' Cam asked.

'No, seriously. We all think she's somewhere close enough that she knows what's going on with the kids. I mean, the whole reason she's doing this is to protect David. So if you take him in for questioning, she might think he was about to get charged and come racing out to save him. She'd feel like she'd have to come out and confess or something, to get him off the hook.'

'It's a good idea, Kate,' Ken admitted. 'But I can't just haul a kid in for questioning. There are very strict rules about how we handle kids.'

'But what if we could get his father to agree?' I asked.

'Katie?' Cam cautioned me. 'Weren't we going to leave this up to Ken to handle?'

'Yeah, whatever.' I brushed him off and turned back to Ken. 'What if we get David's father to agree to let you pretend to take David into the police station. And you don't really have to question him. Maybe he just spends a nice long afternoon at the Police Interpretive Centre and Museum? And how about if he gets there in the back seat of a police car as a special treat? What's important is that, if Carrie is watching, she thinks that David is being investigated and charged.'

'You think you can get the father to agree?' Ken asked.

'No,' Cam said.

'Yes,' I said. 'Come on, Cam, we all want the same thing. We want Carrie out in the open, back with us where we can get this all straightened out. And we want Hank to leave us alone and we want this whole thing finished and behind us. Don't you think this would work?'

'Yes, I think it might work,' he allowed. 'But I think it gets you right back in the middle again. And that is where you promised me you would not go again.'

'How?' I asked, feeling my ire rise.

'Well, it's you that's going to Alan and telling him all about this. And you who talks him into it when he won't agree to it at first? I'm guessing it will be you and me babysitting Emily while they are off on this adventure. No matter what you say, all the arrows point back to you. And Hank has already taken one round out of you. And what about Carrie? Don't you think she might be getting a little desperate herself?'

'Ken, tell him it's safe,' I instructed him. 'Tell him that nobody is going to think I'm involved in this.'

'I can't,' Ken said. 'I can't guarantee any of that. Especially since the other thing I need to tell you is that Hank is out of jail.'

'What?' I asked. 'When did that happen?'

'He broke into our home,' Cam said.

'Well, really you let him in,' Ken explained. 'But, either way, his lawyer got him out and apparently Hank's really pissed off. So you need to be very careful.'

'I always am,' I said.

Cam actually laughed out loud at that one but held his tongue for now. I was pretty sure I would hear something later, however.

'Well, let's leave it at this for now,' Ken said. 'Your idea might work but I won't do anything without the full cooperation of the father. If you happen to run into him and get anything resembling his cooperation, just give me a call.'

'No guarantees,' Cam said. 'We probably won't see him for another week or so.'

'But we'll try,' I promised, knowing I could arrange it.

'And Cam, you'll keep an eye out for Hank? Maybe check Kate's office and stuff. You don't really have the best security in this building from what I've seen so far.'

'No problems there,' Cam said. 'But if he comes after her again, I cannot guarantee that I will have the self-control I had the first time.'

'I understand,' Ken said. 'But I do have to inform you that self-defense must be of an equal force as the attack. Otherwise, you're going to be the one winding up in jail.'

'I know,' Cam said. 'Criminal justice seems to mean justice for the criminals, not the victims.'

'I'm not going to debate the penal system with you,' Ken said diplomatically. 'Especially since I'm on duty right now. But I am going to remind you that if you wind up in jail, there will be no one here to protect Kate.'

'I understand,' Cam said.

'I've got to get going,' Ken said. 'Just call me if anything comes up.'

197

Ken pulled himself up and headed for Grounds Zero.

'What, first you had a Coke and now you're having coffee?' I called after him.

'Just going to have a talk with Gus,' Ken said. 'He seems to have a lot of information that no one else around here has. I figured it couldn't hurt to talk to him.'

Cam helped me up and we headed for my office. True to his word, he led the way all the way up and checked out the office, the washrooms, the ushers' changing room and the fire escapes. When all was clear and I had the coffee pot on, we sat down, each of us on either side of my desk.

'I don't want you to do this, Katie,' he said.

I picked up the phone and started dialing.

'Cam, I need this whole thing with Carrie and Hank to be over. Finished and done and all tied up. We have other stuff we should be dealing with right now, don't you think?'

'Straight to the guilt?' he asked. 'Are we going to do nine months of this? Of you bringing up the pregnancy every time you want me to do something? Or crying?'

'I thought you were going to cut me some slack?' I asked. 'I may actively choose to use guilt on you of my own free will, but the crying is something I cannot control. I thought you said you understood all these hormone things.'

'Well, maybe I'm getting a little tired of it already.'

'You're not tired of it,' I said. 'You're just using guilt right back at me. Making me feel guilty and making me think that I'm putting the baby at risk.'

'I saw you with Hank yesterday morning, Katie, and that scared me.'

'And we're going to go back over all that again?' I asked, still holding the phone.

'Are you going to keep using the baby to get your way?' he asked.

'Probably,' I admitted, a twinkle in my eye. 'Especially if it works.'

'It works,' he said. 'You're right. Let's do this and then for the next nine months you promise me you will keep your nose out of everything except for your own business.'

'I promise. But only if I'm allowed situational withdrawal.'

'What the hell is that supposed to mean?'

'Well, if something extraordinary happens, I can't be expected to keep my promise, can I?'

'Yes, you can.'

'Cam, you just don't understand—' I began, but then someone answered the phone. I had lost track of how many times I had let it ring. 'Hello? Alan? Hi, it's Kate Carpenter calling. Cam and I were wondering when we could come over and have a chat with you about a little idea we have.'

'What idea?' he asked me.

'Well, it's something to do with trying to bring Carrie out into the open. We met with Detective Lincoln today and sort of had a bit of an idea that might work.'

'Uh huh.'

'I would really prefer to do this in person, Alan. Just tell me where and when we can meet and we'll be there.'

'Tomorrow morning,' he suggested. 'How about the Starbucks on Twelfth Avenue and Eighth Street?'

'One of my favourite places,' I agreed. 'Ten thirty OK with you?'

'That'll be fine. Look, can you just tell me if everything's all right?' he asked.

'Alan, one thing I've learned from your side of the family is that if it were bad news you wouldn't have to wait for it,' I said, paraphrasing Cam.

'OK, I can live with that. I'll see you tomorrow.'

Cam looked at me, shaking his head slowly as I hung up the phone.

'Here we go again,' he said.

'Here we go again,' I said with a smile.

'Why are you smiling?' he asked. 'This isn't funny, you know? I don't want you taking this lightly.'

'I'm not. I just had a thought, though.'

'Another one?'

'Cam,' I warned him.

'What?' he asked, kindly avoiding any further puns available to him.

'What about Nora?'

'Nora who?'

'Nora, if it's a girl.'

For a minute he just stared blankly at me and then a smile broke across his face, too.

'And her middle name could be Beth, I've always liked Beth or Becky . . .'

'Or Liza with a "z",' Graham added, coming into the office and tossing his bag into the corner. Then he saw the look on both our faces. 'Am I treading in territory where I don't belong?'

'Uh, yes,' I said.

'You want me to go and check the theatre or something that doesn't involve my being here in this room right now?' Graham asked.

'No,' Cam answered for me. 'I've got to get to work, you don't have to leave.'

I stood up and kissed Cam on the cheek.

'See you later.'

'I'll try to come up later,' he said. 'But if I don't, do you need a ride home?'

'I'll get Scott to drive me,' I said. 'I don't really know when we're going to be done here tonight.'

'And walk you up,' Cam said.

'Yes, and walk me up. I'll tell him the whole sordid story and I'm sure he won't mind. What time do you think you'll get home?'

'I'll be home around three o'clock. Don't wait up for me.'

'Even if I tried, I don't think I'd be able to.'

'Bye, Graham,' Cam called, before heading down the hallway.

'Sordid details?' Graham asked.

'Carrie's husband just came over for a little visit yesterday,' I said, hoping that would be enough to keep him happy.

'What?' Graham asked. 'What happened?'

'Nothing, really. He was arrested but Detective Lincoln has just let us know that he was released. So Cam's a little concerned that he might come looking for me or something.'

'Well, I think that's a pretty valid concern,' Graham said. 'Should you even be here?'

'Yes. I am not going to let him scare me. Otherwise he's won, hasn't he?'

'Well, I think I should at least talk to the security desk and they can keep a look out for him.'

'I wouldn't say no to that idea,' I told him.

'You wouldn't?' he asked, eyebrows high with disbelief.

'It's like Cam keeps reminding me, I'm not just looking out for myself anymore, am I?'

'That's right, we can't forget baby Liza now, can we?' Graham smiled, hoping I would see the humour.

'Liza?' I heard Martha say. 'Have we picked out a name already?'

I sat back in my chair, a heavy sigh escaping.

'No, actually Graham came up with it,' I explained.

'Liza like in Minnelli?' Charlotte asked, hanging up her coat and helping herself to a coffee.

'Like Elizabeth,' Graham said.

'No, Cam said Beth, you're the one that made that interpretation. So does anyone really care that I don't want to talk about this right now?' I asked.

'Oh, no, dear,' Martha said, sitting down beside Charlotte with her own coffee. 'It's like a wedding. This really has nothing to do with you and more to do with everyone else.'

'We get to talk about you and touch your tummy and ask you questions that we would never think of asking you before,' Charlotte added.

'Like what?' I asked.

'Oh, about hemorrhoids and varicose veins and urinary frequency,' Martha said with a giggle.

'Goodie.'

'And then we get to suggest names and nicknames and tell you all sorts of horror stories about all our friends who were in labour for three or four days before they finally delivered their children.'

'Those are the best,' Martha agreed.

'And afterwards,' Charlotte said. 'You'll be one of us. You'll be telling everyone about your episiotomy and your stretch marks and how your breasts leak at the sound of an infant crying—'

'I will never, ever talk about those kinds of things with anyone other than my doctor,' I promised.

'Oh, you'll see. After a day or two in the hospital, you'll be lifting your dress for the TV repairman.'

'Never,' I said. 'And I never want to talk about any of these things with you again.'

'Have you thought about Jane?' Charlotte asked. 'I almost called my second daughter Jane.'

'It's one of those good solid old English names,' Martha agreed.

I pushed myself away from my desk and headed for the theatre.

'I'm going somewhere and not telling any of you where I'm going. I'll be back when you're all ready to talk about anything else. Try and be useful until then, OK? By the way, we had all agreed we weren't going to talk about the pregnancy yet.'

'If you and Cam were to get married, that might take a little heat off it,' Charlotte suggested.

'There are twenty-five thousand Christmas ornaments to unpack and hang. Get to work.'

'We could spend countless hours helping you plan your wedding and not talk about the baby so much.'

I screamed and then turned and ran. Although I didn't know exactly where I was running to, since there was pretty much no one in this entire complex who didn't know all about this by now. And, like my faithful staff, no one seemed to be shy to talk about these things.

I was asleep when Cam got home, but I woke up as he was getting undressed and climbed in bed beside me.

'Morning,' I joked.

'I didn't mean to wake you up,' he apologized, getting under the covers and wrapping me in his arms.

'Oh, you're cold.'

'It's cold out. It's almost December, you know?'

'Well, I'm sure once you warm up you will prove to be worth the wait,' I said, snuggling into him.'

'Any problems getting home tonight?' he asked.

'No, Scott was busy so I just hitchhiked home and had old man Johnson down the hall check the apartment for me. He didn't have enough strength to pull his oxygen canister into the loft to check it out but he called up and asked if anyone was up here waiting to kill me.'

'What?' he asked, half sitting up in bed and looking down at me. 'You'd better be joking.'

'I am. Scott and Trevor both drove me home and checked every nook and cranny in this place before they would leave me in peace.'

202

'Good.'

'By the way, they found your porn collection.'

'You are just a laugh a minute for someone who should be sleeping,' he said.

'I know, I'm hot.'

'Goodnight, Katie.' He kissed me. 'By the way, I would like you to know how much I appreciate that you actually agreed with me a couple of times today.'

'Hey, it was my pleasure. You'd best just not get too used to it, though,' I said. 'It's not real easy for me.'

'I know, we'll keep working on it.'

Thursday November 27

W hen the alarm rang that morning, I was already awake. I'd been awake for an hour or so. Mind you, the alarm was set for eight o'clock, like a household that worked evenings, not six o'clock like the regular working world. But I was excited. We'd be meeting with Alan today and I liked forward momentum. I finally felt like we were doing something, rather than just sitting around, waiting and stagnating. But my boyfriend, lying lovingly next to me in bed, was never quite as keen in these adventures as I seemed to be. So I continued to pretend I was asleep. I carefully monitored my breathing and my movements and forced my eyes to stay closed. I snuggled up tightly against him, as he turned the alarm off and made one of those little half-asleep and half-awake noises. It would be better if he didn't realize how excited I was about all this. Better for me, at least.

'Give it up, Katie. I know you've been awake for at least an hour.'

Or I could just give up the pretense and run for the shower, which I did. Trying to be caring and considerate, however, I did stop in the kitchen long enough to get the coffee going before I got in the shower. And maybe this morning sickness was all in my head, because this morning I seemed to be just fine. I guess I had more important things on my mind.

When I came out of the shower, Cam was sitting at the table with the newspaper and a coffee.

He patted the chair beside him, 'Care to join me for breakfast?' he asked.

'I should get dressed.'

'Katie, we're not meeting him for two more hours and the Starbucks is only ten minutes away. I think you have time to have a quick coffee and a little something to eat.'

I begrudgingly sat down beside him and he poured me a coffee.

'Are you drinking decaf?' I asked.

'It's the least I could do, join you in your suffering, don't you think?' He smiled.

'Yes, I do think. Especially since I pointed that out to you a couple of days ago.'

'Can't let me just be chivalrous, can you?'

'Nope, especially since you caused this whole problem.'

'Right, I keep forgetting that part.'

'Have you quit smoking, too?' I asked.

'Pretty much.'

'Then how come you're not as grumpy as me?'

'Because I've been eating potato chips like they're going out of style while hiding out in my office. It seems to help me but I hear it's not recommended for pregnant women.'

'Nothing seems to be recommended for pregnant women.'

'I know, sweetie. They say it's all worth it in the end.'

'So I keep hearing.'

He kissed my forehead.

'It's going to take a lot more than that to make me feel better,' I told him.

'How about breakfast?' he asked, pushing himself away from the table and checking out the fridge. 'What do you feel like today?'   ·

'Oh, could I please start with a tall glass of milk?' I asked.

'It would be my pleasure,' he said, pouring one for me and ignoring my sarcasm. 'And to finish off with, Your Highness?'

'Are you really giving me a choice or do you have this all planned out already?' I asked.

'OK, you got me,' he admitted. He pulled out a plate from the fridge with half a melon, filled with cottage cheese and topped with strawberries. There was also a wholewheat bagel topped with a slice of cheese.

'Do you want your bagel grilled or cold and with a little mayo?' he asked.

'Well, at least I get a bit of a choice.'

'Which will it be?' he asked, waiting by the toaster oven.

'Like that is just fine with me. Cam, do you have some sort of chart going to ensure I get all my food groups?' I asked suspiciously. At least he put an identical plate in front of himself.

'I keep it all in my head.'

'Yeah, I don't really trust you on this, you know? I'm pretty sure I'll stumble across a notebook or chart or spreadsheet eventually.'

'I know. But give it a couple of weeks and just wait and see how good you feel. Besides, did you see the weight chart in the book your doctor gave us?'

'You've started reading that already?' I asked, feeling guilty.

'Of course. Anyway, there are very specific weight gain goals for you, so this isn't just an eating free-for-all.'

'Well, I am eating for two, you know.'

'No, right now you're eating for about one and one one-hundredth.'

'Very funny.' But I was enjoying the fresh fruit.

'So you really think Alan is going to agree to do this?' he asked me.

'I really do. I mean, just think about it for a minute. He's pretty much in the same position as we are. Nothing is happening, the kids are in limbo, he's probably afraid to let them out in case Carrie tries to kidnap them or something. This way, at least we're trying to do something to bring some closure to this.'

'I hope you're right,' he said.

'I think I am. Cam, I know that the last time I thought I was right I almost got shot—'

'No, you did get shot,' he reminded me.

'A flesh wound.'

'Semantics! Blood was flowing.'

'Blood was oozing, not flowing. And that's not the point I'm trying to make here.'

'OK, make your point.'

'Well, I just was going to admit that maybe my timing is a little off, but my instincts are usually right.'

'Katie, it doesn't matter if your instincts are right if you wind up dead.'

'But see, that's the great thing, I'm not dead!' I smiled triumphantly. He didn't.

'Yet.'

'Well, honestly, right now my biggest fear is you killing me because I'm driving you crazy. But look, this time I'm doing it right. I checked with Detective Lincoln, we're involving the entire police force and I won't be anywhere near the scene.'

'You know, Katie, it always sounds so good when you say it, but somehow when we're actually doing it, it just never seems to work out that way.'

'Cam, sweetie,' I said, wrapping my arms around him. 'Go have a shower. I'll do the dishes.'

He gave me a dirty look but did head for the bathroom. I was happy to do the dishes when it involved two plates and a couple of coffee cups. I was tempted to put them in the dishwasher, but I knew that really would make him crazy. He figured that if there were only a couple of dishes you might as well wash them. That was not my attitude toward the dish-washer but, since I was trying to keep him happy just now, I washed the dishes. I only had to keep him happy for another couple of hours. I managed to take care of the dishes just as the phone rang.

'Hello?'

'Hello, pregnant lady,' Sam chuckled. 'How are things in incubation land?'

'Well, I have to admit things are a little easier since Cam found out.'

'I hate to say I told you so—' she began.

'So don't.'

'What are you up to today? I've got a couple of hours open and I think I could manage to fit you in.'

'Oh, today's not good, Sam,' I said. 'We're kind of doing a thing.'

'A thing?'

'We're kind of working on a plan to get Carrie out into the open and we're just on our way to have coffee with her ex-husband.'

'When you say "we", are you using the royal we or does Cam really know about this?' she asked me.

'Cam really knows about this.'

'Kate . . .'

'I swear. As does Detective Lincoln and probably the whole police department. I swear, Sam, I am doing this the right way this time.'

'OK, well, are you going to be all day with him?'

'No, after we're finished we're setting up Christmas in the lobby at the theatre and it's taking forever,' I explained. 'My plan was to have it mostly done by now but we've barely got the upper lobby done.'

'Well, how about if I drop by with muffins for a coffee-break later?' she asked.

'I'm pretty sure we would all be amenable to that,' I laughed. 'You know how my ushers feel about your food.'

'I'm just about ready,' Cam said, poking his head out of the bathroom door. 'Who's on the phone?'

'It's Sam,' I said and then turned back to my conversation. 'I'll see you later this afternoon and tell you how everything went, OK?'

'Bye.'

So for once I succeeded in keeping everyone happy. My guy was happy, my friend was happy and we were dressed and at Starbucks, sipping coffee, on time and with no stress. I'd never realized that you could get almost anything in decaf. I didn't know why you would want to, unless you were in my situation, but at least I could still get the flavour I was craving. I sipped a caramel macchiato while Cam had a full strength, just because he could. I could almost feel the caffeine surging through his veins. And we waited quietly for Alan to appear. Cam had grabbed a newspaper and I was kind of reading it upside down, which is why neither of us noticed when Alan finally walked in.

'Cam,' he called out, striding quickly across the floor.

'Alan.' Cam smiled, standing up and shaking hands with him.

'Kate?' he asked, shaking my hand, too.

'It's me,' I smiled up at him. 'Nice to see you again. Have a seat, Alan.'

'I'm just going to grab a coffee. I don't seem to be sleeping well right now and I think it might help.'

'You have a seat,' Cam offered. 'I'll get you an Americano and you'll be feeling better in no time.'

'Thanks,' Alan said, taking him up on his offer and having a seat beside me.

'So how are the kids doing?' I asked.

'The kids are fine, all things considered. And as much as I could usually talk about my kids all day long, I have to tell you that I'm really curious about why you've asked to see me today.'

'Yeah, I understand that. Have you been in touch with Detective Lincoln recently?' I asked.

'Yes, he was over a few days ago. He told me he thought David might have been in the room when the shooting happened and they wanted to take his clothes for testing.'

'Yeah, I knew about that,' I admitted.

'I don't know what's up with Carrie. I mean, I knew she and Hank had some problems but I just can't believe what she's put them through all these years. And now this.'

'I don't understand either.' I was trying hard to stay noncommittal. 'But I don't know any of the history. Have you heard anything from Carrie? Or has she called the kids?'

'No and, if I did, I'd turn her over to the police in a second. This whole thing is crazy and it needs to end. The kids are in limbo, we're going to counseling, but not knowing where their mother is is hard for them.'

'I'm sure it is. I'm glad you feel that way, though, about trying to bring some closure to this situation. We really feel the same way and that's what brings us all here today, I guess.'

'So have you told him?' Cam asked, sitting back down at the table and setting a coffee in front of Alan.

'I was just about to.'

'And I'm anxious to hear about it.' Alan added.

'OK. We saw Detective Lincoln yesterday and we all think that Carrie is around somewhere close enough to keep watch on the kids. So I had this crazy idea that if she saw David being taken in by the police she might come out of hiding to try to rescue him.'

'That's a very good idea,' Alan said. 'But I'm not going to have David taken into police custody just to entice his mother out of hiding. He's fragile enough right now.'

'I know he's having a rough time right now. And I didn't mean that he would really be arrested, just that it would look like it to someone watching from the outside.'

'We could tell David that the police department is giving him a special day because of what he has been through or something,' Cam said.

'Right,' I added. 'And that he's getting a ride in a police car. And they could take him down to the police station, but the two of you could actually spend the day at the Police Museum and Interpretative Centre. Carrie would never know. She would just think that he had been taken away in a police car and was being interrogated. Alan, I really think this might be enough to bring her back out into the open, don't you?'

'It might be,' he agreed. 'But I need to think about it. The kids have been through a lot and I don't want to do anything that might upset them any further, you know?'

I was disappointed. I had wanted him to say 'yes, great idea, let's do it.' Patience wasn't my virtue. And this wasn't Cam, who I could bully and cajole and tease and flirt with until he would do anything for me. So I had no choice but to honour Alan's decision.

'I totally understand,' I said.

'Me, too,' Cam said. 'Look, why don't you give us a call if you decide you want to give it a try. We can get in touch with Detective Lincoln and he will arrange everything. We can look after Emily for you, too, if you like.'

'Let me just think about it,' he said. 'I promise I'll give you a call in a couple of days for sure.'

A couple of days, I thought, I can't wait that long. But out loud I managed to say, 'That would be great.'

'OK, well, I hate to drink and run, but I have to get back to the office.'

'No problem,' Cam said. 'I should be getting back to work myself, too.'

The men shook hands and then Alan trotted off down the street. Cam sat back down to finish his coffee.

'Oh, Katie, it's not the end of the world,' he said, noticing the disappointment on my face.

'What do you mean?' I asked.

'That look on your face. You don't like it when you don't get your own way, do you?'

'No. Does anybody?' I asked. 'But am I that obvious?'

'You are to me,' he admitted.

'There goes my feminine mystique.'

'Look, Alan will decide yes or he'll decide no. Either way, you have now officially done all you can. Now drink up your coffee and let's get to work.'

'Can't I take my coffee with me?'

'You know the rules about my car. No food or drink.'

'What are you going to do when we have a baby?' I asked. 'No bottles for the little one, either?'

'I guess I may have to rethink those rules a bit, huh?'

'Can we even put a car seat in your car?' I asked. 'Doesn't there have to be a sort of bolt or something to attach it to?'

'You can retro-fit those,' he explained. 'I've checked that out.'

'You have?'

'Yes, I have.'

'I should have known that.'

I finished my coffee and tossed it into the garbage, following him out on to the street and settling into the car.

'So I think you'd better let me start drinking in the car, just so you can get used to the whole idea.'

'Yeah, well, when you start drinking your coffee out of a baby's bottle, then we'll discuss it.'

'Can we Scotchguard the upholstery?' I asked.

'Not today.'

Cam dropped me at the theatre door and then parked the car and disappeared into the building himself. I let myself into the theatre and found Graham was already in the lobby, setting up a Christmas tree and humming something about Good King Wenceslas. I dropped my stuff in my office and then joined him in the lobby, sitting on the floor with a box of ornaments in front of me, painstakingly unwrapping them one by one from their tissue-paper nests.

'This is such a good idea,' I said, trying to put a smile on my face.

'What, the ornaments?' Graham asked.

'Yeah.'

'They suck. Do you know how long it took us to unpack the first five cases yesterday?'

'A long time?'

'A very long time.'

'But its going to be such a good fundraiser,' I said. 'People get to buy an ornament and hang it on one of the trees and all the money goes to charity.'

'That part is a great idea,' Graham said. 'The fact that there are so many of them, individually wrapped, and that they are the most delicate little glass baubles I have ever seen, that's the part that sucks.'

'I was beginning to think that myself,' I said. 'But they were donated for this fundraiser so we have to be grateful for that.'

'Not me. I'm just setting up the trees and pounding nails, the manly things. You and the other womenfolk can take care of all that other stuff.'

'That's wishful thinking there, Graham.'

'Not really. I know you called Martha and Charlotte to come in this afternoon to help us.'

'And Sam,' I added.

'Did I hear my name?' I heard from the lower lobby.

'We're up here,' I answered.

'Did you bring food?' Graham called down the stairs to her.

'I brought food,' Sam said, joining us. 'But I'm not going to give you a single muffin until you bring me down a fresh coffee. Two sugars and cream, please.'

'Boss?' he asked.

'I'm good,' I said, holding up my go-cup.

Graham raced up the stairs to my office. Sam joined me on the floor and started unwrapping ornaments with me.

'How many of these have you got?' she asked, looking around at the boxes littering the lobby.

'Twenty-five thousand, I think.'

'All right. One of those brilliant ideas from the admin offices, I'm assuming.'

'It's a great fundraiser,' was all I had to say.

'So, how'd it go with what's-his-face?'

'What's-his-face? You mean Alan?' I asked.

'Carrie's ex?' Sam confirmed. 'Or ex-ex? These modern relationships get so confusing.'

'Yep, Carrie's first husband and father of her children.'

'So, how did it go?' she asked.

'Not great,' I admitted. 'He wanted to think about it for a couple of days.'

'Aw, I'm sorry,' Sam said. 'It would have been nice to get this all over with.'

'Yeah, it would have. But now it's back to plan B, I guess.'

'What's plan B?' Sam asked.

'Letting the police sort this all out and trying to get used to the whole baby idea.'

'That's not a bad thing, you know.'

'I know. And I'm sure I'll believe it eventually,' I said. 'Now, what kind of muffins did you bring with you today?'

The day had been long and unrewarding. I knew it was because I was feeling down since we'd met with Alan. And probably because I had another 10,000 ornaments left to unpack. I had been dragging my feet all day at the theatre, letting Graham do everything while I spent most of the afternoon and evening on the floor, where I had started out the day, and grumbling at anyone who crossed my path. The one good thing about this mood was that not a soul mentioned the word baby all day long.

Cam and I drove home in silence, which I think was mostly for his own protection. He was good at sensing my moods. We did walk hand in hand down the hall to the apartment, my little peace offering to him. He opened the apartment door and let me go first.

'You going to be this quiet all night long?' he asked.

'Maybe.'

'Well, I'm going to make you a cup of tea and I think we should watch a movie or something.'

'Fine.'

'Would you pick out the movie or should I just do everything?' he asked, a little sarcastically, but I let it pass.

I went into the living room while Cam got the kettle boiling. I picked something that I wasn't totally interested in, and put it in the DVD player. Then I sat on the couch and waited for Cam. He brought in two steaming mugs and a plate of cookies and set it all down on the coffee table.

'Hey, Katie, there's a message on the answering machine,' he said.

I hadn't even thought to interrupt my little pity-party and check the machine. So I quickly turned around and pushed 'play'.

'Hi, guys, it's Alan. Look, I've been thinking about this all day and I really don't know if your idea is the best idea in the world, but I do think I'd like to give it a try. This waiting is making me crazy. Just give me a call after you've talked to Detective Lincoln and let me know what we're going to do. And thanks for everything.'

'Happier now?' Cam asked me.

'Totally.' I smiled at him. 'As a matter of fact, let's just forget about the movie and celebrate, OK?'

Friday November 28

The funny thing is, I was so excited that this big plan of mine was actually coming to fruition and yet, after my romantic interlude with Cam the night before, I had fallen asleep contentedly and not even thought to call Detective Lincoln and leave him a voice mail letting him know that Alan had agreed. I realized I should do that and began trying to climb over Cam to get to the phone, when he grabbed me and pulled me back into bed,

'Where are you going in such a hurry?' he asked.

'I wanted to call Ken and tell him Alan had agreed to my little plan,' I said. 'I meant to leave a message on his voice mail last night but you distracted me.'

'Me?' he asked. 'I don't think it was me that ripped the buttons off my shirt.'

'Well, no, I guess it wasn't.' I blushed. 'But let me go and call Ken now, please.'

'You don't want to try and repeat last night's performance?' he asked, nibbling on my shoulder.

213

'Well . . .' I thought for a moment, feeling a tingling beginning in my loins. 'No!'

I pushed away from him.

'What?' he asked, shocked.

'You're trying to trick me.'

'What are you talking about?'

'I've heard about this. A woman's sex drive can increase when she's pregnant. And you're trying to take advantage of that and trick me into not calling Ken.'

'Hey, are you telling me you didn't enjoy last night?' he asked.

'Well, no . . .' I hesitated. 'See, there you go again, trying to trick me.' I climbed out around the foot of the bed, managing to get out safely, and hurried down the stairs to phone Ken.

'Detective Lincoln,' he answered.

'Ken, hi. It's Kate Carpenter.'

'Hi, Kate. Tell me you have good news for me today. Tell me Carrie is sitting in your living room and is ready to turn herself in.'

'Sorry, Ken,' I laughed. 'But Alan, the kids' father, has agreed to try my little plan and see if we can draw Carrie out.'

'Oh, that's great,' Ken said. 'Not my first choice but it will do. What's Alan's phone number?'

'Why don't you just tell me what you want to do and I'll give him a call and let him know?' I asked.

'Kate.'

'I don't mind helping out, Ken. These people are like my in-laws, you know.'

'I know that,' he told me. 'His number?'

'Five five five, two one two five.'

'Thank you.'

'Hey, don't hang up on me.'

'Why, do you have something else for me?' he asked.

'No, I just wanted to know when you're planning on doing this.'

'None of your business.'

'What?'

'Kate, how many times do we have to have this talk about you staying out of police business? I mean, do I try and run your theatre for you?'

'No,' I sighed. 'But it was my idea.'

214

'That is not the point.'

'Fine.' I gave in.

'OK, that's better. So anything else?'

'Would it help if I begged?' I tried.

'OK, OK. Be at Alan's house at noon today. Then you can find out what's going on at the same time as everyone else.'

'Thanks, Ken.'

'But you're not taking part in anything. I will lock you up and throw away the key if you cause me any trouble. Do we understand each other?' he threatened me.

'We totally understand each other,' I promised, and it was true. I did understand his parameters, I just didn't know if I could live within them.

'Good. I'll see you later.'

I hung up the phone and went into the kitchen to get the coffee started. I figured it wouldn't hurt to make Cam breakfast for a change and try to keep him off my back about this, too. Of course, my bowl of cereal, glass of frozen orange juice and toast with peanut butter wasn't quite up to his standards, but it's the thought that counts, right? I sure hoped so, as I climbed the stairs with a tray. Cam smiled when he saw my head come up the stairs but it turned into a frown when he saw me carrying a breakfast tray.

'What are you doing?' he asked.

'I brought you breakfast in bed,' I tried.

'You never bring me breakfast. As a matter of fact, I don't know if you've ever brought me food that wasn't take-out. What have you got us into?'

'Cam, can't I ever do something nice for you without you getting suspicious?'

'Katie, you certainly can but I don't believe you ever have,' he pointed out. 'Have you this time?'

'Well, no,' I admitted, crossing the room and putting the tray on his lap. 'We're going to meet Ken at Alan's house at noon, OK?'

He just looked at me.

'I'm just going to grab a quick shower while you have breakfast.'

'Aren't you even going to wait to hear what I have to say?'

'Cam, I could almost write out this scene by now. You're

going to say it's too dangerous and I should forget it, I'm going to argue and threaten to do it with or without you and then eventually you'll come along so that you can at least try to protect me. Can't we just skip that and get to the ending?'

'Why do you always have to be involved in these things?' he asked. 'Why do you have to know what's going on with everyone and always be right in the middle of it?'

'Because I worry about everyone. And I just don't feel like anyone will take care of things if I'm not checking up on them, you know?'

'Go have your shower.' He grudgingly gave into me.

'Thank you.' I tried not to smile too big at my victory.

'But, Katie?'

'Yeah?' I stopped half way down the stairs.

'This is something we have to work out, OK?'

'OK,' I admitted, knowing I couldn't win all the time. I was finding it easier to agree now that a baby was coming and I was already planning on severely curtailing my snooping activities.

We showered and dressed and cleaned up breakfast, which wasn't quite so hard since the dishwasher was working again, so I loaded our dishes in there despite Cam's protests that it would be just as easy to wash them by hand. I grabbed my coat and bag and we were off to Alan's house. Being downtown people, we both got a little turned around in the suburbs and Ranchlands was one of those suburbs where every street was named Ranch something and every house looked the same, making it harder to find your way. Eventually, we found our way back to Alan's house. Ken Lincoln pulled up right behind us.

'Right on time, I see,' Ken said with a smile.

'Can't let you have all the fun now, can I?'

'This isn't about having fun, remember?'

'I know, it's about trying to arrest my cousin,' Cam reminded us.

'It's about trying to get your cousin to turn herself in so we can just straighten all this out,' Ken said.

'Let's just do it, not argue about it.' I suggested, moving up the driveway and ringing the doorbell.

Alan opened the door and let us all in. Emily was playing at the neighbour's house, where she was going to stay for the afternoon. David was playing in the backyard, where he could be kept out of the way while Alan discussed the plan with Ken Lincoln. Alan shepherded us into the living room, where everyone had a seat and an uncomfortable silence overwhelmed us.

'So,' I said. 'Should we start with small talk or cut to the chase?'

'I'd like to cut to the chase. I'm not really comfortable with all of this,' Alan said.

'Fine,' Ken said. 'Here's what I'm thinking. I can come back here tomorrow around nine o'clock. I will have a marked police car waiting down the street; he'll come when I call him, when you and your son are ready. I thought we could tell your son that he was getting a special award for being so brave through all this and he was going to get a ride in a real police car and a tour of the station. We'll head out of here with handcuffs and sirens blaring.'

'Handcuffs?' Alan asked.

'I know, we wouldn't normally do that to someone of his age. But if we're going to pull off this charade, we have to go all the way. And, besides, boys love that kind of stuff. As soon as we get out of the neighbourhood we'll take them off and let him play with the siren. He'll be fine.'

'And then?' Alan asked.

'We'll take him downtown, in through the street entrance and the booking desk and then we'll take him to the police museum through an inside entrance. Kids are usually good for about four hours there, if they go through all the forensics stuff. We'll have a tour guide waiting, just to keep him occupied. And then we'll hope that Carrie turns up.'

'And if she doesn't?' Alan asked.

'Then later in the afternoon, Cam will show up and take you all home,' Ken said.

'Easy as pie,' I added.

'It is an easy plan,' Ken said. 'But there is still an element of danger. We don't know what Carrie's state of mind is right now and we don't know what she might do. I plan to keep a patrol car in the neighbourhood all night long.'

'But it might bring her out?' Alan asked.

'If her goal here is to protect David, then she might turn up.'

'And then this will all be over,' he said. 'I think we need to do it. Why don't I bring David in and you can tell him all about this special honour. And then if he seems OK with it, we'll go ahead as planned tomorrow, OK?'

'That sounds just fine,' Ken said. 'Kate, does that work for you?'

'Very funny, Detective Lincoln. Such a comedian but I'd suggest you keep your day job.'

'Funny, I could say the same for you.'

'And then?' Graham asked me.

We were in what was becoming our usual place, the damned lobby with the damned boxes of ornaments. At least I had something a little more exciting to talk about today and that was definitely making the time pass faster.

'And then we brought David in and Ken told him all about this idea,' I continued. 'David seemed a little reluctant at first. I think he might have thought we weren't telling him the truth and maybe he was going to get arrested or something. But Detective Lincoln is good and he convinced him. By the end of it all David seemed thrilled with the whole idea that he got to play with handcuffs and sirens and ride in a real police car. As predicted by me, I might point out.'

'And Detective Lincoln,' Graham added.

We had talked to David for a long time that afternoon, making sure he really was as excited as he seemed about this adventure he was going to go on tomorrow. Alan was finally convinced his son would be fine, and then Cam and I came back to the Plex, as we both had to work this evening. I hadn't had a chance to update Graham until just now, as we had sent the other ushers home and were just finishing up for the night.

'Yes, and Detective Lincoln,' I admitted. 'Look, I'm done with these for the day. I'm going to go up to my office and close things up. Can you get things turned off down here?'

'Sure. I'll be up behind you in a couple of minutes.'

I made my way upstairs and rinsed out the coffee pot and put away all the supplies. I walked across the office to close the blinds on my window. I looked down into the street and froze with what I saw there.

'Kate?' Graham asked, coming up behind me.

'He's down there.'

'Who?'

'Hank.'

Graham hurried over and looked out of the window.

'That guy?'

'Yes.'

'He's brazen. He's just standing there looking up here at you. He's not even trying to hide.'

'Call security,' I instructed Graham.

'I'll call security and I'll call Scott,' Graham said. 'He's parked underground so you guys won't have any hassles getting out of here. Hank won't even know that you've left the building.'

I dropped the blinds down and closed them tightly, feeling a shiver go down my spine, while Graham took care of everything. Scott and Trevor appeared in the office almost immediately. When we peeked out again through the blinds and saw him still standing there, they tried to convince me that they should just go down and have a talk with him. I managed to convince them that they should get me home and leave Hank for security and the police to deal with, and they finally acquiesced.

Once home, though, I realized I was much more unnerved by this than I'd thought, as I tossed and turned for an hour or so in bed, every noise spooking me. But I didn't hear Cam come home, so I didn't have to decide whether to tell him that I had seen Hank or not. That was a decision better put off for another day anyway, when I was calmer; I was pretty sure Cam would be anything but calm about that piece of news.

Saturday November 29

'Katie?' Cam called down to me from over the low wall in the loft. His hair was tousled and his eyes still clouded with sleep.

'What?' I asked, looking up from the kitchen where I was cracking some eggs in a bowl.

'What are you doing up so early?'

'We have to be at Alan's by nine o'clock,' I reminded him. 'You can't tell me you forgot about that already?'

'No, but it's only seven minutes past six right now. You could sleep for another hour and a half easily, you know. Or at least I could if you weren't banging things around so much down there.'

'Well, I had to get up to throw up, anyway, and then I felt the urge for eggs for breakfast.'

'You're actually cooking?'

'Well, I was just going to scramble some eggs and maybe cook some bacon. Do we have bacon?' I asked him.

'It's in the freezer,' he said.

'I looked there already. I didn't see a package of bacon, though.'

'I've got it divided up into single-serving packages in Ziploc bags.'

I opened the freezer again and found the bacon. I pulled out three bags and then found a second frying pan, dumping the frozen bacon in the pan and turning it on high.

'Have you ever been investigated for obsessive compulsive disorder?' I asked him, noticing all the other little packages of goodies he had filled the freezer with.

'Katie, that's three packages of bacon,' Cam said, as he heard me dump them into the pan.

'Oh, sorry, sweetie, did you want some too?'

'How high do you have that burner turned on?'

'High. You know, Cam, I did manage to feed myself before I met you. I can manage some basic things at the stove,' I said, my bravado fading as I slid the egg pan off the burner as the butter started smoking and turning brown.

'I'm coming down. Don't touch anything else.'

Cam pulled on his robe and trotted down the stairs. He slid me gently aside, turned down the burners to low and washed out the pan with the burned butter.

'OK, what exactly is it we're going to make here?' he asked me.

'Scrambled eggs and bacon,' I said, holding up my bowl with the cracked eggs. 'They were going to be fried but I broke too many of the yolks.'

'All right, give me the bowl and I'll get these going for you,' he said, holding out his hand.

'No, I want to help,' I said. 'Teach me how you would do it.'

'You want to cook?' he asked. 'Katie, are you feeling OK? Should I call the doctor?'

'I'm fine. I just don't want to feel helpless and stupid.'

'You're not stupid,' he reassured me. 'I told you, I was just angry when I said that the other day. Besides, I didn't say you were stupid, I said you did stupid things sometimes. Like melting butter on high and not watching it.'

'OK, but, regardless of that, I want to be able to cook something and not have people laugh at me.'

'All right.' He sighed, realizing that breakfast was going to take a lot longer than he had originally thought it would. 'Do you know what a whisk is?'

'Cam, don't patronize me.'

'How about this one then, do you know where the whisk is?'

'No, I don't,' I admitted. 'As a matter of fact, I didn't even know I had a whisk.'

'You didn't. You do now. It's in the second drawer over there.'

I pulled the whisk out of the drawer and brought it over to the bowl with the eggs. I started to beat them, but I was a little sloppy. Cam tossed me the dishcloth but refrained from making any comment.

'Now, just add a little bit of milk and that will give them a nice creamy texture.'

I poured in some milk, I assumed too much by the look I got from Cam but, again, he held his tongue, until I picked up the bowl to pour the eggs into the pan.

'Wait,' he said, pulling the bowl from my hands.

'What?' I asked.

'First we melt the butter and gently heat up the pan.'

'You are so anal,' I said, cutting up some butter and dropping it in the pan.

'Maybe I am, but I've never heard you complain about my cooking.'

'Do you just have to be right about everything this week?'

Cam had the butter melted and finally allowed me to pour the eggs into the pan. He handed me a wooden spatula and held my hand, showing me how he liked to stir his eggs. I managed to perform the task without any further error while he finished the bacon and made some toast for us. He plated it up and sat me down at the table with the most heavenly looking breakfast I had ever seen.

'Do you think this is my first craving?' I asked, greedily digging into the eggs.

'Could be,' he said, setting a glass of milk in front of me and a bowl of fruit salad.

'Can I have some ketchup?' I asked, before he sat down.

He brought the bottle and sat down beside me, watching in horror as I buried my eggs under a sea of red. I dipped the toast in the ketchup, too, discovering a whole new taste sensation. Cam averted his eyes to his own plate, ignoring what I was doing to my food.

'So,' I asked, my mouth full and manners forgotten. 'What time do you want to head up to Alan's house?'

'You want to get there early, I'm guessing?' he asked me.

'Better than late, right?' I used my toast to soak up the last of the ketchup that was on my plate where the eggs had been. Then I added some more ketchup on the other side of my plate, to dip the bacon into.

Cam cleared his plate and stood at the sink, rinsing the dishes and leaving them on the counter to dry.

'We should probably leave around eight fifteen, then,' he suggested. 'What is it with you and all that ketchup?'

'It's really good,' I said. 'You should try it.'

'I think I'll pass. But I don't think I've ever seen you use that much before.'

'I know, I guess I don't know what I've been missing. We'll have to start buying the one and a half-litre bottle, I think. This little bottle doesn't seem to last very long.'

'I'm going to go have my shower now,' he said. 'I can't stand to see you eating that.'

I shrugged my shoulders and grabbed one last piece of bread to clean up my plate with, which I did with gusto. I finished my milk, but covered up the fruit salad and put it back in the fridge. I did toss a couple of apples into my backpack for later, though. I rinsed off my dishes and dried everything and put it away. Cam finished in the bathroom and I had a quick shower. I pulled on my jeans, which felt really tight after that huge breakfast, and put one of Cam's work shirts over the top, so I could undo the button on the jeans if I had to, and the shirt would cover it. We grabbed our coats and braved rush-hour traffic on our way to the north end of the city.

We actually had made better time than we expected, but Alan was up and had the coffee on. From the look of his

222

house, he hadn't slept much either and was ready to get this all over with, too. We sat around the kitchen table, drinking coffee and waiting for Detective Lincoln to arrive. Emily had been dropped off at the neighbour's again, a nice elderly lady down the street who had been filled in on the whole story and would not give Emily to anyone except Alan. David was in the living room, playing with his X-Box and anxiously looking out of the window every time he heard a car go past.

Ken Lincoln pulled in promptly at nine o'clock and joined us in the kitchen, passing on the coffee but accepting an orange juice. We exchanged pleasantries and small talk and all sat on pins and needles, anxious to get going.

'OK, Cam, I'd like you to stay home today, in case Carrie calls you there or maybe even shows up. Katie, I want you at the theatre, covering your phone. And Alan, do you smoke?' Ken asked.

'A little.'

'Good. I'd like you to go out on to the street just outside the police station every couple of hours today for a smoke, just in case anyone is watching. That will suggest David is still being questioned inside the station.'

'Not a problem,' Alan agreed.

'So, are you ready for me to call the police cruiser?' Ken asked, looking around at all of us.

'We're ready,' I said.

'Let's do it,' Alan agreed.

Ken pulled out his radio and talked briefly on it. A minute later, the police cruiser raced down the street, sirens and lights flashing, ensuring no one in the neighbourhood would miss it. The two officers left the car idling in the driveway, sirens down but lights still flashing, and Alan let them in through the front door. David was just about jumping out of his skin with excitement as the officers pulled out their handcuffs. They let David play with the cuffs and also let him talk on their radio to the dispatch officer and showed him everything they carried on their utility belts.

'David, do you want to wear the handcuffs and we'll take you to the car like you're a bad guy?' Ken Lincoln asked him. 'Like we talked about yesterday?'

'Do I still get to work the siren?' David asked.

'Absolutely,' Ken promised him.

'OK, that would be kind of cool,' he said, and turned around and held his hands behind his back, waiting for one of the officers to lock them.

We all went and stood on the front step as David was led out to the police cruiser, which then pulled out of the driveway, sirens turned back on, just in case anyone in the neighbourhood had missed its arrival. From the count of all the faces peering out of all the front windows up and down the street, I didn't think there was anyone who had missed it.

Ken led Alan into his car and followed the police cruiser down the street. We stood on the stoop, waiting for the dust to clear.

'I hope this works,' I wished out loud.

Cam squeezed my hand and then walked me to the passenger side of the car and opened the door for me.

'Hi there!'

I turned around and saw good neighbour Stan racing down his front steps and over to us.

'Morning,' we both said at the same time.

'Wow, that was some excitement around here this morning, wasn't it?'

'Yeah,' I agreed, getting into the car and trying to look sad and scared, like the good aunt. Cam closed my door but I rolled down the window, not to be left out of this conversation.

'Did they take David away in handcuffs?' Stan asked.

'I don't really know what happened,' Cam said, enigmatically.

'Everything OK?' Stan pushed for more information. 'Is there anything Alan needs?'

'I don't know,' I sighed. 'Alan's really upset.'

'Yeah, we're just on our way downtown to be with him. I don't know if there's much we can do but he shouldn't be alone right now,' Cam said.

'I think the police and the lawyers have everything else under control,' I assured him.

'I just wish we knew where Carrie was,' Cam said. 'She should be with her son right now.'

'Look, we've got to get going,' I told him. 'I promise we'll let you know if Alan needs anything.'

Cam came around and got in the car, starting it up and putting it in reverse.

'Nice seeing you again.' I smiled up at Stan as Cam backed out of the driveway.

A huge wave of relief passed over me as I watched Stan race back into his house. If I was right our message was about to be delivered to Carrie.

We stayed at our positions for most of the afternoon, a very boring, frustrating and unrewarding afternoon, until finally Cam drove over to meet me at the Plex. I met him at the stage door with a kiss and walked him down Tin Pan Alley, to the stairwell that led to his office.

'I'm glad you're here,' I told him.

'Yeah, I couldn't sit at home any longer.'

'Weren't you going to drive Alan home?'

'They're going to send him home in an undercover car, just to make sure everything is OK at the house. Don't be disappointed, Katie,' he added

'It didn't work.'

'No, it doesn't appear to have worked, but at least we tried something. Now, we'll just leave it to the police to finish up and we're going to stay out of this, right?'

'I promised that's what we'd do if my plan didn't work,' I agreed.

'Well, have a good evening,' he said, using his key to let himself into the stairwell. 'I'll try to get up for a coffee later if you're not too busy.'

I wandered through the backstage area and poked my head into the green room, on the way to my office, not running into anyone today, which was a strange occurrence. But it was typical Murphy's Law. Today I actually wanted someone to talk to and so, of course, there would be no one around. I opened my office door and got the coffee going, feeling brave since I hadn't been bothered by morning sickness at all that day, since early that morning. When the coffee was set and brewing, I sat at my desk and pulled out some inventory sheets and some time sheets for the night. Then the phone rang.

'Hello,' I answered, half expecting it to be Cam.

'What the hell are you doing to my son?'

'Carrie?' I asked, drawing in a deep breath, excited that my plan had actually worked but not sure what to do about it since there was no one around.

'I know you were there, at Alan's house, when they took him away. I want to know what you are doing to my son.'

'Carrie, I'm not doing anything,' I tried to explain. 'The police took him down to headquarters today. I think they just wanted to ask him some questions.'

'You leave my kids alone.'

'Carrie, I think you should talk to the police about this, not me. I can give you the detective's cell phone number and I'm sure he can straighten everything out for you.'

'So he can trace my call and find me?' she asked. 'You must think I'm pretty stupid.'

'Well, if you want to help David, you're probably going to have to come in from wherever you are right now, don't you think?'

There was silence on the other end of the line.

Please don't let me have blown this, I prayed silently.

'I'll call you back.'

'Carrie!' I called, trying to keep her on the line a little longer, so I could find out more. But she was already gone.

I disconnected the line from my end and dialed Detective Lincoln's number.

'Detective Lincoln.' He answered quickly.

'Ken, it's Kate. I just got a call from Carrie.'

'Good,' he said. 'Let me just get on the line with the phone company and see if they got the number. You stay there and I'll get right back to you.'

'Ken!' I called, but he too had already hung up on me.

I tried Cam next, knowing that not only would he not hang up, but that he would probably come up and keep me company while I waited to find out if they could trace Carrie's whereabouts. And he did in record time.

'Well?' he asked, standing at my office door, huffing and puffing from his run through the building.

'Nothing yet. No one has called me back.'

Cam poured himself a coffee and sat in the chair across from me.

'What did she say to you?' he asked.

'She said I shouldn't mess with her son.'

'See, I told you these things never work out like you say

they will. She's already blaming you for this.'

'Cam, it's OK. She's nowhere around here.'

'We don't know that for sure, do we?' he asked.

'No. Ken Lincoln hasn't called me back either.'

We both stared at the phone for a couple of minutes.

'Well, this is pointless,' he said.

'You can always unpack Christmas ornaments while we wait,' I said. 'It helps the time pass.'

Cam pulled one of the cartons closer to him.

'What are you doing with them?' he asked.

'Take them out of the tissue paper and put them in the basket,' I said, sliding it across the top of my desk, closer to him.

'How did I know you would manage to rope me into doing this before the week was out?'

'I'm good that way, aren't I?' I said with a laugh.

It was another ten minutes before anything happened. When the phone rang and broke the silence in the office, I almost dropped the ornament I was holding. That would have been my third five-dollar donation. This was going to be a very expensive Christmas for me.

'Kate Carpenter,' I said, grabbing the phone with one hand while I gently set the ornament in the basket with my other.

'It's Ken.'

I could tell from the tone of his voice he didn't have good news.

'Hi, Ken,' I said, waiting for him to share his news.

'She didn't stay on the phone long enough for us to get anything,' he said. 'I'm really sorry.'

'Me, too,' I said. 'But she said she'd call me back. Maybe there's still hope.'

'Maybe. You just have to try and keep her talking as long as you can,' he instructed me. 'We need at least twice as much time as you got out of her last time.'

'I'll do my best.'

'So you guys can probably go home now,' Ken said. 'I don't think we're going to get anything else out of Carrie tonight.'

'What about Alan and David?' I asked.

'We sent them home a few hours ago in an unmarked car. They're fine.'

'How is Alan holding out?' I asked.

'He's disappointed, like you are. But he's all right.'

227

'Well, thanks Ken.'

'Kate, don't feel too bad about this,' he said. 'We tried. We knew there was a chance this might not work, but we tried.'

'Thanks, Ken. I guess we'll talk to you if we hear from her.'

'Or if you just need to talk.'

'OK. Goodnight.' I said, setting down the receiver.

'So?' Cam asked.

'He said we could probably call it a day if we wanted to. He didn't think anything else would happen tonight.'

'Are you ready to go home?' Cam asked.

'Pretty much,' I admitted. 'I'm exhausted. This has been one of those quietly stressful kind of days. How about you? Are you ready to go home?'

'Yeah. Mike was covering for me today, so I'm good to go whenever you are.'

'How about we stop and pick up some Vietnamese on the way home?' I asked.

'You don't want to cook again?'

'I think once a day is more than enough to start with. I might go into shock or something.'

'Or I might.'

'OK, well, give me five minutes to get things cleared up here,' I said.

'I'll just run downstairs and get my stuff. Meet me at the stage door?'

'Deal.'

'Inside, Katie,' he warned. 'Please don't go outside until I'm there.'

'I promise,' I said. And then I started to clean up my office for the night.

Sunday November 30

'Morning,' Cam said, as I turned over and opened my eyes. He was sitting up in bed, reading the newspaper.

'Morning,' I groaned.

'You OK?' he asked.

'I have a headache,' I said, struggling to sit up and prop up the pillows behind me.

'Want some Tylenol?' he asked.

'Can I have Tylenol?' I asked.

'They're OK in moderate doses.'

'Then yes, please. And some caffeine. I think that's my biggest problem. Oh yeah, and nicotine, too. I'm really missing the nicotine. Can you take care of all of that?'

'I'll take care of it,' he said, disappearing downstairs for a couple of minutes. He came back with Tylenol, orange juice and tea.

'There you go,' he said, setting everything on the bedside table for me. 'Painkillers for the head, orange juice in case your blood sugar is a little low and tea because this brand has just a tiny little bit of caffeine in it. Not enough to hurt anything but maybe enough to break your headache if it is a caffeine-withdrawal headache.'

I couldn't decide whether I should kiss him and reward his kindness or take the painkillers. The Tylenol won out. I swallowed them with the juice and then settled back with the cup of tea. Cam joined me back in bed and picked up his newspaper again.

Yesterday had ended in a frustrating manner. Detective Lincoln had called just after we got home to let us know that he was sticking to his word and I did not need to be involved in this. We had sat up for hours, me falling asleep in Cam's arms, hoping Carrie would call us back. She never did. Cam woke me up and put me to bed just after midnight. I suspected he'd sat up for a while after that, hoping she would call. I totally understood how he felt, because I had snuck the upstairs phone out of its cradle and slept with it under my pillow.

I reached under me to see if the telephone was still there, and to make sure the battery still had a charge. I pulled it out from under the covers and checked for a dial tone. Everything was working, it was simply that no one was going to call me.

Cam finished the newspaper, put on his robe and started puttering around in the kitchen. I got up shortly after he did, put on my robe and joined him, telephone in hand.

'I'm so frustrated,' I said, sitting at the table and taking the

coffee he offered me. The tea hadn't helped my head; I was
hoping the pills would kick in soon.

'Katie, we did everything we could. Carrie will either call
back or she won't.'

'But I almost had her.'

'Like I said, you did everything you could; now you just
need to not worry about it.'

'Why do you think she blames me?' I asked. 'She said I
was interfering with her children. Not you or Alan or even
the police, but me.'

'Hmm?' he asked, his head in the vegetable drawer in the
fridge.

'She asked me what I had done to her son. Why do you
think she blames me? I mean, it was the police that took him
away, not me.'

'She knows what a snoop you are, like the rest of us,' Cam
said with an affectionate laugh.

'I suppose you're right.' I sighed, realizing that knowing
why didn't really help.

'Do you want the crossword puzzle?' he asked me.

'Or maybe it does help . . .' I said, wishing I hadn't.

'What?' Cam asked.

'Sorry, I was just thinking out loud. Look, I can't really
concentrate this morning. I think I'll have a shower and head
into the theatre a little early, if you don't mind. There are a
thousand things left to do before previews start next week and
I think that might be therapeutic for me.'

'You have to have something to eat first,' he nagged me.

'I know I have to eat. I'll grab a muffin and some fruit at
Gus's, OK?'

He looked at me, trying to figure out if I was trying to pull
something over on him or if I was being honest. Finally he
leaned over and kissed me.

'Do you want a ride in?' he asked.

'No, it's nice out, I think a walk will do me good.'

I showered and dressed, trying not to seem in too much of
a hurry. Cam was very good at reading me, and I didn't want
him to think that anything else was up. So I headed out just
after noon for the theatre. Once I was actually on my way, I
realized I wasn't in such a big hurry, because I was, after all,

only playing a hunch. And if I was right, she would wait for me, no matter how long I took.

Cam had stayed at home, as I hoped. I knew he had found Carrie's address book behind the sofa and he wanted to go through it and see what he could find. I think he was hoping her friends might have more to say to him than they had to the police. But I had another idea, a hunch, a woman's intuition thing. I had a feeling Carrie might be looking for me; she wanted to deal with me personally right now. And if anyone was looking for me, they knew I would always turn up at the theatre sooner or later. So I kept walking toward the office, not sure what exactly I would be facing.

I walked a couple of blocks and then got on the C-train at the 5th Street station. I rode it right down to the Plex and started up the street to the stage door. As I was walking down the street, I saw a light shining through a crack in the blinds in my office window. I suddenly felt a little surge of adrenaline race through me.

Nick, the security supervisor, sat at his desk at the stage door entrance, pretending to watch the security monitors. I was pretty sure he had the hockey game playing on one of those televisions. After the Flames' near-win in the race for the cup last year, hockey fever was abounding in Calgary.

'Hi, Nick,' I said, crossing over to the security desk and watching him scramble with the remote control, obviously hoping I hadn't seen anything. 'Mind if I use your phone for a minute?'

'Not at all,' he said, sliding it across the desk to me.

'So who's winning?' I asked, nodding at the television set.

'I have no idea what you're talking about,' Nick said with a laugh, turning the TV back on. 'But it seems to be another good year to be a Flames fan.'

'Good.'

'Why can't you use the telephone in your office?' he asked. 'You're almost there, you know.'

'Because I think I have a bit of a surprise waiting for me in my office and I just wanted to call Detective Lincoln and have him come on over.'

Nick sat up at attention, all thoughts of the hockey game gone from his mind.

'What's going on Kate?' he asked.

231

'Well, I can't say for sure yet,' I told him, 'But it might be a really good idea to get a security guard on each entrance to the Centenary Theatre and not let anyone in until Detective Lincoln gets here.'

Nick turned to his walkie-talkie and I dialed Ken's cell phone number.

'Hi, Ken, it's Kate Carpenter.'

'Hi, Kate, what's up?' Ken asked. 'Did you hear from Carrie again?'

'No, but I think I know where she is,' I told him.

'What are you talking about?' he asked. 'You were going to stay out of this, weren't you? What have you done?'

'I know I'm supposed to stay out of this because you and Cam have told me that at least a hundred and fifty times. But since I think she's waiting for me in my office, I seem to be right in the middle of it again. And I thought that maybe you could come over and help out. I want her to go peacefully, not in a hail of bullets.'

'Kate, where are you right now?'

'I'm at the security desk and I'm just going up to my office at the theatre. I'm pretty sure she's waiting up there for me. I know she blames me for what happened yesterday.'

'Don't you go up there,' he warned me. 'We'll be there in just a couple of minutes.'

'She's not going to hurt me, Ken.' I tried to calm him. 'If she were, she would have done it long before now. I think she just needs some help right now. She doesn't know how to get out of this and I think that's why she's coming to me. She thinks I can help her.'

'Kate, think about the whole mother lion thing. Think about how protective they are. She is trying to save her son. Now don't go up there!'

'OK, I'll meet you in the lobby, if that meets with your approval?'

'I'd like you to wait on the street, actually,' he told me.

'Yeah, well that's not going to happen, Ken, sorry. Just get over here, I've got to get going before she runs out of patience and we lose her again.'

I hung up on him, thinking how much shorter my arguments with Cam would be if I could just hang up on him, too. I

232

smiled at the thought of the fights that would cause us, as I hurried down the backstage corridor to the Centenary Theatre. I didn't run into a single soul as I made my way through the backstage area and then the front of house. But today I thought that was a good sign, because with fewer people around there would be much less chance of anyone getting hurt. I didn't worry about unlocking the doors downstairs for the police. I knew Nick already had security guards down there and they would ensure Ken was able to get in. I hurried across the lobby and then up to my office. I know I said I was going to wait, but I didn't trust that Carrie would have either the patience to wait too long or what her reaction would be if a police officer was the first one through my office door. So I thought I would go up there first and check things out. I made lots of noise coming down the hallway, not wanting to surprise her and have some horrible accident happen with me being on the receiving end of it. I stood at the end of the corridor, my hand on the doorknob, pausing for a moment, trying to find the courage and bravado I had felt a moment ago. I finally opened the door to my office, slower than I normally did, my courage fading quickly now that the actual moment had arrived.

Carrie was sitting at my desk, holding a gun pointed directly at the slowly opening door and me behind it. I entered the office and carefully closed the door behind me, hearing the lock click into place and feeling my stomach sink as the reality of this situation set in upon me. I walked over to the chair on the other side of the desk. I sat down, trying to normalize my breathing and slow my racing heart. Suddenly, I was very aware of the fact that I was pregnant and there was this other life that was depending upon me to keep it alive.

'Mind if I sit down?' I asked her, trying very hard to sound cheerful and casual.

'Make yourself comfortable,' she said, the gun following me as I crossed the office.

'So, what's up?' I asked, pretending there was no gun in between us.

'You should have just kept your nose out of this, Kate,' Carrie said. 'I tried to tell you I was going to handle it. But you just wouldn't let it be.'

'That's a big downfall of mine,' I admitted. 'Carrie, I just

233

thought I was helping you. I didn't want you to go to jail. I knew you didn't do it. I am so very sorry about all of this. I just never suspected it might have been David that fired that gun.'

'But if you didn't realize who did do it, why couldn't you have just listened to me and left well enough alone?'

'That's not the way I work, Carrie. I seem to have this theory in life that I know better than everyone else,' I told her. 'But if you ever tell Cam that, I swear I'll deny it.'

'Well, I think you should rethink your theory. It doesn't seem to be doing you very much good right now, does it?'

'You can't do this, Carrie,' I said. 'It's wrong. And it's not you.'

'You don't know anything about me.'

'I know that if you were a violent or dangerous person, you would have done something far worse to Hank than just walking out on him.'

'I don't have a choice anymore. You've gotten us all in a mess and you've brought the police into it and I'm not letting my son go to jail.'

'You have to tell the truth,' I advised her. 'Trust me on this one. I'm not really that good a private-eye type person so, if I can figure out what happened, the police surely would have, too.'

'I'm not letting my son go to jail,' she repeated, and I believed her.

'You have to talk to them,' I repeated, much braver than I felt.

'No, I don't. I'm getting my kids and getting out of here. I've already got plane tickets booked for New Zealand.'

'And what about me?'

'I'll kill you if I have to,' she said. 'So please don't try and stop me.'

Glad I asked, I thought.

'Then you'll spend the rest of your life in jail,' I said, forcing that bravado again. 'You don't want to do that.'

'What does it matter? If I can't get out of here I'm just going to confess to the shooting, and what difference will two shootings make? Nothing personal, Kate, but what will shooting you get me after I tell them I've already shot a police officer?'

'It'll get you a sentence you don't deserve.'

'And it will get David off the hook.' There was a quaver in her voice, and she took a deep breath, trying to regain control.

234

'His life is not going to be ruined because I was too scared to protect him, to take him out of that house where that horrible man threatened us and tortured him psychologically. I mean, what kind of a mother am I? He shouldn't ever have had to see me getting beaten up by anyone. So, in a way, I am guilty and I do deserve to go to jail for what I've done to him.'

'Carrie, we need to talk to the lawyer about this. Eli will be able to tell us what to do. And David probably won't go to jail. There are lots of extenuating circumstances and he's a minor. You have to get him the help he needs and you're not going to do that by killing me and going to jail for him. We can't let him keep this a secret any longer. You have to talk to the police.'

'I can't,' she sobbed. 'He's my son and look what I've done to him.'

'Carrie, isn't it keeping a big secret that got you into this mess to begin with? Please, let's just start telling the truth about everything. I'll help you, Carrie. Both Cam and I will be there to help you.'

'No, Kate. You don't have kids, you couldn't possibly understand.'

'I do understand. Carrie, I'm pregnant. Cam and I are going to have a baby. I understand this more than you think I do.'

'Oh, my God,' she said.

'I understand that David is going to have to live with this for the rest of his life whether you admit to it or not. Do you want him to have to live with the guilt of you going to jail for something he did, too?' I asked. 'Carrie, you know this isn't the answer.'

'I don't know what else to do,' she cried.

'Start by giving me the gun, Carrie,' I suggested. 'Then we can go downstairs and talk to the police. I think it would be better if you told them yourself what happened.'

'But my poor little boy . . .'

'We'll make sure that he is taken care of, OK?' I asked, holding out my shaking hand, praying she would hand me the gun. 'We'll get him the best lawyers or the best doctors or the best schools, whatever it is he needs.'

'Are you sure?' she asked.

'Detective Lincoln is in the lobby. I told him you needed to talk to him. He'll make sure that David is fine. You have to trust me,' I said.

Her hand shook, as if she was struggling inwardly with the decision, but finally, very slowly, she reached over and put the gun in my hand. The feel of the cold metal against my warm skin sent a shiver up my spine, but I held on to it tightly, pointing it away from me and toward the floor. I stood up and held the door open.

'You people have far too many guns,' I joked.

She laughed and wiped away the tears that were forming in her eyes.

'Shall we go talk to Detective Lincoln?' I asked.

'I don't know if I can,' she said, tears staining her cheeks.

'Come on, Carrie, you've been so strong through all this. Don't fall apart on me now. You have to do this for your son.'

Carrie stood up and took two shaky steps toward the door. I put my arm around her waist and led her slowly down the hall. We walked down the stairs, where both the Detective and Cam were pacing, waiting for us.

'Katie?' Cam asked. 'Nick called me and told me something was up. What's going on?' And then he saw his cousin.

'Carrie, are you OK?' His voice was steady, belaying the surprise he must have felt at seeing her with me.

'It's OK,' I said, and I held the gun out to Detective Lincoln. 'Ken, will you take this, please.'

He looked quizzically at me but took the gun. He popped out the cartridge and checked the barrel before slipping it into his pocket.

'Ken,' I continued. 'Carrie needs to talk to you about the shooting. I think she's ready to tell you what really happened that day.'

'It's the right thing to do.' Cam smiled at her.

'Do you want to tell me what happened?' Ken asked.

Carrie looked at me.

'It's OK,' I assured her. 'You have to do this.'

'David did it,' she whispered. 'He was trying to protect me from Hank. But he's only eleven and he's never shot a gun at anything except an old tin can. He was scared, he was shaking so badly, and he missed. I was so relieved when the shots went through the window and I thought nothing had happened. David just dropped the gun and I told him to get out to the car. I didn't have to worry about Hank or the other officer, because

236

they were in the
came rushing in
and the gun w
actually fair
Officer Dar
just started
And then

    Ken l
lookin
     'W
'We

f

'Yo
I will be ng.
    'That's fine,' n
a call before you leave.

    She nodded and Ken took n.
theatre and out of the front door.

    I stayed at work, despite Cam's protest
in to continue working through this Christn
mess we had gotten ourselves into. And now that thn
going to be back to normal, I craved a normal night.

    Cam met Eli at the police station and made sure Carrie was
OK. So I worked the night and Cam was waiting for me at
the stage door to drive me home. I got into the apartment and
flopped down on the couch, physically and mentally drained
from the events of the past couple of weeks.

    'How are you doing?' Cam asked, flopping down beside me.
'I feel sick.'

    'Do you want some crackers or something?' he asked.
'Not that kind of sick,' I said. 'Heart sick.'

Monday

I lay in bed, staring u
for probably a goo
same thing, lying
It was done.
working thing
days. Forma
we would
and orde
both de
slept t
got
av

December 1

...p at the ceiling. I had been lying this way ...d half an hour. I knew Cam was doing the ...eside me, but he hadn't said a word, either. ...t wasn't over, but Eli and the police were ...out and a judge would finish it up in a few ...charges would be laid, sentences handed out and ...ll be able to move on. We had gotten home late ...ed in a pizza, which we had picked at until we'd ...cided to just give up and go to bed. We had almost ...e clock around, I discovered, when I turned a little and ...look at the alarm clock. I cuddled into Cam but we still ...oided talking, not wanting to break the peace we had finally ...ttained. I lay there, the warmth of the man beside me comforting me, my bladder aching and my stomach churning. Yes, everything was finally back to normal.

I got up and made my way to the bathroom, brushed my teeth and found Cam at the table with coffee and the newspaper when I finally came out.

'You OK?' he asked.

'Yeah, as OK as I'm going to be for the next few months, I suppose.'

'Do you want the crossword?' he asked.

'Yes, thanks.'

We sat there, blissfully, peacefully; I read the entertainment section and did the crossword, while Cam checked in with the rest of the world. I was sure he would update me if something really important had happened somewhere.

'This is the way it has to be now,' Cam said, out of nowhere.

'What do you mean?'

'Our lives,' he said. 'You're pregnant now, Katie. It's not just you that could have been shot yesterday.'

'I know that,' I admitted. 'I kept thinking that over and over and over while I sat up in my office talking with Carrie.'

'Good.'

'It's not so bad, you know?'

'What?' he asked.

'This life. It doesn't always have to be an adventure, solving a mystery, chasing somebody. Just being here with you is good.'

'I'm glad.'

'And there's lots of stuff going on at the Plex,' I said. 'I'll still get to gossip and stuff like that, won't I?'

'Yes, you will,' he said with a laugh.

'Then I'm OK with that.' And just to prove it, I finished my crossword puzzle in ink. A definite omen for a good day ahead.

We finished our leisurely morning and walked into the Plex together, enjoying another day of late fall sunshine. We were bold Calgarians, wearing only light sweaters, though I did have a nice heavy coat with me to wear on the walk home, knowing the weather would normalize to seasonal once the sun went down. Cam walked me up to my office, stayed for a coffee and then kissed me and was off down the fire escape, taking a short cut to his office.

I wandered down into the auditorium and checked out my theatre. The disaster that had been covering the stage all week was slowly coming together and starting to look good. The boys would be in bright and early tomorrow to put the final touches on everything for the dress rehearsal the following afternoon, followed by the first preview that evening. Then I made my way into the lobby, to unlock the bar fridges so Graham could help the guy from shipping and receiving load our liquor order into the fridges. We were hoping the eggnog with rum was going to be a big seller this month. I heard someone rattling at the main lobby doors and I went down to the lower lobby, thinking Graham had forgotten his keys. Instead I saw Hank standing there, rattling the door.

'What are you doing here?' I asked through the door, fear spiking the timbre of my voice.

'Where's Carrie?' he yelled through the door.

'She's not here,' I told him.

'That's not true, someone told me she was here with you.'

'Yesterday, Hank. She was here yesterday. Now go away or I'm going to call security.'

'Let me in,' he demanded.

'No,' I said firmly. 'Go away.'

'I'm sick of you lying to protect her. She's my wife and I want to talk to her.'

'She's really not here. She's at the police station. Why don't you go look for her there?'

Hank had been pulling roughly at the door, checking out the tenacity of the lock. A particularly violent rattle seemed to loosen the lock a little and he attacked the door with renewed vigor.

'I'm going to call security,' I threatened him and then turned to run up the stairs.

Another violent rattle and I heard the door give way behind me. Now I was scared and my body released a huge burst of adrenaline as it urged my feet to move faster up the stairs. I hesitated a moment at the top, trying to figure out if I should try to make it to my office or to the phone in the main lobby.

'You're hiding her up there, aren't you?' he yelled, still behind me but getting far too close for my comfort.

'I'm calling security,' I screamed, racing across the lobby and grabbing the phone behind the bar. I was desperately winded and wishing I had done more jogging with Cam as my shaking hands tried to dial the extension for the security desk.

He ran after me and grabbed my arm as I was still dialing the phone, pulling my hand away from the number pad.

'You are going to take me to Carrie,' he ordered.

'I told you she's not here!' I tried, hoping a little resistance from me would make him back down.

His hand came out of nowhere and hit me across the face. I spun into the bar, holding myself up, and felt a sharp sting in my cheek. I frantically held the phone to my chest, hoping I could still call for help, but he tore it from my grasp and threw it across the lobby.

'You're awfully brave when it comes to beating up women,' I said quietly, the same silent rage welling up inside me that I had seen in Cam a couple of times.

'Tell me where she is,' he demanded again.

'I told you, she's at the police station. Which is where

you're going to be spending an awful lot of time soon if you don't get out of here right now,' I threatened.

He grabbed my arm and dragged me across the lobby toward my office. I frantically tried to pull away from him. He flung me up against the wall and wrapped his hands around my throat.

'Why is it so hard for you to do what I ask?' he growled through clenched teeth. 'You're just like that stupid bitch I'm married to. If you'd only listen and just do what I say you could avoid all this trouble.'

'Let me go,' I whispered, seeing the world start to swim around me.

'Where is she?' he growled.

'She's really not here, I swear,' I whispered, wondering why no one was coming to help me and realizing my phone call might not have even gone through.

His eyes narrowed in rage and he crashed my head against the wall and then let me go. I sank slowly down the wall, my legs not willing to support me any longer. The room was still spinning, so I slowly rolled over on to my side and lay on the carpet. Less distance to fall, I figured, and I prayed for Cam to come running up the stairs, or Nick, or anyone at this point.

'Get up and show me where your office is,' he ordered me.

'I can't,' I said. 'I can't get up.'

I saw him come closer.

'I said get up,' he screamed.

'I can't stand up,' I whispered.

He kicked me, landing the blow right in the middle of my abdomen. I felt suddenly sick and gasped for a breath.

'Katie?' I heard Cam call from the broken door downstairs.

'Cam,' I croaked, with the last of the breath I had in me, praying it would be loud enough for him to hear.

I heard him race up the stairs. I looked up and saw him stop for a second, looking at Hank standing over me, and then he let out a primal scream and dove for Hank. The man didn't even know what hit him and Cam had him on the ground and out for the count with a couple of punches. Cam didn't even look back as he raced over to where I was lying.

'Katie, can you hear me?' he asked.

'I'm fine,' I lied, trying to get a grip on the carpet so I

241

could push myself up into a sitting position and prove I was OK.

'I think you're lying to me again.' He smiled at me, brushing the hair away from my face. 'Don't move, I'm going to go call security and we'll get you an ambulance.'

I watched him cross the lobby and pick up the phone from the floor. I pushed myself up into a sitting position and propped myself against the wall. He came back and knelt down beside me, trying to assess my injuries.

'Where does it hurt?' he asked.

'Everywhere,' I whispered, my throat still raspy from where Hank had tried to strangle me.

'Security will be here in a minute,' he assured me. 'They called an ambulance.'

'I don't need an ambulance,' I argued. 'I'll be OK in a minute.'

'Humor me on this one,' he said. 'Let's just get you checked out and let the doctor decide if you're OK or not.'

'Cam.'

'What?'

'I hope you noticed that I didn't let him in?' I said. 'The door was locked.'

'I did notice that,' he said.

'So I don't want to hear any I told you so's here.'

'No, you won't. I promise.'

'OK.' I caved in, a wave of nausea passing over me. 'You win this one. I'll take an ambulance ride.'

Security came running through the back of the house. One guard stopped and made sure Hank wasn't a threat; Nick came running over to where Cam and I sat.

'Kate, if nothing else you are going to have a great shiner,' Nick said, smiling at me.

'Did you call the police and an ambulance?' Cam asked.

'They're on the way,' Nick confirmed. 'How are you doing, Kate?'

'I've been better,' I said, feeling another wave of nausea. I stopped talking and took some deep breaths. I finally heard sirens in the distance, thank God.

'Cam, I want you to go to the police station,' I told him. 'Make sure that bastard gets locked up.'

'Stop trying to be a martyr, Katie, I'm staying with you.'

'I need to know I'm safe,' I tried to convince him. 'And I don't want him blaming Carrie for anything.'

'I think she'll be OK.'

'What are you going to do at the hospital?' I asked. 'Pace in the waiting room for an hour while they examine me? Please go to the police station and then you can come to the hospital as soon as you're sure Carrie is OK and Hank is locked up. Please, Cam, do this for me.'

'No way, Katie, you're not going to win this argument.'

'If you don't agree, I'm not going to the hospital,' I informed him.

'I don't think you're in any position to argue,' he said, moving aside as the paramedics knelt down beside me.

'Neither are you,' I told him.

'What happened here?' one of them asked.

'She got in the way of his fist,' Cam said, pointing to Hank. There was a police officer cuffing him.

'Looks like more than his fist made some contact,' the paramedic said. 'Can you tell me your name?'

'Kate Carpenter,' I said. 'Cam, I want you to go now. I'll see you at the hospital later.'

'Do you know what day it is?' the paramedic asked, as he took my pulse.

'It's Monday, the prime minister is Paul Martin and I am in the main lobby of the Centenary Theatre. Oriented to person, place and time.'

'Where did you get hit?' the paramedic asked me.

'My face, he tried to strangle me, the back of my head made some contact with the wall and he kicked me in the stomach.' Then I turned to Cam. 'Please go, Cam. I don't want him back out on the streets again.'

'Is she going to be OK?' Cam asked the paramedics.

'It doesn't look too bad,' he said, pulling my head forward and feeling the back of it. 'A couple of stitches here. We'll take some x-rays and check for internal bleeding.'

'Katie, I don't want to leave you,' he said.

'Please, Cam, just go and make sure that bastard is locked up. I'll be waiting for you at the hospital.'

He leaned close to me and kissed my forehead lightly, trying not to hurt me.

243

'I'll be quick,' he promised me.

'I love you,' I called after him. 'Ouch, take it easy, guys.' The paramedic taped a pressure bandage to the back of my head and wrapped a blood pressure cuff around my arm.

'There's something else you should probably know. I'm pregnant.'

'How far along?' he asked.

'About five weeks, I think,' I told him

'We're going to get you on the stretcher now,' he said. 'Do you think you can stand if we help you?'

'I think so,' I said, much more bravely than I actually felt.

They each put an arm under my shoulder and helped me to my feet. I was overcome by another wave of dizziness, followed in short order by more nausea. This wasn't a lot of fun. They helped me quickly on to the stretcher and started to strap me in.

'And about this pregnancy thing,' I said.

'Yes?' one of them answered me.

'I think I'm bleeding,' I said.

'Let's just get you to the hospital and we'll let the doctors have a look,' he said, covering me with a blanket and strapping me in.

I don't remember much of the ride to the hospital. I was too busy praying to Saint Anne once again, something I continued to do as they wheeled me in through the emergency entrance and found a bed for me. Nurses began cutting away my clothes and poking me with needles.

'She was attacked in the Centenary Theatre,' one of the paramedics told the doctor. 'Blood pressure one hundred and twenty over seventy-five, pulse eighty-five, respiration normal. She has bruising around the throat from manual strangulation, a laceration and contusion on the back of her head, bruising to the lower abdomen. She informed us she's five weeks pregnant and there is some bleeding.'

'OK, let's get an x-ray of her skull and her face, and get the portable ultrasound in here. Can someone page obstetrics?' the doctor called. He moved to the head of the table and smiled down at me. 'How are you feeling, Ms Carpenter?'

'I've been better,' I told him.

'Any dizziness?'

'Lots, and nausea. What about the baby?' I asked.

'We're going to check everything out. We've got a doctor

244

coming down from obstetrics. But, meanwhile, I'm a little worried about your head,' he said, shining a bright light in my eyes.

'You don't have to worry. It's very hard.'

He laughed. 'Well, at least you still have a sense of humor. How's this cheek feel?'

'Better when you don't poke at it,' I said, trying to turn away from him.

'OK, well, we're going to take some x-rays of that and see how the bone looks.'

'Can you call my doctor?' I asked.

'We need to finish with you here first. But tell me who he is and we'll get one of the nurses to call him when we have you settled, OK? What's his name?' he asked me.

'Dr Benson. Please call him for me.'

'I think you're in luck.' The doctor smiled at me. 'I just had coffee with him before you came in. Nurse, would you page Dr Benson and see if he's still in the hospital?'

'Yes, doctor,' she said, crossing over to the phone.

'OK, now we're just going to send you to radiology and get some x-rays,' he said. 'I'll be back as soon as they're developed and let you know what I've found.'

'OK,' I agreed, not really having any other choice.

I lay there for what seemed like hours, while they took x-rays, started an IV drip, did an ultrasound and then finally left me alone for a few minutes. I closed my eyes, hoping that if I went to sleep, I would wake up and find it was all a dream.

'Kate.' I felt a hand on my shoulder and reluctantly opened my eyes.

'Brock, thank God you're here. Can you please tell me what's going on?' I asked. 'I haven't seen a doctor for hours.'

He slid a stool up to the bed and sat down beside me.

'I've got your chart right here. I've been over it and seen the x-rays and the ultrasound. The good news is that your skull is still in one piece, as is your cheek. We'll just do a couple of stitches to close up that scalp wound. Your voice will have that sexy raspy quality for a few days, but there's no permanent damage and you should be fine. And it doesn't look like there's any abdominal bleeding. But Kate, the pelvic ultrasound doesn't show a heartbeat. I'm afraid you've lost the baby.'

'Oh, God.' I stifled a sob. 'Oh, God, this is going to kill Cam.'

245

'How about you?' he asked, holding my hand.

'I'm OK,' I lied, a small sob escaping my swollen throat and betraying me.

'Kate?' he asked.

'I'm not OK,' I cried. 'What am I going to do now?'

'You're going to get better,' he told me. 'You're young, there's no other damage. You can try again within a couple of months if you want to. I'm just going to go out to the waiting room and see if Cam's here. I think you two should be together right now.'

'Brock, will you tell him, please. I don't think I can.'

'Kate, I'm going to bring him in here. You two need to be together right now.'

'You have to tell him for me,' I insisted, fear filling my soul. This would be the second child Cam had lost before he had even had a chance to hold it in his arms. I didn't know what he might do or say.

'I'll tell him,' the doctor promised as he left the room.

I steeled myself for his entrance, afraid of what directions our lives might take in the next few minutes. When he came in the door, the look of pain in his eyes just about killed me. But he was ever the dutiful mate and hurried across the room, taking me in his arms and letting me cry into his shoulder. But I will never forget that look he had in his eyes.

They released me the next day, pushing me out to the front door in a wheelchair. I tried protesting but it didn't do any good. Cam was waiting out front, the car idling in the loading zone. I got out of the wheelchair, thanked the nurse and reached into my purse. I pulled out the package of cigarettes I had bought in the gift shop and lit one up. Cam could wait another minute or two.

Spring

Life is funny. Months pass and yet things don't ever change. Officer Strachan was still in the hospital. Mind you, it was the rehabilitation hospital, so there was a little progress being made there. Carrie, David and Eli were still going to court, though they never seemed to get there; and Carrie, David and Emily were going to counselling, though they never seemed to get cured. Carrie was going to stop seeing Stan, but she was bringing him to Easter dinner. And I was going to stop being so apathetic and get on with life, but . . .

It was April. Life was being renewed everywhere as rain began to fall and the snow melted, revealing the bed of green grass it had blanketed for the winter. The leaves blossomed, like they did every year, and the flowers bloomed. This was normally my favourite time of year. This year, I just didn't care. I hadn't cared about much for a while. I made our first Christmas together a non-event. New Year's Eve was no big deal, spent in front of the television eating potato chips. Time just passed and every day was the same. That was kind of how I felt about everything right now, as if nothing mattered. All that mattered is that I had cost Cam his second baby.

My mother had even come out. I don't know who told her, whether it was Sam or Cam or even Graham. I had pretended I was fine and she'd pretended she believed me. Neither of us was fooled and she had finally given up and gone home.

During the daytime, in front of everyone, we held hands and carried on as normal. But at night, when Cam reached out to touch me, I felt fear in the pit of my stomach. We had made love awkwardly once or twice, but that was all. Normally, I slept tightly curled into a ball, on the far side of the bed. He never gave up, though, reaching out to touch me, trying to make me feel like he still loved me and still cared. He was an incredibly understanding man, and I wasn't sure why. I knew he was going to leave me. I knew this was something he would never get over, just like the last time with his wife. And I also knew it was all my fault. If I had stayed out of it, like he had begged me to do, none of this would have happened and we would be happily awaiting the birth of our first child in another month or so. The child Cam longed for more than anything else in the world. Sam told me things would start to look up for us once I got past my due date. But I wondered if she even really believed that any more.

So every day, though I acted like the old Kate, I waited for him to say it, that he couldn't stand the sight of me any longer.

He would do it when enough time had passed and he wouldn't look like a cad. I knew it would be soon. But Cam was a gentleman and he continued to wait for just the right time.

I stood on the street, outside the stage door, waiting for him to come out of the parkade and pick me up. His car appeared and I let myself in, sitting silently beside him.

'Katie, I know things have been rough,' he said.

Oh, God, I thought, here it comes. And even though I knew it was coming, I still wasn't ready for it. He had insidiously wormed his way into my life and I did not want him out of it.

'Katie, I want us to get over this,' he said.

'I told you I don't want to go to a counselor,' I said, afraid to look directly into his eyes, afraid of what I might see there.

'I want us to go away,' he said. 'Maybe if we can get away from everything and everyone for a while, we can get beyond this. Don't you think a little holiday would make you feel better?'

'Maybe,' I said, but I didn't really mean it.

'You've got some time off coming up at the theatre.'

'I've been thinking I might find a part-time job this summer,' I said. 'Or maybe apply for one of the summer festival jobs.'

'You said we would talk about it before you made a decision.'

'You said we would talk about a vacation before you made a decision.'

'I've been looking at cruises or bus tours,' he said, ignoring my animosity. 'Is there any place you really want to go?'

'I don't know,' I said.

'Well, maybe we can go to the travel agent together tomorrow,' he suggested. 'Just to have a look at some brochures or something.'

'I have to work.'

'Katie, please,' he begged. 'Tell me what I have to do to help you with this.'

'Cam, can we talk about this tomorrow?' I asked. 'I've got a bit of a headache.'

'Fine,' he said, starting the car and pulling out of the loading zone. 'But we are going to talk about this.'

He leaned forward and took an envelope that had been sitting on the dashboard and shoved it angrily into his jacket pocket.

'Cam, what is that?' I asked.

'Nothing.'

'Oh, my God, Cam, what have you gone and done?'

He pulled the car over to the curb, right under the No Parking sign across from City Hall, and put it in park.

'What have I done?' he screamed, losing complete control of his emotions. 'I would really like to know what the fuck I have done. I thought I had been the supporting boyfriend, holding your hand and trying to get you through this loss. But no matter what I've done to try and help, all I get is scorn and sarcasm. So maybe you could tell me what I've done?'

'Cam, please let's just go home.'

'We don't have a home anymore, Katie. We have an apartment. But if you want to go and spend another frigid night there, pretending everything is normal while you cringe every time I accidentally touch you, then that's what we'll do. Because we all know that my life right now is about nothing more than trying to please you.'

'Fuck you.'

'No, fuck you. It's you that won't talk, won't deal with any of this.'

'If you're so unhappy, why don't you just leave?'

'You want me to leave?' he asked.

'No!' I screamed. 'I don't want you to leave. But you're going to anyway so why don't you just quit dragging out this agony and get it over with.'

'You think I'm going to leave you?'

'Yes. I lost your baby. Why would you stay?'

'God, if I was going to leave, I would have left way before now. Katie, is that what you're so upset about? Do you think I'm going to leave you?'

'Yes.'

'But what about all the things I've tried to do to make it work out between us?'

'You're just being a gentleman. I know you would never leave me if you thought I couldn't handle it. You're just waiting until you think I'm strong enough and the proper amount of time has passed. Well, I'm fine, so just get on with it.'

'Katie, I will never leave you,' he said. 'I don't care how hard things are, I am going to work to make our relationship last.'

'I cost you your family,' I said. 'Cam, I know it's all you really wanted. How can you even stand to look at me?'

He got out of the car and came around to my side. He opened the door and pulled me out on to the street. He held both my hands in his and his face close to mine, forcing me to look him in the eyes.

'Katie, do you know what I learned this year?' he asked.

'No,' I sobbed.

'I learned that I didn't want a baby. What I wanted was a family. And with you, that's what I have. We are family now. Anything else is a bonus.'

'We are a family?' I asked. 'You're not leaving me?'

'Not that easily.'

'Oh, my God, Cam, you better not be lying because that is one of the most beautiful things I have ever heard anyone say to me.'

'I love you, Katie,' he said. 'Do you still love me?'

'More than I could have ever believed possible.'

He pulled me close and wrapped me in his arms, holding me tight while I sobbed tears I had been saving up for months. We weren't OK yet but I knew we were finally on our way there.

Epilogue

'Kate, you know it's OK to be here.'

'Uh huh.'

'You didn't do anything wrong and you don't have to feel any shame. It's just part of life to have to do this every once in a while.'

'I know,' I whispered. 'Doesn't mean I have to like it.'

'No, it doesn't mean you have to like it. But it's not that bad, you know. A few hours here and there. You might even be a better person for it in the end.'

'I highly doubt that.'

'So you don't want to talk about it?'

'Do I have to?'

'It would help, you know. It always helps to talk about these things.'

'But you know I hate talking about this stuff.'

'Try, Kate, just reach straight into your soul and pull out whatever is hiding down in there. Tell me how you really feel about this.'

I took a deep puff off my cigarette and put it out in the ashtray.

'I hate this stuff,' I admitted. 'How's that for honest? I get roped into doing this every year and I always hate it and I swear there is no way I'll let it happen the next year.'

'But why, Kate, why do you feel that way about this?'

'Because, Graham, it is a colossal waste of my time.' I got up from my desk and filled my go-cup with coffee. 'But the deal is I have to take part in these annual job fairs every year. Doesn't mean I have to like them.'

'Well, you don't seem to have a problem dragging me along for the day.'

'Yeah, funny how that doesn't cause me any guilt at all, huh? But if we have to spend twelve hours today interviewing potential staff for next year, I think it's important that you take part in that. It is one aspect of management that I feel is important for you to learn.'

'You're a funny girl,' he said. 'I've missed that. I'm glad you're back, Kate.'

'Yeah, and you used to be scared of me,' I said, teasing him but feeling warmed by his compliment.

'Don't you prefer respect rather than ruling with fear?' he asked.

'I'll take what I can get. Now why don't you run down to the concert hall and tell them I'm on my way and I'll be there in a few minutes.'

'Don't you dare do like you did last year,' he threatened me.

'What do you mean?'

'You sent me off and then you didn't come down until two o'clock in the afternoon.'

'Graham, I told you I had a family emergency. You know I would never abandon you to interview over five hundred applicants on your own.'

'If you're not there in ten minutes I'm coming to find you,' he threatened me.

'I'll be there.'

He took off in one direction and Cam appeared from the stairwell in the other direction.

'What are you doing here?' I asked.

He leaned over and kissed me, taking my hand as we walked towards the concert hall. It did feel good to be back.

'I should be asking you that. Aren't interviews supposed to start at nine sharp?'

'Everyone else is there on time. And I always stay late to make up for it.'

'No, you don't.'

'Well, I have good intentions of staying late.'

'OK, I'll give you points for the good intentions.'

'So, are you going to distract me for a little while?' I asked, hopefully.

'No, actually I'm just doing a wall survey. Seeing what needs painting over the summer. I'm not even here to see you because I thought you'd be down at the job fair already.'

'OK, OK. Man, you guys are all such nags.'

'Don't forget your cell phone,' he said.

I hated cell phones. But Cam had given me one for Christmas. And it had come in handy a couple of times. So we backtracked to my office, I pulled it out of my backpack and shoved it in my jacket pocket.

'Have fun,' he said, giving me a quick peck before he patted my bottom and sent me on my way.

I sauntered down the hallway, stopping to stare at all the shop windows as I tried to put off the inevitable, longest day of my year that was awaiting me at the concert hall. And then, just as I arrived, my cell phone rang.

'Hello,' I said, turning away from the concert hall doors and taking the call.

'Hi, Kate, it's Sam.'

'Hey, Sam, what's up. I'm just going into the job fair.'

'Kate, I'm in a bit of a bind and I'm afraid I may have made a promise on your behalf that I'm really hoping you can keep.'

'Oh, Sam, what have you done?'